Don't Take The Girl: by L.A. FERRO Published by Pine Hollow Publishing

Copyright © 2025 by L.A. FERRO

All rights reserved.

This is a work of fiction. Names, characters, businesses, places, events, locales, and incidents are either the products of the author's imagination or used in a fictitious manner. Any resemblance to actual persons, living or dead, or actual events is purely coincidental.

Cover by **K.B. Barrett Designs**

Proofreading & Editing: Jenn Lockwood

Published by Pine Hollow Publishing

Cataloging-in-Publication data is on file with the Library of Congress.

 Formatted with Vellum

Don't Take the Girl

Dedication

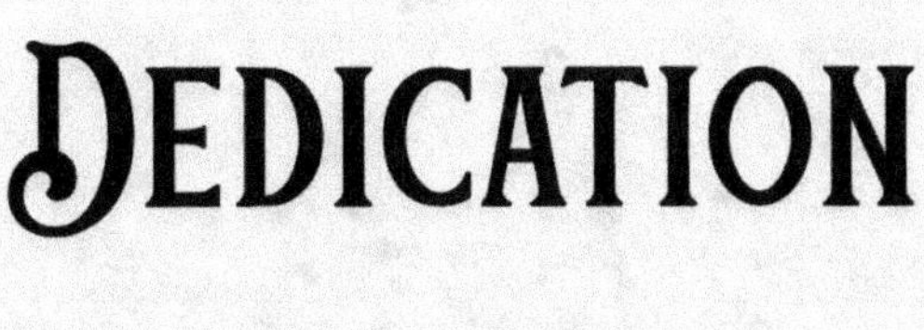

For those who know that sometimes
the boy who runs away with your heart has to
become a man before he can come back for
your soul.

LANEY

PROLOGUE

AGE TEN

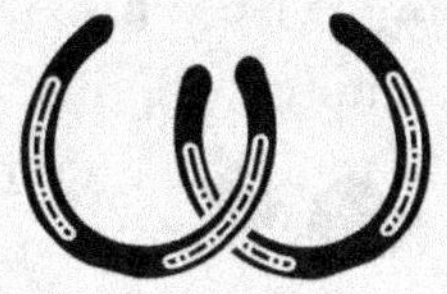

"Aw, man. Dad, come on. Do we really have to take her?" my neighbor London complains as I stand beside his dad's pickup truck.

"Yes, London, she's going. The more the merrier," Mr. Hale says as he loads the fishing gear into the back of the truck bed.

"But you said it was just going to be me and you, like old times," he whines.

"Well, the plan has changed," he says with a hint of annoyance at his son's nagging, and I cringe.

I didn't ask to play the third wheel on their fishing trip. We might be neighbors, but London and I are not friends, and I didn't think my mother and Mr. Hale were either, but somewhere between her mowing the lawn this morning and a call from the hospital to pick up a shift, I got shafted and Mr. Hale was tasked with babysitting me. I told my mother I didn't need a babysitter. I begged her to give me a chance, but she refused. Now, here I am, the unwanted spare on a father-son day. I've dreamed about the day London Hale would look up and notice me, but it never looked or sounded like this in my dreams.

"Then can I bring Fisher? I'm sure his mom will say yes if I call him up," London pleads.

His dad sighs before he concedes. "Fine, run inside and call Fisher. Make sure he knows we are leaving now, then bring me my cell phone when you're done. I left it on my nightstand."

"Yes!" London hisses excitedly before running past so fast it creates a slight breeze in the stifling Texas summer heat.

"Laney," Mr. Hale calls from the back of the truck.

I shove my hands in the back pockets of my jean shorts and walk toward the tailgate. "Did you change your mind?" I ask.

His kind eyes find mine. "Don't tell me you don't want to go either." I shrug, not wanting to say no and add to the headache my presence has already caused. "Don't worry about London." His eyes flash up to the house. "He'll come around." I don't say anything, my anxiety getting the best of me. He closes the cooler. "Do you have a hat?"

"I do, inside."

He nods toward my house. "Go grab it. The sun reflecting off the water gives you a double dose of its intensity. I don't need you getting sunburned on my watch."

"Sure," I say before running back into my house, grateful for the small reprieve of doing something other than standing beside his truck, looking pathetic. I take an extra second to put on sunscreen when I grab my hat, not wanting to end the afternoon looking like a crab. Those extra seconds spent lathering my skin grant me a few glorious moments in the comfort of the air conditioner to cool my heated flesh. Still, the relief is short-lived, because the second I step out my front door, I'm thrown right back on the coals as I walk across my front yard, and the screen door to the Hale house swings open.

London sulks out of his house, his steps heavy on the wooden porch. "Fisher is sick," he mopes as he kicks a pebble. "I don't want to go anymore. Let's just stay home. I'd rather do that than take a girl."

Mr. Hale closes the tailgate as London trudges down the front steps. "Laney, what do you say we put this to rest?" Mr. Hale says, stepping between the truck and me. "Do you want to go fishing?"

I dig my nails into my palms. I want to say no, but he just finished packing a cooler and loading up the back of the truck, and saying no after he went through all that hassle feels rude, so instead, I give him another honest answer.

"I've never been fishing."

His eyebrows rise in surprise before he clasps his hands together. "Then that settles it. We're going fishing."

"She's never even been fishing?" London groans as his dad rounds the truck to the driver's side, leaving me in plain sight of his son's scornful study. London Hale notices me for the first time since I moved in, but the offense in his glare as he leans, arms crossed, against the truck makes me wish he didn't. I'd rather be invisible than on the receiving end of his annoyance. When his dark eyes finally connect with mine, they lock and narrow slightly before a scowl takes over his face. He disappointedly shakes his head before pulling open the front door of the truck. Climbing up, he mutters, "This is the worst."

Adjusting my baseball cap to hide my discomfort, I get in the backseat and mentally echo London's sentiments. It's the worst day ever.

"No, no, no. Don't take the bait. Drop it," I whisper-yell at the fish as though it were a dog that would release its bone.

We've been fishing at the lake for almost an hour now, and no one has caught anything. The last thing I want to do is catch the first fish. I can already see the fit London will throw if I catch the first fish on a pole that's not mine, with bait I refused to touch, on a line I didn't cast. I set the pole down, walk to the water's edge, and squat to see if I can see a fish.

"What are you doing?" London startles me, and I shoot up.

"Nothing." I tuck a stray strand of hair behind my ear. "I was just seeing how cold the water is."

His brow furrows as he pulls up the hem of his black t-shirt to wipe the sweat off his brow. "Are you sure that's what you were doing?"

I roll my lips and rock back on my heels. "Mm-hmm."

His eyes flick between mine and the water. "So you weren't trying to see if there's a fish on the end of this line?"

My eyes widen, and I shake my head. "Oh, I don't a have fish." I chuck my thumb over my shoulder and look back at the water as I search for a lie. "It got stuck on something at the bottom of the lake," I say nervously before running with it. "That's why I was checking the temperature of the water. I figured I'd go in and unsnag it so you guys didn't have to help me."

He stares blankly, like he can't believe the words that just came out of my mouth, before picking up my pole, but to my surprise, he doesn't make fun of me. "That bobber dipping underwater was a nibble, and now that it's fully submerged, it means you have a bite," he says as he starts reeling in the fish. "I'm sorry about earlier."

"Did your dad send you over here to say that?"

"No…" he says, his tone lacking a true defense.

After the fit he threw about me coming, I know that's a lie. He didn't suddenly have a change of heart. I saw him sitting on a bucket while his father was re-stringing a pole and giving him an earful. I'm positive whatever verbal lashing he was receiving was about me. I'm not mad at London. I get it. I crashed his afternoon with his father.

"You don't have to do that," I say in response to his lie. "A lie isn't any better than a meaningless apology that I didn't ask for."

He looks over his shoulder and purses his lips before he returns his eyes to the fish he's currently reeling in. "Fine, he may have told me to apologize, but that doesn't mean I don't agree you deserve one. I was a jerk."

I cop a squat on the large flat rock I'd been sitting on before I noticed my line moving in the water. This rock is the entire reason I chose this spot. I didn't want to sit in the grass and get eaten alive by the bugs.

"I can't believe the girl who has never been fishing is the first one to get a bite."

"It's not a big deal. I'm sure it's something small, like a crappie."

"It doesn't matter if it's small. A catch is a catch," he says as the fish I caught breaks the water. "And that's not a crappie. You caught a catfish."

I get to my feet to get a better look as he grabs the line, and the fish flops around in the grass.

"How are you going to get the hook out of its mouth?" I ask with a grimace. "Won't those things on the side of its face sting you?"

He laughs, and for once today, I'm grateful for the heat. My cheeks were red before he laughed at my expense. He does a double-take when he sees I don't find my question nearly as amusing.

"Sorry, I forgot you've never been fishing. I've never been fishing with someone who doesn't know about fish." He pulls a pocket knife out of his shorts. "Didn't your father ever take you? I mean, I know you're a girl, but…"

"Tell your dad you caught the fish. I'm going back to the truck so I can sit in the shade," I mutter as I hastily slip my Keds back on.

"Hey, Laney…" I can tell he's about to give me another shallow apology that I don't want to hear, so I ignore him. "It's Laney, right?"

"Yesss," I drone, finally getting my last shoe on. "You didn't want me to come, and I don't want to be here. We don't have to pretend." I drop my hands to my hips and roll my eyes, deter-mined to hide the hurt his mentioning my father brings.

He grabs my arm as I turn on my heel, and I swear a tiny buzz of electricity zings through my body. It's an awareness I've never felt, probably because a boy has never touched me before, especially not one I liked or thought I liked. "Stay. I swear I wasn't laughing at you."

My eyes study the hand wrapped around my wrist. There's dirt under his nails from putting bait on hooks, and God knows what kind of grime is on his knuckles. It's gross, but the hum I feel from head to toe remains. I trace his arm back to the body it's attached to, cataloging every freckle and the tiny scar on his bicep before my eyes finally reach his rich brown eyes. The agitation I saw in them earlier has faded, and now, as they stare back at me, they almost feel warm. The way he's looking back at me is how I'd hoped he would look at me the first time he saw me. I don't know what I want him to see, but whatever he sees is better than what he saw earlier. *"Do we really have to take her?"*

His words from earlier flick through my mind, and I pull my arm out of his grip. "I'll stay, but we don't have to talk." I don't need any more forced apologies or reminders of how he never wanted me here to begin with. I'm trying to make the best of an afternoon I didn't choose either.

"Okay…" He furrows his brow and pinches his lips. "But I was going to tell you about the fish and show you how to take the hook out."

"Yeah, sure. We can talk about fish."

"The whiskers on a catfish aren't what sting you," he says as he grabs the fish by its stomach. "It's the spine and the tips of the fins. If you don't touch those parts, it's just like any other fish." He holds the fish between us and examines it as it opens and closes its wide mouth. "Sometimes when you catch a fish, the hook gets lodged deep in its throat, and you can't get the hook out. In that case, we have to cut the line to release the fish."

"Wait, does that mean he's going to die? I mean, the hook is lodged inside of him."

"Yeah, he won't live that long if we throw him back."

"If? What does that mean? What else would we do with it?"

He looks at me and flashes me a grin, a sincere smile that makes my tummy turn. "We eat him." And just like that, the butterflies are gone. I eat meat. I understand things must die in order for me to enjoy them, but being the hunter… I don't know how I feel about that. "We don't have to; we can release him," he adds when he sees the unease on my face.

"No, it's okay. We can eat it. I'd rather his life serve a purpose. If we eat him, he fed us; if we let him go, he dies for nothing, and I don't like that."

"Good choice. My dad makes the best fried catfish." He tips his head behind me. "Can you grab that bucket? It's better to keep them in water when it's this hot." When I return with the bucket, he says, "Think you can catch another one?"

I shrug. "I can't really take credit for the first one. Your dad baited the hook and cast the line. I literally sat here and held the pole."

"Holding the pole is ninety percent of fishing," he says as he puts the fish in the bucket. "So, where are you from? You just moved in a few months ago, right?"

"Um, I'm not really from anywhere. We've never stayed anywhere long enough to call any place home, but I was born in Tennessee."

"That's kind of cool, though." He puts another worm on a hook. "Seeing new places all the time sounds like fun."

"Maybe." I reclaim my seat on the rock. "But it gets lonely. It's just me and Mom, and we never stay long enough for me to make any real friends."

"I'll be your friend," he says as he casts the line.

A snort escapes. "You'll be my friend now?" I question skeptically. "You didn't even want me to come today." I tap my chin. "Let's see, I think you said, 'Don't take the girl.'"

He runs his hand through his dark hair, closes the distance between us, and extends the fishing pole to me. "That was before."

I push at the pole. "No, that's okay. I don't want you to be my friend because you feel sorry for me." I draw up my legs, wrap my arms around my knees, and look anywhere but at him.

He taps me with the handle of the pole. "That's not why I offered to be your friend. You're good at holding a fishing pole and picking a spot. Plus, you didn't freak out when I suggested eating the fish. I totally expected you to lose it." He laughs. "Most of the girls I know would have."

That makes my lips curl. I've never been a girly girl, but I wouldn't say I'm a tomboy either. The only hobby that has stuck is junk journaling. Moving around all the time makes it hard to settle into anything, but I enjoy collecting mementos from the places I get to see. With that in mind, I take the rod. Why not? I'm wasting time being self-conscious and embarrassed. If London Hale wants to be my friend, I should take it. When and if something terribly tragic happens where I embarrass myself beyond repair, my mom will accept an offer in a new city, and all of this will be nothing more than a forgotten memory.

"Friends," I say, taking the pole. "For now, anyway."

"For now?" His brow furrows.

"Yeah, you'll get attached, and then I'll have to marry you someday."

That makes him laugh a deep belly laugh that has my whole face lighting up. I know what I said; he doesn't have to know a small part of me would love that ending. Right now, I'm just a girl who knows how to pick the best spots to cast, isn't grossed out by eating fish, and loves to crack jokes. For now, we're just friends.

"You're funny, Laney, but I can't marry you."

"And why not?"

"Easy. I'm never getting married. If you like someone, the secret to keeping it that way is never marrying them." I'm not sure what to say to his stance, and when I say nothing, he side-eyes me expectantly. "No argument?"

"No, that sounds fair. We're ten." Trying to convince him he's wrong isn't a battle I care to have.

"Speak for yourself. I'm eleven." He mindlessly flips open his pocketknife, opening and closing its different parts. "Your parents were married, I guess," he says as he uses the edge of his blade to clear dirt from the crevices of the soles of his tennis shoes.

"No, I never met him."

"Did he leave or something?"

I don't like talking about my dad. It's why I was ready to head back to the truck earlier. I'm sure he picked up on that, but his persistence now feels different. Something about it feels genuine, so I don't storm off. However, I also don't want to talk about things that make me sad.

I hold up my fishing pole. "Look at me. Who would leave me?" I laugh, but even London can tell its false bravado. Rejection hurts, and for the first time today, I sense he knows a little something about what I'm feeling. Unlike him, I pay attention. I've noticed there isn't a Mrs. Hale.

His mouth tugs into a sympathetic half-smile before he says, "I won't leave you." My smile fades as my stomach twists into knots, and I hold my tongue. His words feel true, and I don't want to mock them, especially when I want to keep them. He returns his eyes to the water. "If I ever do get married…" He hurriedly gets to his feet, and my heart starts to beat out of sync as it hangs on his every word. "She'll know the best spots to fish." His eyes sparkle as they dart back to mine. "Reel it in this time. We got another one."

My eyes hold his until I feel the tug on the end of the pole, and I do as he says, my smile mirroring his. Perhaps "don't take the girl" weren't the bad words I thought they were. Maybe that's just how boys are. Maybe their words say the opposite of what they mean, because I'm pretty sure London Hale just said if he ever got married, I'd be his girl.

PART ONE

LANEY

CHAPTER 1

FRESHMAN YEAR

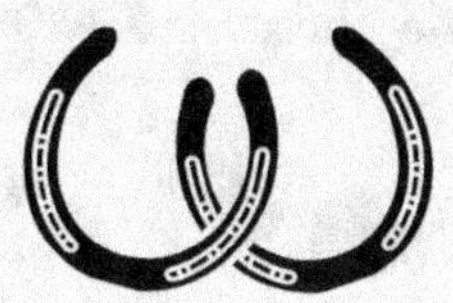

AGE FIFTEEN

"You have to do it if you want to make the squad," Sydney says as we walk down the dark street toward my house.

"Yeah, I got that. I'm rethinking how much I want to join the team right now."

"Come on." She bumps my hip. "We just finished Justin's house, and we didn't get caught. We both know London's not home. That's why you chose him, right?"

I stare down at the pavement and try to stick to the shadows, my mind focusing on anything other than Sydney's question, because the answer is pathetic. I've had a crush on London Hale since the day I moved into the house next to his, and for the past five years, we have been friends. I got to tag along on more than just fishing trips. If he was going somewhere, I was going. That day, when he said, "I'll be your friend," he meant it—at least for a while, anyway.

Things changed last year when he started high school. He stopped inviting me to grab ice cream on Wednesday nights at the Twisted Cone, and if he was hanging out with Fisher, he no longer asked me if I wanted to join him on the walk there, even though my new best friend was Fisher's sister. He also stopped going fishing.

"You still like him, don't you?" Sydney jumps in front of me and catches me by the shoulders stopping me in my tracks.

"Syd," I groan. "We've been over this. It doesn't matter. He doesn't see me that way."

"And how would you know that? You've never told him you like him."

"Pfft, okay…" I mock as I grab the straps of my backpack. "So that's what girls are doing these days? Oh, hey, I like you…let's date."

"Some do. That's badass. We don't have to wait for guys to make the first move. If you say it, and he turns you down, then you have your answer, and you can move on."

There's logic in what she's saying, but… "I don't know. It's not my style. I guess I'm old-fashioned in that way."

"Or chicken…" she offers as she tucks her arms and taunts, "Bawk, bawk, bawk."

I shake my head and roll my eyes. "I'm not chicken." Well, maybe a little, but that's not what is stopping me now. "It's not just that. Sydney, you know better than anyone. Making friends was never my strong suit, with my mom always following her career and the money. London is the longest friendship I've ever had. Heck, you and I may not even be the friends we are were it not for him letting me tag along when he came over to hang out with your brother." She exhales a heavy breath, and I know she can read the direction my thoughts are going. I don't want to ruin what I have, and that kind of confession feels like it could. I'd rather have him at a distance than not have him at all. "Plus, the ball has been in his court since the day we met."

That earns me a laugh. "You can't be serious. You're basing your future on a conversation you had when you were ten. I can promise you that boy doesn't remember a word from that day." I furrow my brow. She's probably right. Girls feel things differently. Words don't just stick. They cut deep, and in my case, they were forever engraved on my foolish, young heart. "Hey, no doom and gloom. Look, I'm Team Laney. Whatever you want, I want that for you. All I'm saying is London Hale isn't going to make the first move—at least not with you, anyway."

"What's that supposed to mean?" I say as I look down at myself. I'm not stick thin. I have thick thighs, a tummy that says I enjoy food and don't starve myself like most girls my age do, trying to achieve a thigh gap, and I've always had bigger breasts, but I've never been ashamed of my body. I'm comfortable in my skin…or I was until about ten seconds ago.

"Oh my god, you took that wrong. I'm pretty sure I tell you on a daily basis I wish I had your boobs." She slaps my arm as we round the corner. "What I mean is you're too close. He's a year older and is best friends with my brother. He looks at you like a sister, and that's why he won't ever make a play. If he's anything like Fisher, he feels protective over you, so you can probably kiss dating goodbye too."

"Does this conversation get better or…"

She flashes me a mischievous grin. "That depends on you. He might see you like a sister now, but that doesn't mean you can't change his mind. You just have to make him see you differently."

"And how do I do that?"

"I have a few ideas in mind, but first…" She tosses me a toilet paper roll. "We have a yard to TP."

"Laney, catch," Mindy says as she tosses a roll over the big oak tree in London's front yard.

After she finished TPing the houses on her list, she and Skylar cut through the backyard two houses down to get home. They spotted us and decided to help. Needless to say, if they're handing out grades for the best TP job to make the cut, I have my spot in the bag. Every inch of London's front yard is covered, even the hedges.

"Guys, I think we're good. There's literally no green left in sight," I say, standing back to admire our work.

"Yeah, yeah," Skylar chimes in. "But we still have this roll to use up. Can't walk in the front door with evidence."

"She has a point," Sydney says, chucking her empty roll onto the lawn.

Skylar and Mindy snicker as they toss the last roll back and forth, wrapping the base of the oak tree.

"I wonder when he'll be back. School starts next week," I say to Sydney as I put on my now empty backpack.

I spent all my time hanging out with Sydney, learning dance routines in hopes of making the dance team with her. She's my best and only friend. For a while, I thought maybe she had taken me under her wing because London had asked her to, but even if that was true once upon a time, I know it's not why we are friends now. Let's be real: I'm not winning any popularity contests. It's been five years, and I'm still the new girl in a small town, and Sydney…well, she's Sydney Downs. A carefree, outgoing extrovert who can turn a complete stranger into a friend in seconds. We are polar opposites. I'm content being on my own. I'd be perfectly happy junk journaling in my room or reading a book on our porch swing. Sydney might push me, but I like the excitement she brings to my life. She is the yin to my yang—two peas in a pod who were always meant to be friends forever.

With her, the summer has flown by, as it always does. We were at the lake, soaking up the sun and listening to music, when we weren't practicing dance routines or driving out to her cousin Cooper's house to ride horses. It took me two weeks to notice that London and I hadn't simply been passing ships in the night, treading by unnoticed. Our windows look directly at each other. His blinds have remained open all summer, but no lights have flicked on, shadows haven't passed by, and his bed has stayed made. When I asked my mother if she knew what was up, she suggested he may have gone to camp or visited family, but after another month passed, I knew that wasn't the case. What camps literally last longer than six weeks?

"I know Fisher plans to give him an earful when he returns.

They had planned to work out together this summer to better their odds of making the varsity football team this year, and then London ghosted him."

A light flicking on in the front room catches my eyes, and my heart sinks as my adrenaline kicks in. "Caw-caw," I call out to get Mindy's and Skylar's attention.

Their eyes dart to mine, a mix of shock, fear, and excitement. I snap toward the window and start pointing for them to run to the left toward my house, knowing it's their best shot of getting out unseen. They don't hesitate. "Go to the back door," I whisper-yell, and we all jog toward the back of my house.

I'm just past the hedge when my foot catches, but not over a branch, over another foot. Strong arms wrap around my waist, and I'm pulled against the shadows of the house.

"What are you doing?"

My thoughts scramble to process what's happening as his voice reverberates through me. His body pressed against mine is disorienting.

"London," I pant as my fear ebbs, and I attempt to stabilize my racing heart.

"Were you expecting the boogeyman?"

My eyes widen as I moisten my lips and get my bearings. Pounding my fist into his chest, I say, "No, but I wasn't expecting a ghost either."

The smirk that was there fades, and something unrecognizable passes over his expression as his grip on me loosens. He's been gone all summer, and we haven't been as close as we used to be this past year, but I can tell something's different. I just wish he'd tell me what's going on or where he's been. The London two summers ago would have. But since he doesn't, and I'm not sure who's standing in front of me now, I nod to the front. "It's just a prank. I'll—"

"You've got to be fucking kidding me," Mr. Hale curses as we hear the front door slam shut. London's hold on my arm tightens as he pulls me closer to the house and closer to him once more.

"London!" he calls, "You're cleaning this mess up. I'm sure this is one of your punk friends or rivals, and I have work." London holds his finger to his lips, motioning for me to keep quiet as my pulse storms through my veins, listening to Mr. Hale curse under his breath and pace the front porch in a few long sweeps before the screen door opens, and he returns inside.

When I'm sure the coast is clear, I say, "I'll clean this up tomorrow."

He releases me. "You said it was a prank." He shoves his hands in his pockets as I discreetly take in all the ways he's changed since I saw him last. His hair is longer, and his skin is darker, which tells me he wasn't kept in solitary confinement wherever he's been. But the biggest change has to be his build. He's never been scrawny, but he's definitely filled out. My body is still humming in the areas where his firm chest bumped mine. When my eyes finally drag up to his, there's a hint of amusement, one that reminds me he asked me a question, and I'm standing here, gawking.

I clear my throat. "Yeah, you know how Syd has always been a dancer. Well, she finally convinced me to try out so we could do it together. She spent the entire summer training me, and tryouts ended last Friday. Tonight, we were pulled out of our beds and tasked with TPing one of the football players or a guy we liked, so I'm assuming we made the team with the completion of this task." I tuck a strand of hair behind my ear and take another step back, realizing my word vomit. "All of that..."—I wave my hand toward the front yard—"is the whole rite of passage, hazing ritual thing they do every year." I rock back on my heels. "So..."

"And you don't know any other guys?"

I can feel my face heat immediately. What kind of question is that? Does he think I can't pull a guy? I swear, sometimes I question why I'm so infatuated with this man.

"You haven't been home all summer. Therefore, your house was the perfect target." Since he was out of town, tonight should have been me TPing a house that a guy from school lived in that would have been none the wiser of my shenanigans, but because fate seems to want to play jokes here, I am caught red-handed. His eyebrows slightly knit together as he mulls over my words, and I say, "If you're not going to rat me out to your dad tonight"—I chuck my thumb over my shoulder toward my house—"I'll be over first thing in the morning to clean this up."

I turn on my heel to leave, but his words stop me. "You said football player or a guy you liked. I missed tryouts, which means I'm not a football player."

I squeeze my eyes closed but don't turn back. "Don't worry about it. I interpreted their words according to their basic meaning, not figuratively. They said *liked*—that's past tense, not present."

I open my eyes and face him, content that my lie has satisfied his curiosity. When I turn around, prepared to walk the five steps between his house and mine backward, his studied gaze is inexplicable. I can usually read all his expressions, but this one is new.

"So you don't want to marry me anymore?"

His response catches me off guard. Just moments ago, I was convinced he'd indeed forgotten the day I'll never forget and the words we shared. I could shoot my shot, be the badass Sydney dared me to be. I could lay it all at his feet, tell him how mad I am that he started high school last year and forgot about me, or how he left me all summer without so much as a word, and I can tell him how that hurt me because he means something to me, but I don't because a memory isn't a declaration. This isn't him telling me he feels the same way. So instead, I test the waters and save face.

"I'm not ten anymore, London, and you're not looking for the best spot to fish."

The last part of that statement sends my heart racing, and my palms instantly start to get clammy. Those were his words, ones that I always believed were meant for me.

He purses his lips, his back leaves the wall, and he inhales deeply before running his hand through his hair. "Yeah, you're definitely not ten anymore, heartbreaker."

What did he just call me? London has never called me anything but Laney, and now, of all the times to assign me a nickname, he chooses that one. The chosen name hangs in the air between us, and I can't tell if it's an accusation or something akin to admiration—maybe it's both. All I know is, for the first time in five years, it feels like London is seeing me the way I've always seen him, and the realization is dizzying. His gaze lingers as though he knows what he called me was no accident.

"Laney," Sydney's voice whispering my name off the back porch has my head snapping toward the sound.

"I should go. They're looking for me," I say, but when I turn back, he's gone.

I'VE BEEN OUTSIDE FOR OVER AN HOUR AND STILL HAVEN'T SEEN London, but I know he's inside. Last night, after Mindy and Skylar went home, Sydney hung back, and I told her what went down between me and London before I came inside, except the part about him calling me heartbreaker. The nickname felt personal, and I wanted to keep it for myself while I worked through if it was dismissive or intimate. The latter is what felt real at the moment, but the entire night had me off balance, and that's the excuse I'll use when I get around to telling Sydney, because I will eventually tell her.

After the surprise of him being back in town wore off, Sydney filled me in on her ideas for getting him to see me as more than a sister. In her opinion, his words last night meant that part of him, small or not, noticed we weren't kids anymore, and that was half the battle, according to her. So, this morning, when I got out of the shower, I put her plan into action and walked into my room with my curtains wide open, wearing only my towel. Usually, I took a change of clothes to the bathroom, but Sydney advised me to change my routine. London's window is directly across from mine, and I needed to use that view to my advantage and show him exactly how grown I was and what could be his if he wanted it. Stepping into my room, knowing I was going to cross the room to my dresser in nothing but a towel, past an open window, was intimidating as much as it was exhilarating.

As I searched through my drawers for my underwear and bra, I took my time, and the way my skin pebbled, I knew he was watching. I could feel it, and if the sensation of being watched wasn't enough, when I turned around, I saw him sitting on his bed, arms crossed, staring directly at me. My eyes widened. Believing he was watching and catching him in the act were two completely different emotions. One was the thrill of being caught, the other was the act. His expression was impassive, much like most of our interaction last night, but the fact that he didn't move said something—or at least I thought it did when I came outside an hour ago. The high I felt when I walked outside is long gone, and now I'm questioning everything.

Last night, London admitted we weren't kids anymore, and I've replayed every ghost of an expression that crossed his stoney face since the words left his mouth. I may have taken liberties, letting my eyes drift over all the parts of him that had changed over the summer, but his eyes blazed a trail over every inch of the exposed skin on my tanned thighs to my braless breasts covered only by the thin material of my sleep tank.

It's that endless loop that has me anxious to see him again. A summer of no contact, as shitty as it felt, may have been exactly what we needed. Absence makes the heart grow fonder. I thought he was forgetting me, but maybe it was fanning the flames. Maybe in our time spent apart, he felt the same as me. Being apart sucked, and now I need to know if I'm destined to be a dreamer or if last night was a turning point in our relationship.

Honk, honk, a horn sounds, and I turn around to find a red convertible I'd know anywhere pulls up to the curb. Long auburn hair, red lips, and frosty blue eyes that mirror the frigid heart that beats inside her cold chest giddily bounce out of the driver seat. Riley Heron. She's a sophomore, like London, and captain of the junior varsity cheer team, a title that's really a technicality because of her year. With her dad running the football program, she walks the hallways like she owns every brick, making the varsity team look like mere accessories to her reign.

Before our eyes can connect, I finish pulling the toilet paper off the base of the oak tree and stuff it in the trash bag I've been hauling around. The last thing I want is to be on Riley's radar. The girl is as fake as they come. If she's being nice, it's never for your benefit but for hers.

"Lyndsey." I hear her footsteps come to a halt behind me, and I cringe.

I roll my lips as I slowly turn. This morning started out great, but my day is quickly turning to shit. "It's Laney."

She flips her long red hair over her shoulder. "What is?"

My eyes widen. I knew she was a mean girl, but I didn't realize she was stupid too. "My name is Laney. You called me Lyndsey."

"Right…" She flashes me a big fake smile. "So you did all of this to make the dance team, right?"

I look around at what remains of the mess I made last night. Toilet paper still hangs from every branch above my head, but I highly doubt she's here to congratulate me on my TPing skills, and I'm starting to regret my choice to correct my name.

"Yes," I answer cautiously as the screen door opens, and London waltzes out with a quickened pace.

"Riley," he greets as he meets her on the sidewalk, wearing a crisp V-neck, dark jeans, and white sneakers. The shadows that hung around him last night as we stood between our windows have faded, and in their place is what looks like the London I used to know…until my eyes meet his. They're still different. "I thought we said we'd meet at The Twisted Cone?" He shoves his hands in his front pockets.

"I know, but I was right around the corner, and I remembered you mentioning that you don't get your license for another week, so I thought I'd pick you up."

Wait, he was planning on meeting her? Since when is London

friends with Riley Heron? His eyes stay pinned on hers like he's lost in thought, and I can't tell what he's thinking. Hopefully, he's plotting his way out of whatever plans they made because I don't like it. I hate it. She's the last person on the planet I'd want to see him with if he didn't choose me. I'd learn to deal with anyone—anyone but her.

"Did you have other plans?" Her eyes drag back to me. "I thought you were asking me on a date, but now that I'm here…"—she holds her palms out—"maybe your plans have changed. I mean, everyone knows there's only one reason the dance team upholds this silly tradition—"

"He was out of town. That's why I chose this house," I cut her off in hopes of ending this conversation so that the two of them will go away, and I can sulk in peace.

"Sure," she says condescendingly as her eyes drag down my body. I'm wearing a pair of athletic shorts and an oversized band t-shirt while she looks like she's ready for a night at the club, wearing a black mini skirt, cropped tank, and those stupid platform shoes everyone thinks are so cute. They're hideous, but it doesn't matter what I think. All that matters is what he thinks. "So are we leaving or what? It's hot out here, and I'm starting to sweat," she whines as she checks her phone.

"You caught me off guard. I need to grab a few things. Wait inside. I'll be right behind you."

She quirks a brow and twirls her keychain around her forefinger before conceding. "Fine. Don't keep me waiting. I don't like it."

He watches her walk up the pathway toward the house, and when she reaches the steps, he throws his hand in his hair and tugs at the roots. "Hey…" He turns back to me. "Sorry, I can't help clean this up." He pulls his grandfather's knife out of his back pocket. "You might need the chief to help cut the twine around those yard bags." He hands me the knife. "Just leave it on the porch when you're finished."

'Sorry, I can't help you clean this up. Take my knife.' Really, that's all you

have to say right now? Not you went MIA all summer, and now you're back for less than twenty-four hours and taking the meanest girl in school on a date? What the actual fuck? Those are the things I want to say, but I don't.

"It's fine. You didn't make this mess. It's not your responsibility to clean it up." His dark pools lock on mine, and while they're different, the hardness I saw before has softened, but something else is there too. I don't know what it is or why it's there, but I know that puzzle will not be solved standing on this front lawn while Riley Heron impatiently waits inside. All this is doing is dragging out my mortification.

Logically, I know he can't read my thoughts, but I feel incredibly exposed right now. It's as though he sees through every lie. Yes, I TPed your house because I like you. Yes, I still dream about marrying you, and yes, I walked in front of my window this morning hoping you'd see me. Instead, I say, "You should go. Wouldn't want to keep your date waiting," I say with a sarcastic tone that speaks to my disdain.

My eye catches a subtle clench in his fist, my words hitting a nerve. I just wish I knew on whose behalf he was offended. I can tell it's on the tip of his tongue to say something. London is not the guy who will spare you his words to save your feelings, so his silence now is as bemusing as it is infuriating. Words I can process. This version of the boy I used to know, I can't. He turns back to the house, and I go back to picking up toilet paper when he pivots on his heel back to me. "Oh yeah, and Laney…" I look up and meet his eyes. "You should probably close your curtains."

His midnight gaze collides with mine for one electric heartbeat before he deliberately tears it away, those obsidian depths guarding secrets I'm desperate to unravel. His message is a warning that only makes my defiance burn hotter. Why give it at all if he was unbothered? I won't be closing my curtains.

LONDON

CHAPTER 2

FRESHMAN YEAR

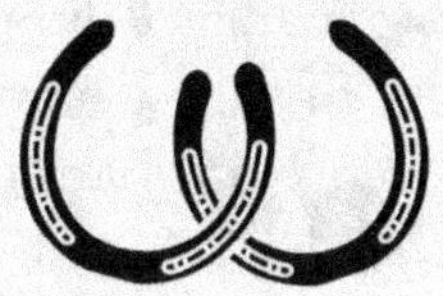

AGE SIXTEEN

Fisher: You're alive! Holy shit, man, where have you been all summer?

London: I don't want to talk about it.

Fisher: You missed football tryouts. How am I supposed to play without my best friend?

London: I'm handling it.

Fisher: Want to come over and I'll catch you up?

London: I'm out front.

"Out of all the places you wanted me to drive you, Fisher Downs' house was not where I thought you'd have in mind," Riley prattles as she looks over the red rims of her obnoxiously big sunglasses.

I resist the urge to say the first thing on my tongue: *Jealous?* Fisher Downs is one of the most genuine guys around, but beyond that, we both know why she doesn't want to be here, which I'm hoping will play in my favor. Fish comes from old money. Willow

25

Creek might be a small town, but it has its hierarchy and back-woods royalty, and Fish's family sits at the top. I know, without a doubt, Riley's snide comments are rooted in envy. If anything, her snarkiness now is because, in Fisher's world, she doesn't exist, and Riley Heron can't stand it when she's not the center of attention. I dig my fingers into my thigh as I slip my phone back into my pocket and remind myself I consciously made this choice. There will be no going back. I ripped the proverbial Band-aid off this morning. That was the hard part. The part that felt like I killed something inside of me, something I didn't know I had. My jaw tightens with my chest, and I swallow hard to push it out. What's done is done. Now I have to play my part.

"You don't have to stay. I haven't seen Fish all summer, and I wanted to get a rundown on how the teams are shaping up this year and see what I missed."

She sinks back into her seat and flips down the sun visor to open the mirror. "If you're worried about your position as quarterback…" She pulls out a lip gloss tube to reapply another thick layer to what already exists. "Don't be. Daddy said he would give you your position back at lunch."

That's not exactly what he said. He said I have a place if I earn it. The entire lunch, I questioned if I had made the right decision when I called Riley Heron. By the end of it, I had decided it didn't matter, but I did learn something. Coach Heron doesn't exactly enjoy his daughter's company either. That told me I could please him by taking up space in her life, because it accomplished two things: it pleased her and took away from the amount of time she had to nag him. However, that doesn't mean I plan to worship the ground she walks on. Riley might be the queen of the school, but I have a reputation too. I don't date, and I know she sees that as a challenge. She wants to be the first girl to break the trend, but what she doesn't know is that I'm counting on that. She'll put up with whatever I throw her way to earn a title, and for me, nothing will change.

I see Fisher open the privacy gate around the back, and I open the door. "Stay or don't. This is where I'll be for the rest of the day." I don't wait around for her to respond. I don't care what she does. Riley Heron is here to serve a purpose, and today, she played her role. Now, she is free to go.

"London," I hear her call out as I walk toward Fisher, but I pay her no mind. I said all I had to say.

"Bro, tell me that's not Riley Heron, the coach's daughter," Fisher says, pulling me in for a pound hug while looking over my shoulder at the car parked on the street.

"The one and only," I say, stepping around him and making my way into the backyard, praying like hell I hear the sound of wheels peeling out instead of the slam of a door.

"Don't tell me she's the reason you couldn't bother to call your best friend all summer."

"Not exactly," I say as I begin to empty my pockets on the patio table.

"Okay, what the hell is going on with you? I feel like you're talking in code or some shit. Why aren't you saying what you mean?"

I know what he's asking, but I don't respond. I can't give him an answer I don't have. This past summer came out of left field. Never in a million years did I expect my father to pull a stunt like this. I thought he'd fight for me, and not only did he not stand his ground, he took everything, and now I feel like I've come home to nothing. I can't give my best friend answers I'm still seeking. I've spent most of the summer being angry and depressed. I thought coming home would feel better, but instead, I just get to add sadness to the lineup of shitty things I feel.

"I didn't call you because I couldn't. I didn't have my phone. My dad took it before he shipped me off."

His eyes widen with the gravity of my last words, catching him off guard. Luckily for me, we've been friends long enough that he knows how to read me, and he leaves it alone, but not before dragging his nail over the itch my brain can't scratch.

He puts his hands on his hips. "So, what do you have to say

about that?" He gestures toward the front yard. "You're back, and what… Riley Heron is your girl? What happened to—"

"Don't," I bite out.

"Nah, you don't get a pass on that one, London. I'm your best fucking friend, and in the years we've talked about anything and everything, Riley Heron has never made your list. We both know only one girl occupies space in your mind."

"Things change." I shrug and turn toward the pool. The sound of wheels squealing out front is music to my ears, and for the first time since I've come home, I feel like I've finally found favor with some deity.

"Not that much!" he says, his tone ringing with absurdity. "I know for a fact the girl you want wants you back."

"Not anymore," I say as I pull my t-shirt off and slip off my shoes.

"Wait, wait, wait," he says, cutting me off before I jump in. "We are talking about the same girl, correct? My sister's best friend and your neighbor, the one with blonde hair as bright as the sun and light brown eyes that reflect its flare, Laney Hart."

"Same girl." I try to keep my tone unbothered when I'm anything but after he quotes my words.

"Not possible. I watched her—"

"Stop." I hold up my hand. "I don't want to hear it. The words came directly from the source. I asked if she still liked me, and she said no."

"But—"

That's all I hear before his words are muffled by water as I jump into the pool and let myself sink to the bottom, wishing like hell chlorine had the power to wash away what has been the worst summer of my life.

London

CHAPTER 3

SOPHOMORE YEAR

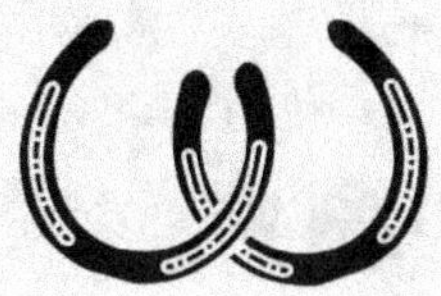

AGE SEVENTEEN

"Bro, what's up with you tonight?" Fish says as he chucks a toy football at me across the balcony.

"I don't know what you're talking about," I lie as I look down at the people gathered around the bonfire for the last party of the year.

"We've been best friends since kindergarten. I know better, so why don't you tell me the real reason your head is anywhere but here?"

Fisher comes over and leans onto the rail beside me. I don't answer him. The school's baseball team just won state. We're here tonight to celebrate with his cousin Cooper, who pitches for the Cougars. I thought coming might make me feel better, though I'm not sure why, since masking shit never fixes anything. Eventually, the mask falls, revealing what we thought we could hide. But it's not the fall I'm worried about. In fact, it's the reveal. Will I still be me, or will he be removed too?

A loud cackle catches in the wind, and we spot the source at the same time.

Fish chuckles. "Oh, now I get it. You're hiding from Riley. I still don't understand why you're still letting whatever the fuck you have going on with her play out. There is no way Coach Heron can afford to lose you next year. You're literally the only person in town that can throw a football worth a shit, and you've already got your full-ride offer to Stanley."

I watch Riley laugh and dance with her entourage around the bonfire as she shakes her ass for anyone who will look her way, and I cringe. Teenage popularity makes no sense. Is Riley Heron attractive? Yes, every girl wants to be her, and every guy wants to date her, aside from me and Fisher Downs. It's funny how I have something everyone wants, and I don't want it. I haven't wanted it since the day I got it. One would think the easy answer to getting rid of things they don't want is simply getting rid of them, but I'm not cruel, even if my intentions were never altruistic. I think that's why I haven't been able to bring myself to cut the cord.

Riley Heron may play the unsuspecting, naïve, head-in-the-clouds card well, but she's smart. She knows what I hope to gain by having her on my arm, the same way I know what she expects from me. In small towns, in the heart of America, traditions die hard. The captain of the cheer team is supposed to date the quarterback. They're supposed to be prom king and queen, the envy of the school, which is part of the crux of the dilemma I've found myself in. Her dreams are not innately evil. Misguided perhaps, but not ugly. I've stuck it out, hoping to find my redemption for entering this situation with ulterior motives. However, at what point have I done my time and paid my dues for a mistake? When do I get to say, "I fucked up. This isn't working." Every day that ticks by as I wait for my sign, I feel like I'm losing pieces of myself. I'm not this guy, and she is not my girl.

"Hey, hey, hey, what are you fuckers doing up here on my deck? The party is downstairs," Cooper says, strolling out onto the deck off his bedroom.

Fisher's dad and his brother own horse-racing tracks in Kentucky, and not just any tracks—the big ones. What I've never been able to put together is why they choose to live in Willow Creek.

"We came up here looking for you, to congratulate you on an immaculate ninth inning when the Cougars were only up by one," Fisher says, pulling Cooper under his arm and roughing up his hair. "Whose house?" Fisher yells.

"Coogs house!" Cooper and I say in unison.

"Alright, alright, come on, let's get this party started," Cooper says, ducking in the door and pulling out a bottle of whiskey. "Let's do a quick shot before we head down."

I snatch the bottle from his hand. "Where did you get this from?" I ask as I check the label.

"I raided Dad's cabinet. If he notices—which chances are slim —I'll remind him of the meeting he had last weekend. He has so many bottles out at all times he won't remember what he served, let alone how much and when."

"It's warm," I say.

He swipes it back. "So are hot toddies, buttered rum, and Spanish coffee." He pulls the cork and mocks, "*It's warm*. You sound like someone who needs a shot."

"That's because he does," Fish piles on. "Pass it this way." He takes the bottle before Cooper has finished his shot to take his own. After knocking back a hefty swallow himself, Fisher passes me the bottle. "You're up, Hale."

I hadn't planned on drinking tonight. I've taken two swigs off the beer Fish shoved in my hand the second we arrived. I'm not in the mood, which I know is beyond pathetic. For the most part, we can score alcohol when we want, but it's not a guarantee, which is why you don't turn it down, and you sure as hell don't show up as the buzz kill. The spices of the amber liquid are more pronounced warm, and while it's still poignant, the warmth mellows the burn. I take a look at the label. I've had warm whiskey and hated it. Whatever expensive shit this is…it's good. There may be a burn, but I had zero urge to wince. I bring the bottle to my lips for one more taste, hoping to knock my anxious thoughts down a notch, when Cooper's words cause me to choke on the spicy spirit.

"Holy shit! Is that Hart who just showed up with Syd?"

My eyes find her instantly, and my heart starts hammering against my chest when I see she's wearing my old t-shirt like a damn dress. A barrage of emotions attacks all at once, and my ears begin to ring as I try to sort through the fact that she decided to show up in my t-shirt, looking hot as fuck. She said she was over me. I search my mind for the words she gave me and replay them, confirming I didn't miss something. Laney said, *"Liked, past tense,"* I'm sure of it, but this isn't like her. She doesn't pull stunts like this, and finding out I wasted any time on someone else when she could have been mine all along has me on the edge of spiraling.

"Shut up, Cooper," Fisher says, punching him in the arm.

"What? You don't see what I see. She looks like she wants to be my next girlfriend. Laney might be like a little sister to you but not to me." He crosses his arms. "And she likes to ride my horses. All I need is one trail ride to move things out of the friend zone."

I grasp the rail on the balcony hard, using it to rein in the growing anger I have no right to feel, but it's there all the same.

"Laney is taken," Fish tells him, attempting to make him back off.

"Since when? Donovan might like her, but the feelings are clearly not mutual. Otherwise, they'd already be something, and since they're not..." He excitedly runs his hands together and turns on his heel to leave when Fisher catches his collar and pulls him back. "What the hell, man?"

He clears his throat, and his eyes nervously flick between Cooper's and mine as he waits to see if I'll jump in. When I don't, he says, "I said she's already taken. That's London's girl."

Now it's Cooper, whose eyes are as big as saucers, moving between me and Fisher's. "That's a joke, right?" He crosses his arms, waiting for a confirmation that won't come. I get why he thinks it's a joke. From the outside looking in, I'm with Riley, not Laney. Riley may not have the fancy title she wants, but she's next to me in the cafeteria, walking with me in the hallways, and hanging around whenever we're at the same events—not Laney. "If that's true, prove it."

I raise a brow. "Prove it," I repeat as I watch her walk toward the keg with Sydney.

"Yeah, pick a lane, Hale, because you don't get two girls," Cooper presses. His tone might be light, but he doesn't want to follow Fisher's advice.

Laney is a sophomore like him, and in our small town, dating options are limited. Most people pair up early, and dating someone's ex gets messy.

Even though Laney has been here a few years, she's still considered an outsider. Sydney Downs knows everyone and is picky about her inner circle, mainly because the Downs family has money, which attracts people with ulterior motives. Laney was clueless about who the Downs were. Sydney's friendship could've given Laney access to any social group, but she's stayed under the radar.

"Let it go, Coop. That t-shirt she's wearing..." Fish's eyes swing to mine as he leans on the balcony, watching the girls, and I see it. I know, without words, that he sees what Cooper sees, what every guy will undoubtedly notice—she looks good...too good not to take a shot. Fish gives me a head start. "That shirt is London's. She might not be interested in Noah Donovan, but I'm not sure the same can be said for London. A girl doesn't show up wearing a man's shirt if she's not trying to get his attention."

When we first met, I thought Laney needed saving. It was just her and her mom, like it was just me and my dad. She was new in town and didn't know anyone, and who doesn't want a friend? But I quickly realized Laney Hart never needed rescuing; she stays on the sidelines because she prefers it there. The first half of her life was spent picking up and moving around the country, following her mom wherever her work led. Making friends was pointless. She didn't get to keep them.

Shit. My eyes dart back to Laney, who's no longer with Sydney but Noah, and I rub my thumb along my bottom lip as Fisher's words and my thoughts collide. *She didn't get to keep them.* That's why she shot me down. I thought it was because she wasn't into me, that she had moved on after a summer apart, but Fish is right. He has to be. Why would she wear my shirt tonight if not to get my attention?

"Well, if that's the case, make your move, golden boy. If she's yours...prove it."

"You think I won't?" I say, keeping my eyes trained on her and Noah beside the keg, watching for any sign I'm reading this wrong, anything that says don't do it, not because you don't want to but because she's happy—happy with someone else.

"I got a Benjamin that says you won't." Cooper pulls his wallet out.

"Is that a bet?" Fish asks.

I walk over and grab his shoulder. "I don't want your money, Coop, but I'll take your bet." I squeeze his shoulder and head downstairs with a renewed pep in my step. I'm not betting on her. I'm betting on me. I'm making a play. You play to win. You might lose, but dammit, you play. I can't predict how she'll react. It doesn't matter if the odds are in my favor. I'm going to do it anyway. She means too much not to. She's important, and I'm done watching her from the sidelines. Laney made a move, showing up in my shirt. The proverbial ball is in my court. It's time to play. Noah Donovan doesn't get to take my girl.

"I'M GLAD YOU CAME TONIGHT. I'VE BEEN WANTING TO TAKE YOU out on a date," I hear Noah say to Laney as I follow a few feet behind them, sticking to the shadows as they make their way down to the boat dock where Sydney is hanging out with her boyfriend, Justin, and a few other random party goers.

They had already started walking toward the boat dock when I got downstairs. Noah Donovan has been a thorn in my side for the past year. There is nothing notable about Willow Creek. It's a small town that tourists accidentally happen upon on their way to the more desirable Lake Texoma towns, but his family sure has taken an interest in it.

Noah's father won the mayoral election by a landslide, and it was no surprise to anyone, seeing as how his family is loaded, and the town isn't. Mayor Donovan offered a lot of promises on his ticket, the main one being jobs. I wondered why a man with his fortune would be interested in a Podunk town off the beaten path until three new stores opened this past year: Donovan Hardware, Donovan General Store, and Donovan Flowers. The mayor is slowly buying the town, and I have no doubt he plans on making it a tourist destination with his name stamped all over it. We don't get to choose our family, and I don't dislike the guy because I think his dad has ulterior motives. I dislike him because he's all too happy to ride his coattails. He's not above using his influence to gain Laney's attention, and I don't like it. I didn't think Laney would either. She's not the type to give a shit about money and status. However, I haven't interrupted whatever this is to talk to her, because maybe I'm missing something, and I need to know. I need to know if part of her wants him.

"Yeah, I needed to get out——" catches on the wind before she trips over the transition between the ramp and the shore.

It hasn't gone unnoticed that things have been off with her the past few months. I convinced myself it was all in my head, that the unease crawling up my spine whenever she entered a room was just my perception shifting. Somewhere along the line, she became more than just the girl next door, more than just a friend, and because of that, I stopped trusting my own judgment when it came to her. But hearing those words confirms it wasn't just me.

"Sorry, the dock grabbed my foot," she jokes as Noah stabilizes her with his free arm.

"It's not a problem. I like it when you touch me," he lays it on thick, and I shake my head.

I don't want to hear this. The last thing I care to listen to is another guy flirting with my girl. "Shit!" I pinch the bridge of my nose. My subconscious is already claiming her, and she's not even mine. "Or is she?" I question, returning my gaze back to them. *She is wearing your shirt. It's why you came down here.*

"You're cute, Noah Donovan." Her back is to me, but I can hear it in her voice. She's smiling.

"Come on, I saw her go this way," Riley Heron's unmistakable high-pitched shrill says somewhere behind me, and I duck behind a tree.

I've been avoiding her all night, and the last thing I need right now is for her to find me. She'll latch on, and that'll be it. I could lose my chance to talk to Laney, and I refuse to lose the opportunity to ask her why she showed up tonight wearing my t-shirt while she's in it. Once she and her entourage pass, I move closer to get a better view. It's dark now, but the dock has Edison lights strung all around the metal roof and the railings, which helps, but still it's hard to see. I quickly scan the group gathered on the dock, curious who her target might be as she tramps down the ramp on a mission. My curiosity is short-lived when I see her stop right behind Laney.

"Shit," I mutter as I start toward the dock.

"London." Two hands slide around my bicep, catching me off guard. "We've been looking for you all night," one of the girls from Riley's cheer squad says in a seductive come-hither tone.

I stare at her blankly. I've seen her face a million times, but I can't remember her name for the life of me. I also don't care to remember it. She's pretty, but I'd never be into a girl who would go behind her so-called friend's back and try to bait the guy she's talking to. If she's genuinely trying to help Riley find me, there's no need for the flirtatious tone or the batting of her eyelashes.

"Yeah, I think I found her," I say, nodding toward the dock when a splash followed by Riley's obnoxious laugh meant to garner attention has both our heads turning toward the commotion.

Everyone is now staring over the edge into the water when I ask, "What the hell was that?"

"Probably time for skinny dipping," she guesses.

I'm scanning the onlookers, searching for Laney, when Noah dives in. "What in the actual fuck?"

I brush her hand off my arm and continue toward the dock, only to take off in a sprint when Noah pops up out of the water and yells, "She's stuck!"

I don't need to search the dock to know which shadowy figure is missing. Laney.

I'M BEYOND SOAKED, MY CLOTHES ARE A SECOND SKIN, WEIGHING me down, determined to drag me back into the depths that nearly claimed her. My lungs aren't just burning; they're screaming for mercy with each ragged breath while my muscles tremble and threaten to give out completely as I battle against the shoreline. Her blonde hair is plastered against her face, and blood is streaming down her right leg, but it's the faint, erratic flutter of her heart against my chest that terrifies me most. I have to focus on that fragile drumbeat because if I don't, I'll lose myself to the panic that gripped me when I thought I might lose one of the only people I've ever truly cared about. Each shallow breath she takes, each weak thud of her heart as I carry her toward safety, is the only thing keeping me from completely falling apart.

If I hadn't been there…if I hadn't had my grandfather's knife in my pocket… I shake the thought away. I don't want to know what an existence without her looks like, and I sure as hell never want to feel it. I feel her fingers tighten around my neck, and I look down at her motionless body. Our eyes lock, and though no words are shared, something profound passes between us, a silent acknowledgment of what was nearly lost. Not just a life, but a future. Our future. My eye twitches with the thought, wondering if the "our" part is flicking through her mind the way it is mine.

In the distance, I hear familiar voices. "Laney, thank god you're okay," Sydney says, coming to my side, but I don't stop walking. I won't. I can't. Not until she's safe. I can't be sure what put her in that lake, but I know damn well I don't trust anyone else to take care of what is undoubtedly the reason my heart beats.

"London," I hear Noah call out, his footsteps heavy as he runs up the grassy hill beside me as I reach the yard. "Thanks for helping. I can take her home. I offered to take her home. What happened back there didn't change that."

My fingers instinctively grip her tighter. "Go home, Donovan," I grind out without slowing. There's no way she's leaving here with anyone but me.

"I'm her date, Hale!" he attempts to assert, but I ignore it. Laney didn't come here with him. She came with Sydney. His wanting this to be a date and it being a date are not the same.

"You can stop staring, asshats. You're all gawking like you've never seen someone get wet," I hear Sydney say at my back as she follows behind us as we pass the people gathered around the bonfire.

The sound of the music fades once I get past the backyard, and Laney asks, "Is there anything sticking out of my knee?"

"No," I answer, eyes forward.

"Well, how would you know? You didn't even look," she argues as she squirms to get a better look.

My jaw tightens with the memory. The second I came out of the water with her in my arms, my eyes scanned her entire body from head to toe, ensuring I was pulling her out the same way she went in—in one piece.

"Trust me, Laney. I looked," I say, my tone a little thorny.

I may have saved her, and an unspoken moment of what we almost lost might have been shared, but it doesn't change the fact that I still don't have an answer for her clothing choices tonight. It's her choice of outfit that has me marching straight back to my truck. My forearm has been firmly plastered against the lacey underwear covering the soft milky skin of her ass since I swooped her into my arms. There's no way in hell I'm pulling it away with an audience.

"Noah can take me home. You've done enough. You don't need to drive me home," she says meekly, misreading my tone and words for annoyance with her.

I'm more than annoyed, but not with her, with this entire night. If I hadn't second-guessed myself last year, if I hadn't paused again tonight, allowing doubt to creep in, she might never have ended up with her ankle stuck in an abandoned fishing net beneath dark murky water.

"Yeah, I got it, man," Noah piggybacks onto her suggestion, and I ignore it as I reach the old truck my father gifted me for my sixteenth birthday last year.

I carefully set her down at my front, pinning her between myself and the truck so no one sees what she's wearing beneath my old shirt. "Hold on a second," I say with one arm firmly wrapped around her center as I pull open the door before lifting her by the waist onto the backseat. "Don't move," I instruct before disappearing to the back to grab a med kit.

"Laney, I'm so sorry. I jumped in to help you when I noticed you weren't coming up, and then when I found out you were stuck, I went back up to get help and—" Noah says, quickly invading the space I vacated and leaning against the door, only to be cut off.

"London, what's going on?" Riley interrupts with her minions at her back.

I pay her no attention. I'm unsure what happened, but I know she's not innocent. She fucking laughed, and now she dares to ask what's going on as though she didn't bear witness to pure horror. I return to the side of the truck with a first aid kit. "Do you mind?" I gesture for Noah to step back so I can reclaim my spot at her front.

"I can do that," Noah offers.

"I got it. You can leave. I'll be taking Laney home."

"You can't be serious," Riley says exasperatedly. "Noah just offered to take her home."

I rifle through the first aid box in search of the supplies I need to patch her up until I can get her home. I have nothing to say to Riley, and the things I want to say are awful. I knew she could be an arrogant brat, but this…this is a new low, even for her. All this time, I thought I owed Riley something, but I didn't. She's a big girl; she knew what the deal was the second she answered my call. There was a mutual benefit to our arrangement, but that's gone.

"Are you really choosing her over me?"

My hands find my intended target: an Ace bandage. I squeeze it in one hand before closing the box and setting it on the floor. I raise off my knee and turn around slowly.

"Am I serious? Are you?" Her mouth opens slightly. "Laney almost died back there in an incident you caused."

I may not have seen it, but I can combine two and two. Riley stormed that dock and found Laney. A few seconds later, Laney was in the water.

"I didn't push her in the lake," she counters coldly, hand settling on her hip in practiced innocence, her eyes flicking over everyone gathered around as she calculates the impact of her words as though the fact that she caused the fall is merely an inconvenient technicality.

"I'm not doing this with you." I shake my head and turn back to Laney.

Riley grasps my wrist. "London..." she says my name as one last plea.

My eyes lock on where her hand touches my skin, her touch igniting a fire in my veins. I never liked it, but now I hate it.

"If you want me to choose between her and you, fine…" I pluck her hand off my wrist. "HER. It will be her every time."

"You're going to regret those words, London Hale."

"Not possible." I turn back to Laney, immediately tending to her knee and avoiding her eyes. I don't have time to analyze whatever I do or don't see there. I have things I want to say but not here. "Go home, Donovan. I'll be taking Laney home, no one else," I say, knowing he's still at my back, waiting to swoop in.

"Is that what you want, Laney?" he asks.

She's quiet, and it's that silence that has my heart rate spiking and my eyes drifting to hers. I just chose her in front of everyone without hesitation or regret, but her choice remains unspoken, hanging in the air between us. I want her to choose me with the same fierce certainty that drove me into the water for her. Not because I'm standing here dripping and desperate, not because I saved her, but because something in her recognizes something in me that makes all other options impossible.

"London can take me home," she says, her eyes pinned on mine with what feels like recognition, until they're gone, and I'm downgraded to a convenience when she adds, "We're neighbors, and you live on the other side of town. Thank you for helping me tonight. I'm sorry you had to get wet."

"Okay…" Noah stutters out dejectedly. "Call me later."

"Yeah." She nods in agreement. "I'll call you tomorrow."

"Well, if you're leaving, so am I," Sydney says, stepping up to the side of the truck.

"You should stay. The night is still young, and Cooper is your cousin. I'm wet, and my knee hurts. I'll be fine," Laney offers.

I finish wrapping her knee, and Sydney jams her finger into my chest. "Get my best friend home safe, Hale, or I'll have my brother kick your ass."

I grab her finger. "I'm pretty sure your invite is the reason she's in this situation to begin with."

"You know what I mean, Hale."

My eyes narrow slightly before releasing her finger. "I have no idea what you're talking about, Sydney," I dismiss her pointed comment. Any ownership of feelings I have for Laney will be given to her first. They won't be acknowledged in a flippant comment, because she deserves more than that. I open the front door of the truck and reach across, grabbing my football hoodie before returning to Laney and tossing it on her lap. "It's all I have. I figure it's better than being wet."

I watch as she clutches the fabric in her fists, staring at it in her lap before her big brown eyes latch onto mine. "Thanks."

"Call me when you get home," Sydney says before retreating to her boyfriend's side. "Let's go, Justin. I'll say hi to Cooper, and then we can leave."

I watch them return to the house, my gaze lingering a little longer than it should as I take a minute to collect my thoughts. It's not until my skin starts to prickle with that unmistakable electricity —that sixth sense of being observed—that I turn back to find Laney curiously staring at me.

Her fingers nervously twist in the drawstrings of my hoodie. "You didn't have to—"

"Don't even think about finishing that sentence. There's no alternate ending where I let anything other than you coming out of that lake alive happen."

"Right." She nods in agreement before dropping her gaze to her lap. "What I was going to say is, Noah would have—"

"Would have been too late." I tip her chin up until my eyes are on hers. "He didn't have the chief with him." I pat my pocket. Standing here, staring into her eyes, unravels me. I swear I can almost feel the ground shift beneath my feet. It's that off-balance feeling that pulls me back. "Do you need help?" Her eyebrows rise in surprise, and I close my eyes, realizing my mistake. "I didn't mean with the shirt. I meant turning forward in the seat." I gesture to her knee.

"Oh, no, I got it," she says, slowly pulling her legs into the cab before I close the door.

I would love to say I don't care to relive tonight or that if given the choice to go back in time and erase it, I would, but that would be a lie. If tonight showed me anything, it is this: It feels like she could fall with me. I don't know what the future holds, forget about life. I don't know about love, but I know about madness, and that's what I've felt since she said she didn't want to marry me anymore. But the depth I saw in her chestnut gaze makes me believe falling might be the answer to all of it.

~

LANEY

CHAPTER 4

SOPHOMORE YEAR

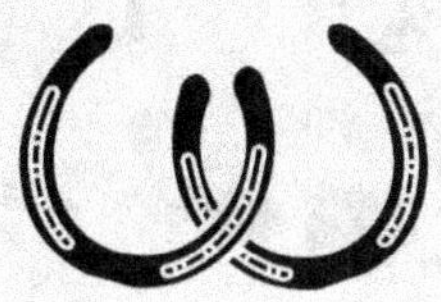

AGE SIXTEEN

The crunch of gravel beneath tires fills the silence as London navigates the winding road away from the lake house. I reach for the hem of my sopping-wet shirt and squeeze my eyes shut. Just a few seconds…that's all I need to wallow in my regrets. I told myself no drama tonight, yet here I am, drenched and trembling in the backseat of his truck.

There are many reasons I've been a ghost for the past few months, and not all of them orbit around the man behind the wheel; however, right now, he eclipses the rest. London Hale is an enigma wrapped in contradiction. One minute, he was the phantom at the edges of the party, sight unseen, and the next, he was plunging into the dark water, his hands finding me in its murky depths.

I know it's stupid, and the last thing I should be worried about right now is what feelings London does or doesn't possess when it comes to me. I nearly drowned tonight. My lungs still ache with the memory of water rushing in. Death brushed past me with cold fingers. Yet all I can fixate on is whether saving me was merely an inconvenience to him and if choosing me over Riley has already turned into regret. The silence stretching between us feels like both might be true, or maybe it's my insecurity from the judgment I felt from everyone who watched me spectacularly fall tonight. I peel my shirt away from my skin, hoping that removing it will help me escape the humiliation threatening to consume me. At the very least, I won't be cold.

I toss the wet shirt on the floorboards, a crumpled testament to tonight's disaster. Sitting in nothing more than my wet bra and panties, my eyes catch a flash of movement in the rearview mirror. London's eyes, dark and unreadable, are locked on mine. Something electric crackles between us, my pulse quickens, and I nervously tear my gaze away first. Allowing him to watch me through my bedroom window is one thing; sharing the small space of his dad's old truck is another. He's close enough that I could touch him. Just as the thought that he could touch me too flits across my mind, so does my desire to chance another look.

This time, when our eyes collide, something shifts in his expression. His jaw clenches tight enough to see the muscle twitch beneath the stubble now lining his jaw. He wrenches his attention back to the road, knuckles blanching against the steering wheel. But that stolen moment of intensity felt like a spark of desire mirroring my own. Maybe it's the near-death experience loosening my grip on self-preservation, or I'm simply tired of the tightrope walk of pretending I don't feel what I feel. But I don't believe his lingering gaze was rejection. I think it was restraint. Tonight feels like free-falling through a reel of my worst impulses —what's one more reckless decision to add to the collection? If I'm destined to make a fool of myself again, I might as well dive headlong into the humiliation.

I reach for his hoodie and pull it over my head. The soft fabric slides against my bare skin, enveloping me in the warmth that carries his scent. It's both refuge and torment. I push my arms through the sleeves and grip the headrests, determined to propel myself into the front seat in one fluid motion without bending my knee. The second I'm in the passenger seat beside him, the space between us collapses to inches, and with it, all my careful defenses.

"Christ, Laney, you're going to hurt yourself," he scolds, eyes wide, as I settle into my seat. His harrowed look softens as his eyes rake over my body, and I can't help but wonder if it's because he likes how I look wearing his things.

"You have the heat on up here," I say, holding my hands against the vents. "I was cold." I have a list of other things I want to say, but sitting this close, I feel pieces of my bravery slipping, so I start with an apology. "I'm sorry about what happened with your girlfriend tonight."

"Are you?" he asks flatly. "You wouldn't have shown up to a party wearing nothing but my shirt if that were true."

I'm unsure what I expected him to say, but going straight for my wardrobe selection wasn't it. I roll my lips when I feel his accusatory gaze boring into the side of my head. "I didn't start anything with her tonight. She came after me. It's not like I approached her, tapped her shoulder, and announced I was wearing her boyfriend's t-shirt."

Anger coils tightly within me as the cruel irony of my words registers, and my mind floods with the vivid memory of her approaching me on the dock.

"The only heart up for grabs is the one standing next to you," Sydney's boyfriend lightheartedly joked, with Noah pulling me into his side and kissing my forehead.

"No, actually, it's not. Everyone knows her selfish little heart already covets my boyfriend." I cringed when I heard the voice that belonged to maybe the only person I've ever hated. Riley Heron.

I knew she'd be at the party, but I didn't think she'd be wasting her time on me, especially when London was nowhere to be seen. The second I turned around, my rational thought betrayed me.

"Riley, what the hell are you talking about? I haven't seen London all night, though I'm sure if I did, his face would be attached to yours."

I could have chosen better words. The ones that came out definitely sounded like fighting words.

"You might think I'm stupid, but I'm not, especially when it comes to men," Riley defended, showing up unprovoked, set on making a scene for the small crowd that had gathered on the dock to escape the bonfire. "You TPed his house last year, you never close your window even though you know his looks directly into yours, and tonight you wore that. The fact that your outfit is a tired trend is beside the point. Everyone knows Lyndsey Hart doesn't dress provocatively." Her eyes dragged down my body with disgust, and she waved her hand. "You wore that to get attention."

My right eye twitched. She knew my name and deliberately called me the wrong one out of spite.

"Newsflash, biatch. If Laney wanted to steal your man, she could," Sydney snapped in my defense.

"Please…" Riley rolled her eyes as though the statement was preposterous. "There's no competition, I'm the captain of the cheerleading team, and London is the quarterback—"

Noah cut her off, his hand finding my arm. "Is what she's saying true? You want Hale?"

That was the last straw. I had promised myself no drama, and everything about her confrontation was the very definition, so I tried to bow out.

"You know what? I'm not doing this," I said, raising my white flag. I had no energy to fight over someone who didn't belong to me. It only would have taken me three long strides to pass Riley and escape the drama I was determined to avoid, but before I passed, I couldn't bite my tongue. "You came here to warn everyone about my heart, but it's yours you should be worried about. You can judge mine all you want, but it's yours I feel sorry for. Not because it's cruel, but because it doesn't know its worth."

Pining for London was different than being his and knowing his heart wasn't all in. Her eyebrows rose, and for a second, I thought she heard my underhanded jab for the truth it was, but then her snobbish superiority returned, and I knew there was no way she'd let me have the last word, which was fine; she could say them to my back. I only made it one step before hands were on my back, and I was sailing forward to my knees.

"We're not done here, Hart."

Those were the last words I heard before searing pain ripped through my right knee as I landed on a nail. My heart palpitated as my body fought the desire to pass out. I rolled to my side, clutching my leg, and plunged off the ramp into the lake.

"I know," London says on a long exhale, snapping my thoughts back to the truck cab.

"You know?" I ask, trying to blink away the anger the memory brought to the surface. "That's all you have to say? Your girlfriend is an evil witch. I can't believe you'd even—"

"She was never my girlfriend."

"Okay…" I say sarcastically. "Fuck buddy, whatever you want to call it. It's all the same."

"It's not at all the same." He grips the wheel hard, my words clearly touching a nerve.

"How is it not? You shared yourself with her intimately, gave her your free time, and—"

"No, Laney. I spent most of my time hiding from her. I was never home because I took every opportunity to stay late after practice and help the coach. When I wasn't training, I was tutoring in the library, and the few nights you did see me with her, it was so I could stomach being in my room after I asked you to close the window."

"Ouch." I turn my gaze back out the window. That stings.

"That's not what I meant." He releases a frustrated breath. "You don't get to put this on me. You're the heartbreaker, Laney Hart, not me."

"What's that supposed to mean?" I snap back.

"Last summer, when I came home, I caught you TPing my house, and I asked you…" His eyes flash over to mine for a split second. "I asked you if you still wanted to marry me, and you said no."

My mouth drops open. "You can't be serious. That was your way of asking if I was still into you?" I feel like I'm in a twilight zone.

"Yes, and I didn't get the response I expected. Instead, you went into an overexplanation about being contextually correct with the team's use of the word 'liked' being past tense and not present, and how I was out of town, so my house made perfect sense. You had a million reasons about how I wasn't your guy."

I'm stunned. I had no idea those words had cut him so deeply. That night replays, and I sift through how I felt and what I said, wishing I could get a do-over. Had I said what I truly felt, the next day may have looked a lot different. Perhaps it would have looked the way I dreamed it to be. I breathe deeply and turn to him, only to be met with the slamming of a truck door. I was so lost in my thoughts I hadn't realized we were home.

He comes around the truck and opens my door. When he extends his hand, my voice is barely a whisper.

"London." His name hangs in the air between us, weighted with regret.

I trace my fingers along his hand, savoring the exquisite buzz that always comes when he's touching me, but it's not until my eyes lock with his that I see it. Not only does he care...he cares deeply.

But right now, that's enough. There's something else lurking behind his obsidian stare, and I can't help but wonder if all of this is too little too late when he answers, "Not now, Laney," through clenched teeth.

The second my feet hit the ground I'm hoisted into his arms. I could walk, but I don't argue. It would be futile. He won't allow it, and truthfully, cradled against his chest with his heartbeat steady beneath my ear, there's nowhere else I'd rather be.

Walking through the front door of my ranch, he strides straight to my room the way he's done countless times over the years, each step assured and familiar. His scent surrounds me, a comfort I've known since we were young. Then, nudging the door open with his foot, he navigates the familiar path to my bed. His warmth vanishes far too soon as he sets me down. The mattress dips beneath me, and his fingers linger at my shoulder for a fleeting moment, reluctant to break contact completely. His eyes, usually guarded, reveal a flicker of something that makes my breath catch, and then he's across the room, rifling through my drawers.

"Why did you wear my shirt?" he asks, his tone giving nothing away.

"It was Sydney's idea." I try to match his indifference.

"Uh-huh, but why did you agree?"

This time, there's a faint hint of curiosity in his voice. He's fishing, and the last time I didn't give him the truth, we lost a year.

"I wanted you to see me."

He turns around. "I've always seen you. Why this way? Why tonight?"

I know what he's asking. Of all the ways to step out of my comfort zone, why did I choose this avenue? That answer isn't easy. It's twisted in a multilayered fear. Fear of misstepping, losing my best friend, and never knowing what it's like to be his.

"I'm scared of messing up." I sigh. "I think my mom is considering taking a new job again. I didn't want to give her any ammunition to say yes."

"Wait, I thought she took a full-time offer at St. Anthony's. Doesn't that mean her traveling nurse days are over?" He closes the distance between us and hands me a pair of shorts. "Put those on," he says before giving me his back.

"Why?"

"Laney…" he draws out my name. "Please. Can't you see this isn't easy for me?"

"I didn't ask you to stay," comes out before I can think it through.

He turns around, his eyes wild as they snap to mine. "But I want to," he says intensely before closing them and pulling air through his nose. "I need to make sure you're okay."

I can see he's worked up. I just wish I knew the roots. Is he worked up because he wants a chance at us, or does he feel obligated to protect me? It could be both, but one of those reasons weighs more than the other.

I pull off my damp underwear and hide them under one of

my extra pillows before pulling on the shorts and saying, "You can open your eyes now."

He opens his eyes cautiously, keeping them keenly trained on mine, ensuring he doesn't see a trick before dropping to his knees to remove the Ace bandage he put around my knee at the party. His hand barely touches my calf, and my whole body begins to tingle from the contact. It's not until my chest starts to tighten that I realize I've been holding my breath, waiting for this moment to become a figment of my imagination because there is no way London Hale is on his knees for me, in my room, while I'm swallowed up in his hoodie wrapped in his scent. This has to be some kind of alternate universe. The slight tremble in his hand as he unwraps the bandage is the only sure way I know this is real because, in my dreams, I don't make him nervous. He makes me nervous.

"Why do you think your mom will make you leave?"

"If I answer one of your questions, you have to answer one of mine," I counter.

Those midnight eyes flash up to mine. "Deal."

"A few months ago, she left her computer open, and one of the tabs was for jobs, but not just any jobs—the traveling kind. The ones she used to take before we settled down here. I think she's considering leaving again, and I don't want to give her any reasons to pull the trigger." He's quiet, and when I draw my eyes away from his face, I see it's because my knee is exposed. "Oh my god, I think I'm going to be sick."

"Lie down. I'm going to clean it up," he says, getting to his feet and quickly crossing the hallway to the bathroom. Blood has always made me queasy, but it isn't that so much as it is the small indention from where the nail head broke the skin. He rushes back in with supplies. "I think it looks worse than it is. Once I clean it up, I'll know if we need to go to the ER." I throw my arm over my eyes. That's the last thing I need. "If it comes to that, you tripped and fell on the porch."

"Okay," I agree with a grimace.

"This might sting a little, so I will talk through it. Your mom's job search…is that why you've holed yourself up in your room?" he asks as I feel the cold liquid drip down my leg before the sting settles into the open wound.

"Yes," I answer with a wince as I roll my lips and pull a lungful of air through my nose. "But it's my turn to ask a question." A towel starts to trail up my leg, catching the excess liquid, and I ask, "Why the shorts?"

"Of all the questions you could have asked, that's the one you chose?"

Maybe it sounds out of place, but it's the most direct-indirect question I can ask to find out what side of the fence we fall on after all that happened tonight. The question hovers between us, deceptively simple after everything we've confessed. The answer to this one feels the lightest on what's already been a heavy night. Yet somehow, this seemingly innocent question carries the power to define whatever fragile thing exists between us now.

"Because being on my knees in front of you wearing nothing but my hoodie is difficult enough; the shorts make this bearable."

I throw my arm off my eyes and push myself back into a seated position to see him. The honesty and vulnerability I just heard was unexpected, however, if those words mean half of what they mean to me, you wouldn't know it by looking at him. I'm sure he can feel my eyes boring into the top of his head as he tends to my knee, but he doesn't acknowledge it. I give it a few more seconds, waiting to see if he'll say something, anything, that tells me that admission was a loaded one, and when he doesn't, I ask my next burning question. It doesn't mean he'll answer, but at least I won't lose sleep over the regret of not asking. "So we're not going to talk about it?"

"Talk about what?"

"Us," I answer boldly. He doesn't get to act like he hasn't said a lot of things tonight that weren't cloaked in admissions, ones that echo the same sentiments I've had since the first day I saw him.

"There isn't an us," he says flatly, and I stifle my desire to audibly growl my frustration with his dismissiveness. He's strung me along all night, only to shut me down the second I ask for the slightest clarification.

"I get that, but what if I had said I still wanted to marry you that night?" I ask, going in for the kill.

"You didn't." He uses a cotton swab to wipe away the dried blood. "I don't think we need to go to the ER."

"I know what I said, London, but—"

"No buts, Laney." His eyes find mine for the first time since I sat up; I see the plea in them before he adds, "We're not doing this tonight."

Those eyes that cause my heart to stumble every time they fall upon mine stay pinned for moments. I wish I could hold onto them a little longer before they're focused on my knee once more. He starts covering the wound, and I consider his silent petition to let it go for tonight, but I can't. I've played the passive hand, but not now. I can't play it safe after I've come this far.

"I don't understand. Why not?"

"Because you almost died," he states loudly as his hands slam onto the bed beside me, and I startle. "I almost lost you, and I'm struggling to work through what almost was while staying grounded in what is."

He closes his eyes as his hand fists in my blankets, knuckles whitening with the strain. The weight of all the words he gave me, sparse and carefully chosen as they were, crash into me. I knew he cared, but it's the realization of its depth I hadn't fully understood until now. The tremble in his fingers against my bedsheets and how he can't meet my gaze now are confession enough.

"London…" I reach for his cheek, and the tension in his jaw loosens. I lean my head against his. "I'm sorry. I won't push."

His head subtly shakes as his hand covers mine. "You have nothing to be sorry for."

"I overthink everything and—" His eyes pierce mine straight through to my soul as his thumb brushes over my bottom lip.

"Never apologize for how you feel, especially if I'm the one that made you feel it."

With our foreheads pressed together, his eyes slowly search for an objection. They wait. They're patient, taking their time to allow for second thoughts, but with our lips mere inches apart, he finally makes a move, obliterating the madness that separates us and crushing his mouth to mine. The move is fast, like he made it before he could talk himself out of it, but the kiss is anything but. His lips take their time parting mine as his hand delicately slides down my jaw to my neck, sending a trail of goosebumps down my spine.

My head swims, but it is the muffled groan that escapes his throat the second his tongue dips into my mouth that has me drowning. I don't care what kind of storm London Hale is; I could dance in his rain or cry its downpour. The second he walked into my life, he struck like lightning, fast without warning, scorching the earth and leaving its mark. This might be our first kiss, and you never know which one will be your last, but I know this one will forever be burned on my heart. I never want it to end. I could be happy just like this for the rest of my days. Maybe it's all just a crush, one that would eventually fizzle out if I let it, but he's not just my favorite daydream. He's someone I can't stop thinking about. No matter how hard I've tried, I always come back to him.

My hand reaches for his chest, and the second it does, I wish I hadn't because he pulls away. "I have to go." He gets to his feet.

I reach for my swollen lips, and my cheeks tinge. "You didn't like it?"

He runs his hands through his wild hair. "What? No. Laney, you have no idea how long I've wanted to kiss you like that, but I can't stay."

His words from earlier seep back in. "Because I almost died."

"Yeah." His hands fall to his hips.

"Isn't that more reason to stay? Life is too short. You never know when your chance might be taken from you."

"That's one way of looking at it; the other is I don't want to fuck this up. You're too important to me, and I'm a mess right now. You deserve the world and everything you want, and if any part of that is still me, I want it to be real. Not because I saved you, not because we were strung out on the adrenaline from everything that happened tonight."

"So, tomorrow, when I want to kiss you again…" I pull on the strings of his hoodie. "You'll let me?"

Tongue in cheek, he drops his head. "You're making my choice to walk out of this room feel like punishment, heartbreaker." I want to say *good*, but I don't. He kissed me. We kissed, and he liked it. For tonight, that memory will be enough. "Come on." He nods toward my pillows. "Lie down. I don't want you walking around on this knee tonight. It's late. Get some rest." He pulls back my covers, and I lift a few inches to get on the other side and crawl beneath. Once I'm settled, he pulls my hand to his soft lips and kisses the back of my hand.

"For the record, when I ask for a kiss tomorrow, that's not where I want it."

He pinches his lips together to stifle the smile pulling at the corners of his mouth, but he can't hide the slow smolder in his eyes. "Tomorrow, then," he says before releasing my hand and shutting off the light.

I don't bother mentioning it's already tomorrow, but the few short hours that stretch between now and dawn will most certainly be a small eternity, because there will be no sleeping tonight. All there will be is counting down the minutes and seconds before I get to be his again.

~

WHY HASN'T HE TEXTED ME BACK? I ASK MYSELF AS I FLIP MY phone over in my lap for the hundredth time this morning.

I texted London hours ago, letting him know I went to the ER. Of course, the second my nurse mother saw my knee, she was unwrapping it for herself, and the second she found out a nail was involved, we were en route to the hospital. Apparently, I needed a tetanus shot and an x-ray to ensure no small pieces were embedded in my knee. I knew there were no fragments in my knee, and I think she did too, but my mother has always been over the top when it comes to my health. I've always thought it was because of her career. Being a nurse, she sees a lot of worst-case scenarios, but the older I get, I see it differently. Now I know it's because I'm all she has. We're all each other has.

"What has gotten into you today? You've been on edge all morning," my mother asks as we drive down Main Street, finally on our way home after spending hours at the hospital.

"I'm not on edge. I just don't like hospitals the way you do," I say as I watch Mrs. Donovan place a bouquet of flowers in the front window of her shop as we pass by.

"I wouldn't say I like hospitals. It's just where I work. I do, however, enjoy helping people. I think you can at least relate to that, given you're considering going into counseling."

I roll my eyes and lay my head against the window. It's not that I don't want to talk to my mom. My mother and I get along just fine, but right now, all I really want is to get home, and that desire is so strong it leaves no space for anything else. I suppose that has left me a little edgy, but it can't be helped. I want to know how, last night, London Hale treated me like I was something special— something he couldn't live without—and now I'm being left on read. No text asking if everything is okay, no worry or concern, not even a *when will you be home?* Nothing.

"For someone not on edge, you're about to bounce that good knee through my floorboard."

It's on the tip of my tongue to tell her I want to see London, but I don't, and that's not easy because I'm used to telling her everything—well, almost everything. Over the past year, I haven't brought up a few things—one being the job search I found on her computer. However, not telling her about London is different. I don't want to lie any more than I already have about last night, and telling any bit of what happened leaves a lot to be questioned. Plus, her knowing I have a crush on the boy next door and that boy turning into my boyfriend will most definitely raise flags. I don't want her to see him as anything more than he ever was until it's a certainty, and maybe not even then, because I'm sure he'd be banned from entering my room the second he went from friend to boyfriend.

"It's Sunday. I feel like I just wasted half my weekend, is all."

"Did you forget you're on summer break?"

Because the Mustangs went to state, their season ran until the end of school. The party last night almost felt like another day of walking down the hallways with familiar faces and social anxiety, which for me was only piled on by Riley's confrontation and my epic fall. The slightest bit of tension releases as the knowledge of having twelve weeks before I have to face anyone from school settles in.

"Yeah, I guess I did," I mumble, my thoughts scattered as she turns down our street. My heart quickens, a sudden tension I wasn't prepared for.

"Does pizza sound good for dinner? I don't feel like cooking tonight."

When my mother pulls into the driveway, I see London in his backyard, shirtless, splitting wood. My annoyance instantly kicks into overdrive. For starters, it's summer. Who splits wood in the summer? There's no way he couldn't spare a minute to text back? It's not like there's a cold front on the horizon. And secondly, I know he heard my mother's car pull into the driveway, and he hasn't even spared me a glance.

"Sure, pizza sounds great, Mom," I say. My hand grips the door handle, and I strengthen my backbone, reminding myself of all the words I promised to give London when I saw him, no matter the consequence. No regrets.

My mom starts toward the house and then pauses, remembering my leg. "Laney, do you need help?"

I wave her off. "I'm fine, Mom. I'll be in shortly," I say, my eyes laser-focused on London as I stomp my way across the yard as best I can with a bum knee.

The second I'm a foot away from him, and the axe he's been swinging is on the ground as he gathers the split wood, I push my finger into his shoulder. "Why are you ignoring me?"

"I'm not," he says, not even bothering to look at me as he puts the wood on the rack.

"I texted you," I say, crossing my arms.

"I don't have my phone." He swipes a bead of sweat off his eyebrow and finally spares me a glance. It's a sideways glance, but it's a look all the same, one that melts me even though I'm so mad I could spit. I hate boys. It's unfair how much they can affect us and how hard it is to let them go when they're not good for us.

"It's right there." I arch a brow and point to it laying on his discarded shirt.

"I've been busy," he blows out exasperatedly.

"You expect me to believe you've been chopping wood all morning?" I put my hands on my hips as he puts another log on the chopping block.

"No, I mowed the grass and vacuumed the pool first. Now I'm doing this."

He refuses to meet my eyes, so I force him to by stepping in front of the chopping block. "You left me on read."

His eyes slowly come off the ground and find mine, but his expression is unreadable when they do. He's not seeing me. He's looking through me. He doesn't want to look at me, let alone talk. I swallow down the hurt. When I went through all the scenarios that might play out the second I got home, this was one of them, and it sucked then as much as it does now, but if this is it, I'm not walking away with things unsaid. He's going to own his part.

"That's it, then? You slept on it, and the way you see it, last night didn't happen? Nothing has changed?" I state firmly, and he stands, unmoving. I clench my fists so I don't punch him instead. Rejection sucks. Last night, he seemed concerned about our friendship, but right now, it feels like the end of the road. "Whatever, I'll get your hoodie back to you," I add as I step around him. "I won't be—"

His arm wraps around my waist. "I don't want my hoodie back. I like it when you wear my things."

"And I don't believe you. You're only trying to placate me because you think you'll hurt my feelings. You not making up your mind isn't killing me; it's just wasting my time. And I deserve better than that," I grind out as I push his arm away.

Both arms wrap around my middle, and he spins me toward my house and directs my gaze to my windowsill, where the shirt I wore to the party last night sits neatly folded. His lips brush my ear, his voice low and deliberate, "You were saying?"

"Why give me your shirt and not respond to my text?" His arms loosen, and I turn around. Ghosts of annoyance still mar his stupidly handsome face, but the shirt and the fact that he didn't let me walk away mad tell me there is something else. "I still want you to kiss me."

He inhales deeply and closes his eyes. "I can't."

"Why not?" I ask, and he subtly shakes his head. "Will you stop avoiding me and just tell me? I'm a big girl, London. If you changed your mind and are having regrets, just say that."

His eyes flash open. "My dad wants to take your mom to dinner."

"Okay…" I draw out, not understanding how that affects us.

"My dad hasn't gone on a date since my mother walked out and never looked back. He deserves a shot at happiness. There can't be a you and me if there's a them."

"That sounds like a cop-out if I ever did hear one. I saw you first. I want you, and I think you want me to."

He swallows hard, and the way his coal-dark eyes lock on mine, I know I'm right. "It's not that simple."

I step into him. "Yes, it is. You were mine first," I say as though that settles it.

"Is that so?" A soft smile tugs at the lips I've dreamed of kissing again since the moment they left mine.

"It is," I state without waver.

His eyes search my face as he battles with what he wants for his dad and what he wants for himself. "You win." My mind barely has time to process the words before his perfect mouth collides with mine. Strong arms envelop me, and my body hums as the hard lines of his body meld against mine, and he holds me the way I've always dreamed he would. His hands ball in my shirt as his tongue seeks entrance that I eagerly grant, desperate to get closer. "You'll always win, heartbreaker."

Seconds dissolve into minutes as we kiss deeply on the cool grass behind the shed for hours. When our lips part for air, our bodies stay tangled, neither wanting to let go of what we've found. We fit together perfectly, heartbeats synchronized as my fingertips trace the outline of his jaw while his arms keep me tightly pressed against his front. It's the best night of my life—then he is gone.

LANEY

CHAPTER 5

JUNIOR YEAR

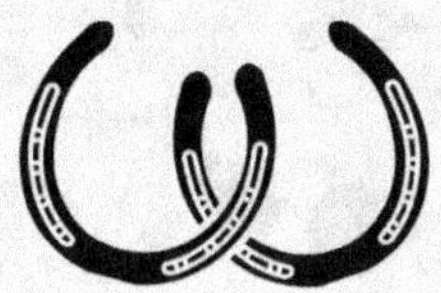

AGE SEVENTEEN

"Thanks for letting me stay for dinner," Noah says as my mother serves him a bowl of white chicken chili. It's August. Most would consider chili a fall dish, but Mother insists it's a year-round dish when you live in Texas.

"Noah, do you mind passing the cornbread?" Mr. Hale asks from his seat across the table.

"Yes, sir," Noah replies, passing him the bowl as I take a big bite of my muffin so I don't smile. I can't help it. This dinner is awkward, and I tend to laugh at the most inappropriate times.

"So, Laney, your mother tells me you plan on attending the University of Oklahoma after graduation," Mr. Hale starts up the small talk.

"I haven't made any official plans yet, but it's fairly close and has the top psychology program in the state."

"Have you considered Penn? The University of Oklahoma might have the best program in Oklahoma, but it's Oklahoma," Noah chimes in.

"Penn, as in the University of Pennsylvania? Uh, that would

be a no. I don't need to study psychology at an Ivy League school."

"Why not? Never sell yourself short, Laney. You have the grades, and I could help you find scholarships," Noah offers.

It's kind, but... "Are you sure you're not just saying that because it's where you plan on going?" I shoot him a knowing side-eye.

"I mean, I might have ulterior motives, but posturing aside, it is a better school."

"It's also halfway across the country," I point out. It's not that I'm against going away for school, but I also don't want to leave my mom.

"Are you saying if you go to the University of Oklahoma, you plan on making the two-hour commute home twice daily?" Mr. Hale asks before taking a swig of his beer.

Now I regret asking Noah to help me with my school project. At the time, his coming here sounded better than me going to his place. Don't get me wrong, his house is great, but every time I've been there, I feel like his parents are interviewing me, and when they're not quizzing me, being alone with Noah isn't any better. I don't want to lead him on. I like Noah but not the way he likes me. Being at my house, I set the tone. However, right now, I'd take the minor discomforts of his house over being put on the spot in front of my mom about leaving.

"I wouldn't make Laney drive to me. That doesn't make any sense. If she wants to go away for school, I'll go with her."

My eyebrows raise, and I nearly choke on a piece of chicken, but before anything else is said, the kitchen's back door opens, and in strolls London. His eyes dart around the table, taking account of who's all here before lingering on me as he walks to the table and pulls out an empty chair like this is a typical Friday night, and he hasn't been gone all summer.

"Thanks for inviting me, Ms. Hart," London says as my mother gets another place setting.

My eyes may as well pop out of my head. I'm sure they're

about the size of saucers. Once again, London disappeared all summer without so much as a goodbye. We spent one afternoon that turned into night, inseparable, lying behind the shed in his backyard, getting to know each other on a deeper level. I'd never felt more connected to someone in those few hours than I had him. We laughed, he held me in his arms, we talked about anything and everything, and I thought we were something, and then he was gone.

"You invited him?" I question my mom when she sets a bowl in front of him.

London's dark gaze locks with mine, and the usual butterflies I get every time his eyes land on mine are mere flutters because right now, I'm pissed. He left without a word, no contact all summer, and apparently, my mother knew he was coming home today but not me.

"Is that a problem?" London raises a brow, his eyes floating to Noah at my left before returning to me.

My eyes narrow on his. He thinks I'm with Noah. Good. If he's even the least bit jealous, then he deserves it. He can sulk in that feeling for a while, and it still wouldn't equate to how I felt being ghosted all summer.

"Not at all," I reply, tacking on a smile for added indifference.

He's taller, tanned from a summer I know nothing about, and apparently perfectly content with acting like he didn't put a crack in my heart. He smiles at my mother as she passes him a bowl of shredded cheese, charming her with dimpled cheeks and manners. Mr. Hale starts carrying on about football without missing a beat, as if London's three-month disappearance was nothing more than a weekend trip. I watch him doctor his chili as he nods along to his father's season predictions. A ringing fills my ears, and the room blurs.

This can't be happening. There's no way London Hale is sitting across from me, chatting easily with his father about football like we're nothing more than childhood friends who occasionally share the same air. Riley Heron was never technically his girlfriend, and after hearing his reasons for entertaining any sort of relationship with her, I understood it. It may have been ill-thought-out, but I got it. But I thought I was different. I thought I meant more to him—he told me as much, his voice breaking with what I thought was sincerity. He has to know he hurt me. He has to feel something when he looks at me, even if it's just guilt.

The table chatter continues, spoons scraping bowls, ice cubes clinking in sweet tea with every sip, everyone around me oblivious to the storm brewing inside me. I push my chair back from the table, the legs screeching against the hardwood floor like they're screaming for me, and every head turns. London's gaze finally meets mine fully, and I see something flicker there for a second. Recognition. Regret, maybe. But it's gone before I can be sure it was ever there.

"Excuse me," I say, my voice steadier than I feel. "I need some air."

"Can we talk?" London says, hot on my heels, following me into the yard.

I stop dead in my tracks, and before I can think it through, my fist is in his stomach. He makes a guttural, muffled *oof* as he inhales sharply. "Okay, so you're mad."

"I'm not mad," I respond quickly. Technically, I'm pissed, but not for the reasons he probably believes. The difference between this summer and the past two summers is that I know where he was this time.

"Then what was the right hook for?" he questions as he straightens.

"Leaving and not thinking I could handle it." His eyes flare in surprise before realization sets in, and then there's sadness. "Don't look at me like that. Unless the night before you left meant nothing, you should have told me."

"Laney..." He steps toward me, but I take one back. If I let him get close, I know I'll crumble. My walls will fail me because it's him, and even when I'm blinding mad, seeing him already has me mixed up, wanting to forgive and forget, but I can't. He hurt me. "It's not what you think. I was going to—"

I shake my head. "Don't lie. When exactly were you planning on telling me? This was your third summer going to see her. Were you going to tell me next summer or just disappear again?"

He puts his hands in his pockets. "I won't be going back to visit her next summer."

"Why not?"

"Because I graduate this year, and I can decide for myself, and I don't care to know the woman who walked out on her two-year-old son and husband to start a new family with someone else."

My heart splinters, and it takes great willpower not to close the distance between us and hug him, but I don't. He might be hurting, but so am I, and I don't understand why he wouldn't just tell me.

"My mother is a gold digger who married a wealthy man, and suddenly, she wants to make things right between us. She walked out of my life. She sent zero birthday cards…no visits…hell, she couldn't even pick up the phone. She was dead to me, and then three years ago, out of the blue, she called my father and wanted a relationship." He angrily rubs his chin. "He didn't even ask me if I wanted to go. What I wanted didn't matter. He packed my bag, and I was shipped to Florida." His eyes come back to mine. "I've been playing happy family in a million-dollar beach house that belongs to my mother's new husband for the past three summers, hating every second, wishing I could come home. But this summer was the hardest."

"Why?"

"Because all I wanted to do was spend it with you."

Now, the stupid organ inside my chest is galloping, and the butterflies have returned in full force, and I have to mentally remind myself not to let him off the hook. I might be young, but I know a young heart is easily fooled by a devilishly handsome guy and the right words. It's actions that speak the loudest. I know what I want. The question is, does he?

"I'm not asking why you wanted to come home. I'm asking, why didn't you tell me where you were going all this time? That's what people in relationships do, London. They tell each other things."

He tries again to step closer, his hand barely brushing my arm, and I shrug it off, taking another step back. "Are you trying to torture me?"

"You're doing that to yourself. They make these things called phones. You could have picked one up at any time if missing me was truly unbearable while you floated around in your pretentious beachside pool all summer."

He runs his hands through his dark hair. "I didn't not tell you to hurt you. I didn't tell you because I wanted to keep you," he says, vexed.

"That doesn't even make sense, London. You visiting your mother the past three summers has nothing to do with me."

"It has everything to do with you. Don't you get it..." His hands find his hips as his gaze drops to the ground. "It's what bonded us. I didn't have a mom, and you didn't have a dad. We were the two kids with parents who abandoned us. I didn't want to tell you about my mom suddenly coming back into the picture because I didn't want it to change things. I didn't want to lose something that felt like us. We laid on this grass countless days, went on more fishing trips than I can count, and took the long way home from Fisher and Sydney's house more times than not, talking about life and what that looks like with one parent, the weight we bear, the guilt, the expectations..." His eyes slowly rise, meeting mine. "I didn't want to lose us, but more than that, I didn't want to hurt you. You say you can handle it, but because I know you, I know a small part of you would be envious and sad, because I know what you wish for. You wish to find your dad. I never wanted to be a source of anything that didn't bring you happiness."

That was a loaded answer and not one I expected. I anticipated my lack of having a father to be part of his reasoning for keeping secrets, but the rest of my mind is struggling to keep up. "I wasn't abandoned. He doesn't know I exist," I argue, his words cutting deep because the more time passes, the more I feel they are what's true.

My mother stands on the hill of not knowing, but if that was all it truly was then why not look for him? What mother wants to raise their child alone or, better yet, wouldn't want to give their kid a chance at knowing the one other person in this world who could love them unconditionally? Over the years, I've tried to bring it up, but she hasn't strayed from the script: I don't know who he is and wouldn't begin to know where to look.

"Fuck, Laney." Before I can react, he's pulling me into his strong arms, the same ones I've dreamed about falling back into all summer.

I spent a large part of my summer being upset about how he left things, and doubt made me wonder if he left things unsaid so he could have a carefree summer to do and see who he wanted. The depth and care he spoke with now feels like he's always seen me, just like it did the night before he disappeared. That felt like a dream, like we were always meant to be, but in leaving, he also taught me something: to be careful with my heart.

"I didn't mean it like that. My mother abandoned me. I didn't mean to project that on you. Nobody could ever abandon you. You're unforgettable, heartbreaker." I let myself soak in the way his body feels pressed against mine and inhale his musky scent, letting it wash over me and calm the storm that has been brewing inside me. "I'm sorry, Laney. I'm bitter and mad. I'm twisted up inside, and none of that is your fault. But if I've learned anything from all of this, it's this: there's power in knowledge, but there's also peace in ignorance because you can't undo what has been done. Once you know—you know. Good or bad, it's what is."

"Getting to know your mom was that bad?" I murmur against his chest, clinging to him a little longer, hating the pain I hear in his words.

"I wish I'd never met her. Sure, for years, that wasn't the case.

When I was younger, I wanted her to come home, but at some point, I stopped wanting the things that didn't want me back, and that was her. Never knowing her would have been better. The mother I reasoned her to be was better than the woman she is."

His words hang in the air between us, raw and final, as I steal a few more seconds, melting into the embrace as if my touch can somehow absorb the years of hurt he'd carried. I want this. I want to be his safe haven, but I'm hurt too. I take one last deep inhale, drinking him in and storing away all the tender pieces because I'm going to need them. I'm going to need them when I push him away.

I pull my arms up and press my hands to his chest to break us apart and watch as his eyes search mine. "I need to go back inside. Noah is in there."

"Are you saying you're with Noah?"

I push a strand of hair behind my ear. "That's not what I'm saying, but you don't get to just walk back in," I say, stepping around him to head back inside.

He reaches for my hand. "What do I have to do to make it up to you?"

I roll my eyes with a sigh. "I don't really know. All I know is I can't let you back that easy—not because I don't want you, but because…" I want to say my heart is not ready to be broken again, but he didn't break it, not really. To break it, he'd have to have it, and that's not an admission I'm ready to give. "You need to grovel."

"Grovel?" he repeats slowly.

"Yeah, boyfriends do that when they're in the doghouse."

"Boyfriend?" It sounds like a question, and I can't tell if his tone is skeptical or receptive.

I just flippantly labeled our relationship. We spent one night making out and a summer apart, and with one sentence, I may have ended everything before it began, but I guess if that's true, then it answers the question of what he doesn't want: ME.

I hold up my hand and start up the steps. "I said what I said. Grovel or don't."

❦

"OH MY GOD, THE ENERGY IS CRAZY HERE TONIGHT," SYDNEY SAYS as we leave the field.

"I know. The year's first football game is always a big deal around here, but you're right. Tonight feels extra." Willow Creek is small. The high school football games are the Friday-night events around here, but there's a buzz in the air tonight that can't be ignored. Maybe it's because this is our last first game cheering on Fisher and London since they are seniors this year, or perhaps it's because London is back, and every time he goes to the bench, he looks for me. All I know is that tonight's game is already leaving a memory I won't soon forget. "It helps that we're currently winning."

"Yeah, that pass London made to Fisher right before halftime was epic." She bumps my shoulder. "London looks good out there. Does that have anything to do with pre-game make-out sessions, or is he still in the doghouse?"

I roll my eyes. "To be in the doghouse, we'd have to be something. We shared one night kissing, and then he left for the whole summer, and need I remind you, I already kind of—sort of—called him my boyfriend, and let's just say he looked like a deer caught in headlights, and it hasn't come up since."

"I wouldn't read too much into that, Lanes. He was caught off guard, is all. You're right. It was one night before he left, and the night before that was complete chaos, but one thing is for certain: that boy has it bad for you. He's been driving you to and from school all week, picking you up after your shifts at the flower shop, and if that isn't enough, there's no denying that his eyes have been scanning the field for you all night. I'm pretty sure the entire stadium knows where his focus is when he's not playing."

"I know," I say as I release a long sigh and watch him get into position for the snap. "I've already given him so much power over me, and he hasn't even really been mine. London Hale has been the forever I've dreamed about since the first day I saw him. Maybe I'm not in a hurry to find out that not all dreams are meant to be lived. Sometimes, they're only meant to stay in our heads."

"That sounds a lot like fear. It's his senior year. He's going to be gone before you know it. You don't want to waste the few months you have left wondering what could have been." I watch him throw the ball downfield, and her words hit deep as he completes the pass, and our wide receiver goes down at the twenty-yard line. "And look at it this way: if he's not your forever, wouldn't you rather know now than spend forever waiting to find out? Come on, Lanes, these are our days. We're supposed to be reckless and carefree, not worrying about tomorrow or what comes next."

I pull in an anxious, deep breath, and before her rightness has time to settle, someone else is stealing my attention. "Hey, Laney. Do you have a second?" Noah calls out from the raised platform of the bleachers above the track.

I look over at my coach. Technically, we don't have to go back on the field to perform, but we're supposed to stay and watch the game from the sidelines as a team. I really want to know what he has to say. I nod toward the end of the bleachers, and he follows.

"Did you find anything?" I ask as soon as I step away from the crowd.

"I did," he says, jumping over the waist-high chain-link fence. "I have two leads."

"Leads…plural?" I squeal excitedly and go in for a hug. "That's amazing."

"Don't get too excited—"

"Stop," I cut him off, not wanting him to discredit himself. "It's more than I had three weeks ago."

The crowd roars, and we turn around to see our team running into a huddle. The Mustangs just won their first home game of the season, and while all eyes are on the field, one dark pair is keenly zeroed in on me and the guy with his arms wrapped around me. I was nervous about coming back to school this year after the way sophomore year ended, and while I get the occasional side-eye or stare that lasts longer than social norms would deem acceptable, it's more awe than anything else.

The story made its way through the school, and since I played the starring role, their stares are rooted in curiosity more than anything. Even Riley has kept her distance thus far. Don't get me wrong, her glares are most definitely filled with hate, but I think even her black heart has a boundary. That, or she's keeping her mouth closed, fearing I might press charges. What she doesn't know is that I never would. That would mean telling my mom what happened, but the low profile I've managed to maintain feels like it's seconds away from disappearing, because London isn't celebrating. No, he's walking off the field, and his target is clear. ME.

I subtly shrug out of Noah's hold to avoid being rude right before London reaches us. London pulls his helmet off. "Donovan, what business do you have touching my girl?"

My eyes widen in surprise as my stomach flips. It's possible I didn't hear him correctly. It's loud as fuck, and the attention he's garnered from making a beeline straight for me has my anxiety pounding loudly in my ears, its beat matching the tempo of my racing heart. Dancing in front of people as part of a team is a lot different than being the solo act, and that's exactly how I feel now that so many curious eyes are pinned on us.

"Your girl?" Noah questions skeptically.

Noah's become one of my closest friends, and honestly, I don't know what I'd do without him. He tried to save my life, and now he's helping me with a project that means everything to me—something I'm probably way too obsessed with but can't seem to drop. Plus, he got me a job at his mom's flower shop this summer, so I can actually save money for college, which is huge.

We've gotten close, and Noah has made it evident that he

wants more than just friendship. And I've been just as obvious about turning him down, which sucks because I hate hurting him. I keep telling him it's not about him, it's about me, and that's true. Noah would be perfect for someone. He's sweet and funny, and he actually cares about me. Any girl would be lucky to have him. But he's not the one who makes me feel like I'm going to combust just from being in the same room. He's not the one who's had me completely messed up since the day we met. That's someone else entirely—the boy who makes my heart do this stupid fluttering thing every time he so much as glances in my direction.

"Did I stutter?" London says with a possessive bite to his tone that sends those flips I was feeling into full-blown butterflies.

"Sorry, I assumed if she was your girl, you would have made it so after you pulled her from the lake," Noah says as Fisher and a few other players come over to see what's happening. "But you didn't because the star quarterback is more interested in his reputation. You wanted to play the role of hero. Your intention was never to keep the girl."

London's eyes flash to mine, and I see the second he snaps, and he charges. I rush in between the two of them. Noah may not be a football player, but he's not small either. I might be stupid for getting in the way, but I'm not trying to start a war. I'm not naïve. Noah's willingness to help was rooted in his hope we'd become more, but I refuse to let them fight over something neither of them have: ME.

"Laney, get out of the way," London grinds as my hand hits the pad protecting his chest.

"No, it's not what you think. Let it go," I say, attempting to push him back a step.

I watch as his incensed glare stays locked on Noah before finally dropping to mine. "What does it suggest that you had to say that?"

"Nice," Noah chides, and I grind my teeth. It's like he's asking for a fight right now while I'm trying to prevent one. "You're not fooling anyone with this act. What you want and what is are not the same thing. She's right, London. Let it go…or should I say, let her go. Leave her alone so someone else can treat her right."

"Someone like you?" London spits.

"Yeah, I have real feelings, unlike you. She means more than a bet to me."

There are audible gasps from the crowd that's gathered around us. "Now it all makes sense," I hear Riley say somewhere in the distance. "Who leaves the captain of the cheer team for a nobody?" Her words don't even faze me. I don't care what Riley Heron thinks. Hell, I don't even care what all these people watching me live my moment of horror think. I only care about what the man standing before me has to say.

My hands fall from his chest, and I find the strength to look him in the eye when every part of me wants to crumble. "Bet… What is he talking about, London? Am I a bet?" There's a tick in his clenched jaw as his nostrils flare. With every second that passes, and he holds his silence, I have my answers. I was a bet, but I refuse to hear it from Noah Donovan. If this is where we end, I want to hear it from him. "Answer me!"

He flinches. "Yes."

The crowd oohs, and Fisher pushes through. "Fuck, Laney, it's not what—" Fish starts, but London holds up his hand, silencing him, his eyes never leaving mine.

"If I told you it's not what you're thinking, would you believe me?"

Gah, I want to scream. Inside, I am, because everything is on fire. My body is hot, my ears are ringing, and my heart is pounding so fast it feels like it's one pump away from giving out on me. For years, London Hale has been an enigma to me. His actions and words were always out of step when it came to me— or at least that's how I saw it. But after the night he saved me and the next where he finally kissed me, what I thought was out of sync started to look like expectation. I expected him to act a certain way, to make moves, and when he didn't, I was let down. You see, that's the thing with people. We can shut out the good by boxing them into our expectations. Fisher was about to cut in, and London stopped him, and if I had to guess, he stopped him because he doesn't want me to trust words. He wants to see if I trust what's inside me...if I believe in what we have…what I felt. There will always be an enemy ready to pull apart all that's good, and tonight, that enemy is a friend.

His eyes search mine, and I know he sees I want to say yes, but the words aren't coming. He takes a step closer, and his arm falls to my hip, where he pulls me closer so only I can hear when he says, "Heartbreaker, I'll grovel until the end of time if that's what it takes to heal the hurt I caused, but if you trust me..." His tongue darts out and licks the lips I've replayed covering mine all summer. "I was wondering how you feel about grand gestures?"

"I trust you—" hasn't even finished leaving my lips before his are colliding with mine. My brain momentarily turns to mush, the prying eyes, taunts, and whistles not nearly enough to pull me from the hypnosis his mouth covering mine blanketed over me. It's not until the hand that was on my hip slides down the spandex of my dance uniform and firmly cups my ass, giving it a heady squeeze that leaves a sting, that I come back down to reality. He pulls back and swats my ass. "Allow me to clarify. The only bet ever made was one where I bet on myself and went after the only girl I ever wanted." Then, turning to Noah, he adds, "And just so we're crystal clear, my girl means my girlfriend, which means MINE."

The crowd of teammates from my squad and his team has grown, and the oohs pick up in a crescendo.

Noah rolls his eyes, unimpressed by London's show. "Less than ten seconds ago, you didn't trust her."

The football coach blows his whistle. "Mustangs, locker room now."

Everyone glances back to the coach except London. "I trust my girl. It's you I don't trust."

"Hale, let's go!" the coach calls out, and London's arm draped over my shoulder disappears.

He kisses my cheek and lingers by my ear. "Meet me at my truck." Then, holding his helmet toward Noah, he says, "Watch your hands and your mouth. That's my girl. Whatever favor you found with her doesn't extend to me, Donovan."

I watch him walk off the field, breathless and stunned, like the rest of the people still looking on. The town's golden boy, who doesn't do titles, just gave me one. I'm London Hale's girlfriend, and while I might be his, he's mine too.

LONDON

CHAPTER 6

JUNIOR YEAR

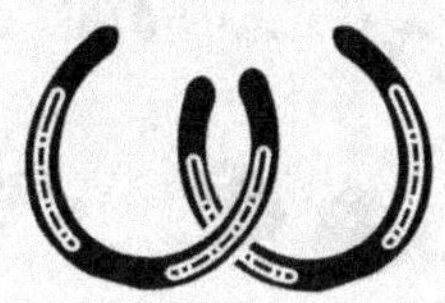

AGE EIGHTEEN

"You're upset," I say, tossing my gym bag into the truck bed behind her, the thud punctuating the tension between us.

"I'm not upset," she says, uncrossing her arms and flexing her fingers before dropping them on the edge of the tailgate. "Stunned, confused, and nervous are a little more fitting."

I move to stand in front of where she sits on my tailgate so she can't avoid my eyes and give me half-truths. "What part are you confused about?"

"The part where you called me your girlfriend. Why did you say it?" Her brown eyes pierce mine. "Why that moment?"

My eyes widen. I know what she's asking, but the topic I expected to make the top of her list when I came out of the locker room was the bet.

"Do you want a list? Because there's more than one reason."

She leans back, bracing herself on her palms, the shift putting space between us. "No, I just want the one at the very top."

"Because I want you to be," I say without hesitation. There's the semblance of a small smile, and I step between her legs hanging over the tailgate. "Does that smile mean you're not mad anymore?"

"I told you I wasn't mad."

She tries to keep the smile from curling her mouth, but we both know she'll fail. It's one of the reasons I'm hooked. Her smile is contagious, but her eyes intrigue me the most. She looks at me like I'm a puzzle she's dying to solve. It's the intense desire I see in them that keeps me holding on. No one has ever looked at me the way she does, she wants everything I have to give. I only wonder if she knows I see everything I want in this world when I'm staring back at her.

My hands find the frayed edges of the jean shorts she must have slipped on after the game. "Semantics." I smile as my hands find a stray string on the shorts. "Want to go somewhere?"

I watch as she pulls her bottom lip between her teeth, a lip I'm eager to have pressed against mine again as I wait with bated breath, hoping she'll give me the answer I want. We spent a summer apart, of which I spent every day counting the hours until I knew I'd see her again. I knew coming home after the way I left things wouldn't be easy. I was well aware I'd have things to answer for, but I wasn't prepared for the space she'd put between us.

She nods just once, and I fight to contain my relief. I've languished in friendship purgatory for two weeks, carefully trying to rebuild what I broke, desperately seeking the trust I'd squandered. Tonight feels like the first real step back toward us.

"What's the deal with Noah?" I ask as I pull out the bag of snacks we stopped at the gas station to get before coming to the lake.

"Deal?" She asks, rummaging through the bag for her candy.

"Yeah, first I come home, and he's sitting comfortably at your mother's dinner table. Now I'm winning my first home game of the season and looking over to find my girl wrapped around him."

She smiles as she tears open the bag of chewy Nerds, and I can't help but mirror it. Calling her *my girl* is new, but I like it. It feels like a title that should have been there all along.

"We're just friends." She pops a piece of candy in her mouth. "We were lab partners in Biology last semester, and we were assigned a summer project for AP Biology this year." She shrugs and pours a few pieces of candy into her hand, sorting the colors before adding, "He's nice, and he's helping me. It's nothing more than that."

"Yeah, well, we were once just friends too," I say, pulling my bottom lip into my mouth and biting down so I stop talking. I told her on the field, I trust her, and I do, but I'm a guy. I know when another guy is making a play.

"You sound jealous," she teases.

"So, what if I am?" I release an anxious breath. "I'm not afraid to admit that. Jealousy means I know what I stand to lose."

"You don't need to be." Her eyes hold mine.

"Yeah, well, you're all I think about, heartbreaker. I've had a crush on you for years."

"How long is that exactly?" she questions, trying her best to hold back the smile that's tugging at her mouth.

I've always seen Laney. She has meant something to me since the second I laid eyes on her, but once eighth grade hit, I couldn't keep her in the friend box anymore. Not when the desire to be more than her friend was greater, so I started putting space between us and waited. I waited for her to give me a sign that she felt the same way.

"Long..." my eyes search hers, scanning their depths. I know I hurt her this past summer. If I could do it over, I would, but I can't. All I can do is move forward and make sure I give her no more reasons to doubt what I know she feels between us. "I realized I had a crush on you when our friendship was no longer enough."

Her eyes widen with her smile before she ducks her head, dropping her gaze to her lap as she sets aside her bag of candy, and I want to reach out and tilt her chin back up. I hate that I can't catalog every reaction and feel it with her.

"Well, now I don't know what to do with my face," she says before her brown eyes pierce mine. "Friendship was never going to be enough for us."

Our eyes stay locked as the vulnerable honesty we both shared rewrites everything between us in real-time. I can practically feel the walls of *just friends* crumbling around us, and I never want to go back to pretending again.

She breaks first, sinking her teeth into her lip and reaching for a soda can, and when she attempts to pop the top, the tab snaps off before the can opens.

"Here, let me have it." I reach for the can and pull out the chief. Flicking open the blade, I press it into the aluminum and open the can.

"The chief saves the day once again," she says, grabbing the can and taking a long, slow drink.

I want to change the topic. I don't want to talk about anyone else when I'm with her, but I need to speak my piece first. "Laney, I'll never tell you who you can and can't be friends with, but you should be careful. Noah doesn't care about a title. If he wants something, he thinks it is his for the taking. Guys like him don't take no for an answer, and because you're giving him the time of day, he's not going to let it go."

Laney sets her soda aside and reaches for the snack bag again. "I know," she says, her tone a bit too cheery, given the warning I just gave her as she digs through the bag. "But you still haven't told me about this bet you made." Her eyes swing to mine. "Maybe I'm just keeping my options open."

I tackle her onto the truck bed. "The hell you are, heart-breaker. You're mine. I made it so, and now you're stuck with me." I grab her knee and squeeze right above her kneecap, making her laugh and squeal. Her laughter is like music to my soul. It washes away all the ugly things that are collected from everyday life, taking with it the weight of the things we can't change. When I'm with her, I'm happy, and the upward curve of her mouth as she laughs and struggles against my weight, trying her best to reach my hips and find her counterattack, tells me I make her happy too. When it's her and me, the world falls away.

"London, stop, it hurts…" She struggles to get the words out between laughs, and I release her knee, but my hand doesn't fall away.

Her laughter fades as my hand glides up her thigh, my eyes tracing its ascent as I watch her skin pebble beneath my touch. "When I saw you wearing my shirt at the party, I couldn't take my eyes off you. A million thoughts had already been running through my head, and then you showed up wearing that. I knew the second I saw you wearing it, I would find out why." My fingers reach the hem of her jean shorts, and my eyes finish the journey, finding hers. "I assumed you wanted my attention, and you had it."

Her pouty lips part slightly as her eyes explore the depths of mine. "Cooper Downs was going to try to talk to you, but Fisher stepped in and told him you were off limits because you already belonged to me."

"Why would Fish say that when it wasn't true?"

My hand aimlessly starts playing with the fringe of her shorts again as I find the courage to tell her everything. "Because he's my best friend, and he knew I'd only ever wanted one girl. I just didn't have the guts to own it. I was afraid shooting my shot would ruin our friendship, or worse, I'd ruin your happiness if that was what you had found. But the more I watched and listened to Cooper rattle on in the background, I knew I couldn't go one more day without telling you how I felt, so by the time he dared me to prove it, I had already decided I would pursue you. I didn't know what would happen when I walked downstairs. All I knew was I wasn't proving to Cooper that you were mine. I was proving to myself that I wasn't going to go another day without finding out if it was me that you wanted. When I came downstairs, you and Noah had already started walking down to the lake...and you know what happened after that."

I make a mental note that I still need to have a talk with Cooper. Noah could have only known about that conversation through him since they play baseball together.

"Maybe you didn't bet on me then, but on the field tonight...I bet on you."

"How so?" I ask as I lean on my arm beside her, making myself at home with her body tucked against mine.

"I've never been able to figure you out. There have been times when I thought I knew what you were thinking, what you wanted, but then you'd go and do something that said the opposite. All these years, I wanted you to see me the same way I saw you, and tonight on the field, I had to sift through all the times I thought you did, all the times that made zero sense, like when Riley Heron showed up on your front lawn."

"Hey, can we not—"

Her finger presses against my lips. "I get it. I'm not trying to rehash what's done. I'm only saying I had to bet on the man I thought you were, the one who didn't always let me in."

My hand finds her hip. "I did let you in, and it scared the shit out of me every time. I'd be lying if I said it still doesn't."

She smiles softly. "Good, at least we're on a level playing field." Her hand reaches for the one I have on her hip, and she brings it to her chest. Placing it over her heart, she says, "This is what you do to me every time you look at me."

"It's racing," I say, my fingers splaying over her soft skin.

"It always does when you're around."

"I want to kiss you, Laney Hart."

A small smile turns her lips upward. "You're in luck because I want the same thing."

It's not our first kiss, but damn if it doesn't feel like it. I'm hooked, addicted, and still completely terrified—the same way I was the night in her room. I don't know if having her will ever shut out the fear. If anything, in a way, it makes it worse. Before, I feared her not wanting the same things. I feared never knowing what it was like to have her, and now I fear losing her. I can't lose her.

As our kiss deepens, her hands wander, and fuck if I don't love every inch they explore. My hands do the same, memorizing the curve of her hips, the softness of her stomach, and the heat between her legs when she throws her thigh over mine. Shit. A groan I can't contain rumbles from deep in my chest. She's too perfect, and I want everything. The soft fingers that were exploring my chest dip to my belt, and I release her mouth.

"Laney…" is all I manage as I close my eyes and try to temper my body's reaction to her.

"Did I do something wrong?"

"God, no, you could never do anything wrong."

"Then why did you stop?" Her hand suggestively slides along my waistband, and I grab it. "Oh." Her face drops.

"Don't do that. You have no idea how hard it is to say no to you."

"Then don't. Don't you want to?"

I roll onto my back, putting space between us, and cover my face with my hands. "It's not that. You mean a lot to me."

"Well, isn't doing stuff a way to show how much you care about someone? You did stuff with Riley. Are you saying you give your body to people you don't care about?"

"What? Who said?" I drop my hands. "Never mind, it doesn't matter. I didn't bring you here for that. I brought you here so we could be alone and talk and find each other again. I wanted to close the distance that spending the summer apart put between us." I grab her hand and intertwine our fingers. "I have you, and you're enough just like this."

"Okay," she says somewhat dejectedly.

I'm about to question her and demand she tell me exactly what she's thinking. I'm done guessing. I chose her, I want her, and that means everything. I want every insecurity, every argument, and every bad day, so I can make it better, because that's what existing in her world does for me. She makes it better.

Her eyes flash to mine. "But you do want to..."—she nervously clears her throat—"do those things with me?"

"Yes, Laney. I want everything with you."

Her eyes slowly flick between mine, and then she lays her head on my chest. "Me too."

She makes herself comfortable, listening to the beat of my heart, and it's on the tip of my tongue to tell her it beats for her, but I don't. We have time. I plan on keeping her. I plan on giving her the world.

Laney

CHAPTER 7

SENIOR YEAR

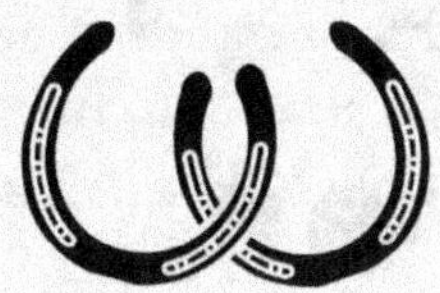

AGE EIGHTEEN

"I'm glad you crashed tonight," I say, swinging my legs off the back of his tailgate in my yellow prom dress.

"I never wanted to miss it, but prom fell the same week as finals," he says, hopping up on the tailgate to join me.

"I know," I sympathize as we stare at Lake Texoma, parked in what became our spot eight years ago. "I'll be at Stanley with you in a few months."

He's quiet, and my insecurities start to take root. We haven't seen each other as much over the past few months since he left for college. Our dynamic has changed. I wouldn't say it has been bad, but the distance that separated us physically feels like it's seeped in —in other ways.

"Are you sure that's what you want?"

My head snaps to him. "If you don't want me to come, just say that."

His eyes widen as his hand tightens around my fingers. "No, Laney. That's not what I'm getting at. I want you there if you want to be there…" he trails off.

"Then what? Did you find someone else?" The second I found out he was going to college three hours away, my heart sank into my stomach. The year difference between us in high school wasn't a big deal, but after graduation, that year felt like ten. I suddenly felt like a little girl compared to him. What college guy wants to date a girl in high school when he can have a woman. I'm sure the girls on campus are experienced and better suited to care for his needs. My stomach starts to churn at the mere thought of him touching someone else.

I try to pull my hand away, and he grips it tighter. "Are you serious? Why would you say that? Of course there's no one else."

"Well, what am I supposed to think? It feels like you're sitting here telling me you don't want to be with me anymore when I'm excited about eliminating the space between us. We'll be on the same campus and won't have to sneak around."

"That reminds me... Do me a favor. Don't sneak out tonight." My body starts to get hot. Did he really just say that? My sneaking into his room was his favorite thing a few months ago. Now it feels like that's the last thing he wants. I turn my head away from his to hide the hurt, but then his free hand is on my chin. "Hey, that was ill-timed. I didn't mean it the way you're thinking. You mentioned sneaking out, and my mind went to the text my dad sent me earlier. He told me to keep an eye on you tonight because a drifter has been spotted around town in the last few days. I didn't want you climbing out of your window in your pajamas. I'll come to you."

His eyes slowly flick between mine, checking to ensure he's eased my concern. "Okay, but don't come because I want you to."

I should let it go and take his words for what they are, but I can't. I'm feeling a lot of insecurity. Life after graduation is intimidating. I'd be lying if I said I wasn't scared. High school relationships are not the same as adult ones. Sure, some people marry their high school sweethearts, but many don't. I'm scared of finding out which one we become.

"I know you got accepted to Lindenwood." His eyes stray

away to the sky. "I spotted your acceptance letter peeking from beneath your history book last time I was in your room." When my mom agreed to relocate for my education, I broadened my college search—mostly for show. Deep down, I wanted to follow London, though Mom insisted I apply to Lindenwood after she caught me researching their campus and programs. "I don't want you to prioritize me over the future you want for yourself."

"You're part of my future," I say softly but surely. "I thought I was part of yours too."

He jumps down off the tailgate and pulls me to the edge. "You're the only future I want, heartbreaker. Don't ever think for one minute I want anything or anyone else. It was you from the second you said, "I'm going to marry you one day.""

"I'm not sure those are the exact words I used," I tease.

"Stop…" His hands wrap around my waist, sending a chill down my spine the way they always do. I crave his touch. It ignites a fire inside of me as much as it soothes me. I feel safe and happy with his hands on me, because his hands are home. "Dance with me."

"Did you really just ask me that?" I smirk and raise a brow.

A faint smile appears, and his cheeks tinge the slightest shade of pink. "I did. Why is that so hard to believe? It's prom."

"Yeah, but there's no music, and we're not at prom. You're stealing a line from some mushy rom-com you saw on TV. I don't want the guy that does what he thinks he is supposed to do. I might be missing prom, but there's nowhere else I'd rather be." I shrug and look toward the sky. "You're enough," I echo the exact words he once gave me in this very spot. He's quiet—a little too quiet—and I risk glancing at him. I'm nervous about looking him in the eye after saying those words but too curious not to know what I'll find. When I pull my gaze away from the stars, I find him smiling from ear to ear. "What?" I try hard to keep my face impassive but fail miserably because his handsome, dimpled smile is contagious.

He holds up his phone. "I have music." He lays it down on the tailgate and presses play, and the chorus to "Kiss Me" by Sixpence None the Richer starts crooning from the speaker. "And I'm not doing it because I think it's what I'm supposed to do. I'm doing it because I'm selfish."

"You're selfish?" I question skeptically.

"Yeah, I needed a reason to put my hands on you." He pulls me flush against his chest, my breath hitching from the swiftness and our new proximity as he slides one hand under my thigh. His lips are mere inches from mine, and all my thoughts begin to swirl before he adds, "And I would regret not making this memory with you. You in this dress"—his lips graze mine—"is the prettiest thing I've ever seen." He lifts me down and sets me gently on my heels. "So I'll ask again. Will you spare me a lifetime of regret and give me the honor of dancing with the most beautiful woman I've ever seen?"

I roll my lips, attempting to stifle the giddy smile that has my heart melting, but it's useless. "I'd never say no to you, and I'm pretty sure you know your hands don't need a reason to touch me."

I'm always the one pushing the boundaries with London, and he's always the one pumping the brakes. We only recently made it to third base—a base I've been dying to explore again—but I can tell it makes him uncomfortable. So, I've left it alone, settling for the touches he does give me. He wraps one arm around my waist, the other finding my hand and lacing our fingers together. "Can I ask you something?" I say as we begin to sway.

"Anything?" he answers without pause.

"Why this song? It came out before we were born."

"Classics never die, and I already told you..." He leans his forehead to mine, and my heart skips a beat as his eyes lock on mine. "I'm selfish. I want to kiss my girl beneath the stars while I spin her around a moonlit patch of grass, beside the same lake where she ran away with my heart."

"London—" I start with words I don't even have. Did he just say I ran away with his heart? Was that an admission?

"Don't," he murmurs against my mouth. "Kiss me, heart-breaker."

LONDON

CHAPTER 8

SENIOR YEAR

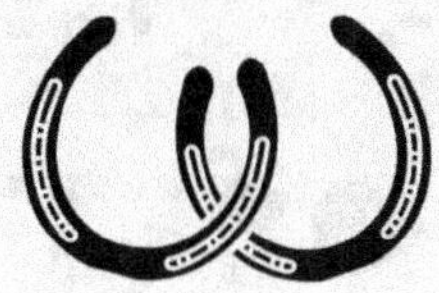

AGE NINETEEN

God, I wonder if she'll ever understand how much she means to me. Her body pressed against mine and our lips locked beneath a star-filled sky feels surreal. If you asked her, she'd say she's nothing special, but ask me, and I'd tell you, she hung the moon and all the stars in the sky, and nothing has ever scared me more. I told myself I'd never fall for a girl. The only woman in the world who was supposed to love me unconditionally couldn't. How could any other? I've never believed in things like marriage or the social constructs of titles, but damn it, if Laney Hart hasn't made me want to believe in the idea that perhaps those man-made constructs were formed not out of theory but lived experience and genuine, all-consuming, irrevocable love that can and does exist when you've found your person. At least, those are the things holding Laney in my arms makes me think.

The tips of her fingers lightly caress my jaw, as her bubblegum tongue slowly swipes against mine, and I force myself to stay present, not to slip away, not to make this more, but when her hand drops to my chest, and she presses me back, stealing her lips away from mine, I can't help but growl and pull her closer. I'm not ready to let her go, not when I just got her back. Not having her next door the way I have for the past eight years has felt like a punishment.

"The music stopped," she says with a smile, her lips pecking mine.

I smile against her mouth. "I hadn't noticed." I kiss her jaw. "I was a little preoccupied," I add, trailing kisses toward her ear. Her hand deliciously snakes up my neck, her fingers splaying through the hairs at the base of my neck, and my entire body shivers. Laney Hart has no idea how much power she has over me or how much it takes to restrain myself from taking everything. I nip the delicate skin on her neck before caressing it with my tongue and pulling away.

"Why did you stop?" she questions, her cheeks flushed and the skin on her chest sexily pebbled from my mouth.

"Walk with me." I take her hand and pull her toward the shore of the lake. If I keep kissing her there, I don't know that I'd have the strength to stop. I know what she wants. I want the same thing. I want everything with her, but I have managed to hold out this long, and I don't intend to break now. If we have forever, then there's time, because there's something I want more than intimacy.

"London," she stops in her tracks. "Is there something wrong with me?"

"What?" I turn back, eyes wide, not understanding the root of her question.

Palms up, she gestures down her body. "Is there something wrong with me? We've been together over a year now, I've known you since I was ten, and you refuse to…" Her eyes hold mine, and now I understand her question. She wants to know why I won't cross the line with her. I don't know what she sees, but I know, whatever it is, she reads it wrong, because she says, "Forget it," as she stomps by and sits on the shore where the grass meets the sand. Kicking her heels off, she digs her feet in.

I give her a second, letting her cool down while I try to find my words. I don't want to tell her no, but I also don't want to tell her how I truly feel. I don't want to coerce her to say the things I need to hear to take things further.

"I'm happy, Laney. You make me happy. I don't need your body. All we share is enough."

Her gaze swings from the lake to mine. "Yeah, you've said that a time or two, but you've also said you want everything with me. When you push me away, it makes me feel like you're not being honest with me."

I shake my head, failing to find the right words but keeping my eyes firmly pinned to hers, hoping she stares into their depths and finds the answers without words. I'm a guy with raging hormones, sitting on the beach with the girl of my dreams looking sexy as hell while telling me she wants to go all the way. It would be easy to take what I want, but I can't give it back once I take it. Her eyes narrow slightly, and I think she sees what I can't articulate, until she smashes that thought to pieces. She's no longer seated beside me. Instead, she's on her knees in front of me, pulling her yellow, satin, backless maxi dress over her head, leaving herself exposed in nothing but a white thong.

"I want you, London Hale. I want you more than I've ever wanted anything, so unless—"

I pull her by her hips into my lap, our bodies fitting together perfectly. "Believe me, I want to..." my voice trails off as I capture her lips with mine, needing to taste her. Her warmth and softness overwhelms me as her sweet mouth covers mine. Her presence fills every space between us as I trace my hands along her thighs, and the electric hum from where my skin touches hers is intoxicating. My breath catches as she moves against me, her fingers threading through my hair, pulling me closer and eliminating any space that remained.

Our kiss deepens, becoming more urgent—more consuming. She's setting the pace, and I am a helpless fool following her lead. My lips leave hers of their own accord, desperate to explore. Her entire body breaks out in goosebumps; I feel them in the softness of her cheeks in my hands and the delicate skin beneath my tongue. Her response to my hands on her body is hypnotic. My mouth travels dangerously close to the curve of her breast, but it's not until I feel her heat against my groin as she subtly rocks against my hardened length that I find the strength to pull away. Her lust-filled eyes burn into me. There's desire, but there's also hurt. She still thinks I don't want this.

"Maybe we should wait," I breathlessly pant.

"Wait?" she questions, her wild gaze studying every emotion that crosses my face.

I lick my lips. "Yeah, maybe you should wait for love."

I tried. I really did. My intent wasn't to lead her to those words, but she's so worked up, vulnerable, and exposed I can't be sure she heard them for the confession they are.

"Is that why we haven't gone further? You're worried about my virtue."

I'm quiet as I battle the tightness in my chest. Sure, I don't want her to say something she doesn't feel, something she doesn't mean, but not hearing it sucks.

Her soft lips sweetly connect with mine as her hands frame my face, and she says, "Don't be. I want to give this to you, and as for the rest..."—her hand rakes through my hair—"we can pretend tonight will never end."

"What if I don't want to pretend?"

Her eyes intensely lock on mine. "This isn't about what I want, is it? You're the one who wants to wait for love. Tell me I'm wrong."

"I can't," I admit as I close my eyes. I refuse to lie to her. I promised I wouldn't keep things from her after she found out about my mom, and she deserves this. She made a big move tonight, and now it's my turn. She might shred my heart to pieces, but at least she'd know it was hers to tear apart. I open my eyes, ready to say words I never thought I would, when she reaches for her dress. "What are you doing?" I ask, holding her in place when she tries to move.

"You want to wait." Her voice is pained. "I'm not trying to force myself on you. I mean, I guess I am. That's what I get for taking Sydney's advice and trying to be someone I'm not."

"Hey, stop. Look at me, Laney." She pulls her dress in front of her breasts, shielding herself in a way that only fuels the storm already brewing inside of me. I never want her to hide from me. "What do you mean someone you're not? Are you saying you didn't want any of this tonight? It was all Syd's idea?"

"No, I want this. I want you. I'm just not the girl who makes the first move, but Sydney said girls these days make the first move sometimes, and I don't know…" she trails off and looks away.

I pull her chin back to center so her eyes are on mine. I take a second to take a breath and shove down the anger that comes from knowing I put the hurt in them. "I want this. I don't want to wait—"

"But what about love?"

"If you're the one I do this with, then I don't need to wait." My heart is hammering in my chest as I wait for the moment my words sink in and what I just admitted resonates.

Her pretty pink lips part as her hands skim up my chest. "You love me?"

"I think I've loved you since the day you proposed at ten."

The sadness that marred her face is instantly gone, replaced with a smile I'll never forget as she swats my chest. "Shut up, I did not."

"You say tomato, I say tomahto. I don't think we'll see eye to eye on this," I tease.

Her face turns serious. "London Hale, you better mean it, because you don't get to take it back. If you say it. It's forever."

"I don't want it back." My thumb skims over her cheek. "I can't wait to do forever with you."

She smiles softly, and the gentle, unhurried collision of our mouths feels like a first. This kiss is different than all the others; it's still vulnerable, but it's secure. It's found its home, and it's sweetened by the promise of tomorrow, and with her by my side, tomorrow feels like the best is yet to come.

She breaks our kiss, and I chase her mouth, not ready to let it go. She laughs as I kiss all over her neck. "Hey, stop trying to distract me."

"It can't be helped," I admit between kisses. "You're sitting naked in my lap, and I just gave you my heart." I kiss my way along her jaw before finding her eyes. "Promise you won't break it."

Her eyes flick between mine. "I could never. Your heart is tethered to mine; breaking it would break mine." She runs her hand through my hair. "You may have said it first, but I felt it first. My heart belonged to you since the first day I saw you."

"Is that right? And what day was that?"

"What day was it? How am I supposed to remember that?"

"I mean, what was I doing when you saw me?"

There's no way she will win this one. I wasn't just a pre-teen boy with an aversion to taking girls fishing the day my father was wrangled into watching the new girl that moved in next door.

"Helping your dad fix his riding lawn mower."

Called it. I didn't fix that lawn mower with my dad until the weekend. Laney and her mother moved in on a Tuesday, and the only reason I remember that is because at eleven, I still played soccer, and we had practice every Tuesday night.

"Well, that settles it, then. I said it first, and I felt it first." She leans onto her elbow. "I watched you unpack your room the first night you moved in. I sat on my bed in the dark so you wouldn't know I was there. Until that day, I had never really thought of girls in any type of way, but there was something about you. I was enamored, and I couldn't figure it out, so when the day came that I found out you were going on my fishing trip with my dad, I threw a fit. I see you now, I saw you then, and in that seeing, I found everything I never knew I was looking for."

Her mouth covers mine, and who saw who first is long forgotten. It doesn't matter who fell first; all that matters is that we're here now. We're both all in. We were all in from the start. It just took us time. We were careful, neither of us wanting to risk what we had and knowing that if what was meant to be was this moment, it would come because the best things are worth waiting for. Have I spent hours wishing she were mine sooner so I could have her longer? Yes, but having her like this now…I can't say I'd change a thing because it's perfect. She's perfect.

Her fingers find the hem of my t-shirt, and she tugs it up, our mouths only separating long enough for her to pull it over my head. I'm suddenly vulnerable under her gaze, my skin prickling with nervousness and anticipation. She's seen me without my shirt on countless times, and her soft hands have traced over every peak and valley intimately, but I know what's next…what she wants… what I want.

"Is this okay?" Her voice is small as her eyes search mine in the shadows, the only source of light streaming down from the moon above.

I nod, not trusting my voice, and reach for her with trembling hands. Despite the certainty that brought us here, there's a moment of hesitation. This is uncharted territory that will forever change us. There's a hitch in the breath that fills her lungs, and then she's leaning forward, her soft lips pressing against my collarbone, the gentleness unraveling something that has been tightly wound inside. I pull her close before flipping us over and positioning myself on top of her.

"We have forever, heartbreaker. I need you to promise me that if any of this is too much, you will tell me to stop."

"Are you ever going to stop calling me that nickname?" she teases, her voice light, creating a small bubble of breathing space between us in this intensely charged atmosphere.

"Not a chance. There's not a day in this lifetime that you won't hold the power to break my heart." My lips peck her cheek, and I murmur. "Now promise…promise you'll tell me."

"I will," she says, wrapping her hands around my neck with tender urgency as her mouth turns to mine. "But it won't be. It's not possible, because it's with you." The certainty in her voice warms my insides, and I let go, helpless to deny her anything she asks.

I press my jean-clad hardened length against her satin-covered center, and my arms shake. This woman will be the death of me. She's been everything to me since she walked into my life.

Her hands abandon my neck and glide down my back, and every hair on my body stands at attention, welcoming its master. The second I feel her hands slide around my hips, my heart stutters, and when her fingers flit over the button of my jeans and dip inside to grab my length, I break our kiss to catch my breath.

"Are you having second thoughts?"

"No." I nip her bottom lip. "But you're driving me crazy."

She smiles against my mouth, her hands pushing the band of my pants down before she squeezes my throbbing cock and strokes it slowly. "Good." Her sweet tongue darts out, and she seductively licks my lips, her eyes never straying from mine. "I've heard sanity is overrated."

My lips find hers, and one kiss flows into another, each deeper, more passionate than the last as my bare cock presses against soaked panties. But then she pulls them to the side.

"Shit, Laney," I hiss, feeling my length glide through her folds.

"What?" Her worried eyes search mine. "I thought—"

I shake my head. "No." Then I reach into my back pocket and pull out my wallet. "Need a condom," I say, setting it beside her head and hastily flipping it open.

"Oh," she says with a sigh of relief.

I bring the foil packet to my mouth and tear the package before sliding my hand between us and slipping it on. Once it's on, I bring my gaze back to hers and settle between her thighs and let the gravity sit between us. Her fingertips lightly glide over my sides, and I patiently await her move. It's hers to define—hers to take, just like my heart. The space between us hums with energy that grows more charged with each passing second, and I still wait.

Her eyes darken and drop to my mouth, and I feel my restraint slipping as I give her all the space she needs before she wraps her legs around my waist, dissolving it all with her unspoken invitation. Our mouths collide passionately as I push inside slowly, taking my time and allowing her to acclimate to my size. Our tongues feverishly glide against each other as our hearts race, both eager for what's on the other side. With each slow thrust, I get a little deeper, but so do the nails digging into my back, the bite of their sting telling me what her lips won't—it hurts.

"Laney…" I pull back, breathless with concern.

She shakes her head. "Please don't stop. It's not all pain."

I can see the honesty in her words, and I drop to my forearms and hover above her before laying my forehead to hers, our breaths mingling. "No?" I ask as I push in a little more, almost fully seated, watching her face for every reaction.

"No," she pants, her chest heaving. She licks her lips, eyes holding mine. "Is it good for you?"

"Are you serious right now? Don't ask about me. There aren't enough words."

I flip her over so that she's on top and in control. I need her to understand the depth of what I'm feeling. "Find what you like. There's nothing you can do that isn't already everything I envisioned my first time would be."

Her eyes widen with realization. "You haven't... I mean…I'm your first?"

"I'm a little offended you think I'd give this to anyone else—" My hands glide up her back, pulling her close and eliminating any space between us. Her mouth eagerly covers mine, and a new intimacy settles between us. This is ours. No one else has had these parts of us.

She starts at a slow pace, which can only be described as pure euphoria. I can hear and feel the moment it transforms for her, when what was discomfort turns to bliss. A delicious moan floats through our kiss as a rush of wetness seeps down my shaft. Her hands wind through my hair, nails dragging over my scalp as her pace quickens with a newly found confidence.

"Slow down, heartbreaker," I murmur against her jaw, gently holding her hips. "If you keep going like that, this isn't going to last." Her brow furrows slightly, misunderstanding. "You feel too good," I clarify, showing my vulnerability.

"Oh." She smiles, her eyes brightening with understanding. "So do you." Her tongue glides against mine before her hands press into my chest, and she pushes me back with playful confidence. "We can go again."

I toss an arm over my eyes, overwhelmed by the sight before me—one that's better than anything I've ever imagined, one that's fueled my private thoughts more times than I can count. The view of her naked, sitting atop me while I'm buried deep, is enough to make me lose all control.

"We can go again, but not here, not now. I only have one condom."

There's a small groan of disappointment that washes away the tendril of regret I have, admitting I only have one condom. I love knowing she wants more and that I'm the one making her feel good. I feel her nipples brush against my chest before her lips find my neck. "I hope you have more at home," she whispers. "This can't be our first and last before I leave."

I remove my arm and find her gaze locked on mine, a mixture of desire and something deeper reflected there. "It won't be," I promise. "I'm keeping you, Laney Hart...forever."

The weight of my words hangs between us, not as a burden but as a promise I intend to keep with everything I am. I'm with the only person I want until the end of time.

"Then I guess we have time," she says, returning to a slow pace that has my mouth parting in complete rapture. Her fingers trace paths along my skin, like she's memorizing a map she never wants to forget. In the dim light, her eyes find mine, vulnerable yet certain, and the world around us falls away.

"Forever," I confirm as I let her take what she wants, how she wants, because it's what I want. There is only us, only this moment stretching into infinity.

LANEY

CHAPTER 9

PROM NIGHT

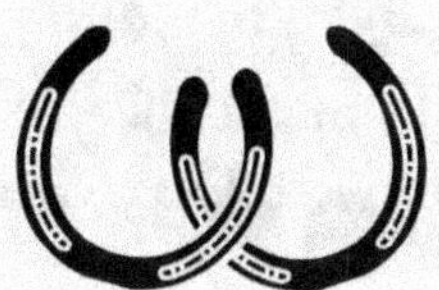

"You should put your seatbelt on. We're almost to town," London says, his voice laced with concern, though his arm remains firmly anchored around my shoulder, contradicting his words. I snuggle deeper into his warmth, my body fitting perfectly against his. I want to preserve this night, and I'm willing to break the rules to keep it.

"Is that what you want?"

"No," he says, placing a kiss on top of my head.

"Good, me neither," I say, lacing my fingers through the hand of the arm draped around me.

The town lights start to come into view, and my chest tightens. I'm not ready to let go of the night. I want to fast forward ten years, where I am his, and he is mine, and I don't have to let him go because we're living under the same roof, sharing the same bed and the same last name. I know that's a big jump. I know we're young, and we still have a lot of living to do, but sometimes the heart just knows. I know there will never be anyone I want by my side more than I want him.

"Hey, can we stop for ice cream?"

"Ice cream?" he questions skeptically.

"Yeah, it's only 11:45 pm. Mom gave me a 1 a.m. curfew for

prom, and Twisted Spoon doesn't close for another fifteen minutes."

They start staying open later when the weather turns warm. Willow Creek doesn't have many hangout spots, and the ice cream shop is happy to fill that void and bring in the extra revenue with extended hours.

I lean forward enough so he can't avoid my face when I say, "Please... I'm not ready for the night to be over."

He smiles a slow, sexy smile that leaves every part of me he touched tonight buzzing. "I intend to sneak in your window tonight and hold you until you fall asleep."

"London Hale, I never would have pegged you for a hopeless romantic."

"Yeah, well, the craziest thing happened eight years ago. I met this girl who proposed to me the first time we hung out. It turns out she was my soulmate, and now I'm living a fairy tale. Grand gestures are effortless, and the passion is all-consuming. If this is the face of a hopeless romantic, I'll wear it proudly because I don't want anything that doesn't feel like what I have when I'm with her."

I bite my lip, but my ridiculous smile can't be contained. He does a double-take and quickly kisses my lips. "London—"

"Hey, is that the guy?" he cuts me off and nods out the passenger side window as he slows enough to catch a glimpse of the man who's been seen around town wearing a long, dark trench coat.

Willow Creek starts to see tourists pass through this time of year, so seeing an unfamiliar face doesn't raise flags. What has people paying attention, aside from his mussed hair, dark sunglasses, and oddly timed wardrobe, given the warmth that's already started to set in, is the fact that he walks everywhere. He's lurked down every street, almost like he's looking for something or someone, but he never asks for directions or stops to talk to anyone. He's just there, watching. His head pivots our way as

London slows, and his dark eyes connect with mine for a second, sending a chill down my spine.

My hand grips London's thigh. "Drive," I mutter through clenched teeth, fearful the eerie man might read lips.

The last thing I want is for him to haunt my street again. That happened once last week. It felt like something straight out of a Michael Myers movie, minus the mask and unnerving thriller music. Sydney dropped me off after school, per usual, but it was Tuesday, and this semester, her father started pulling her into the family business, so she had to go straight home. It wasn't until I got to my front porch that movement out of my peripheral vision caught my eye. He stood at the end of my street, leaning against the stop sign, smoking a cigarette, and watching my every move.

I wanted to haul ass inside my front door and lock the door, but I didn't. I didn't want him to see my fear. So, I did what my mother always told me to do if someone was following me. I looked him straight in the eye and made sure he knew I was aware he was there. I wasn't going to cower. I wasn't going to show weakness. I wasn't going to become bait. I held his gaze for a count of ten and then walked inside, seemingly unfazed, before closing the door, locking it, and rushing to the back door to do the same. I was thoroughly unnerved.

Even with London beside me now, the guy gives me the creeps.

"Remember what I said. Don't sneak out tonight, and as much as I hate to say it, I need you to close your curtains, Laney. Something's off about that guy, and I don't like it. Maybe we shouldn't stop for ice cream."

I'm quiet, still rattled from sharing another locked gaze with a stranger who has the entire town on edge. But the second we turn down Palomino, we see the parking lot packed with cars and teenagers wearing prom dresses and tuxes. This must be where the after-party went.

"We have to stop now. You crashed my prom, showing up in

the parking lot, wearing jeans and a white t-shirt. We can't miss the after-party. Plus, I see Sydney's Jeep."

He pulls into the parking lot and finds a spot on the side of the building. When he opens the door, I slide out on his side, anxious to see Sydney and hear what I missed tonight, but then he opens the back door.

"Here, put this on," he says, pulling his letterman's jacket from the backseat.

"I thought you liked my dress," I say coyly.

He drapes the jacket over my shoulders before pulling me flush against his front. "I more than like you in this dress. I love it. You in this dress is scarred into my mind, never to be forgotten, but it dropped a few degrees, and you're not wearing a bra."

His lips brush over mine softly, and I let my insides melt from the tenderness, soaking in the moment and relishing it for its inexpressible charm before dipping my tongue in for more. One kiss, one touch, will never be enough, because I've lived a life of what feels like stolen moments, always moving, always onto the next, never knowing when one could become my last. His tongue caresses mine the same way it did back at the lake, slow and unhurried, as though time is on our side, and we have forever to kiss under the stars. It's that thought that reminds me we don't—at least not yet, anyway.

His lips fall away, and my heart aches. Cupping my cheek, he says, "You're breaking my heart every time you look at me like that, heartbreaker. I'm not going anywhere. Where you are is the only place I want to be. We have until Friday, and then it's just a few short weeks until we're back together at Stanley."

"You promised we weren't going to talk about this," I remind him.

"I'm not. We're not. I only want to see you happy, and I can't tell if you really believe I don't love this dress on you or if you're having a hard time obeying your own rules."

He's right, and I hate it. I hate that I can't pretend I'm not moving this Friday. I should be happy I at least got to stay in

Willow Creek through graduation. I should be grateful for the summers I had with Sydney, Fisher, and London, but this summer was supposed to be ours. One summer to finally be the young, carefree couple I dreamed we'd be. The last summer before reality hits, and we're college students. Technically, London is a year ahead of me, but his dad doesn't make him work since he's going to Stanley on a full scholarship and taking a full course load. His only responsibilities this summer are chores—the same ones he's always had—and I'd planned on being glued to his side for all of them. Chopping wood to dry out for fall fires, mowing the lawn, and long, lazy days spent beside the lake, picking the best fishing spot and swimming out to the floating dock when the water got too warm and the fish stopped biting. Me and him, that's what it was supposed to be, and now it will be just me—alone—again.

What I can't believe is my mother isn't moving closer to Stanley, where I'll be attending school in the fall. Instead, she's leaving the state of Texas and heading out west to California, which shocked the hell out of me. It makes zero sense with how close we are, but London is right. I'm not playing by my own rules by letting what's to come steal what time we have here and now.

"You're right. I'm sorry." I shake my head and raise up on my heels for a kiss.

His hands frame my face. "Don't be sorry. You have nothing to apologize for, especially when wearing my jacket. I like seeing you wear my things, especially ones with my last name printed in big letters across the back," he says before pressing his lips to mine once more, his hand drifting down my back to grip my ass. "Come on, if you want ice cream, we'd better get it before I change my mind and take you home instead. I'm selfish, and I don't care about sharing you with the world tonight."

I fist his shirt in my hands and steal one last peck. "Let's go. I'll be quick," I say, grabbing his hand and pulling him along only for him to spin me over to his left.

"Why do you always do that?" I laugh, swatting his chest playfully.

"The sidewalk rule?" He grins, eyebrows raised.

"What's that?"

"You seriously don't know this?" his voice peaks with amusement, like I've just told him I've never heard of birthdays.

"Enlighten me, oh wise one."

"I walk closest to the street to protect you from cars," he explains with mock gravity, gesturing dramatically toward a parked car. "Or puddles when it's raining. It's chivalry 101."

"Well, I don't like it," I say, though I'm still smiling.

"And why not?" He slides his arm around me, pulling me closer as we pass under another streetlight.

"Because what if something happens to you? I don't want you getting hurt because of me." My tone stays light, but I mean it. "I couldn't handle losing you."

We reach the front of the ice cream shop, and he turns to face me, his grin softening into something more tender. "And now you know why I walk on the streetside," he says, tucking a strand of hair behind my ear. "Same reason you don't want me there." I never thought a debate about walking positions could make me melt, but apparently, I was wrong. Laughter from the crowd floats to where we stand and his gaze flicks past me. "Hey, don't leave my side tonight, okay?"

I glance over and know without words what he's asking. I have a feeling the jacket is part of his petition. The day I saw that man watching as I walked into my house, I immediately called him on the phone. He doesn't want me to stand out and catch unwanted attention. I lighten the mood and use his words. "Where you are is the only place I want to be."

He smiles, and no sooner than we turn the corner, Sydney has spotted us from a table right near the front of the shop. "Lanes!" she squeals, bouncing off the table and all but mowing me down for a hug. "You came. When you didn't text me back, I assumed you were..." she trails off, remembering London is holding my hand. Then, with a wicked smile, she says, "Occupied." I can feel the flush in my cheeks, but London keeps a poker face as though he has no idea what she's suggesting. She rolls her lips and changes the subject. "Noah was crowned prom king and—"

"Do you want me to get you an ice cream before they close?" London interrupts.

"Yes, please, vanilla with confetti sprinkles." His eyes scan the crowd, and he looks between us and the front window. "Go, I'll stay right here. You'll literally be three feet away."

He kisses my cheek, and then his mouth skates slowly to my ear, sending a shiver throughout my body. I'm suddenly grateful to be wearing his jacket, because I know my nipples are standing at attention, remembering exactly where that mouth was not long ago. "You better be right where I've left you, heartbreaker."

London has barely stepped out of earshot when Syd pulls me close. "So spill. What happened? Did you guys get vertical or what?" My face gives away more than words ever could. "Oh my god, you did!" She slaps my arm. "I'm so freaking jealous. It's prom, and I have no desire to smash anyone here," she says dispiritedly, and I can't help but feel responsible.

It turns out that the reason Noah caught wind of going down on the deck regarding the bet Fisher, Cooper, and London made was that her then-boyfriend, Justin, blabbed a conversation he had with Cooper to Noah. Justin and Cooper both played baseball for the Mustangs, and I guess as rumors floated around about what went down that night at the party—my near drowning and London's rescue—the bet came up. Needless to say, Sydney cut ties right away without question. The Downs take confidence very seriously, and knowing someone close to her who was supposed to care for her broke it was non-negotiable. Family comes before all else; you cross one, and you cross them all.

"Syd—"

"Don't. We've been over this. You did me a favor. Besides, we're about to be free of this small town and the dusty, used, entitled, wannabe men that live here."

"Do you have to go to Kentucky? Tell me again why you can't study with me at Stanley."

"Because the tracks are in Kentucky, and that's where Dad wants me."

When Sydney told me her family's money comes from horse racing, my mouth hit the floor, instantly assuming they must have ownership in Churchill Downs, the most well-known track in the United States, given their surname. However, she quickly enlightened me that most tracks have the name Downs, as the word refers to the track's terrain. Her last name is a happenstance, though horse racing has been part of her family for generations. They own three tracks in Kentucky and one in Florida. Another detail I found interesting is that in Willow Creek, they don't even own a horse. Apparently, they used to have horses here, but before she was born, something happened, and her grandfather sold the horses and the land here. Of course I wanted to ask what happened, but I could see the shadows that crossed her face when it came up, so I left my curiosity at bay.

"One vanilla ice cream with sprinkles," London says, sneaking a cup in front of me from behind.

"Thank you." I take the cup, and he steals the spoon. "Hey." I turn around, and he sticks it in his mouth with a big smile.

"Sorry, it looked too good. I had to try it."

"You messed up," I say, swiftly snatching the spoon. Then, with deliberate slowness, I dip for a fresh scoop and bring it to my mouth. "I bet it would have tasted better on my lips."

"Eww, oh my god, you guys need to get a room...seriously," Syd taunts.

"I like how you think, Syd," London says with a smirk. "In fact, if you could convince my girl, we'll leave right now."

Sydney rolls her eyes. "I was getting ready to leave when I saw your truck pull in. The better after-party is starting up at the lake house, so I'm heading over there."

London pulls out his phone. "Is Fish going? I texted him when I got in this evening, but I haven't heard back."

"Yeah, the dipshit jumped in the pool with his phone in his

pocket when he got home from the airport. His new one arrives in the morning."

She hops off the bench and chucks her thumb over her shoulder. "I'm parked that way. You guys going to come?"

"Umm." I drop her gaze and try to find words. She's my best friend. I don't want to lie, but I also don't want to ditch her invite for a guy. That's equally as shitty.

"God, just go," she groans, rolling her eyes dramatically as she backpedals. "But for God's sake, wrap it up. I'm not ready to be an aunt."

London drapes his arm over my shoulder. "You heard the lady. Let's go," he says quickly, stealing another bite of my ice cream.

"Yeah, let's go," I say, taking one last look at everyone before we head out. Besides Noah, there isn't anyone else I care to catch up with, and even that will have to wait. Even though London and I are exclusive, there's still bad blood between them, and the last thing I want is to ruin his night or ours with futile drama.

London opens the door of the truck for me to slide in, but before I manage a step, I'm yanked back against a hard chest, and a gloved hand is covering my mouth to stifle my scream. It takes London mere heartbeats to recognize the nightmare unfolding.

"LET HER GO!" he roars, eyes blazing with terror and rage, as his fists clench at his sides, ready to fight.

That's when I feel something press into my side. "I wouldn't come any closer if I were you," a male voice scrapes against my ears—gritty, deep, and hoarse, sounding like a man who sucked down a pack a day his whole life. If the menacing gravel in his tone wasn't enough of a giveaway, the sickening stench of tobacco seeping from the leather glove pressed against my lips would betray his identity. Recognition hits me like a physical blow—it's him, the drifter, the shadowy figure whose eyes I felt boring into my back just days ago as he stood motionless at the end of my street, watching, waiting, memorizing, before I disappeared behind the door.

"Do you want money?" London pulls his wallet from his back pocket and tosses it at our feet. "Take it. Just let her go."

"If I wanted money, there's a slew of unlocked cars and unattended purses around the corner," he answers with a snicker.

"Then what do you want?" London pats the front of his jeans. Finding his keys, he reaches into his pocket. "Take my truck. You can have anything you want…" he says vehemently, chest heaving, tossing the keys with his wallet. "But you can't have her."

"I have what I want," he snarls, yanking me backward against him as ice-cold terror floods my veins, while hot tears begin to stream down my face as my heart hammers in my chest.

This is all my fault. I put myself on his radar. I challenged him when I should have just ignored him. I should have walked into my house like I didn't see him. He takes another step, and I lose my footing. A muffled cry escapes as his arm tightens around me, and the barrel of his gun presses harder into my side.

"Don't." London lunges forward with desperate courage, ready for battle, only to freeze mid-stride as cold reality strikes him. His fists remain clenched, but he knows they are useless against a gun. "Don't take the girl," he pleads.

"What are you going to do, boy?" The question slithers from his lips as his pocketed hand swivels toward London with unmistakable intent.

London raises his hands in defense, his defiance taking a hit, but he doesn't relent. "And what about you?" He licks his lips, his panicked gaze flicking between mine and my abductor. He's stalling. "We saw you on the way in. You don't have a car, and I'm not going to let you walk away with my chief."

London's gaze locks with mine as I battle the violent tremors consuming my body. Through the fog of terror and adrenaline, a crucial realization breaks through: he didn't say "my girl," he said "my chief." My eyes widen with sudden understanding. He gives me an almost imperceptible nod of confirmation. I have his chief. I'm wearing his jacket, which means I have a weapon too.

I force my eyelids shut, struggling to tame my thundering

heart with this new thread of hope. But the terror remains, a living thing with its claws embedded deep. The knife's presence feels like a cruel joke. What good is a Hail Mary when fear has practically turned my limbs to stone?

"This is the part where the hero always gets it wrong. He tries to think like a villain. I'm not trying to get away. That's your miscalculation…" Something in my brain clicks, and my desire to live, my desire to fight, overtakes my fear. This man isn't trying to escape and take me hostage. Whatever chip he has on his shoulder is about to come full circle, but I refuse to be the martyr in his story. London's eyes catch the movement of my arm as I sink my right hand into the pocket of his letterman in search of the knife that's already saved my life once.

"So what is it? Why are you here? Why her?" London demands, attempting to distract my assailant as he drags me around the front of London's truck into the empty street.

My trembling fingers locate the cold metal of the pocketknife, and a desperate flicker of hope battles against the paralyzing dread. When my captor steps off the curb, his hand slips just enough, and I don't waste my breath on screaming. Instead, I bite down on his thumb—hard.

"Son of a bitch!" he snarls through clenched teeth. "I should have known you wouldn't make shit easy. Fucking brat!" He wrenches my head sideways. "I could snap you like a twig right now."

My thumb slides over the knife, finding the stud that engages the blade. I press it and slide the blade all the way out the same way I've witnessed London do countless times.

"You hurt her, and I'll kill you with my bare hands! I swear it." London charges forward, stopping mere inches from us, once again stealing my attacker's focus. But I won't let London kill for me. Nobody has to die tonight. I just need to escape.

I wrench my arm free, the knife clutched in my white-knuckled fist, as I make the only hit I can in this position and drive the blade deep into his thigh.

"Ahhh!" His blood-curdling scream pierces my eardrum, and his grip on me falters. I slam my elbow into his stomach. He doubles over, and London lunges forward, shoving me clear as he seizes the knife. What happens next unfolds in a blur—both agonizingly slow and lightning fast. London extracts the blade from the man's thigh, crimson already soaking his pant leg, and presses the cold steel against his throat.

"You were wrong. I wasn't plotting your next move. I was plotting hers."

"Then you should know you've already lost the—"

"Laney!" Sydney's unmistakable shriek drowns out his final words as London drags the blade across his neck before dropping the knife and rushing to me.

"Are you okay? Tell me you're okay," London demands, crushing me against his chest where I feel his heart hammering in terrified synchrony with mine.

I nod vehemently, my entire body shaking uncontrollably. "I'm okay. Lon... I was so scared," I choke through a flood of tears.

"I know, baby. I'm so sorry. It's okay—"

"Call the cops!" someone shouts from the gathering crowd.

"What happened?" Sydney asks, shock evident.

"That man tried to take Laney," London answers as more faces round the building to see what's going on.

"Oh my god. Oh my god. Is he...? He's dead, isn't he?" a girl from my dance squad asks, distress in her voice, and I deliberately turn away.

I can't look at his face. If I see his face, it will haunt me forever.

Sirens wail in the distance as London speaks low, his words for me alone. "It was my knife. I stabbed him, do you understand?"

"No." I shake my head fiercely, tilting back to meet his gaze. "London, no. I'm not letting you do that. It was self-defense. I did it... It was my hand..." My body quakes harder, and I clutch his shirt desperately, seeking an anchor. "I flicked the blade and..."

My words disintegrate as terror overwhelms my speech. "You can't —I won't—please," I beg until his resolve crumbles.

His eyes soften. "Shh, shh, shh." He presses his lips to my forehead. "I love you. I love you so damn much," he murmurs, pulling me flush against his chest once more.

"What the hell happened?" Noah demands. "My dad is on the way with the sheriff now."

"Not a word, Laney. Stay quiet until the cops arrive," Sydney warns. "You don't need anyone using anything against you."

"What are you doing? Don't touch him," Mindy from the dance team hisses with revulsion.

I'm tempted to turn, to witness what everyone else sees—the consequences of my actions—but I resist.

"Someone needs to check for a pulse. He might not be dead," Noah argues.

"Ew, there's no need. That's too much blood," someone counters before tires screech to a halt nearby.

The slam of the police car door makes me jolt in London's arms. "Shh, I have you," he soothes.

"Does he have a pulse?" Sheriff Townsend demands.

"No," Noah confirms.

"Who's responsible for this?" the sheriff asks as ambulance sirens grow louder.

"I am," London states without hesitation.

"No." I push back against his chest. "I am. It...it was self-defense," I stammer. "He attacked me when I was getting into the car," I continue, finally summoning the courage to face the scene. London isn't taking the fall for this.

"Self-defense?" Mayor Donovan cuts through the crowd. "Did he have a weapon?"

"A gun," London insists. "He had a gun in his pocket."

The sheriff kneels beside my attacker's body, and I force my gaze elsewhere.

"Okay, that's enough. Everyone back up," Mayor Donovan

commands, dispersing the crowd of prom-goers with sweeping gestures.

"Son, there's no gun," Sheriff Townsend states flatly.

"That's not possible. I felt it. He jammed it into my ribs," I protest. "There's no way."

"You were in shock. Fear has a way of distorting reality," Mayor Donovan dismisses.

Sheriff Townsend crosses the distance between us in three determined strides. "Laney, you mentioned that it was self-defense and that he attacked you. Is that correct?"

"Yes, he attacked me, and then I stabbed him in the thigh to get free." I feel London stiffen against me. I know he doesn't want me to take responsibility, but it's true. I did stab him.

"No, she didn't," London interrupts. "I stabbed him. That's my knife beside his body and his blood on my hands."

The sheriff's gaze flickers between us, uncertain. "It's your word against hers."

"London's telling the truth," Noah interjects, approaching us, and suddenly, I've never despised anyone more. He's lying. I wait for London to explode, to put him in his place as he's done count-less times before when Noah has interfered, but he remains silent. Their eyes lock, and something unspoken passes between them. "I saw everything. London stabbed him in the thigh before slitting his throat."

"Son, I'm going to have to take you with me," Sheriff Townsend pronounces, his tone full of regret and predetermined judgment that chills me to the bone.

"No, you can't take him. If you take him, you have to take me too, because they're lying."

"Laney, Laney, look at me," London says, stepping directly into my path, his hands gripping my shoulders. His eyes capture mine, leaving me nowhere else to look. "It's going to be okay."

"No." I shake my head, my voice cracking. "It's not. They think you killed him."

"I did."

Two words. Two simple words that shatter everything. Tears well in my eyes, hot and stinging, and I blink frantically, wishing I could erase them along with this moment, wishing I could erase the truth.

"Please don't cry, heartbreaker," he whispers, his thumb brushing my cheek. "You're going to live a full, beautiful life."

"What are you saying?" Rage and despair war inside of me. "You're going to live it with me, London Hale. You said you loved me. That's supposed to be forever." My words come out broken, like the heart inside of me as I struggle through the fear and confusion.

"London," Sheriff Townsend's voice cuts through my spiral, his hand landing heavily on London's shoulder. "I have to ask you to come with me, son. I don't want to use the cuffs, but—"

London nods, his jaw tight. "I'll come." His eyes never leave mine. "Can I say goodbye?"

"No, this isn't goodbye," I protest, but my words die in my throat as he pulls me against him. His arms envelop me in familiar warmth, and I feel like I might stop breathing at any moment. I can't lose him. I haven't had enough time. We haven't had enough time. Our lives were just beginning.

"I'll love you until they put me in a casket," he murmurs against my hair. "You're the first girl who ever truly saw me, the first one to ever love me. You're my heart and soul. Where you go, I go, but where I'm going"—his voice catches—"you can't follow."

I feel the tremble beneath his bravado, the fear he's trying to hide, and I hold him tighter, my fingers digging into his back, desperate to keep him with me. This isn't where our story ends. It can't be.

"You're going to fight this. We're going to fight this. It was self-defense." I pull back just enough to find his eyes, to force him to see my determination through my tears. "Promise me, London. Promise me. You're not accepting this. You're going to come back to me."

He swallows hard. "I'll fight." His voice drops to a whisper that belongs only to me. "I love you, Laney Hart," he says, placing a lingering kiss on my forehead before taking a step back.

Sheriff Townsend grabs his shoulder, his expression grim as he guides London toward the waiting police car. London doesn't look back, but his shoulders are straight, defiant even in surrender.

Sydney fills the void he leaves behind, rushing to me and wrapping her arms around me before I can crumble to the ground. I watch, my vision blurred by tears, as they take away the only man I've ever loved, the man who saved my life more than once. He said he loved me, and I believe him. He just sacrificed everything for it. Now it's my turn.

The police car's door slams shut with a finality that echoes through my bones. Through the window, I catch one last glimpse of London's profile—strong jaw clenched, eyes fixed forward—as the car pulls away, carrying with it my heart and the only future I ever wanted.

He's wrong.

Where he goes, I go. If he thinks I'll just continue on with a beautiful life while he faces this alone, then he doesn't know me at all. London may have saved my life, but what he doesn't understand is that, somewhere along the line, he became my life, our hearts and fates intertwined.

"I need to go," I whisper gently as I pull out of her embrace.

"Laney, wait. You can't just—" Her words fade behind me as I stand straighter, my gaze locked on the disappearing taillights.

London stepped between me and danger without hesitation. He chose me over himself, and now he's walking into darkness alone, thinking his sacrifice will set me free. But it won't—it can't—because his punishment is my sentence too. His hell is mine. If he's there, so am I.

Part Two

LANEY

CHAPTER 10

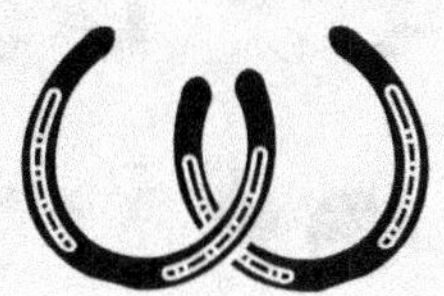

"I can't believe you'll be spending the summer with me in Bardstown," Asha says as we turn onto the gravel road that cuts through her family's property.

"Me neither. Are you sure your dad is okay with me staying here? I don't want to be an inconvenience."

She snorts. "Are you kidding? My dad adores you. Trust me, there is more than enough room at our Fairfield Estate. I'm not even sure he knows who is and who isn't staying here at all times."

I met Asha Fairfield in my second year at the University of Kentucky. We both had an equine-assisted activities course together. She asked if she could borrow a pen and a notebook in class, which left me somewhat baffled until I realized she was covered in mud. I quietly passed her the requested materials, and after class, she broke into a long-winded explanation about her family, stables, and not having time to change. I heard stables, mud, and a horse named Phoenix. Needless to say, we were fast friends. It's hard not to be friends with someone who does most of the talking, especially when talking to people doesn't come as easily as it once did. I'm not shy. I'm just not interested.

My phone pings with a text, and I look down to see who it's from.

> Sydney: FaceTime me when you get settled. I want to see the place you're calling home for the next three months.

> Laney: You'll be here in two weeks.

> Sydney: Yeah, and I need to see if hotel accommodations are in order. She might be rich, but that doesn't mean she has good taste.

I can't help but smile and roll my eyes. Sydney and Asha get along. The three of us have spent almost every weekend and holiday break together for the past three years, living on campus at Louisville, but as much as we all get along, I've always sensed a tiny bit of jealousy from Syd. We were best friends first, and sometimes bringing a new person into the fold isn't easy, but I'm grateful for both of them. Together, they've helped breathe life back into me when living felt like a worse fate than death.

"Is that Noah? Feel free to tell him no boys are allowed. My dad doesn't allow opposite-sex sleepovers," she says as she texts away on her own phone.

"Is that a joke? You're twenty-four," I say, somewhat baffled. "We've lived in co-ed dorms for the last two years."

"Yes, it's a joke," she says sardonically. "But I want you all to myself for a little while." She slides her phone into her satchel and turns to me. "Besides, I don't think you want him here anyway. I'm just giving you an out."

I give her a soft smile and turn my head out the window. She's not wrong. Noah and I are friends, maybe a little more than friends, and as much as I'm grateful for his friendship and support, even when it wasn't easy, I was hoping this summer could be the start of a new beginning, a fresh start for me. I'm here to finish coursework hours to get my certification in Equine Assisted Hippotherapy. I don't know what comes after this—hell, I never planned to be here to begin with. I was supposed to be in Dallas, attending Stanley with London, but there was no way I could go without him.

The truth is, I couldn't bear to be anywhere he had been, not after he was taken from me. The first forty-eight hours after I watched the police car disappear, taking my heart with it, were excruciating. I told London I'd fight, and I did. I went straight home to tell my mom what had happened. I told her she needed to take me down to the police station immediately so we could straighten everything out and get him released, but when we got down there, London wasn't there.

He wasn't there because Willow Creek doesn't have a jail. It has one holding cell mainly used for drunks to sleep off their indecent intoxication or to teach chump kids a lesson when they step out of line. It wasn't for holding real criminals, the kind that murdered people in self-defense.

Gah…almost six years later, and I still can't let it go. Too many things went wrong for anything to ever feel settled. I told my story to Sheriff Townsend, the mayor, and the investigator on his case, and every day, they dismissed me, telling me I was wasting my breath because not only were my fingerprints not on the knife, but there was an eyewitness, and London admitted to the crime.

As planned, my mother and I left five days later to go to California. I didn't want to leave. Leaving felt like giving up, but I couldn't stay. Not only did the people of the town stare at me like I was some kind of disease for ruining the bright future of the town's golden boy, but the memories there were crippling. There wasn't a street I could walk down or an establishment I could patronize that he didn't leave his mark on. The sheriff gave me the name of the prison he would be transferred to, and I wrote him every day. I told him how much I missed him, how I hated what he had done, and how I didn't want a life without him. After a month of no response, he finally replied.

Laney,

Please don't write me anymore. I don't want to remember.

London

After everything, that was his goodbye, and I was just supposed to accept it. I'm still just supposed to accept it. I lean my forehead against the cool glass. The month of May always hits me the hardest. It was the month he was taken from me, the month I lost my heart. If I've learned anything since that day, it's that healing comes in waves. This is a moment of grief; it might linger, but eventually, it will pass.

What hasn't passed is Asha's unvarnished truth about Noah and me, still hanging in the air. I exhale a resigned breath. "You're not wrong, though I'm not sure it's him that's the problem."

At one point in our friendship, before there was ever a London and me, perhaps there could have been an us, but not after. I've found comfort and refuge with him over the years, but in hindsight, they were moments of weakness. I needed to feel something, and he was there, but there are some things you just can't get past.

"Oh, it's for sure him. If he were the one, you'd know it. We always know it." I pull in a sharp breath, knowing her words are true, but I fear, just like you can't live the same moment twice, I won't find the same love twice. "Hey." She jabs me in the arm.

"Ouch!" I grab it and look at her, my mouth agape. "What was that for?"

"You need to get out of whatever funk you've been in since we turned off the highway. Cheer up, buttercup. This summer is going to be fun." Her eyes widen, and she clasps her hands together. "We're here!" Asha leans over to look out my window where a palomino is practicing jumps in the riding arena. He's beautiful, but the sight of a chestnut-colored horse grazing freely on one of the far fields with wooded acres behind him has the anxiety I was feeling moments ago fleeting. This might be another small town, but Bardstown isn't Willow Creek. This is my fresh start.

~

"You're joking right? That is not a barn. It's a full-on backside," Sydney says as I release the curtain in my bedroom that looks out over the stables. I can tell from her tone that she's impressed. "That place looks like their Louisville property on steroids."

I flop onto the bed in my room. "That property is for entertaining and housing horses actively racing during the season. This is where they breed, train, and bring the horses for their seasonal breaks."

I admit that when the treeline broke and the fullness of the property came into view, I was impressed. I knew the Fairfields had money. I've been to their Louisville property many times. It became a second home to me while I was earning hours for my degree, but this place was unexpected. It's a dream. Working with the horses on this property all summer to get my Eagala certification will be a breeze. I already feel lighter being here.

"And the bed is impressive. It looks like there is plenty of room for me to sleep comfortably when I come to visit."

"I was surprised when I saw a king-sized bed in a guest room."

"You shouldn't be. Breeders like the Fairfields host investors and potential buyers. Some buyers like to stay so they can witness the horse's routine and temperament, plus it's good business. If a breeder is willing to give you that kind of access, they're confident they're elite."

I run my hand over the blue suede material on the comforter. "I'm sure you can get your own room if you want it. I counted three other doors before we reached my room, and Asha referred to this as the house's west wing. If her house is large enough to be divided into wings, I'm certain those doors didn't lead to family bedrooms."

"Nah, you know I like to cuddle." She picks up her glass of wine and tucks her legs beneath her on the couch. "How are you holding up? You look like you've been in your head."

"You know the thing that sucks about having you as a best friend?"

"Absolutely nothing," she says with a smile before I finish.

"You know me too well," I answer.

"Which means you were thinking about him, weren't you?" I close my eyes, hating that I can't get out of this cycle, hating myself for not being able to let go. "I had a feeling those wide-open spaces might be triggering, that they might remind you of Willow Creek, but babe, it's okay to hurt. Sometimes, letting it hurt is the best way to let it go. Losing London hurt us all."

God, her comment makes it hard to swallow. I wasn't the only one London cut out of his life when he went to prison. He cut off ties with Sydney and Fisher too. It's yet another reason I feel selfish in my pain. Not only did I cause this, but I'm also the one who keeps it alive by not moving on. I count to three, do what she said, and let it go.

When I open my eyes, I say, "I think I'm going to check out the bathtub and go to sleep early."

"It's only seven o'clock. What are you, suddenly thirty-five?"

"Funny." I roll my eyes. "You know I get up at 5 a.m. to tend to the horses. But horses aside, do I need to show you that tub again? Seriously, it's probably been at least four years since I've soaked in a tub."

There are no tubs in the dorms, and even if there were, I wouldn't dare use one, and the condo Sydney's family has been letting us stay at during the summer doesn't have one either. Instead, it had one of those six-head steam showers, which was heaven after riding, but not the same.

"I'll let it slide this time," she says over the rim of her wine glass. "But when I visit, there will be none of that. We are going to whoop it up. I want to do the Bourbon Trail, so don't go to any of the local distilleries without me."

"I won't," I say, getting off the bed and heading to the en-suite to start my bath.

"Have you talked to your mother?"

"Nope," I pop the P to accentuate my lack of interest in discussing the topic.

My mother and I used to be close. That changed after everything happened. I don't put all the blame on her. I know it takes two people to let a relationship fall apart, but I'm not sure how she expects to have one with me when she moved back into our old house.

Before everything happened, she planned to follow me wherever I chose to go to school, picking up and moving the way we had always done. But when I left California, she didn't follow me to Kentucky.

Instead, she transferred back to Willow Creek—moved into the house she had never sold—with a bedroom that held a portal to alternate endings I spent countless hours dreaming about. My mother had to know I wouldn't come back, and part of me wonders if that wasn't why she did it.

"Got it. Sorry for bringing it up. I just thought maybe with the semester being over, she would have called, and maybe you would have answered," she replies with a hint of hope in her voice.

"You didn't ask if she called." I set the phone on the vanity and kick off my shoes before flipping my head upside down to gather up my long hair and knot it into a high bun on top of my head. "She did." I stand up and secure the bun, tucking in the flyaways. "I don't have anything to say, or if I do, I don't have the right words." I let out a long breath and bring my eyes back to the phone. "Unless you want to see me get naked, I'm going to get off now."

"One, I've seen you naked, and two, I'm not entirely opposed to it. It would be the most action I've seen in months. I'm so ready to be done with school. Two more tests, and I'm out. Fuck getting my master's. It's not like my dad isn't going to give me a job."

I start pulling off my socks. "True, but you weren't ever interested in getting your master's to please him. It was for you."

"Gah, don't remind me. Okay, I'm getting off now. I liked talking better when we were talking about your stuff, not mine."

"Bye," I laugh as I reach to click off the phone, and she blows me a kiss.

"Let it go," I whisper, the mantra dissolving into steam as I approach the bathtub. Stepping in, I close my eyes and sink beneath the surface, letting the words wash over me. "You sulked, you let it hurt, and this is your fresh start. Tomorrow, you'll wake up and start living the life you've been working toward." I take one more cleansing breath. "Now, open your eyes, Laney. This summer is going to be different. This summer, you're going to live again."

I ran until my lungs were on fire, until I thought I might collapse. I had no destination; I just needed to run. When I woke up this morning, I had this anxious energy in my bones. Maybe it was being in a new place, or perhaps it was the act of mindfully letting go of the things out of my control. All I know is at 4 a.m., I was out the door, ready to take the world by the horns. My legs feel like putty, and if I'm not careful, one misstep in the gravel as I head toward the stables, too anxious to see the horses in the first light of morning before dressing, I'm liable to face-plant. But the way I feel right now, I'd welcome the sting. Today's a good day, and it's only about to get better.

As I approach the entrance, my legs muster up the energy to pick up the pace. I've been dying to go inside since we pulled up last night. The scale of the barn is impressive. The doors alone are at least twenty feet tall, with a massive set of medallion door knockers extending every bit of four feet. But the outside could never have prepared me for what I'd find inside. I've seen exceptional barns, living in Louisville, and deciding to go into Equine

Assisted Therapy, I've seen more than my fair share of luxury stables, but this place is next level.

The entire interior is flanked in cedar, the ceiling spanning at least another ten feet above the doors with peaked skylights running down the middle of the barn, drenching the walls with natural light. Iron chandeliers hang beneath the timber trusses, tying in the black stall doors. It's a showstopper, for sure. I can't believe this is their private residence. Then again, I suppose when you're breeding Thoroughbred racehorses, charging hundreds of thousands for a horse, you need to have facilities worthy of the horse.

My eyes connect with a black stallion. He looks like one of the horses I saw in the pasture when we pulled up, though I'm sure it wasn't him. If he's in here, then he wasn't out there. Unless a race-horse is getting its daily workout or working with its trainer, it's not typically let out to run freely. When they're in their stalls, the trainers can monitor their diets and health and minimize their risk of injury.

I glance at his nameplate. "Hi, Duke," I speak calmly and raise my hand slowly, letting him see and smell me before scratching the small star between his eyes. "Are you having a good morning, buddy?"

"I wouldn't do that if I were you," a deep voice from behind startles me.

"Jeez." I huff, running my hands down the sides of my joggers. "You scared the shit out of me."

I intentionally came out to the stables early. I like to be alone, and Asha said the staff didn't start arriving until 6 a.m. This man is dressed in jeans, a dark-gray Wrangler, and boots. He could be a trainer, but something tells me he's not. Most trainers don't wear cowboy boots; they wear riding boots—or at least the ones at high-end facilities like this do. When he crosses his arms, I realize I've stared too long.

"Is this your horse?" I finally let my eyes meet his, only to wish I hadn't, because now I'm staring for an entirely different reason. I know those eyes. They've starred in every dream and nightmare, but the face is different. His eyebrows are bigger, his jaw is broader, and his nose is strikingly straight. It's not bad, just not like the one I know.

"No," he answers, his face indifferent, as though scaring me is inconvenient for him and not the other way around.

"Do you work here?" I ask skeptically. He said this wasn't his horse, but maybe he's a potential buyer who doesn't appreciate anyone touching the horses. I extend my hand. "I'm the new EAP for the summer." He looks at my outstretched hand but doesn't take it, and when his assessing glare narrows on mine, the feeling of familiarity I got the second I saw him returns. That must be what this is. Maybe he's seen me at one of the tracks back in Louisville, earning my hours toward my degree, and by the way he's snubbing me now, I'm assuming whatever run-in we had wasn't a good one. "I'm sorry, have we met before?"

His head tilts to the side, my question peculiarly garnering his attention. "Why? Do I look like someone you know?"

My eyebrows rise in surprise. It's not so much his question that makes my skin prickle with awareness, but the mischievous glint in his eye. I don't know this guy from Adam, but the way he's counter-questioning me is avoidance. I'm only unsure if it's because I'm about to become the butt end of an impending snarky remark or because he does, indeed, know me.

A door closing at the far end of the stable has him sidestepping me. "You're here for the whole summer?" he asks, heading toward the south exit.

"I am," I answer as I watch him saunter away.

"Then I guess I'll see you around."

"Hey, I never got your name," I call out as his boots hit the gravel outside the door, but he doesn't stop. It's not that I expected he would after that odd encounter. "You forgot to mention why I shouldn't touch the horse," I grumble as I turn back to Duke.

"What is wrong with me? Huh, Duke?" I ask, leaning my forehead against the cool bars separating us.

I don't know what it was about him, but I'm certain I'll be playing our brief interaction in an endless loop for the remainder of the day. It's like emotional muscle memory—magnetically pulled toward men who barely register my existence. I don't know him. I can't even say that I want to know him. The rational part of my brain is screaming self-sabotage. The arrogance in his posture, the brooding intensity, and even his non-answer to my every question were borderline rude. The entire confrontation should be warning enough, but something in his familiar eyes tells me I won't listen. Somewhere along the line, I started reaching for what burns me instead of what warms. There's somehow less pain when I knowingly walk into the flames. I'm prepared for it.

LANEY
CHAPTER 11

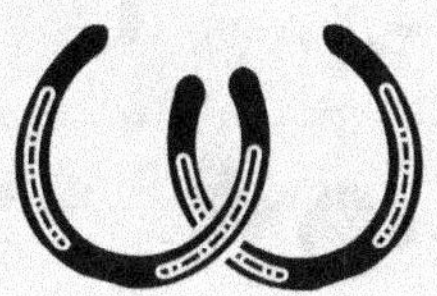

"Laney, isn't it almost break time?" Asha calls out from where she's copped a squat on top of the fence of the training ring where I've been working with my first horse of the summer, Casanova."

One of the reasons Asha asked me here this summer, besides the fact that we are friends and I need to finish my hours to get my Eagala certification, is that she wants to shake things up with how her family runs the business. Her father, Warrick Fairfield is focused solely on investors and breeding and is less concerned with what happens with the horses once they've lived out their racing careers.

Casanova was a racing veteran on the brink of obsolescence. New horses emerge faster and stronger every year, pushing seasoned champions like him harder. Some manage to keep up, while others have already lived their glory days. Asha's family views horses primarily as investments—breeding and racing with little concern for their post-career lives. Her father isn't cruel, but he's also not in the business of repurposing aging horses.

That's where I come in. I'm here to put in hours and earn my Eagala certification, but I'm also here to help Asha challenge her family's traditional approach to retiring racehorses. These horses are athletes, and not all are ready for a quiet retirement. They deserve second chances, and part of my role as an EAP is understanding their behavior, learning their temperaments, and considering their needs as well as potential clients' needs.

My long-term goal is to own my own ranch. All it took was a lone dark horse, standing in a Kentucky paddock on a rainy day when hope had abandoned me completely to transform everything. That day, staring at him stoically, weathering the storm rather than seeking refuge, unlocked something inside me, revealing a deeper purpose. I was given a story that was meant for me so that I would get to that moment and find my reason for existing. Therapeutic trail riding isn't just an activity; it's a journey of connection, healing, and hope.

"Your father gave me a week to work with Casanova. Since he's been retired the longest, he's first to leave. I just want to make sure he goes to the right place," I say as I run my hand along his mahogany coat. Not only is Casanova regal, but he still has a lot of energy. The retirement facility he's slated to be shipped to isn't what he needs. "He's still eager to work and loves taking direction. I know the retirement center your father works with isn't the worst, but..."

"What are you thinking?"

"I think he might be amenable to learning dressage. I've walked through a few exercises, and he caught on to some of the basic commands quickly. But the real test would be someone who could ride him through the movements and see how he performs."

She smiles big, her dark eyes reflecting the sun before she raises her hand to shield them. "I know just the rider."

"You do?"

"I do." She hops off the fence. "I used to compete when I was younger before I started jumping. I'll ride him, but only after you take a break and come with me to lunch."

I roll my eyes. I frequently skip lunch or grab an energy bar, opting to take a break with the horses. Being with them frees my mind. I'm relaxed around them. When I was younger, I loved making junk journals. Since we moved around a lot, it was hard to pick up any real hobbies. Starting a class or joining a team only to turn around and leave right as things got good sucked. I tried painting, but lugging supplies everywhere wasn't ideal.

I can't sing, I can't bake, and I could never focus long enough to learn how to play an instrument. We never had enough money for me to form a shopping addiction, but I always loved being outdoors, and since I moved around a lot, I collected souvenirs of sorts. Coasters from restaurants, passes, receipts, and movie stubs. Originally, I tossed them in a box until I was doom-scrolling one day before getting on a plane to Utah and came across an account where the girl was junk journaling. It became my new obsession. But after everything happened, even the things that used to bring me joy didn't.

"Come on, maybe we will run into your mystery man. I've been itching to run into him. I'm so damn curious who was in my barn. There's only one person I can think of that fits your description, but he wouldn't dare step on my property."

That piques my interest. "And why's that?"

"Our families have been rivals for generations," Asha says, her tone dropping a few decibels.

I catch a flicker of something in her eyes—not just rivalry, but something deeper. Old wounds. The kind that don't heal easily.

"Rivals, how?" I press, knowing full well Asha loves to dangle information just out of reach.

She turns, blocking the sunlight, her silhouette suddenly sharp against the barn. "All I can say is there's a history that extends deeper than simple business rivalry."

Something Sydney said on one of our last calls comes to mind. She liked talking about my drama because it distracted her from her own. I've been doing my best to avoid drama and be left alone, but that hasn't exactly been working for me. Maybe unraveling what Asha isn't telling me is just the distraction I need to escape the haunting thoughts that plague me this time of year.

"Deal. I'll go to lunch, but if this turns into drama, just remember you caused the storm."

She gives me a cheeky smile. "Good thing I like the rain."

I know Asha well enough to recognize when she's plotting. Her smile isn't just playful—it's strategic. She's up to something; sharing lunch is just the first move in whatever game she is planning. The mystery man…the rival families…it's bait, and I know it, but for the first time in a long time, I'm actually curious, and that's saying something. So, I bite.

~

I watch Asha's eyes scour the street outside the window of the coffee shop. She insisted we stop in for an afternoon pick-me-up after lunch.

"I know what you're doing."

Her eyes flick to mine and then back to the street. "I don't know what you're talking about."

"Pssh…you're stalling. We didn't run into my mystery man after someone accidentally parked at the wrong end of Third Street, forgetting the salad place she loves is at the other end."

"I did forget," she insists, her eyes eagerly darting back out the window.

"Uh-huh, and walking rather than circling the block and parking outside the restaurant wasn't intentional, the same way stopping for coffee at the shop directly across from the local tack and feed supply isn't deliberate."

Her cheeks inflate with air before she lets it trill through her glossy pink lips on the exhale. "Fine. You caught me. I thought for sure if we had a chance of running into whoever this dark-eyed, tall glass of water is, it would be here, but seeing as how you aren't looking, and I haven't seen anyone who remotely fits the height and age, I guess we can go." She picks up her coffee and starts to rise from her chair. "After all, it's only your first week here. We have all summer to find this man."

"This is true," I say, lifting my elbow for her to wrap her arm through mine.

The two of us do not match at all. She carries herself with the quiet confidence of someone who knows she's unforgettable: razor-straight black hair grazing her shoulders, and impossible blue eyes that contrast dramatically, practically glowing against her beautiful dark skin. When she's home, she dresses every bit the role of equestrian royalty that her last name is synonymous with around these parts. And then there's me, dirty blonde hair, brown eyes, and a farmer's tan from alternating between t-shirts and tank tops depending on where I was working and the expected attire. I am the epitome of plain Jane next to her, especially today when our outfits are so contrasting. I'm wearing riding pants, a royal blue short-sleeved polo, and boots, while she's wearing a baby blue Lilly Pulitzer number.

We've just stepped out the door when she stops dead. "Crap, I left my phone on the windowsill. I'll be right back," she says, leaving my side to run back in. It's then that a silhouette exiting the tack shop across the street catches my eye, and that sense of familiarity, the same one I had in the barn, instantly returns. He's wearing a cowboy hat, shading his eyes today, but I don't need to see them to know it's him. Everything else is just as it was. Same muscular shoulders tapering to a trim waist, same fitted clothing, tight but not too tight, only hinting at the shape beneath. But those aren't even the most telling signs that I am, indeed, looking at my mystery man. Instead, it's the way he carries himself. He walks with a deliberate yet relaxed fluidity that looks like confidence, but because I heard him speak, I see arrogance.

I hear the bells on the door of the coffee shop ring as Asha steps out. "Got it." Her eyes immediately track mine. "Oh my god, that's him, isn't it?"

There's a flatness behind her surprised tone that betrays her recognition. Her practiced neutrality tells me he's exactly the guy she expected, and when she takes off across the street, heels clicking against asphalt, eyes fixed forward with predatory focus, uncaring about the blaring horns of oncoming traffic, I know my mystery man is also her rival.

I quickly follow suit, waving at cars and apologizing for her reckless jaywalking on my way. "Are you nuts? You could have gotten yourself killed back there," I scold, catching up to her on the curb.

"I'd say that's a fair assessment," the deep baritone voice that I remember all too well from the stables answers for her.

"Trigger Hale, what were you doing on my property?"

"Good to see the prodigal daughter is back in town, but I don't know what you're talking about."

She crosses her arms. "So you weren't in my stable last Saturday morning before any staff arrived?"

His eyes flick to mine knowingly, and my stomach knots. Hale… Is it possible that those dark eyes feel so familiar because he's related to the one Hale my heart refuses to let go of? Or am I making up more lies to keep myself from moving on? Hale isn't that uncommon of a surname, and London told me his dad was an only child like him. I clench my now sweaty palms. They're not related. This isn't a dream, Laney. There's no ending where you wake up tomorrow, London is back, and this man isn't a replacement. Stop holding onto these lies as though they will become your reality. They won't, and even if they did, he doesn't want you anymore—he made that clear.

Those dark eyes narrow ever so quickly, as though he can sense the internal dilemma the mere mention of his name caused, but before that perception can take root, his eyes are trained on Asha. "Did you see me?"

"As a matter of fact, I did." She raises a perfectly sculpted eyebrow.

"Is that so?" He widens his stance and hooks his thumbs into his pockets. "What was I wearing?"

"Are you serious? Don't act cute. You're not that memorable, and we both know you were there."

"Suit yourself." He shrugs. "I'm not going to stand here and be falsely accused of crimes I didn't commit." Then, he checks the time by grabbing his phone from his back pocket. "If you're looking to start a war"—he steps up to her side—"make sure you have evidence." He throws me a wink before walking around her to his parked Ford truck on the curb.

"Dark jeans, gray Wrangler, boots, and no hat," Asha says to the empty space he was standing before turning around.

He steps onto the running board of his truck and looks across the roof. "And here I thought I wasn't memorable." He knocks on the roof. "Glad to hear that was just another lie." She bites her lip, her glare so hard that if it were fire, he'd be ash. Then, with a shit-eating grin, he adds, "See ya around, Laney."

I furrow my brow. His underhanded jab throws me completely. We never exchanged names in the stables, and just now, it didn't come up. So how does he know it? Trigger's truck disappears around the corner just as Asha lets out a wail of frustration, dragging me from my spiraling thoughts.

"Gah! I hate him!" she says, stomping off toward the car.

"Why didn't you tell me the two of you used to date?" I jokingly provoke.

She said her family and his have had a generational feud, but I couldn't help but sense there was more between them. I don't doubt they are enemies, but there's a chemistry there as well that fuels the hate.

"I'm going to pretend like you didn't say that, because there's no way on earth I'd let a Hale touch me."

I swallow hard at the mention of his last name. It's that name that silences my comeback. What Asha doesn't know is that name provokes her as much as it does me. She might be one of my closest friends, but I've never told her about London or what happened that night of my senior prom. Most days, it doesn't seem like I've moved on. There's not a day that has gone by that I haven't thought of him, but it's hard to live with memories that feel alive.

"He knows he was there. It's why he called you by name. Why

didn't you say something?" She stops mid-stride, and I almost spill my coffee down her front. "I saw that look the two of you shared. He was seeing if you'd rat him out, and you didn't."

Was he? I was too stunned by hearing his last name to thoroughly dissect his eye contact. "Asha, you know I'm not good with confrontation—"

She waves her hand dismissively, already onto the next thing. "We're going to use that to our advantage. Trigg is utterly deceived by your feigned doe-eyed fascination. It's obvious he thinks whatever moment you shared in the stables overrides your title as best friend, which is fine with me. Let him think that. That's how I'll find out what he was doing in my stables." My eyebrows raise, and she spins on her heel, continuing like she didn't just elect me to partake in a fake relationship with her enemy in the name of reconnaissance.

"Asha—" I start.

"I'm sorry. He just gets me so riled up." She pinches the bridge of her nose. "Do you like him?"

"Does it even matter?" I ask skeptically. She had an idea who my mystery man may have been from the start based on the description I gave her. There's a reason for that, and I think it goes beyond a family feud.

"That's… It's not…" She tips her head to the sky. "I know it sounds crazy, but saying his name out loud made it real. Saying his name made it more than a hunch."

"I get that," I admit, leaving off the 'more than you know,' part. Lord knows I have countless reasons to never speak London's name again, but this thing between her and Trigger feels different. It feels like hope, especially seeing how worked up he made her moments ago. I am familiar with those feelings that get you hot and bothered because you feel everything while believing the other person feels nothing.

"I'm sorry." She brings her gaze back to me. "It was wrong of me to pull you into this, to ask you to do my dirty work."

I hear her apology, and I know it's genuine. I've been in her shoes. I've been caught between wanting someone's attention and being torn to go after it, but back then, I had Sydney pushing me out of my comfort zone, championing my relationships when I didn't think I had a horse in the race. It's why I say, "Asha, you're one of my closest friends. You were forgiven before you ever said sorry. Our friendship means more than some trivial outburst. As for the latter, there's no harm in asking. If you want me to get close to Trigger Hale and dig up some dirt. I'll do it." I recapture her arm and link up. "Mates before dates." Plus, helping her is two-fold. I want answers about how he knew my name. Small towns talk. If this place mirrors Willow Creek, strangers become headlines within hours. Still, something about his casual use of it feels too intentional to ignore.

She laughs a deep belly laugh. "Did you forget to tell me you were from Australia?"

Her comment has me snorting with laughter. "No, but I have been binging Australian sitcoms."

"It sounds like you could use a little distraction yourself. Shake things up, live a little, and have fun. It's our last summer before we officially become full-time adults with real jobs, rent, and reasonable bedtimes that support functional a.m. activities."

I feel the amusement on my forehead as my brows pull together, and I silently mouth, *wow*. "Some of us had all of that in college too." I may have lived on campus during the school year, but I'll be paying for that housing for the next ten years.

"See, that right there"—she gestures to me with her coffee —"that's what I'm talking about. Stop taking things so seriously. That gives me an idea." She pulls me off the sidewalk and into a boutique clothing store.

"Asha…" I draw out her name with a hint of annoyance. "My lunch hour is up. Can't you shop later?"

"Nope, because I'm not here for me. We're here for you. Clothes inspire, give you confidence, and have the power to change your mood, and that's exactly what you need. No offense, Laney, but you've been rocking the same outfits since we met. You have a hot little body underneath your dirty jeans and button-downs."

"First of all, I work with horses. They don't give a shit about what I wear, and what I wear is not only out of utility but affordability. My clothing budget is non-existent, which is why you've seen me wearing the same outfits for years."

Her lips part as the corners of her mouth pull into a smile, and she holds up a black card. "A perk of having a bestie with money. You get to reap the benefits."

"I'm not spending your father's money on clothes." I turn toward the door to exit. "Plus, like I said, I have to get back to work. I don't want your dad to think I'm exploiting our friendship to cut out of work."

"Well, then, consider this work. You've seen our facilities. Fairfield has an image and a reputation to uphold, and the people working there need to look the part, so just think of this as a uniform fitting. If you'll be working with our horses all summer, frequenting the main stables, you'll need a wardrobe worthy of being seen."

I pinch my lips together and turn slowly. "Fine," I cave. She does make a good argument. I've noticed the trainers and staff all wear cream-colored riding tights and cute base-layer tees or long sleeves, and I wouldn't mind having a windbreaker—in the name of a uniform, of course.

She excitedly clicks her heels on the floor. "Yes!" Her eyes immediately start scanning the store. "And we'll throw in some cute dresses and casual wear too." Her head snaps back to me before I can object. "For dinners and cocktail parties. My father hosts them weekly."

I don't argue. She's right. I need to get out of my own way. I need to let go of what I can't change, and not all distractions are bad; sometimes they are necessary. A change is a good reset, and I could use that.

~

"THANK YOU, AGAIN, FOR WATCHING KATIE DURING THE AUCTION. The auction is as much rubbing shoulders as it is buying a horse," Ms. Cintel says before dropping to one knee for Katie. "I promise we can go to the American Doll store on our way home."

I don't know much about Katie and Ms. Cintel's story, aside from the tidbits Katie has shared with me the past two days her mom has been staying at Fairfield. Every day, she comes out to the training ring in the far field and stands on the fence, watching me work. She talks about anything and everything, but not much about home. However, from the comments I've pieced together, it sounds like her parents are in the middle of a divorce, which could be why Ms. Cintel is trying to sweeten her up now.

"Okay," Katie answers dolefully, which I find somewhat amusing. She might truly be sad that her mother is choosing work over her, but I also know the girl loves horses. She's been stuck to me like glue since they arrived, and I doubt she's as upset about hanging out with me as she's letting on.

"I love you." She kisses her head before standing to full height. "Thanks, Laney. You're truly a lifesaver," she says before waltzing off toward the upstairs VIP viewing room.

Two hours later, we've strolled the entire property and viewed all the horses. They're gorgeous and truly well taken care of. From what I can see, these horses are handled with the utmost care. I've heard stories about that not always being the case, but Elite Equine delivers on its namesake.

"What do you say we take a lap through the inside one more time and see what horses have been sold?" I ask Katie.

"Sure, want to make a bet?" Her big brown eyes sparkle with mischief as she turns on a dime, her pigtails lifting off her shoulders from the force of her spin.

I cross my arms and give her my best poker face. "I'm listening."

"If White Flame sold, then you'll let me ride Hopper tomorrow."

When we walked through the stables for the pre-auction viewing, she asked if I thought any of the horses might not sell, and my answer was White Flame. He's a beautiful horse, but some would consider him past his prime, pushing eight years old. That being said, depending on who the buyer is and the sport they're looking for, he could be an excellent buy. However, Asha said this auction was primarily for buyers interested in racing.

I hold out my hand. "I'll accept on one condition."

She pauses, her hand inches away from shaking mine. "I'm listening."

"Your mom has to approve the ride."

"Deal." We shake on it and make our way inside.

When we turn the corner, she runs down the center of the stable. "Katie," I call after her. "Don't run! Those boots are a little too big," I warn as I jog as best I can in the two-inch wedges Asha insisted I wear with the white floral double-breasted blazer and matching fitted skirt. I'm glad I agreed to let her buy me clothes. I owned nothing that would have worked for this event, but while I'm thankful for the outfit, it's currently not ideal for chasing after a young child with a mind of her own. I catch up to her only for my own shoe to catch in a divot on the stone floor.

"Whoa, there, slow down," a familiar voice says as strong hands catch me by the arms before I can hit the ground. His grip is steadying and lingers a beat too long.

"Thanks," I say, sucking in a long breath that I hold as I step away.

"I don't believe we've been properly introduced." His voice is smooth like honey and it's accompanied by a devastating smile that never wavers. "Trigger Hale. Most people just call me Trigg."

I can't stand that close and smell him. He smells too good, and the last thing I need to do is catch feelings for Trigger Hale. His last name alone affects me more than it should, without the added complication of knowing my best friend has some type of feelings for him. She may not be ready to admit what's written all over her face, but I see it. I see everything.

"Laney." I tuck a flyaway behind my ear. "Laney Hart."

The shift is subtle, so slight I almost miss it, but I know I saw it. His eyes narrowed fractionally when my name left my lips. It could be coincidence, or it could be another instance of my self-sabotage, grasping at invisible threads that might connect back to the man I lost. But the predatory stillness that follows has my skin prickling with warning, and a chill runs down my spine when it hits me. This move was calculated. He said my name the other day at the coffee shop, but neither Asha nor I had supplied it. This isn't an introduction. It's a confirmation of something he already knew. The shift I caught was a puzzle piece clicking into place, and I was the missing piece he'd been waiting to find.

"Are you running from someone?" His tone is momentarily stripped of all that practiced charm.

I pull at the lapels of my blazer, straightening the fabric with deliberate precision as my mind races. I was indeed running but not being chased. He had to have heard me call out for Katie, considering he caught me mere seconds after I stumbled. His choice of words makes my pulse stutter. *Running from someone.* Not *running to* someone, not *chasing* someone. *From.* The distinction claws at me. Each innocent interaction suddenly feels loaded with hidden meaning, each coincidence too convenient to be random.

He either senses my unease or I've truly let my suspicions runaway with my better judgment because his lips quirk into a smile. "I was only joking." The honeyed warmth returns to his voice. "Though, I am curious why you were running."

Katie's small silhouette catches my eye seconds too late. Her finger is already poking him in the arm. "She was trying to keep up with me, mister. Now, if you don't mind, I have a bet to win."

Trigg smiles the first full, genuine smile I've seen from him, and the anxiousness I feel whenever he's been around returns. His smile: it's not just his. It's London's.

"Is that so? Well, I'd hate to keep you from winning. You think I can tag along?"

"Why not? I could use a witness." She shrugs before skipping back to the stall that White Flame was in earlier.

"I apologize for my behavior the other day. I didn't realize you were a Fairfield client."

"Are you saying you treat people with deep pockets differently from everyday people?"

"No… I just meant I thought you were someone else."

"Ah, I see. I hate to break it to you, but you just blew your cover, because the latter is true. I'm not a client at Fairfield, though I am curious who exactly you believed me to be?"

His brow pinches, and Katie steals his words right before he's about to speak. "I win, Laney. Someone bought White Flame."

My eyes zero in on the winning bid card, where the bidder's name is listed in black bold letters. Cintel Estates.

"That's not fair. You stacked the deck."

Beside me, Trigg chuckles. "That's golden. You just got hustled by a seven-year-old."

"Eight," she corrects, making my loss a tad more tolerable. I like her moxie. She may have just pulled a quick one on me, but her loyalty lies with me. "I have one more horse I want to check on; he's on the other end. Can I go see if Brownie Points sold?"

"Sure, just don't leave this area. Stay where I can see you," I say as she's already skipping around us.

We both watch her bolt down the center of the stables before Trigg finally breaks the silence. "So, if you're not a client, what are you doing at Fairfield?"

"Asha is one of my closest friends. I just graduated this past semester with my bachelor's in equestrian science and needed to get working hours for my Eagala and PATH International certifications..." I lift one shoulder. "Since we're friends and she was spending the summer at home anyway, I'm earning them at Fairfield."

"Why both?" He leans against White Flame's stall.

"Initially, I thought I would just pursue my certification with PATH International. I connect the most with horses when I'm riding them, and my dream is to share those connections with others through therapeutic riding, but then I remembered the day that changed my life, and on that day, I didn't ride the horse. I simply watched him stand in an empty field, stoic and strong in the middle of a storm…" I nervously fidget with my hands.

I love helping people find the inner peace I've discovered from working with horses. Listening to their stories and watching them conquer their demons and come out lighter at the end of it is inspiring. While I feel like what I teach has helped me heal, I'm still working on the sharing part. I still haven't managed to get to a place where sharing my experience aloud feels safe. That may never happen, but part of therapy is also realizing that it is okay. Not all stories that we are given are meant to be shared. Sometimes, they are just meant to provide us with the tools to help others, and mine has done that.

"I don't know, that day, staring at the horse, changed me, and then I realized I could return the favor. I could help them too. My work here this summer is twofold. I'm earning my hours, but Asha hopes to show her father, through my work, that mindfully exploring other avenues outside of retirement for racehorses past their prime isn't just good for the horse but also business." I stop my fidgeting and meet his watchful gaze. "When I talk to people like you, I feel silly. I feel like a dreamer or something. In your world, horses are a sport, a stream of revenue, not therapy."

"My world?" His dark, bold eyebrows rise. "You can't judge my world based on Asha's. The Fairfields have their way, but that doesn't mean it's the standard." He turns to White Flame. "So you're a horse whisperer, then? Maybe you could stop by the ranch and look at my friend's horse sometime."

"I don't know," I say, stepping up to White Flame's stall.

"Or I could bring him by Fairfield. Asha might not be too thrilled, but—"

"It's not that. I'm sure you have more qualified trainers on staff. Technically, I'm not a trainer. I assess horses and evaluate their temperaments…" In fairness, I work with them a little, but still not a trainer. "And you're right, working with the competition probably isn't in my best interest, given the hospitality the Fair-fields are affording me."

Yes, Asha asked me to get close, but I'm not sure she meant work-with-his-horses close.

My comment earns me a half smile, and I notice a small dimple as he drops his head and says, "Good to hear Asha recognizes me as the competition, but I think you'd be surprised how different we are. Your career endeavors seem better suited for a ranch like mine. Spending a few hours there might be good for you."

"How so?"

"Well, for starters, I don't have trainers on staff."

"You're bluffing."

He holds his hands up in defense. "I'm not. You're looking at one of the only two trainers on staff. My father taught me all I need to know, and now my brother and I work with the horses."

"Really?" The word escapes me an octave too high.

The training revelation is a surprise, but his casual mention of a brother is the real reason for the pitch in my response. Asha never mentioned that he had a brother.

"WOW, way to knock a man's ego down a few notches," he says, adjusting his cowboy hat.

"I didn't mean it like that," I stammer. "I don't know you well enough. I just assumed—"

"You assumed that because we are breeders, we function the same. Yet another reason you should visit. If you change your mind, let me know."

"Oh, come on, please say yes," Katie startles me, squeezing between us. "I want to see some more horses. We can leave now," she suggests with a big smile.

"I'd love to give you a tour, Katie," Trigg eggs her on.

"Ranch tours?" an impossible voice collides with reality. "The wedding is this weekend."

Time slows as my mind struggles to process. I'm too stunned to move, too scared to turn around and match a face I never thought I'd see again to the only one my heart ever wanted. This could all be a coincidence: the voice, the last name, the revelation of a brother. I haven't been sleeping well, and my mind is still adjusting to staying in a new place. My eyes are pinned on Trigg when he notices my frozen state. There's a slight crease in his forehead before he throws his arm around my shoulder, sensing my sudden discomfort.

"Well, the invitation said I could bring a plus-one. What do you say, Laney? Do you want to be my plus-one this weekend?"

My heart is beating so fast it feels like it's one second away from stopping, the thumping too hard, the pace too exhausting. At the new angle Trigg has pulled me into, I have no choice but to look in the direction of the voice I'd know anywhere. My eyes slowly trail up the dark jeans, his legs thicker, his waist still narrow, but his chest is different. Even through his black button-down Wrangler, I can tell it's more developed, more solid, but it's when I allow my eyes to reach his well-defined, dark, bearded chin that true recognition crashes into me. My fingers have trailed that jawline, my mouth has covered those lips, and those eyes…those damn eyes…I've dreamed a million lifetimes in them. My heart lurches painfully in my chest, and my knees weaken as the world around me goes silent, my senses compressed singularly in shock and disbelief at the sight before me. It's him.

"Dallas, what's wrong with you? You look like you've seen a damn ghost," Trigg mocks beside me.

Wait, what did he just call him? Dallas? That's not his name. That's not even his middle name. He stands rigid, his stillness mirroring my own as the electricity crackles between us with an intensity that threatens to steal my breath. This isn't the reunion I imagined a million times in my head. It's not even close. While I knew he didn't want to talk to me, I thought that desire was rooted in longing—an insurmountable pain—the same pain that lives inside of me over love lost. However, as color returns to his face, his expression transforms. What was once raw shock turns into something more menacing—hate.

"She can't be your plus-one," he finally speaks, his words firm.

"And why the hell not?" Trigg's arm loosens, and he steps back, his eyes darting between us. "Wait, have the two of you met before?"

London doesn't answer Trigg's question, but his silence answers mine. Trigg doesn't know who I am. I don't know how London is here and not behind bars, but I get the impression Trigg doesn't either. With that, I steel my spine and hold out my hand.

"No, we've never met. I'm Laney."

There's a tic in his jaw, as though he doesn't like my response, but before I get a chance to dissect what it might mean, Katie chooses that moment to pop out from my side. "And I'm Katie."

His eyes dart between us, lingering on mine before gravitating toward hers, then snapping back to mine with a flash of something unreadable before settling on her again. "Hi, Katie. I'm Dallas." He shakes her hand.

"I like your hat," she says.

"Yeah?" He drops down to one knee. "Let me guess, you like the braid with the turquoise bead in the middle." She nods, suddenly shy. He removes his hat and sets it on his knee before pulling the braid off. "I hope you'll accept this as my apology." He offers her the braid, and she happily takes it. "Trigg offered something he can't give." Then, standing, he gives me one last glance before pinning Trigg with a menacing glare. "She can't come to the wedding," he says before storming away.

"Dallas," Trigg calls out to him, but it's for not. He won't turn back.

Every footfall as his boots thud against the stone floor is an echo of the night I watched Sheriff Townsend drive him away. He didn't turn back then either, but that's not what's making this time harder than the first. No. This time, he's choosing to walk away. Last time, there was hope—hope that I could plead a case and bring him home. Now there's a wedding.

LONDON
CHAPTER 12

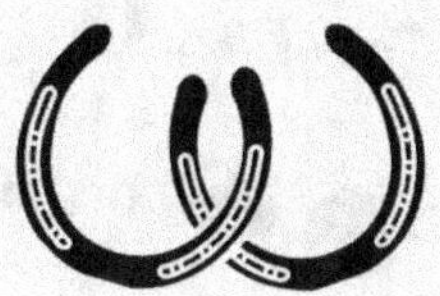

I slam the front door and head straight to the kitchen, where I know I'll find him. It's 3 p.m., so he's either making a fresh pot of dark Folgers or working on his bourbon. Bourbon is what he should be doing. Horses aren't his passion; it was his father's, but the problem with Baylor Hale is he's stubborn. Stubborn, I can deal with. On his good days, he's driven and focused, and on a bad day, it's his character flaw, too proud to be wrong. But today, his arrogant self-righteousness crossed the line. Today, he became a traitor.

I turn the corner and find him leaning against the counter, a cup of dark coffee in hand, staring out at the ranch. "Did you tell Trigg?"

His eyes stay pinned out the window. "You're going to have to be a little more specific," he says, bringing his mug to his lips.

I come around the massive island adorned with copper candelabras and stand before him. "You know what," I say, crossing my arms.

There are a limited number of people who know my story, how I ended up here and not behind bars. The only person in Bardstown with those damning secrets is him, but the way Trigg was pushing me today, his sidelong glances piercing like daggers, scrutinizing my every reaction with what felt a hell of a lot like awareness, I'm not sure that's still true. I may have been temporarily immobilized, my heart hammering hard against my ribcage as panic clawed up my throat, rocking me to my core with dread so heavy I could barely stand. Still, through my fear, I could sense the knowing behind his so-called innocent glare. The air between us crackled with unspoken accusations. I didn't need words to understand the truth: Trigg knew that the woman beside him meant something to me, and that knowledge hung between us like a death sentence.

His eyes, as black as the coffee he's sipping, lock on mine. "Now, why would I do that?"

"Because he's your son!" I shout, unable to contain my annoyance with his lackadaisical reaction when I'm clearly anything but calm. I know he heard the door slam as I walked through the front door.

"Boy, don't go taking that tone with me," he says, setting his coffee on the counter. "I'm not in the business of telling stories that aren't mine to tell."

He stands straight, unfazed by my charge, his hands resting against the kitchen counter, strong hands bearing the small scars and marks of a lifetime working on this ranch. I've only known Baylor Hale for a few short years, but I know those eyes. Deep-set dark eyes, black as coal, peer out from beneath a weathered brow, and I know he's telling no lies. I may not know every trial and tribulation or every secret, but I know those eyes. They're my father's eyes.

"You gonna tell me what's got you all out of sorts?"

I lick my lips before finding the nerve to say it out loud, because it still doesn't feel real. The entire drive home, I felt like I was moments away from waking up from this nightmare, but then I pulled down the old gravel road, and the sound of the rocks kicking up against the footboards of the truck told me this wasn't a bad dream. It's reality. "She's here."

"You sure are doin' a fine job of speakin' in riddles today, but seein' how you're all worked up, I'm gonna go out on a limb and guess that by 'she' you mean Laney Hart. That girl who sent you to me."

"Yes," I hiss, reluctantly confirming.

Out of all the cities in all the states, she had to end up in this one. Why does it feel like the gods are constantly shuffling the deck without rhyme or reason? Why take her away only to bring her back?

"Look, I don't know nothin' about that girl showing up here. I've spoken to your father once since that sheriff dropped you off on my doorstep, and I haven't told a soul about what you did." He reclaims his cup, only to dump the remaining coffee down the drain. His eyes capture mine, his gaze apathetic to the words he's about to say. "I don't know what happened between you and Trigg today or what he has to do with any of it. If I had to bet, whatever it is, is a combination of happenstance and a little bit of knowin'—"

"You just said—"

"I wasn't finished." He reaches for his hat on the center island. "Whatever Trigg does and doesn't know is of his own findin'. But here's the thing with secrets: just as sure as my seed will pop up and grow in rows, so will your secrets. What's buried deep and hidden beneath the soil will eventually surface." Then, placing his hat on his head, he starts toward the back door. "I'll be out in the rickhouse if you need any more savin', but before I go, I'll leave you with this: you can't outrun your lies forever, especially the ones you never should have told."

"I had good reason," I argue, as though he's forgotten the details.

"That's your opinion." His eyes meet mine one last time before he walks out the back door.

The weight of my choices settles on my chest like a boulder, each breath a struggle against the crushing regret that lingered ever since the night I changed our fates. At that moment, I felt like

I only had one option. My path was crystal clear, and I took it without hesitation, but everyone knows hindsight is a bitch.

I've spent countless nights staring at shadows on my ceiling, replaying that evening, frame by frame. The crowded parking lot of that damn ice cream shop. The eerie sense of dread that came from passing the transient on the road. Her smile…before everything fell apart. I've dissected each second and every decision. If I'd driven another route. If I'd told her I didn't want to stop because I selfishly wanted all of her time. If we'd never gone to the lake and instead gone straight home. But "if" is a useless word, and a thousand different scenarios can't wash away what happened, can't undo what was done. Baylor's roundabout advice that the truth will set me free doesn't change anything. Sure, I could give her the truth, but I'd rather have her hate me for the lie.

"What the hell is your problem?" Trigg says, walking up behind me as I exit the flower shop.

"I'm not sure I know what you mean," I say, forcing a levelness into my voice when all I really want to do is turn around and hit him with the third degree, but I can't. If I do that, then he'll truly have the upper hand. Right now, I'm speculating that he knows precisely who Laney Hart is, but all that could very well be a pretense I've manufactured in my head from seeing her.

"You were my ride to the auction, dickhead," he spouts off, clearly peeved.

I turn to face him. He made it back to the house this afternoon, seeing as he's clean-shaven and wearing a t-shirt and jeans instead of the button-down he wore earlier. "I forgot." I shrug. It's not a lie, but I'm also not sorry. "I was thinking about everything I still needed to check off before the wedding on Sunday." His eyes narrow, and he crosses his arms. He's still pissed but maybe a little less offended. "It looks like you made it home."

"I did, no thanks to you."

Shit, he got a ride home. The last thing I need is Laney Hart walking around Hale Ranch. Right now, I don't see her walking down hallways, sprawled on the lawn with her junk journal, soaking in the sun, or sitting beside our lake, casting a line. I don't need new memories to follow me here. I'm barely treading water with the ones I can't forget. One more Laney-shaped memory and I might just drown in what could have been.

"Did your new girlfriend give you a ride?"

He stares flatly, as though he's gauging my reaction to saying those words. They tasted like acid on their way out. In no reality does he get to give her that title, but I have to prod. I need answers —how they met, who she is to him, and why she's suddenly here. Those details won't magically appear unless I poke the bear a little.

"I can't tell if you're jealous or just an ass." I raise a brow, attempting to remain unfazed and act as though the answer to both isn't yes. "Laney had Katie with her, and they had to get back to Fairfield, so I caught a ride with one of Dad's friends..." He pauses to pull out his phone as it pings with a message. Fuck. The little girl...the one who bears a striking resemblance to a young Laney and looks very close to a damning age. My stomach twists as yet another layer of regret is added to the mountain that I'm buried beneath. A smirk ghosts across his face when he reads the message, and he grasps my shoulder. "But hey, if you're worried about un-inviting my guests to the wedding this week-end, don't be. I'm meeting up with her and Asha Fairfield tonight."

She's friends with Asha Fairfield? When the hell would their paths have crossed? But more than that, what game is he playing? While meeting up with Asha may not be a top priority, it would make sense. He got dealt a shitty hand when it comes to her, but what he hasn't figured out is that it doesn't mean he can't still win the game. However, that game part has me saying, "Well, in that case, I'll tag along." Laney isn't a game.

"Are you serious? You're willing to risk the wrath on the other end of that unfinished list to play wingman?"

I shrug. This wedding has grown into something none of us saw coming. The checklist matters very little to me. It's not my list of demands. I've only been working on it when I need a distraction. Its completion bears no consequence. The wedding will still go on as planned.

"I never agreed to play the role of wingman, but I figure I owe you a beer for leaving you high and dry earlier."

His dark eyes hold mine with a smidgen of skepticism before he says, "I'll never turn down a free beer."

"Let's go grab that beer, then," I say, matching his stride as we head toward the park.

Every weekend from May through October, a different patch of grass transforms into a marketplace of food trucks and local distilleries meant to funnel the tourists that flock to this region for the Bourbon Trail to the individual establishments, and tonight, it will also provide me cover. I have zero plans to talk to Laney Hart. I can't. But I do plan on blending into the shadows until I get my answers and see to it that not only does she leave, but that she leaves alone.

We've been sitting beside the food truck Trigg told the girls we'd meet at for thirty minutes now, and I'm starting to think we haven't seen them yet because Laney sees me. She was equally as stunned to see me today as I was her, and while I'm certain she probably has million things to say to me, finding a starting place is crippling. How do you say hi to the man who killed another for you on the same night you gave him your virginity and planned a forever that was taken? When I decided to join Trigg this evening, my purpose was not only clear—it was vital. But the longer we've sat here waiting, the more time doubt has been allowed to creep in and make me question if I have the inner strength to see this through.

Leaving wasn't easy—it broke something inside of me. Staying away has been its own quiet agony. But this separation, this difficult path... It's just how it has to be. Sometimes, the right decisions are the ones that hurt the most.

I take the last swig of beer from my bottle and slam it heavily on the table. "I think I'm going to hit the road. I still have a lot of shit to get done."

His eyes widen with a hint of surprise. "Really? They're going to be here any second. Laney texted that they had to park a few blocks away. They're coming."

I fight the urge to tell him to lose her number, only to quickly remember that he could only have it because she gave it to him. *She fucking gave it to him,* I internally seethe. There's no way she doesn't see the resemblance between us, and if that weren't enough, we share the same last name. Which brings me back to his game and her reason for being here. In the thirty minutes we sat here, Trigg filled me in on a few details she shared with him. I know she didn't go to Stanley like we had planned. Instead, she transferred to Louisville, where she met Asha. I know I'm missing details, but I don't buy that her being here now is all happenstance. Laney and I finding each other once was a mistake. It ended terribly, but finding each other twice…that's deliberate.

"Fine. One more beer," I say, getting up from the table. "You want another?"

"Nah, I'll wait for Laney. She might want a drink."

I give him a clipped smile. "Suit yourself," I say before adjusting my hat, tipping the front of my brim down, and cutting through the crowd toward the truck we passed on our way in.

Most of the vendors here are bourbon trucks—something I've been trying to convince Baylor to look into. He's been blending small-batch bourbon for years but has refused to extend beyond the old farm silo he converted into Hale's Cask. Trigg and I have slowly begun to bring him around to some of our ideas for the future of Hale Ranch, but the man embodies pure, unyielding stubbornness.

But I've found my patience, knowing his obstinance stems from devastating betrayal, which happens to be one of the very reasons I remained ignorant of my uncle's existence until Sheriff Townsend deposited me on his doorstep at eighteen. Baylor's trust isn't merely earned; it's hollowed out through years of proven loyalty. The entire first year I spent at Hale Ranch, his suspicious gaze tracked my every move, scrutinizing each step I took.

Even though Baylor verified my story through one solitary call to my father—the only contact in eighteen years—doubt shadowed his thoughts. Part of him remained convinced my sudden arrival was part of some scheme he hadn't yet pieced together. Then we had our breakthrough: knee-deep in manure and sweat, we discovered our bond forged in mutual contempt for one person —my mother.

"Asha," a visceral voice cuts through my thoughts, and my eyes innately fall on Laney.

She was beautiful yesterday. Time has been more than kind to her. It's been a conspirator. I shouldn't notice the magnetic pull when she's near. I shouldn't feel my breath catch at the sound of her voice. I shouldn't be tempted by something so forbidden, yet here I am, pained by a hunger I have no right to feel. Long gone is the girl rocking band t-shirts and jean shorts, uncaring what her outfit looked like as long as it was comfortable. She looks like she should be onstage tonight, wearing a tasseled, sleeveless, pink suede mini dress and white Tecovas. It's not until she lifts her arm and points in the direction Trigg is sitting that I snap out of my trance.

"Shit." I run my fingers through my short beard. I can't look at her that way—not anymore. I watch Asha lift onto her tippy toes to get eyes on Trigg, and Laney whispers something in her ear before heading back down the row. Now's my chance to get her alone. I spot the portable restrooms ahead and pick up my pace to get in position to make my move.

The second she comes out, I snatch her arm and pull her into the shadows around back between the trees.

"Lond—" she starts, but I throw my hand over her mouth.

"That's not my name here."

The fear in her eyes ebbs like it did freshman year when I caught her off guard after she had TPed my house, and for a second, I'm London again, and she's the girl next door that ran away with my heart when she proposed at age ten.

"What are you doing?" she hisses.

My body tenses instinctively, disliking the tone of her voice directed at me, but it's for the best. Our cruel proximity is unbearable enough—her warmth radiating through the thin fabric between us, her familiar scent flooding my senses, dragging me back through a thousand memories I've tried to bury. If she were all doe-eyed, if I saw a bit of longing in her eyes, this nearness would destroy me.

Her coldness reminds me of why I pulled her aside. It reminds me of my mission: to make her leave town. "Is she mine?"

My words hang between us heavier than Texas heat in the dead of summer.

"Who?" Her expression shifts to confusion.

"Katie." I refrain from tacking on, 'Who the hell else?'

Her eyes widen. "Why would you think that? We used protection, and I don't have any children."

I step back, putting the needed distance between us before ignoring her question. Answering that question hits too close to memories I don't mess with. "Good. Then you need to leave."

"Why?" she asks, genuinely baffled.

"Because I'm here," I state matter-of-factly, taking one last look before taking another step away and turning on my heel. I can't stay any longer. I have the one answer I came for.

"London," she calls out to me, the name burning as equally as the voice saying it.

"What if I had said, 'Yes, Katie is yours'?"

I shrug one shoulder. "You didn't. Goodbye, Laney Hart."

She can't stay, and now I don't have a reason to keep her.

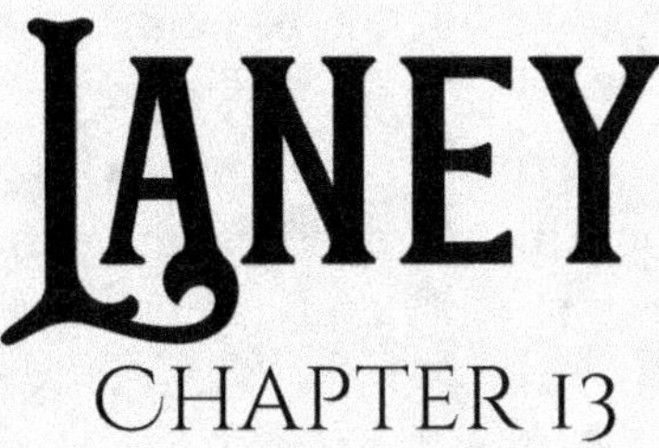

LANEY

CHAPTER 13

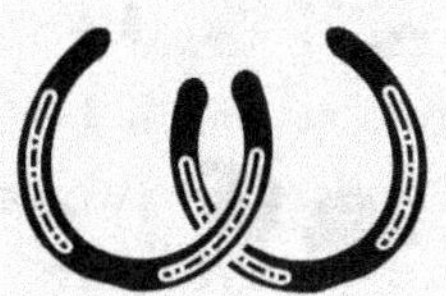

It's a little after 1 a.m., and I can't sleep. At this point, I'm not sure if I'll ever sleep again. My mind is a complete fucking mess, a tangled web of disbelief and deception. Nothing makes sense anymore. Running into the only man I ever loved, a free man, living under a different name, seemingly well, with a new life—one without me. There's no way I could have prepared for that.

The knob to my bedroom door rattles, and my eyes snap away from the white stables outside my window to the door. I know I locked my door. I always lock the door. But the question is, who would be trying to sneak into my room at this hour? I hug my legs tighter, resting my chin atop my knees, my eyes keenly zeroed in on the knob, waiting to see if it will sound again. It's possible there was never a sound at all. I've felt like I've been going through the motions all afternoon with one foot in reality and the other in the clouds, because there's no way any of this is real.

The antique bronze lever dips slightly once more before it's followed by a light knock. "Laney, are you awake?"

That voice—the one that's talked me through some of my darkest hours—pierces through the door. My feet race across the floor, and I fling open the door, and there she is: my best friend.

"Syd," I sigh in relief before crashing into her arms, our embrace fierce and desperate, like a lifeline grounding me to the here and now, her presence reassuring me that everything will be okay.

"Lanes, I got your texts and voice messages after I finished my final and came straight here," she says, hugging me back before releasing me and placing her hand against my forehead. "What's going on? Did you fall? Are you sick?" Her eyes do a quick scan of my body. "You don't look sick."

I pull her into my room and close the door. "I'm not sick and I didn't hit my head." I gesture toward the table beside my bed. "I've already taken my temperature. If I fell, I don't remember..." I turn my arm over and show her the two bruises I've already given myself. "And I may have pinched myself more than once to ensure this isn't a dream." I see the sadness in her eyes, like I've truly lost my damned mind, and I anxiously shake my hands, trying to think of a quick way to prove what I saw. "Wait, I can show you." I rush over to my bed, where I tossed my phone earlier, and quickly pull up a picture of Trigger Hale. I stalked him the minute I found out his name. I scoured his profiles for hours. I never came across a photo of him with London, but the resemblance between them should be enough to convince her I'm not going mad.

She takes the phone from my hands and sits on the bed, her eyes thoroughly scanning the picture before I see her thumb swipe to the next. "Babe, this isn't London."

"No shit. I know that, but they're related. His name is Trigger Hale. I met him a few days ago, and before I ever found out his name, I thought he bore an uncanny resemblance to London, but for the look you gave me seconds ago, I shoved it out of my mind. I thought I was making something out of nothing, and then I got a name—"

"Okay." She sets the phone down and rubs her temples. "In your messages, you said you saw London."

"I'm getting there. I ran into Trigg again today at the horse auction with Asha and her family. I was babysitting one of their client's daughters when Trigg found us and invited me to a wedding with him, and before I could answer, London walked up behind us and uninvited me."

"What did you say?"

"Nothing at first. I was too stunned to speak. Same as you, I thought I was losing my mind, but I promise you, Syd, I'm not. He was there. He's here in Bardstown, living on Hale Ranch."

She stands and starts pacing the length of the bed. "Well, did you ask him how that's possible? How he's here and not wasting away behind bars, the way we all thought he was?"

"Did you listen to any of the messages? The name, the wedding, any of it?"

The first message I left was *London's here, but he's not London anymore. He goes by the name Dallas, and he's getting married.*

She presses her palm to her forehead. "Shit. Yes, I listened to them. I'm sorry. I thought you were having a nervous breakdown, and none of this was real, and now that I'm hearing the facts, I'm…" She drops her hands to her side. "I don't know what I am." She closes the distance between us and hugs me again. "How are you? What are you feeling?"

"That's a good fucking question—one I've been trying to answer for myself all day," I say before taking a seat on my bed. "I thought I'd be sad. It would make sense to feel sadness, considering that's the state I've been living in since everything happened, but I'm not sad anymore. More than anything, I'm mad. I wasted all this time crying over a man that didn't exist, because the one that left me, the one that took a life for me, sure as hell wouldn't be living on a ranch, marrying another woman."

"Good."

"Good?" I question, eyes wide.

"Yes, good. If London has been out here, living his best life all this time, and he's marrying someone else, that man doesn't deserve one of your tears. And that anger you feel…that's exactly what you need to harness your strength. Not all anger is bad. Sometimes, it's the exact power you need to break through the barriers that have been holding you back." She stands and swivels between two doors. "Which one is the closet?"

"The one on the right." She throws open the door, and I can hear the sound of hangers sliding on the racks. It's close to 2 a.m. now. "What are you doing?" I call out. "If you're looking for pajamas, they're in the dresser out here."

She pops her head around the corner. "Oh, I'm not looking for something to sleep in. I'm looking for your wedding dress."

"Wedding dress?" I question before my brain catches up. "No, Syd. I am not going to that wedding. I told you he uninvited me—not to mention he told me to leave town." That last part still stings.

"You said Trigg invited you. I'm sure if you text him, the invitation still stands, regardless of London's dismissal, and if I'm wrong and this Trigg character doesn't have a thing for you…we'll crash it." She holds a dress up in my direction, looking me up and down to see if it's the one. "But make no mistake, you're going, and you're going to look hot as fuck."

Times like this restore my faith. Her friendship is a blessing—unwavering, never judgmental, always exactly what I need. Whether it's tough love, a shoulder to cry on, or someone to carry the shovel, Syd's always there.

"What we need isn't in this closet," she says, her face set with conviction. "We need a damn yellow dress."

For the first time since seeing London, I feel my lips turn upward as a saying from *The Last Jedi* comes to mind. "Let the past die. Kill it, if you have to." There's enough death in my past. I'd rather wear yellow.

～

"Are you sure this is a good idea?" I ask, twisting my

fingers in my lap as the car turns onto the main road toward Hale Ranch.

"Don't tell me you're getting cold feet now. If I need to list all the reasons you should go in there and raise hell, I will."

It's been a week since I last saw London, and in that time, I haven't left Fairfield. The last time I saw London, he told me to leave, and I didn't want to risk running into him again. I want the element of surprise on my side when I show up at the wedding. Trigg texted me a few times throughout the week, but I left him on read until today, when I sent him a text.

> Laney: Are you still looking for a plus-one for the wedding?

His text back left my jaw on the floor, adding another layer to this already twisted story.

> Trigg: I'm glad my brother didn't scare you away. I'd love to have you on my arm today.

Brother! He mentioned a brother the other day, but I assumed it was someone else. London and I may have only been an actual couple for a few short years, but we were close friends before we ever dated. We shared everything, especially the woes of growing up in single-parent households and the weight of being the only child. Sure, he hid his mother from me for two summers, but he explained why. I know he mentioned his mother moved on and had kids with her new rich husband, but that marriage and those children would be younger than London, and Trigg is older. Plus, London used to talk about how he wished he had cousins, another house to visit on the holidays, something besides just him and his dad. One text sent me strolling down memory lane, and it's those good memories that erase the anger I was feeling, but it has also left me with so many questions. The questions are what got me into the dress. I deserve some answers, and if London won't give them to me, I think Trigg will. Maybe those answers will provide me with closure. I've never been able to let everything go, and I think that's because I didn't have a good reason to. Perhaps that's why we've been brought to this moment: for a reason to let it go. London marrying another woman sure feels like a start.

"You're right. I'm good. How about you? Has your teacher posted your test scores yet?"

"No," she sighs with an eye roll. "At this point, I'm just hoping things don't escalate. I'm sure I passed, but she wasn't happy about needing to make concessions for me to take the final hybrid for a 'death in the family.'" She uses air quotes to emphasize her lie.

When she found out London was a free man, there was no way she was going back to Louisville until she saw him for herself. So, she had Fisher call into the school, pretending to be her father, who is a major donor. I've been looking over my shoulder at every corner, waiting for him to arrive. I know it's only a matter of days before he shows up demanding answers too. My heart isn't the only one that was broken in London's absence.

"I still can't believe you haven't let things slip with Asha."

"I told you, he doesn't go by London here. People here know him as Dallas. You know why I don't talk about London, and finding out he has an entirely different identity here didn't change that, but I did ask her what she knows about him. Asha never mentioned he was Trigg's brother. She's heard of him, but her understanding is he was the hot new farmhand, not relation."

She taps her French-tipped nail on the back of her phone. "You know I've been thinking about that. Trigg could have been using that term loosely, not literally. They could be second or third cousins, and he considers him more of a brother than a cousin."

I blow out an anxious breath and lay my head against the seat rest. "Maybe. Your guess is as good as mine."

Her hand squeezes my thigh. "Look, we're here," she says as a sign made of hammered iron with the words "HALE RANCH" suspended from a sturdy wooden frame comes into view before the driver turns down the long, winding gravel road. Asha was bummed she couldn't crash with Sydney today. Her father had a vital investor brunch an hour outside of Bardstown this afternoon, and he insisted Asha attend with him since she is expected to take on a leading role at Fairfield.

The gravel road stretches into the distance, the limestone crunching beneath the tires as traditional pristine white fences pass by the windows on either side. It's nothing like Fairfield. Fairfield commands awe with its grandeur from the moment your eyes glimpse the place. Every carefully manicured detail announces its pedigree—a stark contrast to Hale Ranch. Behind the fence, a few horses are grazing peacefully in expansive paddocks. In the distance, I can see a few barns, their metal roofs reflecting the sunlight. And nestled among a few shade trees ahead is the main house. It's not pretentious, boasting wings for entertaining potential investors. The house isn't boastful like Asha's but, in its simplicity, is everything.

The white clapboard siding contrasts beautifully against the charcoal gabled roof. The silhouette with the backdrop of the landscape is utterly breathtaking, but it's the turret and generous wrap-around porch that add a touch of whimsicality to the property, truly making it something plucked right out of a dream. It's charming. I never would have guessed Hale Ranch was one of Fairfields biggest competitors had Asha not shared that with me. Hale Ranch feels like a step back in time, and I'm beginning to understand why Trigg suggested I'd probably be more comfortable here. I would be—because this is my dream.

"Look over there. That must be where the wedding is going to be held."

I look out the opposite window, and a lake comes into view. White wooden chairs stand in perfect rows along the grassy bank, creating an aisle that leads directly to a dock. At the end, a gazebo perches over the water, draped in baby's breath and elegant white snapdragons.

My heart doesn't just skip—it falters then plummets. The lake was ours. Not this exact one, but back home in Willow Creek, we shared countless days fishing, swimming, and hanging out on the banks of Lake Texoma. So many firsts were spent together on those banks. Seeing him choose this venue for his big day is like a knife to the heart. It's like he's taken our memories and deliberately rewritten them. It's that intention that has my anger returning. How could he be so cruel?

The car comes to a stop, and Syd grabs my hand. "You ready to do this?"

"Yeah, I am," I confirm. I'm tired of hurting, but more than that, I'm tired of living in the past and grieving over a man who clearly no longer thinks about me.

"Good, because there's a fine-looking cowboy headed toward the car."

"That's Trigg."

"Really?" she asks, her tone dispirited. "Damn, he's better than the pictures. Too bad he's a Hale."

I laugh. "Don't worry. After today, we can go into town anytime you please, and you can lasso yourself a cowboy that's not Hale blood."

"I'm holding you to that." She opens the door on her side. "You owe me a tour on the Bourbon Trail."

"I know." I roll my eyes with a smile right before Trigg pulls open the door on my side. He extends his hand. "How'd you know I'd be in this car?"

"I'm familiar with Fairfield's town car." I narrow my eyes, his comment easily being read one of two ways. He sees the direction of my thoughts and quickly adds, "Small town. Not because I've frequented their backseats."

"Right," I say skeptically as I step out of the car. Asha is adamant there never was, nor will there ever be, anything between them, but I can't shake the feeling that he's using me, just like Asha. I don't believe Asha would flat-out lie to me, but I also wouldn't put it past her to leave out details. After all, we all have pasts, indiscretions, and skeletons we wish to keep hidden. It's why I don't press. I have secrets too.

"You look incredible," Trigg says, drinking me in from head to toe with one long glance.

I didn't wear white, but I did wear eat-your-heart-out yellow, fashioned in the same style I wore to prom the night we lost our virginity. London couldn't keep his eyes or hands off me that night, and while I may not have his heart anymore, I know he still looks. His eyes did a long, slow perusal the day we saw each other at the stables and again the night he told me to leave town, and I'm counting on them to do the same thing today when I show up on his brother's arm.

"Ahem," Sydney clears her throat, announcing her presence.

"Trigg, this is one of my oldest and dearest friends, Sydney Downs. I hope it's not an issue I brought her. We can stand under a tree...far away, and we won't touch any of the food—"

"Stop. Dallas is a prickly fucker, no doubt, but there is plenty of food and drink." He extends his hand to Sydney. "You said your last name was Downs. Any relation to Rupert Downs?"

"Yes, Rupert Downs is my father."

"Really?" he says, a tad surprised but not fully. "Small world."

"How small?" she questions with a raised eyebrow.

"Trigg," a cheery female voice interrupts before he can respond. "Is this your new girl?" a petite redhead wearing a short red dress says, strolling up beside Trigg and wrapping her hands around his bicep.

"Madison," he greets. "This is Laney Hart and her friend Sydney Downs."

Her fire-engine-red lips part into a big smile. "So, it is you. You're the horse whisperer I've been hearing so much about."

Trigg coughs into his hand. "I wouldn't say that. I literally mentioned you once at dinner earlier in the week."

Dinner? They don't look related, but maybe she's family.

"Oh, stop." She swats his chest before stepping beside me and wrapping her arm through mine as though we've been best friends forever. Sydney's eyebrows rise in surprise when my eyes catch hers. Most Southerners are welcoming. You can meet someone for the first time and feel like you're part of the family within seconds, but given the venue, I can't help but be hesitant about warming up to anyone here. For all I know, she's a sister I didn't know existed. She slowly starts walking us toward an elaborate wedding tent. "I know we only just met, and you don't know me, but I was wondering if you wouldn't mind looking at my horse while you're here."

"I'm not sure what Trigg told you about me, but I'm not a trainer."

"I know, but he did mention you have an eye for identifying a horse's temperament and retirement needs, and that's what I'm looking for. You see, I've been riding my horse, Gypsy, for years, but he's not keeping pace the way he used to, and it's causing me to dismount in the middle of my performance."

"Dismount? Performance… Wait, are you a competitive vaulter?"

She's a tiny little thing. Her hair and outfit tonight even foot the bill for a vaulter. This must be the friend Trigg mentioned before. I assumed his friend would be a man, though I'm unsure why.

"I am. Are you familiar with the sport?" she asks hopefully.

"Not really. I caught a performance two years ago and thought it was amazing. That takes a lot of skill to get on the back of a horse and do a full gymnastics routine."

She can't be more than five feet, two inches tall, lean, and toned, but now that I know her job, her outgoing personality makes much more sense. Madison is an entertainer. With her flaming-red hair, dress, and painted lips, she looks like a figure skater ready to take the ice. I wonder if she's here today to perform.

"Is your horse here today?"

"Oh no, but he will be in two days. He's currently being driven back from a show we did in California. So, what do you say? Will you take a look?"

"I'm sorry. I wish I could help, but I don't live here. I don't have somewhere for you to drop him off, where I can take a look at him."

"I can bring him here to Hale Ranch."

"I don't think that's a good idea."

"And why not? I know Trigg wouldn't mind having you around more often."

"She's not wrong," Trigg tosses in from her left.

"It's not Trigg that I'm worried about."

Her hand tightens on my arm. "Then who?" she asks with concern.

"I don't think Dallas wants me around."

"If Dallas is your only reason for not working with Gypsy, then consider this settled. Gypsy will be here Tuesday, and you come out on Wednesday, and I'll show you my routine. Don't worry about Dallas. Leave him to me," she says before untangling her arm from mine. "I'll catch up later," she adds before making her way to the main house.

"Who is this Dallas character I keep hearing so much about?" Sydney presses as though she's completely oblivious. I get it. She's eager to see him with her own two eyes. "And who names their kid Dallas anyway?"

I roll my lips to stifle the smirk her subtle jab causes. She's laying it on thick to get the answers she wants.

"Dallas is just a nickname. It came pretty naturally since he's from there." He shrugs like it's no big deal. Willow Creek is not Dallas, but I digress.

"And you are his…" Sydney gestures for him to continue.

"Brother..." he answers, the word lingering in the air as he extends his hand toward the tent entrance for us to proceed.

"Hmm," Sydney answers, walking inside without another question.

"When does the ceremony start?" I ask, curious how stiff of a drink I need to order to survive the vows.

He checks his watch. "We have forty-five minutes, give or take. What can I get you ladies to drink?"

"Two ranch waters, please," I say.

"Make them doubles," Sydney tacks on.

Trigg flashes her one of his charming smiles that I know even Sydney can't ignore. "Coming right up."

Once Trigg is out of earshot, she leans in. "Okay, when he comes back with our drinks, we make up a reason to go to the main house alone so I can lay into that asshole before he walks down the aisle."

"We're doing no such thing. Sitting with the guests, where he has no choice but to see two ghosts from his past while waiting for his bride to walk down the aisle, will be enough. I have no interest in convincing him to choose me."

I can't make my heart stop loving him. We leave parts of ourselves with the people we love long after we decide to walk away. I know pieces of me will always belong to him, but I've also sat with my woes long enough to find my worth. I know what I deserve, and that woman deserves a man who will love her just as fiercely, without waver.

"Then let's ensure we get the best fucking seat out there."

"I can't fucking believe it. I didn't think you were lying, but I also needed to see it with my own eyes. That is definitely him," Sydney whispers as London guides a horse down the aisle, carrying a beaming bride to the groom waiting at the altar. "But he's not the one getting married."

I hate what that little detail does to my pathetic heart. Hope isn't always a good thing. Sometimes it's toxic, especially when it's directed at something that's not good for us. Right now, hope is preventing me from moving on. It's tethering me to a past I need to forget, and worst of all, I now have to sit here and stare at him for the next thirty minutes and try to feel nothing.

Sydney pulls my hand into her lap as we watch the bride's father help her off the horse. "Besides the asshat holding the horse up there, are you okay? I mean, being at a wedding and the whole father-of-the-bride thing?"

From a young age, I have always had this persistent curiosity about the missing piece of my story. I dreamed about finding my father, having a name to fill in the blank spaces, and finding a connection in the mirror with the features on my face. At every age, my reason for finding him evolved, and the year I stopped looking for him was the year I lost London. Visions of my father at my side, walking beside me to give me away to the only man I ever loved consumed me, but when we fell apart, so did my desire to find another man who might break my heart.

Reality, with its complicated humans and messy emotions, would likely shatter the carefully constructed father I built in my imagination. His kind eyes, welcoming arms, and overwhelming joy at discovering my existence lives perfect and untarnished in my mind. The phantom father I molded in my mind possessed the qualities I needed throughout my life. The real man, whoever and wherever he is, carries his own wounds, flaws, and limitations, and I have enough of my own without the weight of his.

"I'm good." I squeeze her hand.

The second he has the horse positioned beside the dock that leads out to the gazebo, he turns around, and the second he does, his eyes instantly connect with mine. He stands perfectly still as time seems to stop. London may not have expected me to show up today after he told me to leave, but the shock that existed a few days ago when we set eyes on each other for the first time in years is gone. In its place is a dangerous, familiar current.

"He's looking at you," Sydney mumbles through clenched teeth.

"I'm aware," I answer as I watch him stand transfixed, as though the world around us has crumbled away.

I wore this dress specifically to get his attention, to make him remember a night I'll never forget, but in my haste to get revenge, I didn't consider how his reactions would feed mine. And maybe that's because I didn't expect him to look at me the way he's looking at me now—like he remembers the taste of my skin, the break in his voice as he whispered sweet nothings while moving inside of me, and the completeness that settled over us as we held each other.

A flex in his hand has my rational side slowly returning. "Distract me." I nudge Sydney.

"Find out whose wedding we're at."

There's a thought. I was so convinced we were attending London's wedding that I hadn't considered anyone else. I lean to my left, and Trigg meets me halfway and drops his arm over the back of my chair. The move sparks yet another subtle reaction from London as he rolls his lips and looks away.

"Whose wedding is this?"

"My father's best friend's daughter."

"Why is Dallas part of the wedding and not you?"

"The bride wanted to ride a horse down the aisle, and Dallas's horse is the only Thoroughbred on the property that's been gentled for trail riding…and Titan is majestic."

The horse is indeed regal, but once again, I find my mind wandering back to the man at its side. If Titan is a Thoroughbred retired to trail riding, and London is his owner, then does that mean he's the one who trained him? Is working with horses his therapy the way it is mine, and if so, is his madness rooted in the same vein as mine?

Stop it, I internally scold myself before subtly elbowing Sydney again. "Remind me why I need to stay mad."

"Because he lied. Because he didn't trust you with whatever truth brought him here. Because he cut us all out of his life like we meant nothing. And if that's not enough, because while he may not be the one exchanging vows today, I don't think he's single. Check out your new bestie."

That will do it. I bring my hands together in my lap and squeeze until my knuckles blanch white. I look over at Madison and catch it. There's an unmistakable heat in her eyes as she watches London, it's a lover's heat. Though I'm not sure how much love can ever really be found when the person he's with doesn't even know his real name. My heart can't help but contradict my mind at every turn. It's desperate to write a new ending than the one I've hopelessly tried to rewrite, the one that doesn't end with him. We could be wrong; I was wrong about the wedding. The truth is neither of us knows who he is anymore.

Sydney discreetly snapping a photo earns my attention. "What are you doing?"

"Sending Fisher the proof that he picked the worst best friend of all time."

Her comment on the heels of me questioning London's ability to find a genuine relationship with someone who doesn't even know his name has me remember something else.

I turn slowly to the man on my left. "Do you know who I am?"

Madison isn't the only one who calls London by a different name. His so-called brother, the same person Asha asked me to dig up dirt on, does too. If they're truly brothers, then it's possible that Trigg is covering for him. But what if he's not?

Trigg's eyes skeptically drag over me, and he lowers his mask just enough for me to see that whatever words are about to cross his lips have been crafted. "No more than you know me." He knows. He may not know exactly, but he knows enough to understand that I mean something to London. The question I have now is, why would he invite me here? Recognition flickers across his face, and he leans in, his mouth a hairsbreadth away from my ear in what I now believe is a move meant to provoke—only, I'm not the target. "We'll talk."

My mind doesn't get a second to process his words before the crowd around us stands and erupts into cheers as the newlyweds are officially announced as husband and wife. I join in the celebration and follow Sydney in a daze as we all exit the ceremony to return to the tent.

A hand slides across my bare back, and I tense. "I need to congratulate the newlyweds. Promise you won't run off?"

"Oh, you don't want me to come with you?" I try to play it cool, like his comment seconds ago wasn't unsettling.

His hand lightly squeezes my hip. "I'd love nothing more than to have you on my arm. I only assumed you wouldn't want to, given my father is standing over there too." There's a hint of mischief in his eyes when he adds, "I didn't think you'd want to meet the parents on the first date."

"I didn't realize this was a date." I can't help but smile. Tricks or not, Trigger Hale is a charmer.

His mouth drops open mockingly. "I asked you to be my plus-one."

"Who actually considers a wedding a date? You didn't even pay for anything."

His free hand covers his heart. "Now, I'm wounded."

I swat his chest. "Stop. Go congratulate the happy couple. I won't leave."

"Good," he says as he starts to walk away. "But now I owe you a real date." He tosses me a wink before turning on his heel to meet the wedding party beside the lake.

"Shit," Syd stops and glares at her phone, her thumb hovering over the call button. "It's my Dad. I have to get this and make sure he didn't catch wind of Fisher's phone call to the school to get me off campus for finals."

"Yeah, I'll be fine," I assure her as she walks away from the crowd funneling into the tent. "Great," I mumble as I quickly scan the people around me. "Guess I'm having a drink," I say, following behind a couple walking into the tent and passing beneath an entrance where mason jars filled with baby's breath hang from shepherd's hooks.

Grievances aside, the wedding itself was romantic, and this tent is pretty magical for a pop-up structure. Billowing white fabric drapes from the peaked ceiling, secured with twinkling lights that seem to float overhead mimicking the sky at night. Through the tent's open sides, I can see the paddocks stretching toward a line of oak trees. But it's the reclaimed barn wood bar, adorned with trailing ivy, that catches my eye, and I make a beeline for a cocktail. There's only so much ambiance can do for my nerves right now.

"What can I get you?" the bartender asks as soon as I reach the counter.

"What is she drinking?" I point to a woman at the other end of the par with an orange drink that looks delicious.

"That is tonight's signature cocktail—an Aperol spritz."

"I'll have one of those, please," I say, setting my clutch on the bar top.

"Sure thing," he says as he starts making my drink.

"I tell you to leave town, and you show up to the wedding I disinvited you to." London steps up beside me, his proximity so close I feel the softness of his cashmere suit brush against my bare arm, instantly pebbling my skin. Fucker. I know he's aware of precisely what he's doing—delivering cutting remarks while standing so close he envelops all my senses.

"If you thought I'd listen, then I guess you never really knew me at all," I say as the bartender slides my drink across the bar, and I take a slow sip of my Aperol spritz, avoiding the penetrating glare that I know is plastered to the side of my face. He's trying to get a rise out of me, but two can play that game. "Did you bring a date?"

"No." His answer is immediate, sharp, like he's already three moves ahead in whatever game this is. "So, you and my brother, huh? Tell me, did you wear that dress for him tonight?"

I push my tongue into my cheek, letting the silence stretch between us like a taut wire. He wants a reaction. It's why he stood so close. I only wish I knew the root of his digs. Are they genuine disgust for our past, for what we once shared, or is he projecting, and deep down, he hates that he still yearns for me with every fiber of his being? Either way, I won't give him the satisfaction.

"Novel concept…" I finally lift my eyes to meet his, and the moment our gazes lock, I know I've made a mistake. The world tilts. My whole body hums with familiar electricity, my stomach flips like I'm falling, and my stupid, traitorous heart sputters against my ribs. But somehow, through the wreckage of my composure, I find my words again. "I wore it for me."

One minute ago, if he'd asked me the same question with even a hint of warmth, I might have given him the truth. I might have admitted that I chose this dress because it mimics the one I wore to prom with him the night he told me he loved me for the first time, the night we danced under a moonlit sky, the night he promised we'd be together forever. But after his delightful greeting, I refuse to dignify his response. I won't let him believe he still has any influence over me, that I still think about him every day, that I still dream about his hands, his mouth, and his whispered promises in the dark.

The lie sits between us like a loaded gun, waiting to see who flinches first, and then leaning in, close enough that I can smell the hint of mint on his breath, he says, "I don't know what you came here for tonight, but you're in the wrong town, wearing the wrong dress, for the wrong man."

His eyes lock with mine, and for one suspended moment, I see something flicker there—pain, maybe, or regret—before his mask slides back into place. The air thickens with unspoken words, and I can barely breathe. Then he straightens, steps back, and without another word, he walks away. I stare blankly at his vacated spot, my mind still racing to unravel the meaning of his words.

When I turn around, he's gone, and Sydney's headed straight for me. Now, his abrupt departure makes more sense. He has no problem doling out painful comments to me, but he's not ready to face her.

"There you are! I've been looking everywhere for you. So we're drinking—"

"No." I link my arm through hers. "We have to get out of here."

"Oh, come on." She stomps her foot. "I wanted to shoot daggers at London all night and then wait for the perfect moment to lay into him."

"You can come back and lay into him on your own time," I say, ushering her out of the tent and toward the stables. "I need to get out of here, but first, I need to tell Madison I can't work with her horse."

"How do you know she's in the stables?" Sydney questions as the gravel crunches beneath our feet as we walk across the road splitting the tent and the stables.

"Her bright-red hair is hard to miss. It caught my eye while Trigg asked me to wait for him."

She stops and pulls out her phone. "I'll call the driver. Shit. I don't have a signal." She holds the phone toward the sky. "I'll get the car while you tell Red to pound sand."

"That's fine. I'll meet you when I come out."

I don't need to keep running into London like this. I want to talk. He owes me as much but not like this—not forced. Plus, date or not, I saw the way Madison was looking at him during the wedding. I heard the certainty in her voice when she said she'd handle London earlier. I have nothing against her. She seems nice, or at least she hasn't given me a reason to dislike her aside from the fact that I think she might be hooking up with my ex, but that's enough reason for me not to come back. I don't need the drama.

I'm turning the corner into the barn when I see her; however, she's not alone. I swallow hard, my saliva doing little to stop the acid clawing its way up my throat from the wave of hurt that crashes into me as my eyes fall upon London's form leaning against the stall, her small frame tucked in the tiny space between as he tips her chin up and kisses her softly.

I consider turning on my heel and acting like I was never here, but instead, I boot up and clear my throat. I'm done running from this shit. Does it hurt? Hell, yes. But things can only hurt for as long as I give them the power to. I don't want to give him that power anymore. Their startled eyes find mine, and she quickly untucks herself from his side and wipes the smeared lipstick from her face.

"Sorry to interrupt," I say anxiously, running my hands down my dress. "I saw you come down here and assumed you were alone." London doesn't move from his guilty position. Instead, his eyes slowly roll over to me as though I've just thoroughly inconvenienced him. Asshole. "I just wanted to let you know I can't work with Gypsy this week after all. Mr. Fairfield has two horses coming back from Louisville this week, and since he doesn't like to keep things that don't make him money, my schedule is full. I'm sorry." I give her a tight smile, completely ignoring the penetrating gaze I can feel staring at me over her shoulder, before turning to leave.

"I'll give you ten grand," she rushes out before I can take more than two steps.

My eyebrows shoot up in surprise as I slowly spin around, catching London mid-reaction—his palm pressed against his mouth, no doubt suppressing the same thought running through my mind: *That's crazy.*

"Madison, I really wish—"

"And you can come after work," she stammers before rushing to my front. "Please, I really love my horse."

Damn it. One, she pulled the horse card. My job is helping horses, and I'd hate to see an innocent animal be pushed into retirement or worse because I couldn't get past my personal issues. And two, that's a lot of money. I have a mountain of student loans to repay, and at the end of the summer, I'll technically be home-less unless I go back to Willow Creek and the house I never want to step foot in again. That money could be the down payment I need for my own place.

"Please," she begs, pressing her palms together, her eyes pleading with mine. This girl really has no clue who I am. Her ask is genuine. She really wants me to take a look at her horse, and because she has that kind of money to throw at a nobody like me, I can't help but believe I'm her last hope, which means I'm Gypsy's last hope too.

"Fine," I clip out. "Tuesday, five o'clock."

She squeals and claps her hands before throwing her arms

around me. "Thank you, thank you, thank you." Her arms are wrapped around my neck, her hold giving me no other choice but to face London.

He tilts his head slightly, and I can see that he's conflicted. It dawns on me then that he didn't challenge Madison's pleas, yet he's made it perfectly clear he doesn't want me here. His restraint now feels calculated. Too bad I stopped caring why when I caught him kissing someone else.

I'm coming back for the horse, not the man.

LONDON
CHAPTER 14

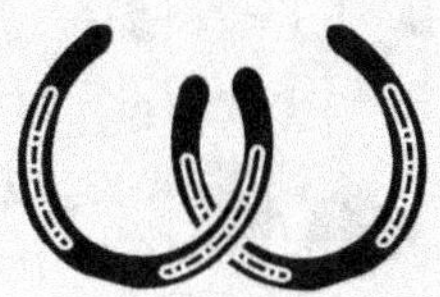

My alarm blares for the third time when I finally decide to put myself out of my misery and get some relief from the pounding inside my head. Yesterday was a complete mindfuck. Processing seeing Laney again after all these years still hadn't fully sunk in, and then she showed up at the wedding. Did I expect Laney to leave town with no questions asked after I demanded she do so? Not exactly. I assumed she would have shown up on my doorstep and demanded an explanation of how I'm here and why, but I sure as hell didn't expect her to show up at the wedding.

She sat in the second row, with Trigg's arm draped over her chair and Sydney Downs on her right. Two fucking ghosts from my past and my brother, whose eyes scrutinized my every move. Knowing he was looking for a reaction already had my blood boiling, but seeing Laney—standing feet away from her and trying not to look in her direction—was like standing behind the gates of hell. I was on fire and attempting to be unfazed by her presence. She wore a satin yellow dress—a replica of the one she wore to prom. Laney knew exactly what she was doing, putting that dress on. She wanted to get my attention. I guess it's a good thing she didn't know she would have it without the dress.

I throw my sheets off, my heavy steps matching the pulsing in my head as I pad over to the bathroom in search of the ibuprofen. I open the drawer, quickly twist off the cap, and toss four into my mouth before turning on the faucet and drinking straight from the source. I take messy swigs, drinking more than enough to wash the pills down in an attempt to quell my thirst. I feel like shit, and when I have had enough water, the reflection I see in the mirror tells me I look like shit too. I close my eyes, hating how I handled things, only to be reminded of why I drowned myself in a bottle of bourbon: Laney.

She's different now. Her hair is longer, still darker at the roots and platinum at the tips, and her soft curves have been replaced with lean muscle from riding. Still, it wasn't her looks or even the sinful yellow dress that had me twisted up inside. It was her smile and how someone else kept putting it on her face. I had no right to be jealous, but every time I saw it, I couldn't help but remember the days when it was reserved for me. I open my eyes, and the images of her disappear. Good. I need carbs and electrolytes.

I can smell Baylor's thick, black coffee as I walk down the hallway, and today, the sludge actually sounds palatable until I turn the corner and find Trigg in the kitchen too. He's the reason this is happening: inviting her here and entertaining conversations. I try to ignore it, even though I want to confront him and make him reveal his intentions. However, I hold back because doing so would also mean revealing my own. I take a coffee cup out of the cabinet and stop at the fridge to pour a generous amount of half-and-half into my mug. Then, I hurry over to the coffee pot so I can sit on the back deck and find some peace before I start work.

"Good, you're up," Baylor says, entering the kitchen mid-pour. "I need ya to come inspect the fields up by Bristol Creek with me today."

My brow furrows, and I pinch the bridge of my nose and repeat his words, ensuring I heard them correctly before saying, "We don't have fields by Bristol Creek."

We have trails by the creek but not fields. There's a thick acre, if not two, between an old pasture that Baylor turned into a barley field and that creek. The land that sits on the other side isn't ours. It's Fairfield land.

"I'll go with you, Dad," Trigg says as I take my first sip of the mud Baylor calls coffee.

"Naw, Dallas knows the land better, and you got a tour to give." Baylor gives us our working orders like he does every day, but today, I can tell by the sour look on Trigg's face that he doesn't like it.

"I grew up on this land. I know the land better than Dallas," he pipes up, his tone ruffled.

"You know good and well that ain't what I meant," Baylor dismisses the comment.

"Then explain it to me, because lately, it's starting to feel like the exiled guest is the prodigal son."

My eyes widen as his comment takes a direction I didn't see coming. Trigg and I aren't enemies, but Laney, and now this… I'm wondering if I haven't misread the relationship I thought we had.

"What in blue blazes has gotten into you, boy? You ain't been interested in farmin' a single day in your life. You handle the horses. He handles the land."

"Not that land," he says with bitterness that has me suddenly wanting to ride up to the damn creek.

Why the hell does the creek named after my father have him spiraling?

Baylor's eyes flick from him to me, and he sets his cup down hard, the contents spilling over the side onto the white granite countertop. "I don't know what's got the two of y'all fightin', but you better listen here. It ain't worth it. Nothin' is worth not havin' your blood." He swallows hard, regrets undoubtedly choking him up. "I reckon y'all know better than anyone that I know the God's hard truth 'bout how accurate that statement is."

Trigg's knuckles turn white as his hand tightens around his phone. "That's rich, considering he's never even told me his real name. Neither of you has ever explained why he's here."

"You never asked me my name!" I point out, my own annoyance piqued.

The week I arrived in Bardstown, he was away in Louisville. Baylor wasted no time introducing me as his brother the second Trigg walked in the front door. We stood there, stunned and looking at each other, realizing we had both grown up believing we were the sole offspring, only to discover we weren't. The hallway's grandfather clock ticked five full seconds before Trigg finally broke the suffocating silence with just three words: "Where you from?" When I answered, "Texas," his lips curved into a smirk, and he said, "Welcome to the family, Dallas." I know he hasn't forgotten that day. He gave me the damn name.

"It's London. My name is London Hale," I answer the first half of the question only to freeze on the second part. I've kept my secret because it doesn't just protect me. It protects her. But Baylor is right. You should be able to trust your blood. The three of us have found our way. Our relationships aren't perfect, and even though my gut tells me Trigg is up to something, that his interest in Laney isn't blind innocence, I don't think he'd intentionally cross me, but his hurt might. "I—" I start to give him the answer he seeks when the doorbell rings.

"That must be your tour now," Baylor says, his eyes locked on Trigg's with a bit of sorriness and tough love.

He sighs frustratedly, and his voice drips with enmity when he asks, "Do I at least get a name?"

"Fisher Downs," Baylor answers coolly, and I spit my coffee.

"I'll get it. I'll do horses today," I frantically rush across the room.

He might be a ghost from my past, but I never wanted to leave things unresolved, and if he's here to collect on words I left unspoken, I'll be damned if he hears them from anyone else.

"How is it you always weasel your way out of being a shitty excuse for a best friend?" Fisher says as he pours a second glass of bourbon from Baylor's small batch.

"I'm not trying to weasel my way out of anything. I don't

deserve your brotherhood, and I wouldn't hold it against you if you walked out of this silo and never spoke to me again. It's what I've earned, what I deserve." I twirl the amber hair of the dog in my glass before tossing it back.

"You've become really good at deciding what you think you deserve." He sets the bottle down. "But you don't get to be the judge and executioner." He takes a look around the refurbished silo that's been converted into a private tasting room for Baylor's bourbon. "So now what?"

"What do you mean?" I tap my glass on the counter.

"You're surely not returning to how things have been. You're going to tell her."

"No," I say curtly.

"London, she deserves to know. She may not have asked it yet, but she will. What are you planning to do, then? Lie? You're telling me you can really stand there and look her square in the eye and lie?"

"No," I grind out, reaching for the bottle of bourbon.

"Are you going to say something more than no?" This time, I don't say anything. I can't lie to him any more than I can lie to Laney. "You have to tell her. You can't just take her choice away."

"Choice?" I question with a wince, swallowing my freshly poured bourbon too soon.

"Yes, choice. That truth, the one that's kept you away from her…from me…from everyone…" His hurt eyes find mine. "It wouldn't have changed things for her. I know it."

Every day, the ghosts of my decisions feel more like a physical burden than a mental one. His proposition dangles the possibility of erasure. Yet, I've made peace with my past choices. The pain remains. It's a constant companion I've embraced, acknowledging what will forever be lost and what was gained. I'll continue to shoulder the burden, not for certainty, but for that singular, haunting "IF" that promises everything while guaranteeing noth-ing. Causing Laney any more pain is not an option.

"I can understand why you made the choice you did, but that

doesn't mean I agree. I want to know why you cut me out too? I would have been there for you in a heartbeat. Anything you needed, I would have made it happen, but you cut me out like I was nothing."

I sent everyone a letter with the help of Sheriff Townsend shortly after I left so that they would stop pestering the Willow Creek police department. My letters could have been written with more care. Out of all my choices, I wish I had handled those differently. They were supposed to be my last words to people I cared about, and they were shit. I know it's not a consolation, but I wasn't in a good place either, and words were hard to come by without sending me into a dark place that threatened to consume me.

"Not saying more than what I did is something I regret most, but it never had anything to do with you. Laney needed you. I didn't."

"I'd say you're a little wrong about that last part. It's been a few years since I last saw you, but it's going to take a little bit more than playing cowboys and screwing pretty girls that ride horses to convince me that you're out here living your best life. I'm not leaving."

"You work in Paris," I counter.

"I can work from anywhere. Besides, I was always supposed to end up in Louisville. I'm the one who convinced my father to send me to Paris to start participating in races there. He's wanted me to come here for years, and now I'm wondering if it's not because he knew you were here all along."

"I wouldn't know. We don't discuss what happened when I talk to my dad." I reach behind the bar and grab a tin of roasted nuts. "Let me ask you something. Growing up, your dad never hid the business from you, and Sydney and you always knew you'd take it over one day. Did you know about this place? Did you know my family's ranch was your sole breeder?"

His brows pull together as he runs his hands over his five o'clock shadow. "I didn't look at the books back then, and when we came to Louisville, we never visited Bardstown, but I had met your uncle. When my father introduced us, I was young, and they addressed each other by first name. After graduating and being pulled into everything, I noticed the breeder was listed as Baylor Hale, Hale Ranch. Considering our father's friendship, I assumed there was a relationship, but I had no idea he was your uncle." I toss a handful of nuts in my mouth before he steals the can, taking a heaping handful for himself. "What's the story there? How come you didn't know about this place?"

"It's a saga, and I need carbs," I say, getting up from the bar.

"Good thing I have nothing but time. You can tell me over lunch."

"Fine," I agree. I usually don't tell other people's stories, but technically, it's mine too.

"And then when we're finished, we can figure out how you're going to get your girl back." He squeezes my shoulder as we walk out, and I stop dead in my tracks.

"I'm not doing that. I can't—"

"You have to let her decide that. You can't decide for her."

"You don't get it. Sheriff Townsend…the Donovan's…coming here and starting over…that's only half of it. The other half—her half—I can't…"

"What do you mean *other half*?" He points to where we sat at the bar. "You're still keeping secrets?"

I drop my head, the weight of my secrets too heavy. "I'll tell you. I'll tell you so you can understand why I can't break her."

"You already did. The question is, are you man enough to fix it?"

That's a good fucking question. I want to be, but some things can't be fixed.

LANEY
CHAPTER 15

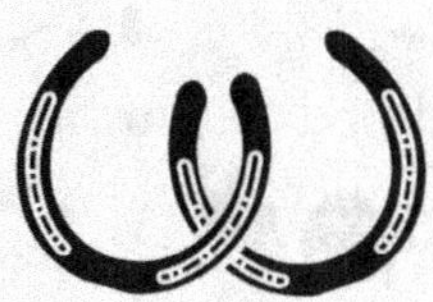

"Oh my god, I swear my father's goal this summer is to keep me from having any fun," Asha says, throwing herself into a cushioned patio chair as Sydney and I share a pitcher of sweet tea.

I've been working in the field all day with a filly named Pria. I had high hopes for Pria when I watched her race last season. She was every bit as fast as her male counterparts. Female horses aren't necessarily a rarity in races, but they're not the norm either. I really want to see her go somewhere she can train. Pria has so many good years left in her. She has a willingness to learn, but her temperament is holding her back at the moment. That's not to say she's a bad horse; rather, she's a product of the habits ingrained into her. She can change, but she needs to adjust to a new routine and unlearn habits that no longer benefit her. It's that last part that has Pria pulling at my heartstrings. Old habits die hard.

"We can't lie beside the pool all day," I say, pushing Sydney's chair with my foot.

"Listen, I can do marketing from anywhere," Sydney prattles, adjusting the straps on her swimsuit. "Today, it just happened to be poolside." Then, she looks around, pushing her sunglasses up farther on her nose. "And intentional."

"You're shameless," I tease. "You're working, alright. Working on getting laid."

"Hey, staying at Fairfield instead of a hotel has its advantages. Between owners, trainers, and grooms, there's a constant flow of sex on a stick walking around this place."

I turn to Asha, mouth agape. "Are you hearing this? You're procuring the goods, and she's not paying."

"Yeah, my pimping services aren't free." She rises from the chair she claimed seconds ago. "Looking will cost both of you three spoons, two pints of ice cream—cookie dough and confetti cake—and one king-sized bed for gossip. My dad texted…" She holds up her phone. "He wants me in his office."

"It's okay. You're not missing much. I'm leaving soon too. We'll catch up tonight," I say as she sorely walks inside.

Sydney pushes her glasses on top of her head. "Okay, but seriously, her dad is one of the hottest guys here."

"He has, like, twenty years on you…" She shrugs. "And he's seeing someone."

"Who isn't seeing someone? Guys like him always have a girl on their arm. It doesn't mean they plan on keeping them." She waves her hand as if it's no big deal.

"Sydney," I scold. "Since when did you become a home wrecker?"

"I haven't. I can look. I never said I'd touch. I'm just saying the brooding, the midnight-blue suits that fit immaculately, and how everyone who approaches him comes prepared or not at all is a turn-on. Call it a kink unlocked." She sits straight up in her chair. "Seriously, do you know I watched two staffers walk toward him only to turn around, realizing without words that whatever task or issue they thought they had was menial and not worthy of his time? It's not the money. We both know I don't need it. It's the man. But enough about my wandering eye. How do you feel about returning to the ranch and seeing London?"

"Well"—my phone pings as I pull it out—"I'm not going there to see London."

I cried myself to sleep the night of the wedding. At first, rage coursed through my veins—rage at him, at her, at the knowledge he'd been breathing the same small-town air as me. I tried convincing myself I was over it, over him choosing her, over the crippling guilt I've carried for the burden I believed he shouldered. Still, once the anger fizzled out, the grief rushed in, an all-consuming wave of realization that cut deeper than any knife: he's been here without me all this time.

That's the thing about grief. It's merciless. We don't get to choose if or when it strikes. It hits without warning just when you think you've found solid ground. I don't want to want someone who doesn't want me back. That's why answering Sydney's question is useless. I can say I'm fine and mean it with every fiber of my being, but the second his eyes connect with mine, it could all fall away. All I know for sure is I can't hide from it, but more than that, I don't want to.

"Who is that?" she asks as my thumb hovers over the screen.

"Noah," I answer dejectedly. "He wants to visit before he goes back to Willow Creek to help manage the businesses since his dad is heading into an election year."

"Let him come," she says with a glint in her eye. "Inviting Noah kills two birds with one stone. You'll make it brutally clear to him that hooking up a couple times over the years was not a betrothal while simultaneously igniting a familiar fire in London's veins. If London Hale has an Achilles' heel that will make him forget his carefully constructed control and whatever fake bullshit life he has here in Bardstown, it's that man. I swear the moment London sees you with him, that perfectly maintained façade will fracture. Just you wait and see."

"I thought we've been over this. I'm not trying to get London back. Secondly, London isn't Noah's favorite person. Noah finding out could be bad for London, and while I might be mad and hurt, I've already spent enough time feeling guilty for what happened. I don't care to repeat the night I watched him get hauled off in the back of a cop car."

"Have you ever Googled London—I mean, his case?"

"No," I say, reaching for the pitcher of sweet tea.

"Well, I did last night, and guess what..." She leans forward with her elbows on the table. "He doesn't have one."

I spit my sweet tea, and she tosses me her pool towel. "How is that possible? You were there. You saw what happened."

"I was there, Laney, but I didn't see what happened," she gently reminds. "But that night, when Sheriff Townsend asked what happened, you said Noah and London shared a look."

"Yeah." I nod in agreement. "But I've always known the look was an unspoken pact, where London aligned with his enemy to lie for me and take the fall for what I had done."

She scans the backyard before crossing her arms and leaning in closer. "I'm not saying you're wrong, but what if there's more to it? Think about it. Noah's family had connections, with his father being the mayor, and we both know Noah was more than happy to remove London's chess piece from the board when it came to winning you."

"Which only supports why inviting him here is a bad idea," I point out.

"Or maybe Noah needs to come here to force both of their hands, and we find out the real truth instead of whatever narrative they've forced us to accept."

"Or...hear me out..." I lay my hands flat on the table. "I could just ask London."

She throws herself against the back of her chair with an exaggerated sigh. "Boring."

"Maybe, but I don't want any more drama. I've lost enough sleep, shed enough tears, and wasted enough time. I'll just ask him." He may not like that I'm here, and he may not want to be friends, but I think he'd agree I at least deserve a conversation. A familiar truck breaks the tree-lined drive, kicking up dust on its way in. "My ride is here."

～

"MY HEART STARTED BEATING SUPER FAST, WATCHING YOU WALK down the hill to join us. Until I saw you, I was half convinced you might renege again," Madison says as I step up to the pine fence bordering the outdoor riding arena.

"I said I'd come," I say with a small smile before chucking my thumb over my shoulder and adding, "It doesn't hurt that you gave Trigg another reason to see me."

"So you like him, huh?" she says, shielding the sun from her eyes.

"He's nice," I say, climbing onto the top rail of the fence. "But I'm only here for the summer."

"Well, maybe he'll be a reason to stay," she says with a wink before calling to her lunger. "Abbey, come meet Laney."

As her teammate approaches, their relation is unmistakable—both barely clearing five feet, with hair like burnished copper and eyes so intensely blue they could pierce armor.

"Laney, this is my sister, Abbey. Abs, this is Laney—the woman who's managed to star in every single one of Trigg's conversations lately."

I tuck that little nugget away for later as it swims around my head, accompanied by the ominous comment Trigg left me with at the wedding when I asked if he knew who I was, and his response was, "No more than you know me." I high-tailed it out of there after I caught Madison and London in the barn, and today, when he picked me up, I hoped we would start where we left off, but he ended up having to take a work call.

"Laney," I extend my hand out. "It's nice to meet you."

"You're very pretty for a horse whisperer." She gives my hand a gentle squeeze, and her gaze lingers a little longer, slowly drinking me in.

"Oh my god, Abs. She's with Trigg. Back off—"

"Actually, I'm not with anyone, but let's talk about Gypsy," I say, wrenching the conversation back to its purpose. I didn't come here to dissect the Hale men or land a date. Though dating a woman has never seriously crossed my mind before this moment, perhaps it should have. Maybe only a woman can be trusted to keep my heart safe. "You mentioned something about his timing changing during your routine. Has anything changed, such as music, new moves, or partners?"

They look at each other and shake their heads. "No, nothing has changed. Abs and I have been partners from the beginning. Every year, we make changes to the routine, but this started three months ago, and the routine we are using is one we've been using for months with no issue, and then *bam*." Madison claps her hands, and Abbey flinches. "He just starts slowing his speed three-fourths into my performance. We're almost to the finish line, and he stops."

"Well, let's do a run-through of the performance, and I'll see if anything stands out."

"Let's do it," Madison says, eager to perform, but it's Abbey's look of detachment that catches my eye. It could be her poker face. All athletes must get in a zone before the game, but it's something to watch. While Abbey isn't the one atop the horse performing, her ability to guide the horse is crucial. If her mind wanders, Gypsy will sense it immediately. Horses possess remarkable perception in that way.

It's one of the reasons why I chose this path: the nonverbal connection, the innate sense of being heard without judgment, and the bond formed purely through emotional resonance. It's grounding in a way few other experiences are.

Abby starts the performance, establishing a consistent, flowing canter using her line and whip to communicate with Gypsy. He does about four circles before she pulls the line closer, and he follows the command effortlessly. Then Madison runs up along-side him before springing into action, gracefully mounting his back in one fluid motion. It's impressive.

I'm just watching Madison stand on his back when I smell him seconds before I feel him at my back. His scent is earthy and warm, like soil after summer rain in Texas.

"If you're here to tell me to leave again, save it. I'm here for the summer."

My heart quickens. I hate how his scent engulfs me completely and how each inhale betrays me, his familiar fragrance still unlocking something inside of me that feels like home despite everything destroyed. But what I hate the most is the invisible, relentless magnetism between us, some kind of cosmic joke that's determined to drag us back into each other's orbit, even though the same cruel universe already tore us to shreds.

"The other day at the wedding, what you saw between me and Madison—"

"Save it. Whatever it is, I don't care."

Not exactly true, but the last thing I want to discuss with him after six years is his intimacy with another woman.

"It's not what you're thinking," he says, resting his arms atop the fence beside where I'm sitting.

Out of all the things he could say to me, this is the one he chooses to start with. I shouldn't be surprised. I'm the one who keeps believing that night shredded him the way it did me.

"Oh, don't give me that bullshit. The whole she's-not-my-girl-friend shit may have worked in high school, but it doesn't now. We're adults. Your mouth was on hers. That means you're with her. Period."

"Fine," he grinds out, jaw clenched as he yanks his hat lower. We sit rigidly side by side while Madison performs, the silence between us electric and suffocating before he finally adds, "I wasn't trying to hurt you."

"Just stop talking. I don't care to hear more lies."

"I'm not lying," he defends adamantly.

"You knew I was there, which means you knew there was a chance I would see."

"And what about you showing up in that yellow dress?" he's quick to snap back, his tone sharp and terse, letting me know my dress of choice hit the mark as intended. "On the arm of my brother, nonetheless. You aren't exactly a picture of innocence," he says gruffly.

"Are you implying I made you kiss Madison?"

I catch his face turning toward me from the corner of my eye, and I find the strength to meet it. His dark eyes are hard, confirming he's mad I'm here, mad I wore that dress, mad I caught him kissing another woman, but as our eyes remain locked, I watch his anger fracture into something worse. Those hard eyes soften into something more dangerous than rage—recognition, remembrance, possibility. His silence hangs between us. A yes would be unexpected; it would be an admission unfitting of the new man he's determined to make me see, the one who no longer thinks about me. But he also doesn't give me a no—a no that could finally set me free.

"Aren't you going to ask me why I'm here? Why I'm not in prison?"

I turn back to the performance I'm here to watch and grant him the silence he gave me. Do I want his answers? Desperately. But saying so means admitting that I still think about him, that he still occupies the darkened corners of my mind I've fought so hard to reclaim. I want all his words, ones I rightfully deserve, but not here, not while I'm perched precariously on this wooden fence, watching his new girlfriend defy gravity on the back of a thundering horse, her body executing remarkable feats that would be mesmerizing if I could feel anything beyond the suffocating weight of his presence beside me.

I pull air through my nose and roll my lips together as I search for the right response, when every possible word feels like walking onto a minefield. It feels like a cruel competition to see who will surrender first, who still cares enough to shatter this brittle silence between us. But then the backs of his fingers skim across my thigh, and even through my riding pants, there's an instantaneous, electric hum that follows a white-hot buzz surging through my veins like wildfire. Just one touch, that's all it takes, and I'm drowning in him all over again, every carefully constructed defense crumbling to dust.

"Laney, I asked you a question." His voice wraps around my name like it has no right too.

Feeling the traitorous tears gathering behind my eyelids, I slam them shut. Damn it.

LONDON
CHAPTER 16

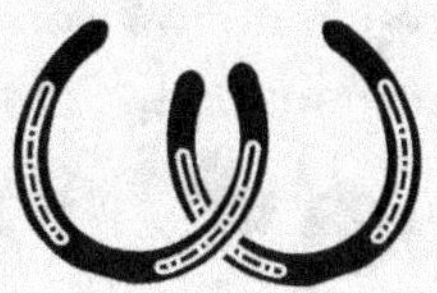

What am I doing? I shouldn't have touched her. Fuck, why did I touch her? When she is near, my mind is useless; every rational thought evaporates. I should have learned my lesson outside those bathrooms the other day, when grabbing her arm to stop her triggered that same devastating electrical current. One touch and all my carefully constructed walls crumble to dust.

She still takes my breath away. My heart thunders in my chest, outpacing Gypsy's stride in the arena. I despise being this hollow version of myself, the one who no longer belongs to her. It's yet another reason I can't stand her being here. Every second in her presence is exquisite torture, a reminder of everything I've lost and everything I can't reclaim. It's killing me to exist as anything other than hers.

Seeing her at the wedding was a special kind of hell where I could look but never touch, speak but never say what screamed inside me. Even now, with her sitting mere inches away in those goddamn riding pants that hug every curve and a navy t-shirt that clings to her like a second skin, my treacherous hand moves of its own volition. Her body still calls to mine like a siren song, magnetic, primal, as though she's still mine to touch, mine to hold, mine to worship all over again.

Her eyes bore into mine with the same penetrating gaze that always made me feel exposed. I can't help but wonder if she remembers everything with the same excruciating clarity that I do, every whispered promise, every shared secret, every moment our bodies spoke a language only we understood. It's beyond fucked up for me to want her to carry these memories, considering it wouldn't change anything, but inside, I'm screaming, *love me, choose me, love me back the way you used to.*

Instead, her voice cuts through my internal plea, cool and detached. "I'm more interested in how you're related to Trigg."

And just like that, I'm reminded why my heart can no longer beat for her, but neither can Trigg's.

"You can't date him," I snarl, wholly peeved with her response. It's been years since we've seen each other, since I was ripped out of her arms, and all she cares about is my brother.

"You can't tell me who I can date," she says plainly, as though my demand means nothing to her, further infuriating me.

"I can. He's my brother," I argue back intensely, attempting to force her to see it my way.

"So," she says, eyes forward, watching Madison and Abbey perform as though our conversation is an inconvenience.

Fine, if she wants to play it that way, so be it. I'll spell it out for her so she remembers everything I haven't forgotten. "So, every time you look at him, it's me you'll see, it's my taste you'll be searching for on his lips, and when he's in your bed, it's me that will be in your head."

She purses her lips, and when her gaze swings back to mine, I see challenge in her eyes. I don't know if it's rooted in the same jealous envy that mine is, or if she remembers just fine and hates the reminder, but her words don't miss. "Sounds like you're talking from experience. You never did answer me earlier… Tell me, London, when you were kissing your girlfriend last night after you saw me in that dress, was it my mouth or hers?"

I feel the muscles in my jaw flex, and I resist the urge to say *yours.* It doesn't change anything, so instead, I ask, "You're really not going to ask me why I'm here?"

She shrugs. "You have not answered one of my questions since I came here. Why would I ask another?"

"Smart ass," I mutter. She raises a brow and smirks, and I tell her anyway. I owe her some answers, even if they're partial truths. "Sheriff Townsend owed my father a favor, so he brought me here instead of taking me to prison. To stay here, I had to keep quiet. I had to be forgotten. No one could know who I was, where I was from, or why I was suddenly here. You don't just get to kill somebody and walk away." She's quiet, and I know I haven't said anything that's probably not obvious. Laney is well aware my name isn't Dallas, and given she knows precisely what happened back in Willow Creek, it's not hard to draw conclusions about why I'm not using that name now. "For the record, I never lied about not having siblings. I didn't know I had a brother until I showed up here. Hell, I didn't know I had an uncle for that matter."

"How exactly is he your brother? I thought Baylor is his father, and if Baylor is your uncle, wouldn't that make him your dad's brother?"

"Yep, sure does, hence why I didn't know he existed. My father and Baylor hadn't spoken in eighteen years until I showed up on his front doorstep. Remember that fantastic mother I tried to hide from you? Turns out she's even more stellar than I knew, because she didn't just royally screw me and my father over; she screwed his brother first."

"No," she says with a gasp.

I take my hat off and run my hand through my hair before putting it back on my head and hanging my arms over the fence. "She hooked up with Baylor before she ever married my father. My mother lost her virginity to Baylor, got pregnant, and then put the baby up for adoption without anyone ever knowing. It's the weight of that secret that I believe ended her marriage to my father. She couldn't bear the weight of her deception. Every day, she had to look at him and keep this despicable secret. You know I spent three summers with her in high school, and she never once mentioned Baylor or Trigg. Even now, she holds onto her secret."

"Wow, I don't even know what to say. Did she love Baylor?"

"I don't think so, but from what I've gathered, I'm pretty sure he loved her. Baylor doesn't talk about what happened, and of course, my father never did; hence, how I didn't know he existed, but from what Trigg and I have put together, there was a party that both my mother and uncle attended. There was lots of drinking, and what we speculate happened is that she didn't want to be inexperienced for her first time with my father. We think Baylor knew exactly who she was, but she didn't know it was him. Seven Minutes in Heaven was played differently around these parts when they were teenagers. When you entered that dark room, you didn't always know who you were going in with, and the time stopped when you came out. Speculation aside, we know she loved my dad first, and because she loved my dad, she tried to erase what happened until finally she couldn't block it out anymore, and she just left."

It's unfathomable to me how she could so easily walk away from two of her children. The second I saw that little girl by Laney's side, my heart sank into my stomach at the possibility she might have been mine. I never could have walked away.

"Does Trigg know who I am? I mean, does he know about our past?"

"No...or rather, I don't think he does. I'm still trying to piece that together myself. The only person who knows who you are is Baylor. I don't talk about you, Laney. I left you in Willow Creek."

Damn it, the second I see her spine straighten, I know I chose the wrong words.

"Ouch, thanks for the reminder." She hops off the fence. "Well, I'm glad we got that cleared up. I need to finish up with Madison," she says, starting toward the center of the arena. "Oh, and don't worry about your secret. It's clear people here know you as someone else, someone I don't know anymore. I'll stay out of your way, and you can stay out of mine."

After six years of carefully constructed distance and cutting ties with everyone I cared about, I finally started to build something that resembled a life after her, and now she's here. This is going to be a long, long summer and an even longer forever after that—if my secrets don't burn it all down first.

LANEY

CHAPTER 17

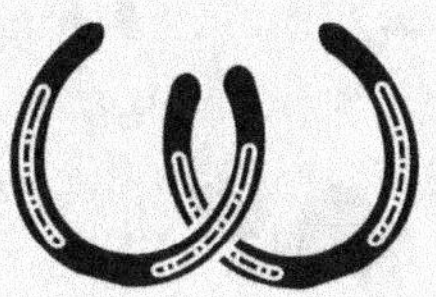

"Christ!" I throw my hand over my heart and stop dead in my tracks on the side of the road.

Bending down, I grab my knees to recenter myself after being spooked half to death by the deer that just darted out in front of me on my morning jog. I'm not a runner; the most athletic I'd been growing up was dancing on the drill team, and I only did that to be with Sydney. I've never been drawn to working out. However, something about the open countryside and the crunch of loose gravel under my feet has my thoughts untangling. The weight of my problems feels manageable, and the rhythmic, steady beat of my heart almost sounds like natural meditation. Right now, I need to quiet the noise more than ever.

I have so many things to sift through, and I don't know where to begin. I knew there was a possibility I'd run into London when I agreed to work with Madison's horse, and when I left Fairfield, I was prepared for that possibility. I had even run through possible scenarios of how to bring up the past and what had brought him here, and while I know even the best laid plans can turn to shit, I studied. I thought I knew what cards he would pull, and I was ready to hit back and demand answers. What I didn't see coming was the part where he acted like he still cared or, even worse, was hurt.

At that moment, I was taken aback, and then I was mad, and because of that, I threw up my walls. I tossed and turned all night, thinking about how all of this could simply be one big devastating miscommunication. I understand why London needed to disappear, to hide—but severing connections with those who matter most to live a life in exile? That's the part I cannot reconcile.

He made his choices believing they served everyone's best interests, but the flip side of those decisions is trusting your friends and having faith that the people you care about will understand. He could have confided in me, in Fisher, in Sydney... We all would have stood by him unwaveringly.

I've also considered that miscommunication might be the least of my worries. Misunderstandings can be rectified, but regret is a different matter. It lingers, remaining constant, until the person holding onto it decides to let it go. It's the regret I believe he harbors for me that eats me alive. I'm the reason he had to leave to begin with, but how dare he make me the villain. It may have been his knife that made the fatal blow, but I'm the one who wielded it. He stole my crime, pushed me away, and now blames me for the life he chose. I never would have asked him for this.

"Damn it." I kick a rock and put both my hands atop my head.

The distinct sound of a horse snorting has me whipping around. "It's kismet that we keep running into each other this way," Trigg says, slowly riding his horse out of the grove along the road.

"I'm not sure that's the word I would use for trespassing," I say, dropping my hands to my hips. "You must be the reason I almost got trampled by a deer."

"So, that's the reason for your delightful greeting," he mocks. "Well, I'm very sorry for spooking a deer. I assure you I did not instruct him to mow you down."

I roll my eyes. "Whatever." I came out here to clear my head, not clutter it by giving more time to another Hale. "Just stay on your own property, and you won't be liable for any collateral damage due to your trespassing." I know I ran farther than last time, but there's at least a mile or two between where I stand and the Hale property.

He chuckles as I pull my foot to my rear and stretch out my thigh muscles before preparing to take off. "Technically, this is my property."

I drop my foot and squint as I look at the land. I work with the horses on the back half of the property, away from the stables where the racehorses and breeding mares are kept. On the second day of working with Pria, I took her for a ride along the perimeter to explore and determine her temperament. I know he's lying.

"I'm not in the mood for head games today, Trigg. I need to get back to Fairfield and get ready for my shift."

"Hey, I'm sorry about the other day. I wasn't trying to blow you off, but I had to take that call," he tries to explain, and I start jogging.

I'm not mad at Trigg, though I didn't love riding back to Fairfield with my ex-boyfriend's new girl. It didn't matter that I was the only one in the car aware of the relationship; it was still uncomfortable. The entire way back, I analyzed her every move, her scent, her laugh and compared myself to everything she is and all I will never be. And then, when I came home, it was more of the same. Girl talk used to be a safe space, but right now, it's just another space to be reminded of all I've worked so hard to let go of. I just need a minute to myself to hear my own thoughts.

"You're upset. Let me make it up to you," he says, riding alongside me, his horse walking as I run at a slow and steady pace. I ignore him in hopes that he'll give up, and I can return to the peace I had found prior to him spooking that damn deer, but then he says, "Unless you'd rather go dress shopping and watch your best friend marry my brother." His words make my heart stumble in sync with my feet, and I lose my balance, tumbling into the grass. "Whoa." He dismounts the horse. "Are you okay?"

"What does it look like to you?" I say as I huff a strand of hair out of my face. "What makes you think I care?" I say irritably.

"You mean besides the fact that you fell over when I mentioned Dallas marrying someone else?" I scowl, hating how my body once again betrays me. "I know he means something to you."

"Yeah?" I say, brushing my palms together to rid them of the dirt. "And how would you know that?"

He extends his hand toward me. "Let me give you a ride, and I'll tell you."

We never did circle back to the talk he promised we'd have, and the fact that London told me his uncle Baylor is the only one who knows who I am and what happened all those years ago tells me I need to get on that horse. From the few interactions I've had with Trigg, he seems nice enough, and London didn't give me any reason to believe he's an enemy. But if he's digging into our past, I want to know why. London saved me last time. Maybe this is how I save him.

"Fine," I concede, taking his hand.

He helps me up, and I wince when I put weight on my right ankle. "What hurts?" he asks quickly, shouldering my weight.

"My ankle. I may have twisted it. I just need some ice, and I'll be fine."

"Then we'd better get you home," he says before helping me onto his horse. "This is Knickers, by the way."

He stabilizes me as I awkwardly try to put my foot in the stirrup while not putting too much weight on my rolled ankle. We're a mess of limbs for all five seconds, but it doesn't go unnoticed that he was careful about where he placed his hands, never touching me inappropriately, even though it would have made my ascent easier. Once I'm up, I scoot back, giving him enough space to hop on. With both of us on, Knickers shifts beneath us as Trigg carefully guides her forward, his hands steady on the reins before turning us around.

"What are you doing? Fairfield is the other direction."

"I know, but we're closer to the ranch, and you're injured. While I'm not particularly fond of my brother at the moment, I don't care to hear about this later."

Wait. My stomach drops. So, London does talk about me with his brother, despite looking me straight in the eye yesterday and insisting otherwise. Not only do I come up in their conversations, but apparently, I "get under his skin" enough for Trigg to notice and comment on it. I file this revelation away. There's something both validating and terrifying about knowing I still affect him, that I'm not as erased from his world as he pretended. But I can't process that right now, not when I'm already struggling to breathe normally just knowing he's living three miles down the same winding road.

I force myself to push the thought down, to focus on this moment, this conversation, because whatever complicated mess of feelings is churning inside me about London, about us, about the lies and half-truths, I'm no closer to unraveling them now than I was yesterday, and I'm not ready to face him again.

"Take me to Fairfield, and he'll never know," I anxiously rush out. "I don't want to go to the ranch… I can't. I need to go to work. I'm not a trust-fund baby like all of you. I don't have an inheritance waiting for me that allows me to come and go as I please. I have to work to pay my bills, which means you need to turn this damn horse around."

"I'm not sure what you heard or what you think you know about me, but I'm not a trust-fund baby either. I work for a living."

I adjust my hold on his waist as Knickers walks in the wrong direction. "Last time I checked, your last name is Hale. You mean to tell me your father isn't leaving you any part of the business or the property? And was it not you who proclaimed moments ago that this was your land?"

"Yes and no. I suppose this spot is as good as any to start story time. I wasn't lying when I told you this property is mine. I have the documentation to prove it. The back sixty acres of the one hundred acres Fairfield sits on is leased to them by us."

"I was under the impression they were your competition, and there was bad blood between the two families," I say as I recall my conversations with Asha. "Why would you lease land to your rival?"

"I didn't. My grandfather drew up the contract, and Mr. Fairfield's father, who owned the front half of the property, signed it. The rivalry wasn't always what it is now. It's grown into this as the expiration date nears."

"Expiration date?"

"Yes, the lease reaches maturity next year, which means the property reverts to us."

"Surely Mr. Fairfield would offer to buy it. They have structures on the land. A good amount of their operation is run on that back half."

"Mr. Fairfield can offer us all the money in the world, and we couldn't take it. Hale property can't be sold. No piece of it can be sold as long as there are living descendants."

If Asha knows this, she hasn't told me, and considering girl talk over ice cream the other night consisted of her grilling me on every detail of the wedding she missed, leaving no stone unturned to determine what Trigg's game was, I think she would have. We spent hours trying to piece together reasons why he was in the stables that morning we ran into each other, and why he's seemingly gone out of his way to date me when there's clearly animosity between them. I tried my best not to take that last part personally. Is it that far-fetched that he might actually be into me? I know now there's more to it, but still. My arms tighten around his waist as I rest my chin on his shoulder, deep in thought. It isn't until I feel him tense beneath me that I realize the level of comfort I just took upon myself.

I clear my throat and ignore it. If I don't make it something, then it's nothing. "There has to be some sort of loophole."

"There is…marriage," he says, his tone indifferent. "If a Hale marries a Fairfield, they can keep the land."

In her vent session at girls' night, Asha mentioned she thought her father was intentionally assigning her menial tasks to divert her attention from my rehabilitation work with the horses. While Mr. Fairfield supports her dream of becoming an equestrian veterinarian, as it will undoubtedly benefit the family business, Asha suspects he's merely humoring her by bringing me on for the summer. She's convinced he does not intend to implement a long-term rehabilitation and rehoming program for their retired racehorses.

What Asha doesn't see is the weight of the land lease bearing down on her father's shoulders. Mr. Fairfield isn't resistant to change because he's stuck in his old ways, but rather, his plate is full with the fate of Fairfield hanging in the balance. Within a year, he will lose sixty percent of Fairfield acreage—prime Kentucky bluegrass that once sustained their champion Thoroughbreds. With the land division, he'll barely retain enough property for their prestigious breeding operation and what I've nicknamed "the showcase stables"—that immaculate barn adjacent to the main house where he keeps his current racing stock and the meticulously groomed sale prospects that command six-figure prices. His urgency to be rid of the retired horses isn't callousness; it's desperation. Each horse requires significant investment to maintain, and difficult decisions must be made with the reduced pastures they'll soon have.

"Does Dallas know about the lease?" I ask, still unsure why he's sharing all of this with me.

"No."

"Why not tell him?" I ask as I sit straighter, as if that's the answer. Two heads are better than one, and while I may not know who London is anymore, I'm sure he wouldn't take their land. He'd find a way.

"Because it's Dallas. There's potential he'd kick them off the land. The feud existed before he ever arrived in Bardstown, but in his mind, one doesn't exist. But I could also see him going through with the wedding and marrying Asha out of some misguided duty. Both of those options go against my plans."

His remark about London's misguided duty hits the nail on the head. He would totally marry her. I slouch against his back. "What are your plans exactly?"

"It's not important right now," he says, expecting my acceptance.

"Asha is one of my best friends. You really expect me to take that as an answer?"

"Yes, because it's all I can give you right now."

I still don't like his response. I don't care if he doesn't have all the answers; I want his notes. But more importantly, I need to know: "Do you like her?"

With my arms wrapped around him and my chest flush against his back, I feel the tension that riddles his body from my question before he says, "Enough."

Enough could mean he'd learn to love her, but I don't believe that's the reason for his indifference now. It's a cop-out. He isn't bringing me into whatever this is for 'enough.'

We turn down the drive to Hale Ranch, and my heart rate kicks up a notch. He may have told me many things I didn't know, but he hasn't answered the one question I want to know. "What does this have to do with me?"

"You broke my brother's heart, and now I need you to put it back together."

"Excuse me. You clearly have no idea what—"

"I've done my research. I know I don't have a brother named Dallas..." he cuts me off. "But I've known for a while that I do have a brother named London Hale from the small town of Willow Creek, Texas. It's funny what you can find online with just a little digging. A simple Google search pulled up a picture of a star quarterback leading his team to a state championship with a Hail Mary pass in the last sixty seconds of a tied game, and wouldn't you know who's tucked under his arm, smiling in her Mustangs dance uniform..." He pauses, but I keep my mouth shut. I remember that night. I remember every night with London, but that one was special. He was on top of the world that night, sharing all his plans for the future—our future. But a picture isn't evidence of heartbreak; it means we have history. "It was you."

"So, we knew each other in high school. I was on the dance team, and he was a football player… that hardly qualifies as—"

"The photo was captioned: *All-Star Quarterback and Mustang's MVP of the year, London Hale, with his long-time girlfriend Laney Hart.*"

"That's why you stared at me that morning in the stables. You recognized me from the photo."

"Sure did. Want to know what else that article said?" I stay silent and wait for him to give me more words. I don't want to inadvertently give him something he doesn't know when I'm not sure what his goal in all of this is. "London Hale will be attending Stanley on a full-ride scholarship in the fall, where his girlfriend, Laney, will join him after graduation. A true-blue, all-American boy with a storybook love story to boot. Cute article. It probably would have been a great story too, but London didn't go to Stanley. Instead, he showed up here in Bardstown, and I'd be willing to bet you had something to do with that. A man doesn't walk in the opposite direction of his dream unless someone crushed it."

His words sting. The reality of a beautiful dream falling apart is something to mourn, but that's not all on me. I didn't crush London's dreams. I used to see it that way. I tortured myself with guilt for years, but discovering he's been here all this time, leaving no trace, no word…that revelation changed things. He abandoned what we built, but maybe worse, it feels like he never trusted my heart. Regardless, none of that matters. He made his choice, and it wasn't me.

"Trigg, I don't know what you expect me to fix. London has moved on and—"

"Madison?" he questions absurdly as we reach the house. "She's not wife material."

"That seems harsh," I say, loosening my grip as he brings Knickers to a stop.

"Let me rephrase that: she's not wife material for him."

"That's your opinion."

"No, that's a fact." He taps my leg, and I scoot back so he can dismount. "You showing up here has him ruffled. He's drinking Baylor's coffee, which is basically mud, puts in his hours, and then spends the evening sitting beside that lake. And to top it off, he hates that I'm spending any amount of time with you."

I despise how desperately I want to believe I'm the reason behind his strange behavior, that London's long hours gazing at the lake are filled with memories of us. But hearts are traitors, always fighting for dominance over the mind, convinced of their superior wisdom when betrayal is their only true mastery. In both love and war, the heart is your true enemy. It's why I have to stay away. My heart can't be trusted. I can't be trusted.

"I'm not doing it," I say, slowly lifting my bum leg over Knickers. "You have to find another way that doesn't include me."

He moves to stand in front of me, his hands resting on either side. "You'll do it because the alternative is your best friend losing her land or attending her wedding to your ex."

I'm so mad I could spit. My past with London is complicated enough as it is, and I can officially say I'm not a fan of blackmail. I try to think through my anger. There has to be a way out of this— something I'm missing because this entire interaction blindsided me. That's when the missing piece clicks into place. The other crucial variable in this plot he's drafting is the player he's conveniently attempted to avoid discussing: Asha.

"Wait, back up a second. I know what's going on here. I have to admit you almost had me, distracting me with remnants of a past and predictions of an unsavory future, but you're forgetting to connect one major dot." I don't miss the way his fists subtly clench at his side, confirming my rightness. "There's nothing to contest. The land would automatically revert to your family. A wedding only happens if you want—"

"When Asha finds out about the lease, there will be a wedding—"

"I don't under—"

"She'll want it," he states firmly, knowing with sure conviction that his words are gospel.

Whatever further thoughts or conclusions I wanted to share are forgotten as the front door swings open, and we're no longer alone. "Laney Hart, I never pegged you for a cowgirl," Fisher Downs says, rushing down the steps of the wrap-around porch. Trigg steps to the side, and Fisher reaches up. "Get in here, girl," he says, lifting me off the horse and pulling me into a bear hug.

"Well, if you'd been better about coming home from Paris. I missed you, Fish." I squeeze him back every bit as hard as he's holding me.

Fisher Downs isn't just my best friend's brother; he's my brother too. I probably called him more times than Syd in the months after London was taken away. London going to prison—or at least so we thought—was hard on him too, more so than me because he had him longer, but together, we found comfort and peace through our shared grief. When he sets me down, I get a better look at him. He's a far cry from the boy I once knew. All man and covered in tattoos now. His muscular arms are adorned with intricate designs that peek out from beneath his crisp white dress shirt. His short, blond hair is darker, neatly trimmed, and styled with a slight side part that complements his face's sharp angles; he also has a mustache now. We're all grown up now, but when his amber gaze connects with mine, I still see the same kind of man I've always known.

"When did you get back?" I ask, forgetting my ankle in the excitement of our reunion, only to let out a sharp shrill and reach for his arm. "Sorry," I apologize, realizing how loud that was in comparison to the injury. I'm not dying, but the pinch of pain was jarring.

"I got back in a few days ago. Sydney didn't tell you?" he asks, confounded, as he takes a step back, examining me from head to toe. "Are you hurt?"

"I just need to put my foot up and get some ice. I'm fine, really," I assure him.

"Here, let me help you," he says, wrapping a muscular arm around my back and taking most of my weight.

We've barely made it two steps when the screen door slams open. "What the hell is going on?"

Dark stormy eyes immediately connect with mine, and I know I'm screwed. I know that look. It's his heart. London wants to fix it, put me back together, and make me whole again, and damn it if I don't want to let him. Flecks of lighter brown near his pupils catch in the morning light and seem to soften momentarily when he sees my pain, tiny beacons of warmth on an otherwise overcast day. There's no hiding from his knowing gaze. It strips away pretense, cutting straight through to the truth I've been running from. It will always be him.

London

Chapter 18

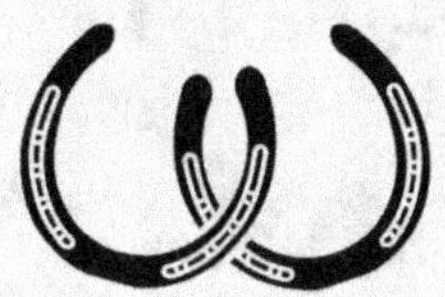

I wasn't going to do it. I wasn't going to walk out that door and lose my temper, even though everything inside of me was screaming to go outside, even if it was just to make her think of me and not Trigg, but then she limped. Somehow, I went from a shadow looming behind the screen door to the man down on one knee, gently squeezing the sides of her ankle. All it took was one high-pitched shrill, and she brought me to my knees faster than I could blink. But the longer I'm here, the angrier I get.

"What happened?" I demand.

"She twisted her ankle out on her morning jog, and I brought her back to the ranch because it was closer than Fairfield," Trigg answers.

"Does this hurt?" I ask as I apply pressure around the side of her ankle.

"Yes, that's tender," she winces.

I slip her tennis shoes off. "How about this?" I work my way up from her toes to her heel, squeezing as I go.

"No," she says, her tone unstrained, confirming she's not being agreeable to be rid of me. "You didn't feel any pain when I was squeezing the center of your foot, which is good. Pain above the bone vs the pain you're feeling when I squeeze here on the sides suggests a sprain rather than a fracture or break. I think it's a soft tissue sprain."

"Like I said…" She clears her throat. "I just need to put my foot up and get it on ice."

My fingers graze over the smooth skin of her calf, and I let them slowly drift down the back, lightly pinching my way down her Achilles tendon, ensuring the pain is centralized to the soft tissue. The exposed skin on her leg breaks out in gooseflesh, and I immediately clench my jaw. Her body responding to my touch is the last thing I need to pile onto all the things already threatening to break my self-control. My eyes trail up her thigh, unable to resist admiring every sun-kissed inch, only for fury to rise when they meet her shorts.

"What the fuck are you wearing?" I rise to my feet.

Her eyes widen. "I was running." She waves one arm down her body. "Have you never seen workout attire?"

I've seen workout clothes. A man had to have invented them. They're practically a second skin, showing off every delectable curve on the female body, or in Laney's case, not covering.

"Your shorts are so high they may as well be underwear, and that's not a tank top. It's a fucking bra," I spit as I unzip the windbreaker I have on from morning chores.

"I'm not wearing that. Fisher, tell him he's acting crazy, and there's nothing wrong with my outfit."

"Dallas, I mean…" He pinches the bridge of his nose. "Fuck, I don't know what I mean anymore, but—" His phone rings, and his words die as he struggles to support Laney and answer it.

I drape my jacket over her shoulders and swoop her into my arms. "This is not necessary; put me down. Fisher!" she calls out for him to save her, but I already know he won't. He's always wanted to see the two of us together, and even after telling him everything, he still believes we are endgame.

"Laney, I have to take this. It's my COO at our Paris location."

He gives her an empathetic smile before taking off toward the house. "I'll see you this weekend for the tour."

I resist the urge to ask which tour he's referencing and focus on the present. "Trigg, run inside and grab me an ice pack."

"Just bring her inside. I'll get the door," he attempts to reason.

"No, she's not coming inside. I'm taking her back to Fairfield. Grab the keys to your truck while you're at it," I say as I walk toward his Ford pickup.

To my surprise, he doesn't argue. "London, put me down. You're acting insane, and this is completely inappropriate."

"Inappropriate?" I furrow my brow, a humorless laugh catching in my throat. Holding her this way, her warmth seeping through my clothes to my skin that's been numb for too long, has awakened parts of me I believed were gone. If anything, touching her is dangerous. Dangerous because each second in her embrace chips away at the walls I've spent years fortifying. Dangerous because I'm suddenly remembering what it feels like to need someone. But the electricity coursing between us, the way my heart thunders against my ribs when she looks at me with those eyes…that could never be wrong.

"Yes, inappropriate," she scolds as I strategically balance her in my arms while still managing to open the truck door. "I'm not your girlfriend anymore. You don't get to call the shots or boss me around."

"We both know I never bossed you around. You called every shot. Now it's my turn, and I say you can't be here, you can't date my brother, and you sure as hell don't get to prance around my town wearing whatever this is." After setting her on the seat, I snap the waist of her spandex shorts. "If anyone is inappropriate, it's you in this outfit."

Our eyes meet when I lean over to click her seatbelt into place, and something electric passes between us, a current of unspoken words. For a second, the anger dissipates, because in this moment, it's not anger at all. It's tension fueled by love and an irrevocable bond that refuses to stay dormant no matter how hard we fight to keep it locked away.

My hand lingers on the buckle, the morning air hanging heavy with the scent of hay and dust as our gazes stay locked, stretching into a small eternity before the sound of the squeaky screen door breaks our stolen moment. I step back, my hand moving from the buckle to the door frame, my heartbeat in my throat as I struggle to find the strength to stay away.

Laney tucks her hair behind her ear, her gaze dropping to her hands. "Thanks for helping me into the truck."

"I've got the ice pack," Trigg says, stepping between me and her, essentially pushing me back. Fucker. He folds the center console up. "Now you can put your feet up." She swivels her legs and rests the ice pack on her ankle.

"You're a lifesaver," she sighs and grabs his wrist to check the time on his watch. "If we hurry, you can get me back before I need to clock in."

"You're not working today," we both say in unison. I clench my fists, pissed that Trigg thinks he has a say.

I snatch the keys out of his hand. "I'm driving her back." I start rounding the truck before he can respond and try to say otherwise.

When I open the driver's side door to get in, he says, "I'll call you later."

His eyes dart to mine, and I swear I see a story behind them. *He knows.* He might not know everything, but he knows enough. I want to call him out right now and demand answers. The only problem is that I can't test his loyalty if I do. I don't want history to repeat itself with him and me. Our fathers don't talk. They've been holding their contempt for years. I don't want that for us. It's why I have to let this play out. Will he use what he knows to hurt me, or is the brotherhood we've found since finding each other an unbreakable bond, one he wants to protect at all costs? If coming to Bardstown has taught me anything, it's this: you need family to survive, someone who'll stand by you even when you're wrong. As his eyes leave mine and return to hers, I see something pass between them. It's not quite a flirt but more of an understanding, and that has me questioning which side he'll choose.

"Better get going so I can get her in bed," I say, hurrying my brother along. They both turn to me with wide eyes. I close the door and grip the wheel. "That's not what I meant. She needs to elevate her foot, pack it with ice, and take some anti-inflammatory medication. I'm just going to get her comfortable."

"Sure," Trigg says skeptically. "Don't pull any shit. She's with me. The only reason I'm not fighting you to drive her back is I need to talk to my dad about something I found on my ride this morning."

My eyes narrow as I consider the path he must have been riding to have stumbled upon Laney during his morning ride. It's the same acreage that Baylor asked me to look at days ago when Fisher showed up. The property there butts up to Fairfield. A document I saw on Baylor's desk months ago comes to mind. I paid little attention to the words 'Land Lease' at the time. Baylor's been experimenting with different wheat varieties and barley. He keeps saying making bourbon is a hobby. We don't sell it to any distributors, and you can only buy it at the old silo he converted into Hale's Cask, but I've always wondered why he hasn't pursued it more. I assumed the lease I saw was him debating on acquiring more land and turning his hobby into more, but now I'm starting to wonder if all this sudden interest in Laney and the border between our land and Fairfield isn't something else.

As Trigg closes the door, I tuck the thoughts away for later. Being alone in a confined space with the girl who has occupied more space in my mind than my own wants and desires is going to take a sheer force of will not to fall under her spell and let it all go, especially with her bare legs stretching out across the bench. I put the key in the ignition and then readjust her feet to lay across my lap.

It's just feet, but damn, it still feels like everything. As I pull down the driveway, I'm jolted back to the memories of us driving down the backroads of Willow Creek with her curled up next to me, the windows down, high on life and dreams. Beautiful fucking dreams.

When I reach the road, she pulls me from the dreams that turned into nightmares—reminders of all I no longer have.

"You can't pull crap like that, London. I can't wear your clothes. People will think we're together."

"That's the point." I bite my lip hard. I can't believe I just said that. The response is too instinctive around her.

"Excuse me?" She tries to pull her foot off my lap, but I lay my arm over her ankles, holding her in place. "London, you can't say things like that to me. You're the one who chose to come here and let me go. You never once tried to come back. You don't get to show up now. It's not fair."

Tongue in cheek, I let her words sting. I want the pain she's carried. I want to feel every ounce, because they were moments spent thinking of me, sacrifices I refuse to ignore.

But her heavy memories are mine too, and apparently, my regret can no longer hold its tongue. "Just because I left doesn't mean I wanted to. I never lied to you. Every minute, every second..." I turn to her, our eyes colliding as they used to when she would peer into my soul. "You have to know..." I shake my head and return my eyes to the road, halfway through an admission I shouldn't be giving. It may have only been fleeting seconds, but I know she saw it. My absence may have hurt her, but I've been dying a slow, torturous death living without her. I want to say so much more. I want to say *I want you back, I want you to be my forever*, but instead, I say, "Our past meant something to me..." and I'd live there if I could, but I can't say that. I won't be cruel. Clearing my throat, I try to save my half-assed admission and attempt to turn it into an apology. "You were a big part of my past, and old habits die hard. We're different people now."

"Are we?" I remain frozen, feeling her gaze burning into the side of my head as the silence stretches between us, its weight heavier than the years we have spent apart. When I still don't speak, she draws a ragged breath. "Why didn't you ever call me? At first...fine...you were scared. But six years, London. Six years. You've been out here, living your life, hiding behind a different name but hardly hiding at all. If what you're saying now is true, if what we had meant something to you..." her voice cracks. "If it wasn't just empty promises between two kids playing at love...don't you think I deserved your truth? I loved you, London Hale. I would have kept your secret."

Her fractured composure destroys me. Each word is a blade between my ribs, carving deeper than I thought possible, dissolving the walls I'd built to justify my silence all these years. The truth in my silence is soul-crushing. There was never a single day I didn't think of calling her. Not one morning did I not wake with her name caught in my throat. I told myself I was protecting her, but hearing the raw devastation in her voice, I question if my absence wasn't protection but instead the cruelest wound I could have inflicted.

"I didn't call because I chose this. I chose to hide. I wasn't going to force you to endure a life of my choosing. You were eighteen, attending Stanley in the fall. You had your whole life in front of you. I didn't want to take that away—"

"But that's exactly what you did by taking away my choice to choose what I wanted my future to look like. Whether I wanted you in it or not, you stole that from me. How was that any better?"

The gravel driveway leading to Fairfield comes into view sooner than I'd like. I messed up. I messed up big, and I don't know if I can fix any of it—or worse, if I should.

I risk a glance in her direction. "Are you saying you would've chosen this...chosen me?"

"Without question," she answers without hesitation, a whole-hearted response from a heart that used to be mine. Knowing does not make any of this easier. It just makes it messy.

"And what about now?"

I turn my gaze back to her as the truck rides hard, crushing the gravel beneath its wheels, the crunching filling the silence as I wait with bated breath, hoping for a response I don't deserve.

"I'm not a fan of masochism, and sacrificing my heart for one that wouldn't choose me back is the very definition. It's like you said… We're different people now."

I can't tell if she's using my words to mock me or if she echoes their sentiment. All I know is I hate that I ever said them. All truths transcend self-righteousness, and she is becoming the most undeniable truth in my life. I don't know the way forward, and I don't know if there's an us after I lay everything at her feet, but not trying only ends with one inevitable destiny—one without her.

"Laney, I—"

"Crap." She sits up straight and pulls her feet out of my lap. "If I asked you not to get out of the truck, would you listen?"

"Depends on why you're asking," I state sharply, gripping the wheel tighter when I trace her line of sight to the black Audi parked in the circle drive outside the main house.

"You don't want to be found, remember." She leans forward in the seat, pressing her hands to the dashboard as if doing so will stop the car. Her breathing quickens, shallow, and irregular. "It's why you shut us all out," she adds anxiously.

Pulling my eyes away from her, I notice a figure exiting the car. He doesn't need to turn around for me to know exactly who he is. Noah Donovan, the man who has always wanted what was mine, the arms I willingly pushed her into, the man who lied in the name of saving the girl. You'd think that last part would garner a little more respect out of me, but it doesn't. He wouldn't save the girl at the risk of losing himself. He saved her for his own personal gain, and I let him. However, while I knew there was a chance he'd keep her the way he professed he would times before, I didn't think she'd keep him.

"Why is Noah Donovan here? Are you together?"

"Does it matter?" Her head snaps back to mine, her wide eyes filled with unspoken accusations.

"Yeah, it matters. I thought you were talking to my brother," I toss back. I don't like that either, but he's the lesser of two evils.

"We're talking. He isn't proposing marriage."

"I'm sure Trigg wouldn't see it that way. If I were talking to someone, I wouldn't want them talking to their ex," I defend. I'm not sure if Noah is her ex, and I'm also unsure if they ever dated after I left, which is precisely why I mentioned it. I need to know.

"You're one to talk. I'm sure Madison would be thrilled with today's conversation."

I don't correct her. She may not be completely wrong, but she's also not right. I'll let her believe what she wants for now. She's seeing what she wants to see, and now that Noah's here, I might need to let that play out.

"So he's your ex, then?"

She rolls her eyes and sets her jaw. She doesn't want to talk about it, and I fucking hate that I'm even asking. I hate that if they were anything, it was because I chose to be her nothing. I deserve the pain that's slicing me open right now. I conjured the storm. I don't get to complain about the damage.

"You left; he stayed." It's not a yes, but it's also not a no. "Look… I'm here for the summer. I don't want to fight with you." I slowly pull up behind Noah's car in the roundabout, and she adds, "Can we just be friends?"

"Friends," I repeat, shifting the truck into park.

The thought of watching her eventually find someone else makes my chest tighten painfully. All this time, I imagined her moving on with her life as I had intended her to, but seeing her now changes things. She might want to move on, but she hasn't, and fuck if I don't want her to. The foreign word hangs between us, and I risk glancing at her. Her earthy brown eyes trigger a rapid succession of memories—her head on my shoulder watching movies, the way her hand felt in mine, perfect afternoons fishing on the lake that started it all…the lake where I realized I was falling in love with her. I drop her gaze to stop the torment, but I don't agree to her terms. Friends is the last thing I want to be. I can't agree to a title I don't want, so I don't.

"Let me talk to him before you get out."

"London, I swear I didn't tell him you were here. I don't want any trouble."

"Neither do I," I say before exiting the truck.

When I step out of the truck, Noah's eyebrows rise in surprise before settling. "London Hale," he says with a long exhale, his tone laced with disdain.

"Noah," I say indifferently.

"I wasn't aware you were here," he says, shoving his hands into the pockets of his khaki chino shorts. The rising sun catches on his Rolex as he shifts his weight, and with little words, I can tell he's still the same arrogant, preppy prick he ever was—maybe more so. Only now, there's something harder about him, something that suggests his privilege has calcified into entitlement. I don't dignify his comment with a response. I'm not interested in entertaining any conversations with him. We were never friends. I knew he'd help me in a time of need because it helped him. Now I have exactly one concern, and entertaining his small talk isn't it.

"Does she know?" I ask pointedly.

His brows tug together, and his head tilts slightly to the right as he studies me. "Not unless you told her." There's an undercurrent of curiosity in his voice, not concern but rather interest in someone who's just realized they might not be the only one playing a long game. I give away nothing, giving him my back to open her door when he asks, "Are you planning on telling her?"

My hand remains frozen on the door handle as I wait to see if he'll say more. Because this is Noah Donovan, there is a chance my judgment is clouded. I'm jaded by our pasts. Perhaps he's changed. In my mind, he'll always be the man who wants my girl, but that doesn't make him a bad guy; it just makes him my enemy by default. But then he speaks again. "I don't know what this is… why you're here…but if you don't stay away, I'll tell her myself."

Liar. His guilt may not run as deep as mine, but there's a

reason he's kept his mouth shut about that night. There's crimson staining his Ivy League hands too, and no amount of family money or carefully curated alibis can change that. He's not some innocent bystander I dragged down with me, which is how I know his threats are empty.

I feel the corner of my lips tug into a smirk as I stare at the door handle. Noah Donovan is still threatened by me. That means a part of her still belongs to me. I'll let him believe he holds the reins—for now, anyway.

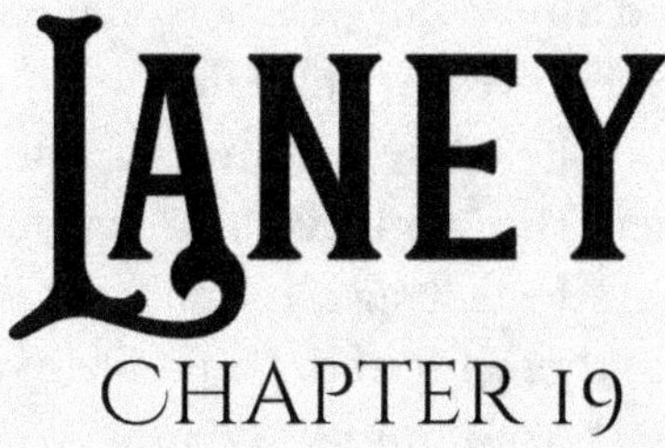

LANEY
CHAPTER 19

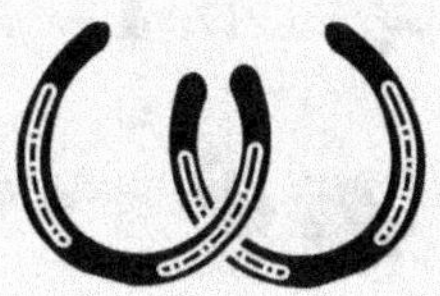

"Knock, knock," Asha's voice vaguely registers, and I try to wish it away as though I never heard it at all. I'm too warm and cozy in my bed until she says, "Oh, I'm sorry. I didn't realize I was interrupting."

My eyes flash open when I realize why I'm so warm. There's heat at my back and an arm draped over my waist. I move to sit up, and when I do, so does Noah. I don't remember him being in my room when I lay down to rest my foot, but he's definitely here now.

"It's fine. You're not interrupting. We fell asleep," he answers with a yawn. "I drove straight through the night. I closed my eyes, and I was out."

She rolls her lips to stifle what I know is an awkward smile. Asha doesn't have a reason not to like Noah. In fact, until I met Trigg, I would have said Noah was exactly her type—pristine Ivy League pedigree with cufflinks that cost more than my monthly tuition, the kind of man whose hands have never known a day's hard labor. But I see the heat in her eyes when she looks at Trigg. She wants a man who has weathered actual storms, rough around the edges, and not afraid to put her in her place. Noah is none of those things, and now he's in my bed.

"Did you need something? Is your father upset I've been here less than a month and already need a personal day?"

"No." She rolls her eyes as though my comment is absurd, which maybe it is, but I don't ever want him to think I'm taking advantage of my friendship with Asha to get out of my responsibilities. "But I am here to deliver a message. He's currently in the gym with his physical therapist and would like you to come downstairs so he can assess your injury. I know you think it's just a minor sprain, but having a professional take a look doesn't hurt."

"Actually, that sounds great. Does he want me to come down now?" I say, tossing the blanket off.

"You can take your time and freshen up," she quips, mocking my discomfort, knowing damn well I've been avoiding Noah, and the last place I want him right now is in my bed. "His session is over in twenty minutes, and the trainer will stick around to look at your ankle." She clasps her hands together and flashes a sheepish smile. "Do you want me to help walk you down?" She finally tosses me a bone.

"I can walk her down," Noah says, stretching his arms above his head.

Her eyes widen, and she says, "Oh, I almost forgot." She ducks back into the hallway and then rolls in a cart filled with flowers. The scent of lilies quickly fills the air.

"You didn't have to get me flowers. It's incredibly thoughtful but completely unnecessary. I'll be fine by the morning, I'm sure."

"Oh, I didn't get you flowers," she says with a shit-eating grin.

"Then who did?"

"Dallas's brother," she sing-songs as she parks the cart in front of my bed.

"Dallas?" Noah repeats the name in question.

"Trigger Hale," she clarifies.

"Trigger Hale?" Noah repeats his name in question. Hale obviously ringing a bell, the other two names not so much.

"Yeah, his brother, Dallas, dropped Laney off this morning. You met him in the driveway."

"Dallas?" he says in disbelief.

"Do you think he'll tag along on the Bourbon Trail this weekend? I was thinking—"

I quickly get off the bed and embellish a hiss of pain as though I forgot about my ankle. I really need to talk to Asha and fill her in, but right here, right now, in front of Noah, is not the time.

Noah climbs over the bed and jumps to my side. "Are you okay? You need to be more careful."

"I'm fine. Maybe we should head down to see the physical therapist," I suggest, trying to change the subject. "Asha, are we still on for dinner tonight?"

"Dinner…" I glare at her eyes wide before she foils my plan. We don't have a dinner date tonight, but we need to talk. "Umm, yes." She nods slowly. "Does 7 p.m. still work for you?"

"Works for me," I confirm.

"Okay, well"—she casually strolls back to the door—"I'll see you tonight, then. It was good seeing you, Noah."

"Pleasure as always, Asha."

The second she's gone, I ask, "Why didn't you tell me you were coming?"

"Why does it sound like you don't want me to be here?" he responds in a terse tone as he offers me his arm, and we start toward the hallway.

"I'm just surprised, is all," I say, attempting to hide my annoyance. His timing couldn't be worse.

Though, I am surprised. Noah and I stay in touch, and although we've been intimate on occasion, we've never put a label on our relationship.

"You're sure that surprise is authentic and has nothing to do with the fact that London Hale is here."

"I had no idea he was here. I was just as shocked to see him as you were this morning."

"I don't know, you looked pretty comfortable in his truck."

I stop walking and release his arm. "What is that supposed to mean?"

He runs his hand through his perfectly unkempt combover. "It means I think you're ignoring my calls because he's here."

I wait for his blue eyes to connect with mine. "Are you accusing me of lying?"

"No, that would require you to respond to a text or answer the phone when I call," he quickly responds, his voice piqued with irritation. This is how it's always been between London and Noah —forever a dick-measuring contest—and I'm sick of it. My reasons for not answering the phone have nothing to do with London. I wasn't answering his texts before I discovered London was my neighbor for the summer. "I'm sorry. I'm not trying to be a dick, but seeing you with him this morning wasn't easy. It brought back many old memories—ones I thought I'd never have to revisit. I don't want to fight with you," he says, taking a step into me and grabbing my hands.

Noah's comment about revisiting memories feels off. We've discussed that night many times, enough for me to know that his recollections aren't as painful as mine. I saw the look he and London shared before he lied and told Sheriff Townsend that he saw London stab the man. It's why I didn't talk to him for almost a year after everything happened. I resented him for helping London lie. I hated the selfishness I felt he possessed to put London behind bars and not me.

Back then, his lie felt like a calculated chess move, one where he strategically played the game to capture me as though I were a prize that could be won. But as time passed and wounds began to heal, I discovered I couldn't deny him the same grace I'd extended to London. The anger still burns when I think of London stealing my crime. It was a betrayal that left permanent scars. However, given the same choice, I would have made that identical sacrifice, putting his chance at a full, beautiful life ahead of my own, because that's what love demands: the courage to place someone else's needs before your own, even when it breaks you.

It's that sentiment that thawed my heart when it came to Noah. Who was I to judge the intentions buried in Noah's heart? Now, history repeats itself with painful familiarity. Some circumstances have shifted, but the core dynamic remains unchanged. I'm trapped in that same suffocating "choose me" desperation all over again, watching the board being set for another round of a game I never wanted to play.

"Why did you come?" I risk asking again.

"It's summer. School ended..." His blue eyes drop to our hands, where his thumb skims over the backs of my knuckles. "And unlike the summers before, we don't return in the fall. I'm heading back to Willow Creek, and I—"

"Ah, there you are," a man with a British accent says as he turns the corner. "My session with Mr. Fairfield ended early, as he had to take a call, so I figured I'd come to you in case you needed help." He looks between me and Noah. "Am I interrupting something? I can wait."

"No, you're not interrupting," Noah says, his voice oddly shaky. "I'm going to check in at the B&B in town. I need to make a few calls. Can I see you later tonight after your dinner with Asha?" I nod in agreement, and he leans in and kisses me on the cheek. "I'll see you tonight, then."

"Okay," I confirm as his blue eyes stay locked on mine. Gone is the pent-up frustration from seconds ago, and in its place is something different, something that looks almost like fear, but before I can read into it any more, he's turning away.

"Shall we?" the PT extends his hand, and I take it.

"We shall."

I never asked for this forced pause, but it's desperately needed.

"I'm sorry I didn't tell you all of this from the beginning." I exhale a cleansing breath as an invisible weight is lifted from my shoulders after telling Asha about my history with London.

For the longest time, I haven't wanted to touch it—its existence is painful enough—but I trust Asha. Unlike Sydney and I, who have known each other since we were young, Asha and I didn't get to meet until we were older, but that doesn't mean our friendship isn't deep. We just don't have the miles on it like Sydney and I do. I trust her, and my reasons for not confiding in her were never because of her but because of me.

"I don't blame you one bit for not telling me." She sits back in her chair, eyes wide. "But I will say I'm fucking speechless. How crazy is this?"

"I know…" I say apologetically. "I didn't mean to put all this on you. I hate to make you a keeper of such a dark secret, but—"

"No, no, no." She straightens. "You're reading me all wrong. Your secret is nuts, but by crazy, I mean fated. I'm going on record now to say I had no idea Dallas's name was London, nor did I know the two of you shared this twisted past. All that being said, you realize this is destiny. The two of you are back together for a reason."

Sydney smacks the table. "And this is precisely why I knew you'd make a great third to our trio." She gestures between the two of them. "Great minds think alike."

"Hold on, you've been just as mad at London for him cutting us out and moving on, and now you're Team Let's Get Them Back Together?"

She swallows her ranch water. "Babe, I'm whatever team makes my best friend happy. I haven't forgiven London. He and I still need to talk. But I'm not the one who was in love with him; you were. Just because I agree that the two of you being brought back together coincidentally is fate, it doesn't mean I'm locked into some fated-mates, written-in-the-stars love story. Fate may have simply brought the two of you back together so that you can put your demons to rest and move on." She brings her straw back to her lips, taking a long sip before adding, "But I will say this: listening to the story again, knowing all that we do now about

London's non-existent arrest record and where he's been, has my heart rooting for the guy I consider a brother again."

I stir my drink. "What are you thinking?"

"We already know everything isn't as it seems, but I think we've been overlooking a key player for far too long."

"Noah!" Asha blurts out. "The night everything happened, he lied, but he's been lying ever since." I lean forward, fully invested in her words. Asha is an outsider hearing all of this for the first time, so her perspective isn't tainted by the years we all spent in school together. "You said things were always different between you after that night, which is understandable. You can't expect your second choice to fill the shoes of your first love, but that's not the only thing that kept a divide between you. It was the lie. Noah's dad was the mayor, you said, and his father showed up with the sheriff. There is no way the mayor of a small town didn't know precisely what happened to London, and because I know enough about Noah, I'm certain that Noah knew too. He may not have known the exact location London was sent, but I know damn well he knew he wasn't behind bars."

"She's right," Sydney agrees. "I don't know how we didn't put all this together sooner."

"Because Noah wouldn't do something like that," I say, sucking the last drops of ranch water through my straw as they both stare at me wide-eyed. I sigh inwardly. "The Noah we knew before that night—the one who got me a job at his mother's flower shop, jumped into the lake to save me, and spent months helping me search for my dad… That guy looked out for me. Sure, he liked me, but he wasn't a saboteur."

I saw that look between Noah and London that night—the silent truce they formed to protect me. I've never been oblivious to Noah's motives, the way he carefully inserted himself into my life. But this betrayal blindsided me completely. It transforms every memory, every gesture of kindness, into a choreographed lie.

Asha's eyes narrow. "Those are always the ones you have to

watch out for. The ones hanging in the balance, waiting to shoot their shot, aren't above scheming to get it."

"It's possible he didn't know," Sydney offers, noting my dejection.

It's a shitty spot to be in when the only two men you've ever trusted have betrayed you in the worst ways. Every relationship feels suspect now, every memory tainted. I find myself replaying conversations, searching for the subtle warnings I must have missed, wondering if I've ever truly known anyone.

Or maybe it's me. I'm the common denominator in these failed relationships. I grew up moving from one place to another with my mother. We had each other, but as far as friends went, I was alone until London came along, and when he was gone, Noah filled the role. Even without the romance between us, Noah has been my safety net, my insurance policy against the void. Our unspoken arrangement comforted me. If the loneliness became unbearable, if no other man ever ignited that fierce, consuming fire London left behind, at least Noah would be there—warm enough to keep me from freezing, if not hot enough to burn. He was my backup plan for a life without passion, my consolation prize, and in some ways, that makes me every bit as bad as him. He may have lied, but I'm lying too, pretending he could ever be my forever.

"So what's the plan, Laney? Do we need to hide a body?" Asha smiles.

"Tempting, but no. I do, however, need to get rid of him. I've been stringing him along, and that's not fair either."

"You've ghosted that man multiple times and side-stepped putting a title on your relationship just as many. Any other guy would have read the writing on the wall and called it quits," Sydney insists.

"That might be true, but Noah and I have history, so he's not any guy, and while I may leave him on read for days or even weeks, eventually, I respond, and we never get off the cycle."

"Well, I, for one, am all for it. I'll happily wait outside the coffee shop while you let him down easy and then drive you to get your man," Asha says, raising her hand to get the waiter's attention.

"I'm not going after London. Why should I chase a dream that doesn't chase me back?"

"You can't argue with that," Sydney says, swirling the cubes in her empty glass.

"That's one perspective, but when I was younger, my mother used to tell me, 'If the dream is in you, it is for you.'" The waitress arrives. "Can we get another round, please?" Asha asks sweetly.

"That's okay, no more for me," I rise from my chair. "There's a dream I need to go shoot down." I grab my purse. "Wish me luck."

Losing a friend, giving up an alternate ending, isn't always easy. It's the end of an era, but when we clutch tightly to relationships that neither nourish our souls nor propel us toward our true path, we can't fully commit to our dream.

I had a dream once. It still flickers inside me from time to time, no matter how much I've tried to extinguish it. It remains unchanged, waiting for oxygen. But I'll never know its full brightness until I stand alone on the edge of despair with nothing beneath me but faith in my own wings. The safety net I've kept stretched below has become my comfort and limit. I won't discover who I truly am until I finally completely bet on myself.

LONDON
CHAPTER 20

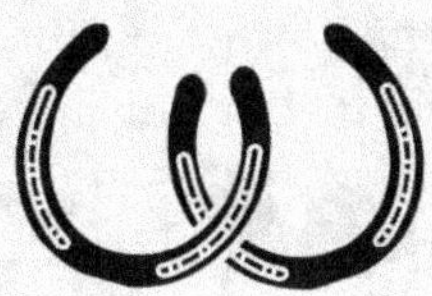

"Shit!" I hear an all-too-familiar voice huff out with a long breath of annoyance as soon as I exit the coffee shop.

I'm never in town this time of day. I'm out in the fields, tending to crops, or busy with morning chores in the stables, but today, I wanted to pick up a new bit for Titan before we started our day. He's been swallowing differently and gnawing at his bit, which is unusual for him. However, now that I'm here, I wonder if I wasn't subconsciously hoping I'd run into Laney. I had a cup of coffee at home, so I didn't need another, but I remembered Trigg droning on about running into Asha Fairfield outside of the coffee shop with her new friend Laney after she first arrived, and wouldn't you know my feet carried me across the street to that same shop.

I watch as she tosses her head back toward the sky with a groan, and I can't help but smile. She was always cute when she got worked up. That hasn't changed. "What did the clouds ever do to you?" I say, approaching her cautiously. I wouldn't say our last conversation ended badly, but it was tense.

"This day just keeps getting better," she says sarcastically, her eyes fixed on the sky.

"That bad, huh?" I question, taking a second to let my eyes scan her body.

Her lightweight canvas jacket hangs open beneath a faded navy polo that has survived countless washings. A scuffed black belt holds up her fitted tan riding pants that disappear into her tall boots.

I know it shouldn't bring me an ounce of satisfaction, but given her attire and that she's standing on the curb, frazzled instead of commanding a field, I'm certain she's running late to work. My presence isn't the source of the storm brewing behind her eyes, and for the moment, I'm not the villain in someone else's morning.

"You could say that I'm currently standing outside a coffee shop, talking to the wrong Hale brother," she says, pulling her head out of the clouds, her brown eyes brilliantly reflecting the rising morning sun.

I roll my lips, her mention of my brother quickly darkening what had been bright. "You were meeting Trigg?"

"Yep," she pops the P. "He asked if we could talk over a quick coffee, and I caught a ride into town with Fairfield's personal chef, and now I'm stranded." She holds up her phone. "It's dead, and Trigg was my ride back."

"Why are you doing this?"

"What exactly do you mean by *this*?" she questions with a furrowed brow.

"Entertaining dates with my brother. I know you, Laney, and—"

She holds up her hands. "You know what? I just remembered Noah staying around the corner. I'm sure he can give me a ride home."

"Laney, wait." I grasp her wrist before she can run, and she freezes, her gaze quickly dropping to the fingers circling her wrist.

The connection between us feels electric, reminding us that the chemistry we've always shared is still very much alive. You'd think time and distance would have dulled its flame, but if anything, it burns brighter. She may not want to, but I know she feels it. I can feel her pulse hammering beneath my touch, its beat mirroring mine. Her eyes finally trail up to mine, and for a second, it's as though we're different people. We're not two strangers standing on the street. Instead, we're back home in Willow Creek, two kids falling in love in the grass that stretched between their windows, but then she blinks, and we're jolted back to here and now.

"Please don't touch me," she says softly, gently twisting her wrist out of my hold.

I close my eyes, giving the sting of her words a second to marinate, because while I hate them, I love them. They made me feel, and most days, all I feel is numb. "Can you just tell me if it was a date?"

Last night, I mentioned to Baylor and Trigg that I'd be running to the tack shop in the morning to grab a new bit if they needed anything. The fact that he knew I'd be in town and pulled this shit isn't lost on me.

She turns to face me, revealing a tiredness I hadn't seen before. "London, can we not—"

"Sorry." I know I'm messing this up, but it can't be helped. She drives me crazy. Being this close and not having her the way I want to is maddening. "Let me rephrase that. Did he mention what he wanted to talk about?"

She looks at me quizzically. "That question isn't any better. What I talk about and with whom is none of your concern. You threw away that privilege; you don't get to demand it now."

"Damn it, Laney." I toss my coffee in the trash. "I know this"—I gesture between her and me—"is hard to put aside, but I'm not prying for the reasons you think. Do I want you to date my brother? Fuck no. And just so we're clear, there is no scenario where the two of you are end game—"

"You don't—"

"I'm not finished," I cut her off as her face quickly reddens with anger. "I'm just trying to understand. I think he's up to something, and I don't want you caught in the crossfire of a war that isn't yours."

Her eyes stay pinned on mine, swirling with a multitude of emotions, all rooted in different pain. I have the urge to tell her everything. She deserves it, but right now, she's not giving me anything. I don't know if she's pushing me away out of fear, hate, or revenge. It could be all of those things, and that's fine. I'll remain the villain in her story if it keeps her whole.

"I see it now," she says, breaking the silence. "I'm not sure how I missed it before. We were never going to be end game. For that to happen, you would have to stop keeping things from me under the guise of protection and trust me." She's right. I've been so caught up shielding her that I never gave her the chance to be strong. The truth and the lie war within me as I struggle to find my words when they matter most. "I guess we're done here," she says, turning on her heel.

"If I tell you what Trigg wants with Asha, will you leave?"

I know she said she wouldn't leave and that she's here for the summer, but I'm losing my strength to fight her. The walls I've built are crumbling beneath her gaze. I never wanted any of this. What I want has never wavered, and it's currently standing right before me, breathing and real, her eyes searching mine for truths I've kept locked away. She's pleading with me for trust, and God, I want to give it to her so badly.

Maybe this is the first step in giving her everything, but before I take it, I have to take one last desperate swing at keeping things as they've been. I never chose this road lightly. The decision to hold back has cost me countless sleepless nights and an endless ache in my chest from where my heart used to beat. If we take this step, there are no roads back to the people we are now. We'll either be transformed into something beautiful and unbreakable or into ruins. I'm not sure either of us will survive.

The fight in her eyes softens as the internal battle that's been raging inside of me for years registers. I may have asked her to leave, but there was an olive branch attached to it: answers.

She shoves her hands into the pockets of her lightweight jacket. "Depends. I'll consider it if you tell me something I don't already know."

"You'd really leave?" I ask, my heart stuttering at the thought.

She tilts her head to one side. "I see what you're doing. If I say yes, you're somehow validated in your choice to up and disappear, but the difference between you and me is I wouldn't leave things unsaid. I'd give Asha the truth before leaving." I press my lips together to stifle an ill-timed smile. It can't be helped. She's always been feisty. I liked it then, and I still like it now. "How is that funny? You know what, don't answer that. I don't have time for this."

"I know about the lease," I say to her retreating form.

She stops dead in her tracks, which answers another one of my lingering thoughts. Laney has her own reasons for entertaining my brother's company. I thought it was attraction, but since she knows about the lease, that feels less true. I did some more digging into my suspicions. Baylor's request for me to ride out to Bristol Creek coupled with Trigg's timely ride the day Laney sprained her ankle were too close to be coincidental, and now I know it's not.

"You do?" She turns around, eyes wide. Then, closing the distance that separates us, she says, "Then you and Trigg really need to talk. He thinks you don't know, and Asha's family is going to lose their land."

"Are you really worried about the one percent losing their land? They have money, and losing that land doesn't bankrupt them. They won't go broke. They'll simply rebuild somewhere else."

"Is that really how you see it?"

"Why does how I see it matter? What's the real reason you're invested in this outcome?"

I know my response lacks the empathy she would expect, but it's not without reason. I want to know how much she knows. Is she aware of the loophole? Does she care if I marry someone else? If we take our land back and Fairfield moves, it gives her no reason to return, no more accidental run-ins, and a true end for us.

"Just forget it. I don't care what happens."

She starts to walk away this time with a determined stride, putting distance between us, and I say, "So you don't care if I marry Asha?" She stops, but she doesn't turn around, and I add, "I wouldn't."

"I'm not sure that's any better."

This time, I'm the one to walk around and stand at her front. "Isn't it, though? If I don't marry her, Trigg can. Marrying her would hurt him, and I don't want to do that."

Her conflicted eyes settle on mine, and I see sadness, but I also see relief. Talking about endings that don't include her and me fucking hurt.

"Wait, I don't understand." Her eyes drop to my jacket as she collects her thoughts. "If he wants to marry her, why wouldn't he? He said the loophole was marriage. You both have Hale blood, so why does it have to be you?"

"Remember how I told you he was a secret, and my mother put him up for adoption?"

"Yes." She nods slowly, trying to keep up.

"Well, it wasn't until he got sick and needed a kidney transplant that Baylor found out he existed. His adoptive parents knocked on his door in a last-ditch effort to find a match and save his life. Of course, Baylor stepped up, but not without his own stipulations. He wanted his son back. They agreed, but Trigg was already five years old by that time, and my grandfather had died. Since my grandfather had passed before he knew about Trigg, he wasn't recognized in the will."

"I don't understand. Why can't an addendum be made? How else do heirs get put on the deeds?"

Shit. I grind my teeth, hating how a primal part of my brain takes over when I hear her speak about heirs. "There can be…" I take a deep breath and push out the memory of the one and only time I had her in a position to make heirs.

"Okay, you're going to have to give me more, because I don't understand if there's—"

"I need to know something," I cut her off as another thought floats to the forefront. "Why is Trigg telling you all of this? This feud has nothing to do with you. You're not a Hale or a Fairfield."

Her eyebrows rise, and I can tell she didn't like my words. "I think I'll keep that to myself for now…unless you want to trade."

"Trade?" The word hangs between us. I stroke my beard slowly, buying time as my mind races through the implications.

"Yeah," she says, one eyebrow arching sharply. "A secret for a secret." Tongue in cheek, I drop my gaze, a heaviness settling in my chest. I know precisely which secret she's fishing for—the one thing I've buried so deep that even I pretend it doesn't exist most days. "Look, if you want to talk, you know where to find me, but if there's any moving forward with us, it won't be with secrets. If you can't do that, then just let me be. I'll stay out of your way, and you stay out of mine, but I need to get back to Fairfield."

After a beat of silence, I risk meeting her gaze again. "Do you still need a ride?"

Those aren't the words she wants, but I'm hoping she sees my offer for the temporary truce it is. There's a conversation we need to have, words that could change everything between us, but it has to be the right moment. Perfect timing for something this fragile and maybe even dangerous. And right now, standing on a street corner with tension crackling between us like static electricity is not it.

"You don't have to," she sighs. "Noah is staying at the B&B around the corner. He'll give me a ride back."

Noah. Heat rises up my neck as I recall his threat. My jaw clenches so hard it aches. He's my fear materialized, but I'm done letting my fear control me.

"Is that what you want?"

A small smile slips through. She knows I'm fishing. After this conversation, I'm about ninety-nine percent certain whatever is between her and Trigg isn't romantic, but I can't say the same is true for Noah.

"I'd love to not have to walk another block."

Her response isn't an outright admission, but it's an inch, and I'll take it.

"Okay, there's just one more thing," I say, rocking back on my heels.

Her eyes narrow. "What's that?"

"You'll have to touch me." She furrows her brow, and I nod across the street. "I rode my bike."

She purses her lips before a real smile—the first one she's given me since being here—spreads across her pretty face. "I've never been on a motorcycle."

"I think we should change that." She nods excitedly, and we cross the street.

This will no doubt be dangerous. Having her wrapped around me for the twenty-minute ride back to Fairfield will be sweet torture, but perhaps it's just the kind of torment I need to move my hands and feet.

I throw my leg over the bike and take my seat. When she doesn't get on behind me, I look up and see apprehension, but I don't think the bike is the source. It's me. "It's just a ride," I offer.

"Just a ride," she echoes, sliding one hand onto my shoulder to stabilize herself as she climbs onto the seat behind me.

I draw in a sharp breath as her arms wrap around my waist, the sensation hitting like a blow I used to take on the football field. God, she has no idea how many times I've dreamed of her hanging onto me like this again, just like she used to do in my dad's old beat-up truck. We still fit together the same way we always did.

I start up the bike and slowly pull out onto the street. This is a certified bad idea. She's not mine, but her soft thighs pressed against mine and her warmth seeping into my back, thawing the ice around my heart, makes that feel like a lie. How could she not be mine when her body remembers how to fit perfectly against mine?

A pothole in the road as we travel down the final stretch of road between town and Fairfield has her arms holding me tighter. I instinctively reach for her hands wrapped around my front and squeeze in reassurance.

I should never have let her go. I should have gone back.

The closeness we're sharing now makes me want to keep driving past Fairfield, past the city limits and far away from Bardstown, back to summer nights when the road ahead stretched into eternity, and it was her and me dreaming about tomorrows full of promise.

I turn onto the white gravel leading to Fairfield, and I feel her shift behind me, her cheek coming to rest between my shoulder blades as I slow. Her body molded against my back feels as natural as breathing, her heartbeat steady against my spine. It feels like the start of what could be a new beginning if we both still want it. Far too soon, I'm pulling up to the lot beside the stables, and I'm nowhere near ready to let go.

As I shut off the bike, we sit, each of us unmoving, savoring a moment that feels like the kind we used to dream about, until a trainer walking out of the stables with a horse on a lead headed toward the training ring breaks the calm, and the connection is severed as she gets off the back.

"Thanks for the ride," she says, her voice a tad strained with emotion.

I watch as she tucks a strand of hair behind her ear that has loosened from her ponytail. The air between us feels impossibly charged, our unspoken words hanging heavy, and I hate it.

"In order to add Trigg's name on the deed, all living heirs have to sign off on it," I break the silence and give her a truth, one with no conditions, no trade, no strings attached, hoping she sees it for what it is—an olive branch. It may not be the exact one she wants, but it's a start. Her eyes widen as understanding flickers across her face. I didn't know I had an uncle because my father hadn't talked to his brother in twenty-four years. "Making that happen is my goal."

"Thanks for telling me."

She swallows nervously, and I can tell she's about to give me more, so I say, "You don't have to tell me anything. It's probably better that you don't."

"Why is that?"

I shrug. Standing outside the coffee shop, I wanted answers, but after riding with her on the back of my bike, I was reminded of what's important. I was reminded of the things I care about, and whatever she has to say doesn't change that. I want a relationship with my brother, which means my mission is unchanged. I need to heal the divide that exists between my family. I still want to know what he's up to, and I want to know if he's planning to cross me, but I can't control other people's moves as much as I might like to; it's not reality. All I can do is lay my cards on the table and give him the choice I once denied her. I don't want history to repeat itself. I'm tired of losing the things I care about.

"I'm not telling you this to bind you with a secret. I'm telling you so you can make your own choices. I can't change what is done, but I can try to be better."

She opens her mouth to respond, words forming on her lips, but I shake my head gently. This silence between us isn't empty. It's filled with everything I couldn't give her before. A choice and a truth. She deserves that much. I start up my bike. Whatever comes next for us can't be built on manipulation.

"I'll see you around," I say before pulling off.

Maybe all this ends with a closed door, but I refuse to close it with regrets and what-ifs. I've carried the weight of unspoken words and unpursued dreams long enough. It's time to take bold steps, because the true tragedy isn't our ending. Instead, it's in the possibilities I never allowed myself to explore.

A door may close, but at least I can say I lived fully on this side of it with intention and courage.

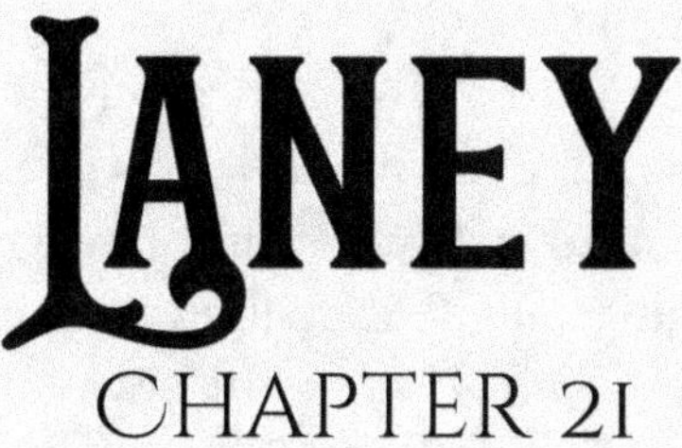

LANEY
CHAPTER 21

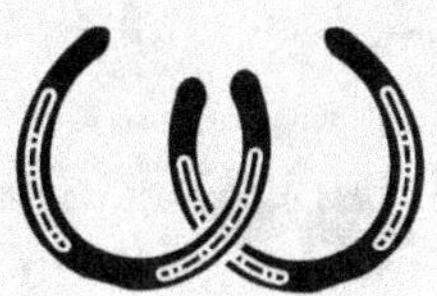

"You know that drink works better if you consume it," Syd taunts, gesturing toward my full glass.

I smile sweetly and take a drink. "Happy?"

"Um, that would be a no." She sets down her glass. "Lanes…" she draws out my nickname. "Come on, it's time for shots. I tried the whole take-it-slow, this-is-a-marathon-not-a-sprint approach, but you need to get drunker faster and get out of your head."

I absentmindedly swipe my phone open, and she steals it. "Hey, I need that," I whine.

"No, what you need is sitting right in front of you. You need to take the edge off, and besides, you didn't mention the exchange of numbers after your little bike ride home, so any number that could flash across this screen isn't one you need to worry about."

I take a long pull of my drink, letting the liquid burn down my throat. Between the conversation I had with Noah and riding home on the back of London's bike, my head has been a mess, and I've been struggling to focus. Noah's uncharacteristic silence is still gnawing at the recesses of my mind. He's never shied away from overstepping and voicing his thoughts. But after our talk… nothing. And the words he did give me felt measured. It could be the conversation I had with Asha and Sydney prior about his potential ulterior motives that has me overthinking all of it. Still, it remains on my mind, nonetheless.

Then there's London. His contradictions are giving me emotional whiplash. One moment, he's reminding me of his desire for me to leave town, practically shoving me out, and the next, there's something magnetic pulling us back together, something that makes my skin prickle with awareness whenever he's near. His dark eyes...they tell a different story than his words. Behind his steely onyx gaze, I catch glimpses of regret, of something that looks like an apology he can't bring himself to voice.

I know what happened between us. Out of all the people he could talk to in the world, I'm the one who could understand, the one who wants nothing more than to be his rock, but still, he pushes me away. I don't know what could be so terrible that he'd rather push me away than simply tell me the truth.

"Can I get two shots of your house bourbon, please?" Sydney asks the bartender with a bit of extra sugar in her tone.

"Yes, ma'am," the bartender replies smoothly, his green eyes holding hers a beat longer than necessary before his lips quirk into an easy smile.

"Is he flirting with me, or have I just been out of the game too long?"

"He most definitely noticed you," I confirm.

"Well, we might have to stay at this bar long enough for me to get a number. Did you see his eyelashes? I wouldn't be mad waking up next to that face for a long time," Sydney jokes. "But back to this." She waves her hand in front of my face. "You look sexy as fuck tonight, and your conversation with Noah the other night went to plan. You did what's always been on your heart, and he may not see it now, but you did him a favor."

I can't help but roll my eyes. She's exaggerating, and I know she's trying to make light of something heavy, but it doesn't change the bombshell he did give me.

"He wanted me to go home with him so we could live together," I remind her. "You realize, in his world, where he lives in the public eye, that's basically courtship. He was ready to take things to the next level."

"Again, that's not on you, Laney. Have you been walking a fine line between friends and lovers for some time? Maybe the two of you were off more than you were ever on, and we both know when you were off, he wasn't keeping his hands to himself." She pauses to take a drink of her old-fashioned, swirling the contents in her glass before adding, "Hell, his silence could have been because he was waiting for you to leave faster so he could call his back-burner chick. We all know she exists. It's only her name that changes every few months."

"I didn't ask him to stay celibate," I point out.

"I get that, but if he were serious about taking things to the next level, he wouldn't have been getting his dick wet elsewhere. Period."

"Two shots of Greenbrooke Reserve for the ladies," the bartender says as he slides our shots across the bar top.

"Where's mine?" Asha says, returning from the restroom.

"Sorry, can you bring us one more?" Sydney asks, this time leaning onto the bar to give him a better view of her cleavage.

I roll my lips to stifle a smile. She totally ordered two instead of three intentionally.

His eyes flick between her and Asha before settling back on her with a slow, sexy smile. "Coming right up."

"What did I miss?" Asha asks, pulling out a barstool to my right.

"I'm getting Laney drunk so she stops feeling bad about breaking off her engagement to Noah," Sydney exaggerates.

"Oh my god, you are being so dramatic." I slap her arm.

"Come on, it's time to let loose and celebrate."

"What exactly are we celebrating?"

She slaps the bar. "Summer and this delightful bar," she purrs, scanning the room. "Which is filled with hot men, in case the two of you haven't noticed."

"I'll be your wingman. It looks like Laney is about to have her hands full with a cowboy," Asha says, and I follow her gaze and find Trigg walking through the front doors with Fisher.

"One extra shot," the bartender slides Asha's third beside the two he brought seconds ago.

"Here's to getting back in the saddle and riding cowboys," Sydney cheers.

"Or two," Asha says with a wink, and we all toss our shots back.

"Remind me what the deal is between the two of you again?" Sydney leans in close so only I can hear.

We've discussed numerous topics over the past few days, and while Trigg has come up in conversation, it has been strictly in a platonic context. She knows the essentials, how Trigg and I first met, his initial interest in me, and his connection as London's brother. But unpacking all of that was complicated enough without revealing the deeper, more tangled layers.

"We're friends," I say with a casual shrug.

I haven't told her that Trigg and Asha are essentially using me as their unwitting double agent, each trying to extract information about the other through me. I have no plans of giving that information up anytime soon. While I've been pulled into Asha and Trigg's drama, it's not mine, and right now, I'm not even sure I plan on sharing the details I learn with them. During my conversation with London outside the coffee shop, he inadvertently confirmed what I'd been suspecting from the start when he said, "Marrying Asha would hurt Trigg." There's something between them.

"Uh-huh," she says knowingly. "If I thought you were a kinky bitch, I might buy that, but that's the extent of my lecturing for the night." She peers around me. "Asha, what's the next stop? Do any of these places have dancing?"

"Dancing?" Trigg questions, leaning onto the back of my stool.

"Yeah, cowboy, you know a spot?" Syd's amber eyes sparkle

with mischief. I love this side of Sydney. The carefree girl who just wants to have fun.

"Actually, I do, but we'd have to skip a few stops to get there," Trigg answers smoothly.

"Yes!" Sydney stomps her feet happily. "I just need to grab a number, and we're out." She turns around, looking for her bartender.

"And whose number is that exactly?" Fisher queries, rubbing his chin and sizing up the men in the vicinity.

"The hot bartender," Asha supplies.

"Jeremiah Greenbrooke? Nope, you can't date the competition," Trigg tosses in as though he has any say in the matter.

"Wait, Greenbrooke… He's an owner?" She taps a manicured nail on the bar top as she thinks it over. "Nah, doesn't bother me, and he's not my competition." She waves him down, and Fisher rolls his eyes.

"How is he competition?" I throw over my shoulder to Trigg. "We're at a bourbon bar."

"Guess you'll find out soon enough," he says ominously before turning to Asha. "Fairfield," he greets sardonically.

Her eyes narrow, fuming with madness, but she doesn't say anything back. Instead, she says, "I'll be in the car."

"No Dallas tonight?" I question casually.

"Nope, he had to work," Trigg confirms.

"It's Saturday night," I remind him.

"I'm aware." Then, with his lips next to my ear, his breath breaking over my skin, sending a chill down my spine, he says, "Careful, Laney. Keep that up, and I might think you miss him."

I don't bother giving him a reaction. Trigg knows we have history, and the more he thinks I care, the better. He doesn't need to know how deeply it's true. He asked me to un-break his brother's heart when he cornered me into doing his bidding. I'm not sure I can do that. Regardless, pleasing him helps me gather more of the missing pieces, so I leave it.

"I'm going to go wait with Asha," I say, getting off my stool.

"Wait." He grasps my elbow. "Does she really think I'm that bad?"

For a fleeting moment, his armor cracks. Beneath that arrogant façade, tight lips, and smoldering gaze, I get a glimpse of something raw and unguarded: vulnerability. I know what it's like to wear a mask and pretend as though you feel nothing.

"She doesn't talk about you, Trigg," I say, meeting his eyes. "So, you tell me."

A muscle twitches above his right eye; it's subtle, but I catch it. He may have preferred I tell him all the reasons she hates him as opposed to not being a thought. But I won't manufacture comfortable lies. Asha has shared very little about their tangled past, and I'm trying hard not to pry, to stay neutral in this war between them, because I think whatever started it is unfinished. This endless feud isn't driven by hate but rather by the phantom pain of what could have been.

"I'm going to go wait in the car with her," I say, chucking my thumb over my shoulder.

He gives me a single nod before deliberately shifting his gaze down the length of the polished bar.

I collect my phone off the bar, and no sooner than I turn around, I hear Fisher say, "Noah Donovan, long time no see. How have you been?"

I close my eyes and count to ten. This can't be happening. I made things abundantly clear to him when I told him I wouldn't be returning to Willow Creek and that there was no future for us. I was intentionally hurtful to ensure he understood this wasn't a conversation we were going to come back from. I wasn't going to entertain his phone call six months from now because I was lonely or needed someone with whom I felt comfortable. I was done. We were done. So why is he here?

"I've been better, but I can't complain too much. I'm done with school and going home to help manage the family businesses so my father can focus on his campaign." I finally chance acknowledging his presence, because I don't want to be rude. His eyes meet mine. "Can we talk?"

"I think we did that already," I say firmly but quietly. I don't want to draw this out any more than we already have.

He takes my hand and walks me away from prying eyes and ears at the bar. "You talked. I listened. Now it's my turn. I thought about it, and I think you don't know what you want. You've had years to tell me we were done, and you choose now to do it… when London's back. I don't think that's a coincidence."

Here he is. This is the man I expected to see when I showed up to talk after dinner with the girls. Instead, he gave me careful responses that told me absolutely nothing. This is the passionate speech I was expecting.

I sigh and close my eyes. This is my fault. I never meant to hurt Noah. I do care about him, but my heart is not in it. However, I don't believe his is either.

"Noah, I—"

"I want a week," he says, his blue eyes pinned on mine with resolute purpose.

"A week?" I raise a brow in question.

"Yeah, a week to show you I'm the man you want." He moistens his lip and reaches for my hands. "I'm the man who stayed."

I release his hands and smooth the front of my high-low white boho dress. "Noah, this has nothing to do with London. I'm not leaving you for London." I pinch the bridge of my nose, regretting my choice of words. "I can't leave you because we aren't now and never have been a couple."

"Hey, babe, are you ready to go?" Trigg surprises me, choosing that moment to stroll over and throw his arm around my shoulder. "I don't think we've met." He extends his hand in greeting to Noah. "Trigg Hale, the man she wants."

Noah's eyebrows shoot up, his eyes darting between me and Trigg. "Is he for real?" He puts his hands on his hips. "This is the same guy that sent you flowers?"

"Trigg, now is not the time," I say with a smile through clenched teeth. His little stunt is not doing me any favors.

"Oh, I disagree. I think now is the perfect time." His arm tightens around my shoulder, and I can see the wheels turning in Noah's head. Trigg doesn't have a clue who Noah is or what he did. He has no idea the shitstorm he's causing with this little spectacle.

I pinch my lips and turn to Trigg, pushing him back a step. "What are you doing?" I grind out so only he can hear me.

"We had a deal," he reminds me.

"Noah has nothing to do with that, and your brother knows you and I are not a couple."

"You told him?" he questions with a hint of intrigue.

"Not exactly," I say. I wasn't entirely careful with my words. I didn't outright tell him I was colluding with his brother or that there's no way I could actually entertain any kind of romantic relationship with Trigg. Still, because we have history, I'm sure he knows. "You'll just have to take my word on this one. He knows something is up."

"Plan changed. Dallas doesn't like him, so he stays," he says, looking over my shoulder at Noah, who is intently glaring back.

"I don't know what you're playing at, but I won't hurt London."

His lips curve into a smile that never reaches his eyes. He slides back to my side, his voice dropping to a murmur meant only for me. "I'm not asking you to hurt him, darling, but it's...revealing...that you immediately assumed that was my intention." His eyes lock with mine, unblinking. "Fascinating how quickly your mind went there."

He tricked me into an admission, one I've yet to fully comprehend myself. I can't hurt someone who feels nothing. But London...London still cares.

"Noah, wasn't it?" he calls out, his arm snaking possessively around my waist as he steers us toward the exit. "If you're determined to stick around, you might as well join us. You have that look of a man desperately in need of a stiff drink."

I don't argue as Noah falls into step behind us, his presence a constant reminder of an everything I've tried to leave behind. Some pasts don't stay buried no matter how deep you dig the grave. They follow you around, patient shadows waiting in the balance for the moment your new life falters. Tonight held the promise of escape. Now that's gone, and I, too, need a stiff drink because something tells me, by morning, nothing will be the same.

LONDON
CHAPTER 22

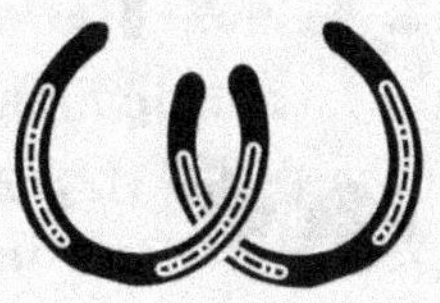

"What game are you playing, Trigg?" I ask when he joins me behind the bar to pour a round of shots for my friends.

"I have no idea what you're talking about," he says coolly, but because I know him, I can hear the hint of piqued peculiarity in his tone. Trigg is fully aware he's playing with fire. He just doesn't know how hot it is. "Hale's Cask is not a stop on the Bourbon Trail."

"I know," he says, deftly arranging shot glasses on a tray. "Sydney wanted to dance, and on Saturdays..." He sweeps his hand toward the back of the distillery where sliding glass doors lead to the outdoor event space where patrons dance on the burnished wooden floors, flanked by wrought-iron gas lanterns that cast an amber hue across the space. This place used to be reserved for cocktail parties and wooing Thoroughbred buyers, and now, every Friday and Saturday night, boot heels pound into the floorboards. "We have dancing."

I'm just about to call him out on his bullshit when Laney's eyes connect with mine across the dance floor. I can tell by the look on her face she had no idea I'd be here. Her blonde hair is in loose curls, falling over her bare shoulders. She's different now, but her eyes haven't changed. They're still that impossible shade of honeyed brown that, when locked on mine, makes time stop. But it's the amount of skin she has on display tonight that's making my pulse pounding heavy in my ears. She's still the sexiest fucking woman I've ever seen.

The bustling around the bar comes to a halt, and the music fades into a low hum as I remember the weight of her head against my chest as I spun her around a moonlit patch of grass beside the lake. She doesn't look away, and for a small moment, it feels like she's in the memory with me.

"Hey, cowboy," Madison says, stepping into my line of sight and breaking my momentary spell. "Mind making me one of your famous bourbon sidecars?" she says, making herself at home on a stool in front of me.

"Sure," I say, my eyes quickly flashing back up to Laney, who is now tossing back one of the shots Trigg brought everyone.

Madison turns around, glancing in the direction I had been staring before making her drink. "So, rumor has it, Trigg finally made things official with the horse whisper," Madison says with an excited energy that makes her words come faster than usual. I drop the glass I picked up to make her drink, and it shatters on the floor, grabbing the attention of everyone at the bar. Her head whips back to mine. "Are you okay?"

"Yeah, I'm fine. The glass was wet," I lie, not returning the gaze I know is squarely on me. I don't need anyone else prying into my emotions. I already have enough of that going on with Trigg and Fish. I grab the dustpan and broom we keep behind the bar for accidents. "I wouldn't believe everything you hear. The tall, preppy boy currently attached to her hip already occupies the space Trigg was vying for."

She turns back. "Really? I don't get couple vibes from those two."

Had Madison said any of this before my shift, I would have said I agreed with that assessment, but before Laney showed up here tonight, I was told she broke things off with Noah, and he went home. Yet, here he is, in all his Brooks Brothers glory, sticking out like a sore thumb. I'm unsure who is annoying me more—my brother or him.

Madison's eyes flick between watching them and me. "Laney Hart..." she says her full name, letting it hang thickly in the air between us, and my heart thuds hard in my chest, knowing the reason for her perfectly timed pause. She is connecting the dots—ones only she could know. "The two of you went to high school together?"

I shake her drink and try to keep my face impassive. I don't want to hurt Madison. She's kind, but I know where this line of questioning is going, and there's no truth that ends the way she wants it to. I could say we were neighbors growing up or that her best friend is my best friend's little sister, but they all sound like cop-outs, ways to skirt around the pieces Madison is putting together in her head. I respect her, and I don't want to give her half-truths that evade what Laney was to me, especially when I think she already knows.

"We did," I answer, holding her gaze to ensure she knows I'm fully aware of the direction her thoughts have gone. Her brilliant blue eyes dim, almost imperceptibly, before dropping to her glass.

We've always been casual, with no strings attached, but that's always easier said than lived. When you share yourself intimately, it leaves marks. She picks up her drink, and I leave her to sit with my unspoken truth. I care for her, but it can never be her. My heart can't unlove the girl who owned it completely. With or without Laney, it will always be hers.

I'VE BEEN WATCHING LANEY DANCE WITH ASHA AND SYDNEY FOR the past hour, my eyes never leaving her as my brother shadows her every move, his boots matching her rhythm just two steps behind her swaying hips. It's been pure torment witnessing the way his hand occasionally brushes her waist or how she tentatively listens every time he leans in to whisper something in her ear. That should be me. My touch. My words making her react. Not his.

But I've swallowed every bitter drop of jealousy because, across the room, Noah Donovan has been standing at his corner table, knuckles white around his beer bottle, looking like he might shatter it or someone's face at any moment. A misplaced primal satisfaction curls inside me. That's right... The thought crosses my mind as I watch his jaw clench when she tosses her head back at something my brother says. She'll always choose a Hale over a Donovan.

It's that ridiculous, possessive thought, so petty it should embarrass me, that drives me forward when I see her break away from the group to head inside. Before she can reach the bar, I catch her wrist, spinning her behind one of the massive steel support columns where the shadows pool deep enough to hide us from prying eyes.

"What do you think you're up to?" I demand, leaning into her.

"You really have to stop doing that," she scolds, catching her breath before adding, "I have no idea what you're talking about."

"Fisher said you and Noah aren't together," I get straight to the point.

"And how would he know?" Her eyes narrow as she smiles condescendingly.

"You think your best friend and my best friend aren't scheming? They're siblings, for crying out loud." Laney knows as well as I do they've both had a vested interest in our relationship from the start.

"What does it matter to you who I'm here with?" She nods toward the bar. "I'm not blind. I know that was Madison sitting at the bar." I want to set the record straight with her about Madison, but the last time I tried, she wasn't ready to hear it. When she's ready to listen, I'll tell her everything. I want to give her all my truths. It's why I pulled her aside to begin with, but when I don't reply, taking too long to figure out what's going on inside her head, she says, "If that's all..." She tries to dip under my arm and walk away, but I lower it and firmly pull her back, this time pressing my weight into her and securing her against the column so she can't run.

"You really need to stop touching me," her voice hitches, only solidifying this move was a mistake.

The second I pressed myself against her, I knew I'd made an error. It's already taken great strength to contain myself, knowing she's in the same town, living on the same road, with only acres separating us. Eliminating any space was never a good idea. I can't think straight when she's this close—never could.

"Friends touch each other." I make another fatal mistake, digging a deeper hole as her scent wraps around me.

"London." Her hands push against my chest, but there's no real fight behind them.

My hands find her wrists, circling them gently, feeling her pulse race beneath my thumbs. "Is it because you don't like it?" My voice comes out rougher than intended, barely above a whisper.

Her breath catches, and for a moment, we're suspended in the space between what we are and what we could become. The air between us feels electric, charged with everything we're not saying. Then, with the lift of her delicate hand, I get an answer. Her fingers hesitate before finally settling on my jaw, and the six years we spent apart suddenly collapse into nothing with her wordless answer. I revel in the way her fingertips flit over the stubble, her touch achingly familiar as they trace over new lines that hadn't existed the last time they were there. I lean into her with careful reverence, my hand gliding up the side of her neck as I rest my forehead against hers, and for a few stolen moments, we share the same breath. In the space between heartbeats, neither of us looks away, too afraid of shattering this fragile connection hanging between us.

With the distance between us eliminated, our bodies quickly remember the closeness our minds still fear. Her eyes drop to my mouth, and mine follow suit, fiending to remember the way they feel pressed against mine. Unable to fight the pull, I close the distance, my lips dusting over hers with such delicacy I'm not sure I didn't just imagine it. I pause and swallow hard as a distant voice echoes reminders of why I should pull away, but I don't. I don't want to stay away, but more than that, I don't think I can.

The next thing I know, her fingers are curled into the fabric of my shirt, and there's no more question of if my lips touched hers. Her mouth covers every inch of mine, and her soft, full, smooth lips, which I've longed to feel again, breathe new life into me, making me believe that we can get through this because the love we once shared isn't dead. It was never dead. We were lost—I was lost—but our love remained, changed but not broken, because that's what love does: it endures. With her fists twisted in my shirt, anchoring herself to me, she deepens our kiss, her tongue seeking entrance that I readily grant, desperate to taste.

The warm notes of bourbon oak and the subtle vanilla sweetness still linger on her tongue. My first taste is familiar and intoxicating, each gentle glide of her tongue against mine leaving traces of amber warmth, its heat spreading from her lips through my body, a slow, pleasant burn that has nothing to do with the proof and everything to do with the girl.

My other hand drifts to the curve of her hip, but before it can settle, an exterior door slamming down the corridor breaks our mouths apart. For a moment, neither of us move, both still processing everything that one kiss held. It was all there—the love that never fully died, the hurt that never completely healed, and the question neither of us has yet to ask: can we find our way back to each other? Or perhaps, the better question: does she want me back?

"I'm sorry." Her hand presses me back this time with a force that wasn't there the first time. She wipes her mouth in a move that pisses me off before adding, "You have a girlfriend."

I can't tell if she genuinely believes Madison is my girlfriend or if the idea of her holding that title is easier for her to latch onto. I didn't entirely disagree with the words she tossed at me the first time I tried to correct her: *'If you're with someone, then you're with them.'* I agreed with it to an extent, but it's the title part I firmly disagree with. If anything, titles mean more now. There's a greater emphasis on compatibility, values, and future plans when one exists. At this stage in life, girlfriend turns into fiancée and, eventually, wife. So, no, that was never going to be Madison, but to her credit, it was never going to be anyone. But something tells me Laney is familiar with the dynamic.

"And you have a boyfriend," I say pointedly. She wants to cast stones and make me out to be a villain, because that guy is easier to keep at arm's length. Too bad. After that kiss, I know her heart. It doesn't belong to Noah Donovan. It never has, and it never will. She rolls her lips and diverts her gaze. She was always shit at lying. "If Noah is not your boyfriend, why is he here?"

"I don't have to explain anything to you, London. He's a good friend," she defends, and it needles at my annoyance. I practically begged for his help that night. I'm just as guilty, but it doesn't change the fact that he wants more. "A friend that wants to fuck you."

This time, she doesn't look away, and I keep my hand firmly planted on the column behind her, my stomach in knots, knowing what she's about to say.

"You don't have the right to decide who I invite into my bed."

"You slept with him, didn't you?" I know it's true, but I need to hear her say it. My legs feel weak in a way they have no right to. I fucking hate that I did this to us. She's quiet, and I press on, needing to feel the pain of her confirmation. "How long?"

"London, stop. You don't get to do this. You left. What did you expect would happen? Did you expect me to stay celibate for the man who told me to stop writing him in prison? The man who stopped fighting for us?"

"You could have chosen anyone, and you chose him," my voice cracks with raw emotion.

She was mine, and he always wanted her, and while I knew

Laney loved me, jealousy and doubt are natural human reactions. There were times when I thought maybe she wanted him too. It may have been small, but in my mind, it existed all the same, and hearing that he had her the way that was only supposed to ever be mine is a blow to a heart I wasn't sure existed anymore.

"Laney, I swear to God, I was never trying to hurt you. Why can't you see that?"

"London, I don't know you anymore. The guy I knew wouldn't have chosen this for us."

"Tell me that kiss just now meant nothing. Tell me you didn't feel anything."

"What do you want from me, London? It can't possibly be that you want me back when you've asked me to leave more than once." Her eyes hold mine, and the fear that's gripped my heart for years returns. I want to tell her, but not here, not like this. She misreads my pause for something it's not. "I can't do this with you," she snaps, pushing me aside.

"Laney, wait. Can we talk?" I rush out.

"Oh, now you want to talk. Are you kidding me right now, London?" she says, running her hands through her tousled hair.

"I've wanted to talk to you since the second you showed up—"

"Could have fooled me." She crosses her arms dramatically.

"I deserve that," I admit. I'm the ass that pushed her away. "But I promise it's true. I only said what I did because we shouldn't talk."

"And you don't feel that way anymore?" she questions pensively.

"Yes and no, but the other day, you said something—something I've contemplated myself over the years—but seeing you again puts it in my lap. It can't be ignored. I didn't give you the choice back then, and I should have."

"This choice…" Her eyes focus on the floor. "This truth you've kept close, why give it to me now?"

"Aside from the fact that you deserve it? I don't think I'll survive losing you twice."

Her rich brown eyes snap up to mine, piercing through years of distance. For a breath-stealing moment, they search mine with the same intensity they once held, as if she's rediscovering something she believed was long gone. I stand perfectly still, afraid to move and shatter the connection where she seems to see what she used to: home. Despite the new town, the new name, and the painful years that have passed between us, my heart has never changed ownership. It never stopped beating for her.

In my raw, exposed gaze, recognition flickers across her face, and for better or worse, a spark ignites behind her knowing stare. It's one I've dreamed of countless nights, one where she sees my sacrifice and my mistakes and loves me anyway. But then her expression hardens, and her vulnerability is replaced with resolve.

"You don't have me," she says, her voice steady, gentle but harsh, as reality crashes into me, the weight of her words stealing the breath from my lungs, threatening to take me down.

I moisten my lips, her taste still lingering, reminding me of all the things I want most in this world, and I'm about to start with an apology and a question when Sydney rounds the corner, her heel catching on the uneven floorboard with a scrape.

"You and I"—she jabs a manicured finger into the space between us—"have a problem."

Her usually immaculate hair has escaped its pins in places, and there's a dangerous glint in her eyes. Damn it. My hands fall to my hips, and I pull in a deep breath to settle the anger that starts to burn hot. Fisher told her what I gave him in confidence. I can't say he told her everything, but she knows something. I've always been able to trust Fisher with my secrets. I should have known better with this one.

Laney shifts, putting distance between us. "He's all yours. He said all he wanted to." Her eyes hold mine, disappointment dimming their honeyed hues, and I clench my fists. She knows damn well that's not true. I know she feels everything I do. "Next round is on me. Don't keep me waiting," she says to Sydney. Then she's gone, weaving through the Friday-night crowd with deliberate steps to put space between us.

I cross my arms as the weight of my obligation settles on my shoulders under Sydney's watchful gaze as I wait for her to say something. There's a small chance that I got it wrong, and her brother—my best friend — didn't reveal the secret I've been holding onto for the past six years. Regardless, I deserve whatever lashing she wants to give me.

"I'm not going to waste time telling you what you already know. You fucked up. I'm not here to threaten you. You still look at her the same way you did the first time you brought her to my house when you were eleven years old, so I know..." her voice cracks with conviction, the weight of knowing my reason warring with the pain she knows I've carried every day. "I know it's tearing you up inside to live a life without her." She looks up and blinks rapidly to keep her tears from falling.

"Sydney—" I reach for her arm.

"No, I'm not finished. I love you, London Hale. You know you're family to me. We've known each other since we could walk, but I came over here to tell you if you think I'm not going to be pressure...you're wrong. You're on a clock. There's no outrunning it this time."

I nod in agreement before pulling her in for a hug. "I know, Syd."

I hold her tight and let my lungs fill with a breath of resolve. I knew from the second I saw her standing next to Trigg at the auction that I'd be laying my secrets at her feet. I've only been lying to myself, believing any of this could have any other ending.

This night has somehow stretched into eternity, one that's had me physically ill and mentally disturbed all at once. Noah has been MIA for most of it, thank fuck, and Trigg has backed off, choosing to watch the girls dance the night away from the end of the bar rather than their heels, but it's the watching that has me on edge.

My jaw has been set all night, my nerves on a slow simmer. When she first arrived and laid eyes on me, her dancing was slow and deliberate. She knew I was watching, and I know she liked it. However, after our kiss and the conversation that ended before I could say anything meaningful, she hasn't looked my way once.

Another man, the third one tonight, leans in, his hand fitting in the small of her back, splayed possessively as he pulls her in. It's nothing I haven't seen. I've watched her entertain a dance and push them away, choosing to let loose with Sydney and Asha. It's the smile on her face that has kept me behind the bar. I want to see her happy. But this guy isn't like the rest. He's either had one too many before he got here, or he thinks he can take what he wants without asking for it. Neither works for me.

Laney tries to push him back, her shoulders tense as her hands press against his chest, but he doesn't budge. Instead, his eyes narrow with a predatory focus as he tries again, this time pulling her into him with enough force that she stumbles against him. Her expression flashes from annoyance to alarm, and I see red.

The bourbon I was pouring floods over the rim, amber liquid cascading across the polished bar top, the bottle crashing to the floor as I vault over the bar in one fluid motion, my body moving on pure instinct as I hurriedly make my way across the bar. I catch him by surprise, one hand gripping his shoulder while extracting her in one swift movement, positioning her behind me before shoving him back hard enough that he staggers.

"What the hell?" he stammers, equal parts shock and fury flashing across his face.

"Take a hint," I growl, trying to keep my voice steady and not make any more of a scene than I already have. "She doesn't want to dance with you." I clench my fists at my sides hard enough that my fingernails bite into my palms.

His eyes flick from me to her, jaw tightening. He's too drunk, too proud to back down. "Are you with him?" he dares to ask her, dismissing me as if I'm not standing inches from him, ready to swing.

She steps beside me. "No," she says, her voice sharp and precise. "He's just the man picking up my tab tonight."

The words land like a slap, but I don't flinch. His clown friends mutter a few choice heckles, but I let them roll off me. My attention is already shifting because, by the time my eyes swing back to hers, she's pushing through the crowd, heading for the exit. I stand rooted, collecting a second to rein in my anger as I watch her retreat. Then, ignoring the assholes behind me, I follow.

The night air hits us both as the door swings shut, sealing off the thrum of the music inside. She's halfway across the parking lot, boots angrily crunching against the gravel, when it happens. The ankle she injured before gives out on the uneven gravel, and she falls forward, but I'm there before she can make it to the ground. My arms circle her waist, pulling her back against my chest before steadying her. For a moment, we freeze like that, her back pressed to my front. I can feel her heart racing, or maybe it's mine, the events of tonight leaving us both reeling as we try to navigate this new territory.

"You okay?" I murmur, not letting go.

She nods, but when she tries to put weight on her foot, she winces. Without hesitation, I sweep one arm beneath her knees and lift her into my arms. "What are you doing?" she asks, but her arms instinctively loop around my neck.

"Taking care of you," I answer simply. Her eyes search mine in the dim glow of the parking lot lights. This close, I can see the flecks of gold in her irises. Her lips part slightly, and for a moment, I think she might argue and demand I put her down. Instead, she relaxes into my hold, her body softening against mine. "Where's your car?"

"I don't have one," she answers, her tone losing the brass it had inside.

"Okay, who drove?"

"Hale," I hear Noah's voice boom from behind us, the noise from inside filtering through the door as he makes his exit.

"I don't want him to take me home," Laney says so only I can hear.

Fuck. Why couldn't he have stayed in the shadows a little longer? Part of me wonders if he wasn't waiting for this moment, one where he could say I finally caught you.

I turn around with Laney in my arms just as the rest of the crew makes their way out. "Put her down, London," Noah demands, as if he has any authority to.

"Sure," I grind out. "Just as soon as you tell me what car. Her ankle is giving her trouble."

I can tell it's on the tip of his tongue to offer to carry her, but shockingly, he keeps his mouth shut. There's no way in hell I put her in his arms, and I think he's too proud to be on the losing end of that war. Her eyes flash up to mine, disappointment flooding her face with yet another rejection from me, but it's not for the reasons she thinks.

"Laney can ride with us," Asha says, catching up to us. "She's staying with me anyway."

"None of you should be driving. I haven't served Noah since he arrived hours ago," I point out.

"Oh, we're not driving," Asha points to the Suburban parked at the back of the lot. "That's my driver, and that's our ride."

"I'll go with Asha and Sydney," Laney cedes.

I call out to Noah, who is standing beside his car a few yards away with the passenger-side door open. "She doesn't want you, Donovan." Sydney reaches the Suburban first, opening the back door for me to put her down. Setting her down, her warmth leaves my body before I'm ready to let it go. "Do you have your phone?" Her hands fall to her sides, plunging into the pockets hidden in her boho dress before nodding yes. "Prove it," I challenge with a plan.

The second her phone is out of her pocket, I send her my number via AirDrop. "Why are you giving me your number?"

"Because we're friends. If you need me"—I pull the seatbelt across her lap and click it into place before finding her face—"call me, and I'll be there, but I can't take you home ton—"

"I don't want to be your friend," she cuts me off before I can explain.

Her face searches mine with a mix of new emotions I can't place. I'm unsure of how to interpret their meaning. Are her words rooted in the same sentiments as mine? The other day, when she suggested we be friends, I couldn't bring myself to agree to the title because I want so much more. Is she saying she wants more, or does she want me gone?

"You heard her," Noah says suddenly, pulling the door wider and invading our moment. "She doesn't want to be your friend, Hale. You've done enough."

Her words and his tone set me off, and all the fucks I had to give disappear as I step into him and push him back hard enough that he loses his footing and falls to the ground. The sound of his body hitting the gravel sends a dark satisfaction through me.

Asha and Sydney shriek, my move catching them completely off guard as the night air now crackles with tension.

"You don't get to speak for her!" I roar as Fisher rushes to my front, pulling me back as Noah gets to his feet. Noah's eyes darken with a hatred I recognize all too well.

This is what he wants. He wants me to lose control, to become the monster everyone already thinks I am.

"You really want to go there," he challenges, the fury in his tone matching my own as his face flushes with anger and something that looks a lot like anticipation. "I don't mind an audience, Hale, but I think we both know the same can't be said for you."

The implication hangs between us like a blade. He's threatening to expose everything. Right here. Right now. The commotion has drawn the attention of a few patrons as they exit. I'm already going to hear about how I handled things inside from Baylor later. I don't need any more problems. And while I'm resigned to giving Laney every truth she deserves, it won't be while she's drunk in a parking lot under the watchful gaze of small-town folk eager to turn our misfortune into tomorrow's gossip.

"It's not worth it," Fisher says, keeping his arm extended across my chest, his fingers digging into my shoulder.

"You should listen to your friend, Hale. You wouldn't want to start something you can't finish." Noah's voice drops an octave, laced with venom, as he glances over his shoulder to Trigg, who's standing a few feet behind him, watching everything unfold beside Asha and Sydney.

I roll my neck from side to side, the vertebrae cracking like gunshots in the tense silence. Fisher's hand twists in my shirt, a silent warning. He knows I'm seconds away from losing my fucking shit, from crossing a line I can't uncross.

"She may not want to be my friend, Donovan," I say, voice dangerously low, "but I'm not the one she told to go home."

Something flickers across Noah's face. I pushed a button. Good.

"She's had years to tell me that." His head tilts to one side, a calculated gesture. "You don't find it peculiar she waited until now to do so?"

I run my thumb over my bottom lip, not bothering to hide the smirk pulling at the corner of my mouth. "If six years wasn't enough time to win her heart, I don't think it's gonna happen for you. If I were you, I'd pack my shit and leave just like she asked before we have a problem."

"Nah, I told you once, I play for keeps, and I don't lose." His words are confident but ignorant of reality.

"That's what you don't seem to get, Donovan. This isn't a fucking game to me. It's my life!" I say, taking a step forward and pounding my chest, my rage hitting a boiling point.

That's when my peripheral vision catches Laney's stare from the backseat of Asha's car. Her eyes are locked on me, quizzical and intense, dissecting every word and reaction as she tries to put together the pieces I haven't given her. The pieces that would destroy her world as surely as they destroyed mine. She deserves to know. But not like this.

I move to close the distance between us, but Noah beats me there, slamming the car door before saying, "Let me tell you what's not going to happen: you and her." His voice drops to a whisper as he leans in. "You may no longer fear giving her the truth..." He looks around before speaking low enough that only I can hear. "But tell me, are you willing to switch places with her that night?"

My blood runs cold. Through the window, I see Laney press her head against the seat. My eyes narrow on his, searching for a bluff. "You'd really do that to her?"

I took the fall. I disappeared. I erased a night, and I have no doubt his father helped cover my tracks and buried the evidence beneath layers of privilege and power.

"Try me, Hale," he spits. "You don't get to take the girl."

I meet his infuriated glare with heat that burns hotter than his. This isn't over, but for tonight, I'll let him have the last word. He doesn't need to know my intentions so that he can sabotage them. I can't think straight with adrenaline coursing through my veins, turning my thoughts to static. I don't think he'd reopen the case and put Laney on trial. He cares for her more than that. But discovering she's in the same town as me is a fresh wound, and his hate for me runs deep.

"If you make good on that threat, it will be the last thing you do," I say, my voice a warning. "I already live in hell. A cell won't change that." I hold his dark-blue gaze, ensuring there's no mistake that my words, unlike his, aren't an empty threat.

Then, turning on my heel, Fisher steps to my side. "Stay with the girls tonight," I tell him. "I don't need him pulling anything that can't be undone."

"Yeah, I was planning on making sure they got home safe anyway." Fisher's eyes search mine. "What about you? Are you going to be okay?"

"I haven't been okay in a long time. This is nothing new." I squeeze his shoulder. "Take care of the girls, and don't worry about me."

The weight of Noah's stare burns into my back as I walk away, each step carrying me farther from Laney but not from the truth that binds us. The night air fills my lungs, cold and sobering. I thought she was in my past. I've mourned the loss of her for six years, but what I'm finding is that the past doesn't die, and if that's true, it's not even the past. It's now.

LANEY

CHAPTER 23

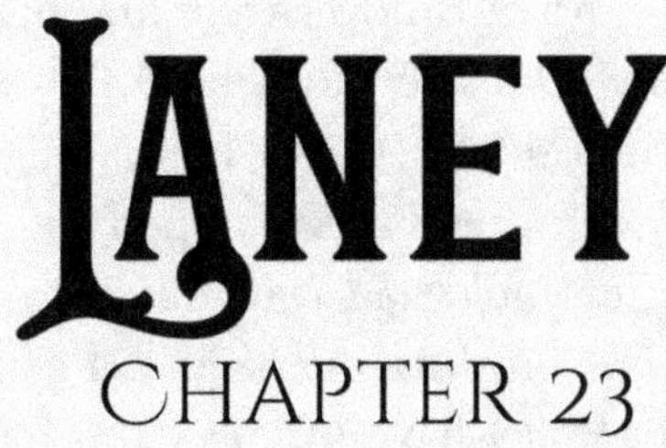

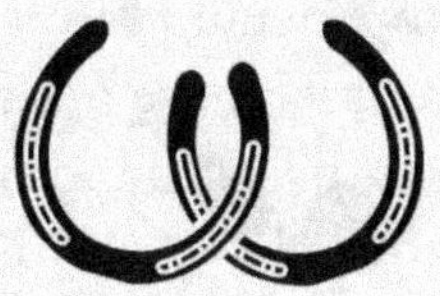

"Come on, Laney." Asha splashes me from the pool. "Get in. The water feels amazing…so good that you might even forget we have two baboons babysitting us."

"Hey." Fish throws his hands up. "What did I ever do to you?"

She rolls her eyes. "Sorry, Fish." Her eyes slide over to Trigg. "You, I'm not sorry."

I know why Fisher came back with us. He's Sydney's brother, and after what I heard London confess in the parking lot tonight, I wouldn't put it past him to have asked his best friend to see us home safely, but Trigg is a different story. He didn't like it when I told him Asha didn't think about him, and I think he's trying to see to it that changes. After tonight, many things that seemed hazy before are becoming clearer. Our loosely fake relationship isn't just about London. It's about her too. If he's with me, he has an excuse to see her.

"Seriously, Laney, get in here and make a memory. Let's end the night on a good note instead of the shit one the guys dealt us," she huffs out before putting her elbows on the edge of the pool.

"If I remember correctly, it was your scandalous dancing that caused a scene worthy of a rescue," Trigg tosses back.

"Are you serious? We were dancing together. Are you suggesting our outfits and our moves were an open invitation?"

"Not at all. I know it kills you to believe I'm not a misogynistic pig, but it wasn't your outfits. It was, however, your come-hither stare-down coupled with that French-tipped forefinger beckoning the next sorry fuck after you'd had your fun."

That makes my lips quirk to one side as I stare up at the stars littering the night sky. They have to know this banter disguised as hate isn't fooling anyone. I wonder if Asha's delayed clapback is because she caught the same detail I did. He's paying attention. A guy who wasn't looking wouldn't have noticed her manicure.

Her response fades into background noise as her mind drifts back to someone else who noticed me tonight. When Trigg and Fish showed up without London, I hadn't expected to see him. I assumed he'd heard I was going and decided he didn't want to go since he's been so adamant about my leaving, so I hadn't prepared for the way my heart would seize when our eyes met across the crowded bar, and I sure as hell didn't see that kiss coming.

My fingers instinctively trace over my lips as the memory of our kiss blazes vividly behind my closed eyes. What did it mean? Does he still feel the same electric current I do whenever he's around, that magnetic pull whispering *you're still mine* even though time and circumstance scream otherwise? Was it a mere habit, muscle memory from our past, or something more?

It was just one kiss. One single kiss. But that brief collision of our lips has me questioning if it holds the power to demolish everything I've built since we fell apart. The past can't be undone, but can it be rewritten, or am I fooling myself again?

My mind tortures me, recalling every second of his body pressed against mine, pinning me between his familiar warmth and the rough brick column that sheltered us from prying eyes. The way his hands cupped my face with a tenderness I'd forgotten then drifted down my body like he was memorizing me all over again. His soft lips meeting mine felt like a homecoming I'd been waiting for. I wanted to capture that moment, preserve it, and let it crystallize into the future I once dreamed about, but it was that thought that slapped me with a cruel dose of reality. We're not those people anymore. I can't let myself free-fall for London again without answers, without certainty.

That realization jolts me upright, and I pat my pockets, remembering how he AirDropped his number to my phone after he put me in the car, his body lingering above mine for a beat too long after he buckled me in. The thought of calling him has my palms sweating before they ever connect with my phone. I need to know if that kiss meant to him even half of what it did to me. I need to know if it's haunting his thoughts the way it's possessing mine and, more importantly, if he's aching to do it again.

The screen glows as I swipe open my phone, and simultaneously, a shadowy figure appears at the far end of the house. My heart rate instantly accelerates, believing it might be him stopping by to see that we made it home safely. But as he draws closer, the landscape lighting illuminates his silhouette, and I recognize Noah's familiar stride. My chest deflates with disappointment as a bitter resentment takes its place.

Fish and Trigg both rise from their lounge chairs when they spot him, my vigilant guardians after tonight's earlier confrontation, but I wave them off.

"I'm fine. Let me handle this," I say as I stand to meet Noah on the other side of the pool.

"Noah, I have nothing to say to you." I cross my arms, not just in defiance but as a shield. "You were completely out of line tonight."

"How so?" His voice carries that academic detachment I once found so appealing. Now, it just feels cold. "I didn't say anything that wasn't true."

"You made egregious insinuations," I state boldly. "I told you none of this was because of London. I'm not with him, but for some reason, you're obsessed with making this about him. Tonight, you were with us from start to finish. You saw for yourself I had no idea London would be at that last stop." I drag my hands through my hair, my nerves frayed. "It's like you're determined to believe I'm lying to you. I feel like you're fighting with a ghost."

"What is that supposed to mean?" Offense flares in his eyes, his posture stiffening.

"It means we're not in high school anymore." I gesture vaguely between us. "This isn't some competition with a trophy at the end, and tonight, you made it abundantly clear that's exactly how you see things."

"Is that what you think I was doing?" A complex mixture of bewilderment and hurt crosses his expression, softening his features in a way that makes my resolve waver, but only for a second.

"I don't know. You tell me." I take a step closer. "You keep tossing around accusations that my timing isn't a coincidence, while the same can be said about you. You had years to ask for more, years to ask me to move home with you, but it was only after you saw London that you suddenly took your shot."

"I was always going to ask you," he says with an honesty that resonates despite everything.

I don't think he's lying, and he isn't entirely wrong in his argument. My timing does appear arguably suspect, and yes, some of that can be attributed to discovering London was here in Bardstown, but not in the way Noah is accusing me. Seeing London forced me to stop running from the truth I've been avoiding for months: I was holding onto Noah for all the wrong reasons. He was never going to make me feel half of what a person should feel when love is real. Drawing things out was bad for both of us. Noah may have planned on asking me to move home all along, but somewhere along the line, his plans changed, just like mine.

"I believe you," I say, letting my defenses down just enough to show my sincerity. "I'm just asking that you believe me too. I was always going to say no."

Something hardens in his gaze. "I don't believe you."

"You don't have to, but you do have to accept my answer,

because it's not going to change." My voice remains firm even though my heart aches. I don't want to hurt him, but he refuses to listen, and I have to close this door once and for all.

He steps into me then, his height suddenly looming in a way it never has before. A darkness I've never witnessed crosses his face as the sound of pool furniture screeching across the stone patio cuts through the air.

"Back up, Donovan," Fisher's voice carries a sharp warning from the other side of the pool.

Noah's eyes stay locked on mine. "You have no idea what you're talking about, Laney. You've never been a game to me." He opens his mouth, as if he has more to say, then closes it, clenching his jaw so tight I can see the muscle twitch. He angrily runs a hand through his hair. "You want me gone? Fine. I'll fucking leave. But when you find out how wrong you are, I won't be there to pick up the pieces."

He lets the gravity of his words settle between us for another beat before turning on his heel and storming off, each footstep a punctuation mark on the end of our friendship.

I watch him disappear into the darkness, hating how everything ended between us. I never wanted things to end up this way, but it's the absolute conviction behind his belief that I am wrong that sends tendrils of fear and insecurity spreading through my chest. My feet move of their own accord, hurriedly rushing toward the back door.

"Laney, where are you going?" Sydney calls after me, her voice full of concern.

"I'll be back. I just need to grab something from my room," I answer without looking back, my voice steadier than I feel.

I just need a minute to breathe. And maybe my fingers are already reaching for my phone, making a call that will either save me or destroy me completely.

～

"Hello," London answers on the third ring.

It's 2 a.m., and I'm sitting on the cold wood floor beside my bed, where I've been for the past twenty minutes, mustering up the courage to make this call. I finally worked up enough strength to press the call button, but hearing his voice filter through reminds me I hadn't planned for what I'd say once he answered. Calling feels personal, and the last thing I told him was, "I don't want to be your friend." After I said it, his eyes flashed up to mine, and for a heartbeat, it felt like he knew what I was saying. *I don't want to be your friend because I can't. I can't when I want to be your everything.* However, our moment was cut short, and given the rollercoaster we've been on, I'm not sure where things stand.

"London…" I start, my voice unsure, a tremble he must pick up, because he cuts in.

"One hundred and ninety-seven," he says evenly.

"What?" I question unsteadily as I look at the moon outside my window.

"It's been one hundred and ninety-seven minutes since I gave you my phone number," he says, the gravel in his tone trailing off.

"I'm not sure if that means you wanted me to call or not."

"Two hundred and fifty-seven," he gives me more numbers, his voice carrying a little more strain. "That's how many minutes it's been since you kissed me."

My eyebrows shoot up. "Excuse me. It was you who kissed me. You're the one who pinned me against the pole, and it was you who leaned in."

"Relax, heartbreaker, I know who kissed who."

"Then why did you say that?"

"I just wanted to see if you were thinking about it too."

I press the phone closer to my ear and close my eyes. I've prayed for conversations like this one, where thoughts of wondering if he thought about me were answered, but now that I have them, I don't know what to do with them. The silence stretches between us like a physical thing, underscoring the years of separation.

"Are you okay?" he asks, the concern in his voice breaking something inside of me. After everything, he still cares. I may not know the details of why he made the choices he did, but I know they weren't made easily.

"It's late—"

"I'm sorry about earlier…" My chest tightens painfully as I immediately assume the worst—he's sorry he kissed me. But then he says, "I couldn't drive you home. I only had my bike, and I would never be able to forgive myself if something happened to you."

"Is that all?" I swallow hard, leaving no stone unturned.

"I'm not sorry I kissed you. If anything, I'm sorry I waited this long." I pull in a stuttered breath that I'm sure he hears through the phone. "Laney…" He pauses, and I listen as he takes a quickened breath. "Can I give you another number?"

"Yeah," my voice cracks with emotion as I collect this moment, one that's literally been years in the making.

"Two thousand two hundred and twenty-one," he breathes out with a sigh that matches the immensity of the number.

"I never knew you had a thing for numbers," I say to knock the tension down enough so I can breathe.

"I don't. I have a *you* thing. That's how many nights it's been since the last time you kissed me."

My eyelids flutter in sync with my heart. "You kept count all this time…" What feels like a million questions bombard me at once. If he kept count, he lived every day remembering, and if not a day has gone by where I didn't cross his mind, why subject himself to this? "Why?"

"It's complicated…but in short, I needed the reminder of what was threatening to kill me so that I could find the strength to continue walking down the path I chose." His voice catches. In the silence, I listen to the soft rhythm of his breathing through the phone.

"I don't understand," I say quietly, my fingers tightening

around the phone as if I could somehow grasp the meaning hidden beneath his words.

"I know you don't…" he trails off with a ruffled sigh. There's a heaviness to it, and I wish he'd open up. I wish he'd stop carrying more than he can bear alone. "Can you meet me for coffee in the morning?"

I hesitate, but only for a second. "Yeah, I can do that."

"Okay." A sigh of what sounds like relief filters through, loosening something tight in my chest.

"Okay," I echo his resolve, the word somehow both a whisper and a promise.

"Hey, Laney…" He says my name like it's something precious.

"Yeah." I press the phone closer to my ear.

"I'm glad you called." It's only four simple words, but they are the exact ones I need to hear. I dialed his number for a reason: I needed to know if he thought of me the same way I thought of him and if there was any reason for me to hold on. And for the first time in a long time, tomorrow feels like it holds infinite possibilities.

"Goodnight, London."

"Goodnight, heartbreaker." The nickname slides through the receiver like a caress, stirring memories I've tried and failed to bury.

After I hang up and rise to my feet, standing motionless beside my window overlooking the stables, I press my forehead against the cool glass, my racing thoughts settling. Tomorrow brings no guarantees, just coffee and conversation with the one person who knows me better than I know myself. The one person who still calls me heartbreaker, as though I hold that power, when all along it was my own heart I couldn't protect.

I crawl into bed, pulling the covers up to my chin. Tomorrow waits on the other side of sleep. Whatever path we've chosen, whatever complicated truths the morning light will reveal, at least we'll face it together. Two people finding their way back to a conversation that never truly ended.

"I'M BEGINNING TO UNDERSTAND WHY YOU SAID NO WHEN I initially asked you to work with Gypsy," Madison says, flanking me on my left as she rides up on London's horse, Titan.

"Yeah?" I say, eyes forward, where Fisher is riding alongside her sister, Abbey, and Gypsy.

"It's hard to control the environment when you don't have your own space," she says, looking behind us where I know Trigg, Asha, and London are trailing. "I should have known the guys would want to tag along the second they saw us tacking up the horses."

"Don't worry about it. The main focus is Abbey and Gypsy. As long as they aren't bothered, that's all that matters. Focusing on their bond and strengthening it is important."

I was surprised when Madison called me earlier in the week to schedule a trail ride. After my initial assessment, I took a few days to research what I thought might be the root of the issue they were experiencing in the arena, and I knew it wouldn't be an easy conversation. The problem isn't with Gypsy. It's not something that can be corrected through training. The issue is Abbey, and only Abbey can fix it.

"I owe you an apology," she says as she leans forward to rub Titan's neck. "I reacted poorly after you told me your suspicions about Abbey, but I just want you to know it's not because I don't respect your opinion. It's because I didn't want to lose my best friend. Vaulting has been our thing since we were kids..." she draws off, and I can hear the pain in her voice as she battles the reality that if Abbey can't trust Gypsy, all their hard work might come to an end. It's easy to overlook the lunger in a vaulting duet when all eyes are focused on the horse and the person performing acrobatic routines on its back as it canters. Still, Abbey's anxiety can be felt every bit as much as Madison's. "I'm just not ready to let this go. I love what I do, and I know Abbey does too, but if she can't get over her fear, then—"

"Listen, the fact that Abbey showed up today, that she's here and willing to try, is a good thing, and while my assessment may have been a hard pill to swallow, that could have been exactly the push the two of you needed. Now that there aren't any secrets between the two of you, you can focus on what's next and healing your bond."

"How did you learn about my fall?"

"Well, after watching your routine in the field, I didn't observe anything that stuck out, so I thought I'd try to find some clips online from around the time you said the issue started, and the first thing that came up when I Googled you was your fall. I didn't think it was a coincidence that, shortly after that, Gypsy's performance in the arena started changing too. That was a nasty fall, Madison. You got lucky. That could have been more than career-ending. I understand why Abbey is nervous. She doesn't want you to get hurt."

She's quiet as she adjusts herself in the saddle, something I said not settling with her, though I'm not sure what. Discussing her fall could be the culprit, but I get a feeling it's not. The air between us thickens with each passing second of silence.

"I see. I just didn't know if someone told you, is all," she says with a shrug.

Someone like London, I think to myself as anxiety coils in my stomach. I know there's something between them, and I hate feeling like the other woman, but what's more, I hate not knowing what something is.

"I should probably catch up with Abbey and see how she's doing." My words hang between us, an obvious deflection.

"Hey, can I ask you something? It's not about horses," she asks.

"Sure." I adjust my hold on the reins and relax my hips to keep pace, bracing myself for whatever's coming.

"How are things going between you and Trigg?" Her question slices through the facade of casual conversation.

I tense a little at her question. "Trigg and I aren't dating."

"Because of Dallas?" I risk glancing in her direction. When

my eyes meet her cold blues, I get a sense of knowing, but to my understanding, she's not aware that London and I have any history. Hell, she still believes his name is Dallas. I let that last thought calm my anxiousness.

"No, it's something else." I open my mouth to offer more and think better of it, the unspoken truth burning my tongue.

"Oh," she says plainly, her face a careful mask, making it hard to interpret how my answer was received. Is she fishing because she suspects something between London and me, or is she genuinely curious? Her eyes flick to mine too quickly, too deliberately. She nods up ahead. "So what's Fisher's story?"

"What do you mean?"

"The two of you seem close. Is there something going on there?" Each question feels like she's circling closer to a truth I'm desperate to hide. Not because I want to, but rather because I don't know how revealing anything unravels the lie London has crafted to protect himself. I never made it to the coffee shop this morning.

"Wow, you are super interested in my love life," I laugh and try to play it cool when, inside, I'm anything but. My laugh is so fake, even I can hear its nervousness.

"I'm sorry, I didn't mean anything by it. I'm just trying to piece together how everyone fits." But it's her eyes that contradict her casual tone. "He's never talked about home, and suddenly, the whole town seems to be showing up."

"Hey," a voice I've been cautiously avoiding all morning rides up on my left, and my pulse skyrockets. "We're going to stop at the lake up ahead. Give the horses a break," London says, his eyes studying mine with alarming intensity before sliding over to Madison. "Everything okay?" he says to no one specifically, but I can hear the nervousness in his voice, the kind that comes from interrupted secrets.

Does he think we were talking about him? If so, why does that make him nervous?

"Madison," Trigg rides up on her left. "Race you to the lake," he challenges.

"Oh, I don't know…" she answers, seemingly uninterested, before a smirk pulls at the corner of her lips, and she's yelling, "Ya," squeezing her legs tight and nudging Titan forward. She gets a three-second lead before Trigg takes off.

I turn back to Asha, who simply rolls her eyes. Trigg didn't have to come back to Fairfield with us last night. In fact, if Mr. Fairfield had caught him, I'm sure there would have been hell to pay this morning, especially if he had seen them passed out on the same oversized lounge chair.

Asha was grilling me for information this morning as I was walking out to meet London when Madison pulled up. Seeing how frazzled she gets around him and knowing what's going on behind the scenes between the two families had me seconds away from spilling things I had promised others I wouldn't. But when I asked her to tell me what had happened between them in the past, she deflected. I know she's keeping secrets, which is why I'm holding onto mine. Plus, she volunteered to come today, knowing exactly where I'd be going and who she might run into, and that says something.

"You didn't show up for coffee this morning," London says smoothly, his gravelly tone making tiny hairs prickle with awareness.

"I know. I forgot I promised Madison I'd go on a trail ride today with her and Abbey to finish Gypsy's assessment," I say, keeping my eyes forward, too scared to meet his gaze.

"You could have called," he says, as though it was the obvious solution.

"You haven't been someone I could call for a long time," comes out easily, my tone harsher than I feel.

"I'm sorry," he says, achingly genuine.

"Sorry doesn't fix things." I swallow hard, hating the reality of the past six years and the distance it's put between us.

"I'm not trying to fix anything," he says squarely.

My eyebrows rise, and I feel a flush rush my cheeks. I anxiously adjust my hat. I thought that's why he wanted to meet today—to fix things, to talk about everything that's happened and where we stand.

"Don't do that," he scolds, his voice dropping an octave.

"What?" I question, a little irritated. I'm tired of feeling off balance, like I don't know which way is up or down around him. The whiplash is utterly dizzying.

"Come on, Laney. I know you." His eyes burn into mine with an intensity that makes my stomach flip. "You're in your head, believing I'm not right where I want to be, with the person I want to be with."

"Oh, I believe you're where you want to be," I say flippantly, and his eyes narrow on mine, their spark dimming subtly with the jab behind my comment.

He rolls his lips before saying, "Trying to fix something insinuates something is broken. You're not broken. I'm not trying to put you back together and make you whole. You're whole on your own. Always have been." His gaze lingers on my mouth as he speaks, and I have to resist the urge to touch my lips.

His words wrap around my heart and squeeze tight. It's unfair how time and circumstance have done nothing to diminish how hopelessly in love I am with this man.

I clear my throat, trying to steady myself against the magnetic pull I feel toward him. "So the talk…"

"Is still something I want to have." His eyes stray from mine only to slowly drag down my body, taking their sweet time before meeting my gaze again. The heat in his stare makes me shift in my seat.

"With a purpose of…" I wait for him to fill in the blank again, hyperaware of how his presence seems to fill all the space between us. I thought coffee was going to be an apology, and since I was wrong, I want to make sure I'm not letting my heart run away with what it wants to hear instead of what is.

"It needs to happen. I owe you an explanation. I owe you a lot of things, but we should probably start there." He leans forward slightly as a gust of wind wafts his familiar scent toward me, and my resolve wavers.

Do I want explanations? Yes. But I also want to know if there's a chance at more. Last night, he admitted he's thought about me every day the same way I have him, but where does that leave us?

"Is that all?" I attempt nonchalance but fail.

He smiles. It's slow and devastating before he purses his plump lips to gain composure. The simple gesture sends a wave of heat spiraling through me. "For now," he says, but there's a promise in his voice that suggests 'for now' might not last very long.

The space between us crackles with everything we're not saying, everything we're both too afraid and too desperate to acknowledge. Six years of distance hasn't dulled this pull. If anything, it has only made it more dangerous. We're no longer the people we were, but sitting here, drowning in his familiar gaze, I'm terrified to discover that some things never really change.

LONDON

CHAPTER 24

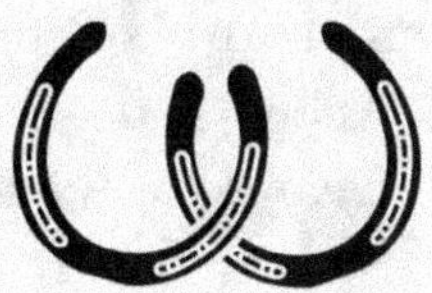

"We need to talk," I say, approaching Trigg from behind as he tacks up his horse.

"What did I do now?" he asks sarcastically, and it rubs me the wrong way.

I never knew he harbored any resentment for me coming here. He's always been easygoing, but all relationships are challenged at some point, and now I'm starting to question if his agreeable attitude wasn't a cover for the things he keeps buried deep. I wouldn't judge him for keeping things to himself. I'm the last person with room to talk. However, I'm unsure whether I'm part of the problem or an easy target. It's true that it's the people we love the most that get caught in the crosshairs of the battles we wage war on within ourselves. I pushed away everything I cared about most, and now I see it was one of my biggest mistakes. It's why I don't want to see that become our story.

"I know about the lease," I say and watch as his knuckles turn white as he tightens the cinch. That tells me all I need to confirm my suspicions about his sudden interest in Laney. I don't know to what extent he's using her, but I don't like it.

"I have no idea what you're talking about," he grinds out—

another lie. I can hear the anger in his tone. I just gave him an intro, and I don't understand why he's not taking it.

"I won't marry Asha." I toss it out there, hoping to cut through the tension and get to the core of what I believe is twisting him up inside.

"Didn't know you were thinking about marriage," he says without missing a beat, but I hear the slight respite in his tone all the same.

"I haven't in a long time," I admit right before a distant scream slices through the thick air. I turn on the spot and spy Fisher sitting on a blanket with Abbey and Madison, and my anxiety spikes as my eyes frantically search for the girls.

"There." Trigg points. "On the other side of the lake by the tree line." My eyes immediately zero in, and I spot Laney and Asha running toward the lake.

Fisher rises from the blanket, his eyes panicked when they lock on mine. "Bees."

"Fuck," I curse as I immediately start hurtling toward the lake.

"It's just bees," Trigg says, hot on my heels.

"Laney is allergic to bees."

"How allergic?" he pants.

"Deadly." My heart thunders in my chest, its beat matching the pace of my feet.

"Is Asha allergic too?" he questions as they both dive beneath the water.

"No idea," I say before bounding off the dock and leaping into the water. I pop up for air and open my eyes, searching for Laney, who keeps bobbing below the surface. "Did she get stung?" I call out to Asha, who's pushing her hair back, eyes wide.

"I don't know," Asha says, wiping the water from her face.

"Are you allergic too?" Trigg's labored tone breaks over the sound of his breaststroke feet behind me.

"No, I just didn't want to get stung."

I'm feet away from Asha, and Laney hasn't popped back up. My heart is hammering, my breaths are labored, and now I feel like I might drown as memories of the night she didn't come back up assault my senses.

"Laney!" I shout her name, panic gripping my chest. I have no idea how deep this old farm lake is or what may be at the bottom, creating obstacles that could cause her to get stuck. Hysteria slowly starts to rise as Trigg and Asha shout her name beside me, each of us treading water in circles. I open my mouth, ready to scream her name again, when the sound of a gasp breaking the water catches our attention as she pops up right beside the dock.

Her chest is heaving when her rich chestnut orbs connect with mine before she ducks beneath the dock.

"Christ." I slap the water, relief flooding my veins before I say, "I'll get her. It looks like a pop-up storm might be rolling in. Get everything ready to head back."

"Sure." A bee buzzes by, and Asha screams. "Oh my god, you have to stop screaming like that," Trigg informs her.

"Well, now that I know it annoys you. I might make it my new habit."

"Oh, I never said it annoys me," I hear him say before I disappear underwater to find Laney.

The next time I pop up for air, I'm under the dock.

"Ouch, shit," she hisses, releasing one of the beams and shaking her hand.

"What is it? Did you get stung?" I quickly grab hold of the beam beside her and take her hand.

"No, it's just a splinter," she manages with a sharp intake of breath as I carefully examine it myself, relief flooding through me as my racing heart slowly returns to normal.

"Wrap your legs around my waist," I command, my voice rougher than intended as treading water becomes secondary to keeping her close.

"I'm not doing that. I'll be fine." She attempts to pull her hand away, but I hold it tighter, my thumb tracing over her knuckles.

"You can listen, or I can make you listen." My eyes lock onto hers, and I see the exact moment her breath hitches. The challenge in my voice makes something flicker across her face—defiance mixed with something darker. "You just nearly gave me a heart attack. I'll be damned if I'm letting you go."

"And how exactly do you plan on doing that underwater in a lake? I'm not scared of you, London Hale—"

Her words dissolve into a sharp intake of breath the second I release her hand, only to slide mine around her waist with deliberate slowness. The water makes her skin impossibly soft under my palm as I pull her closer, eliminating every inch of space between us. My fingers splay across her hip bones before trailing around to her back, mapping the curve of her spine as I sink lower, over the swell of her ass.

I take my time, savoring how her body responds. The way she trembles despite the warmer water, how her lips part slightly when my hand finally reaches the back of her thigh. When I lift her leg and guide it around my waist, her other leg follows instinctively, and suddenly she's wrapped around me completely.

The sensation nearly undoes me. Having her like this, pressed against me, her breath coming in shallow pants against my neck, has been fuel for every fantasy since I was old enough to have them. The water laps around us, but all I can focus on is the heat radiating from where our bodies connect, and the way her fingers have found their way to my shoulders, holding on tight like she's afraid of letting go. Her eyes are fixed on my mouth, and I can see the war inside of her. It's the same one raging in me. Want versus restraint. The knowledge that we're crossing a line versus skirting the magnetic pull that's always existed between us.

"Still not scared," I tease in hopes of lightening the mood and tempering my desire. But my voice comes out strained, betraying exactly how much control I'm losing. The space between us has become charged, every point where our bodies touch underwater sending heat spiraling through me. Her fingers dig into my shoulders as she adjusts her position, and the movement makes us both freeze, the intimacy of our entanglement suddenly impossible to ignore.

"Nope," she breathes, and fuck if she doesn't up the ante by locking her ankles behind me with deliberate intent.

The electricity crackling between us becomes a living thing, as this is no longer an implied situational intimacy. She just crashed through the façade and pressed her pussy against my hard cock with one swift move. The way her chest rises and falls in sync with mine tells me her thoughts are wholly consumed with the same hunger coursing through my veins. We're so close I can feel each erratic breath brush against my mouth like a whispered invitation.

I bring my lips closer, every instinct screaming at me to close the distance, to finally claim what's been mine all along. But another desire, deeper, more primal, wrenches me back at the last second. My nose skims hers, the contact sending shockwaves through both of us, before I force myself to speak.

"Let me see your hand."

I can't help it. Her safety and well-being have always taken precedence over everything else. Ever since the first day, I've always had this innate need to take care of her. It heals something inside of me. Taking care of her feels like taking care of myself, and now that I have her back, I know it's because the heart that beats inside of her is the other half of mine.

She gives me her hand, her heated eyes never leaving mine. The last thing I want to do is turn away. I could stare into her honeyed pools for a lifetime, and it still wouldn't be enough. In her eyes, I am home. I see the man she wants me to be—her man. I find the spot between her thumb and forefinger where the wood punctured her skin, and I bring it to my lips, drawing her skin into my mouth, and her hips ever so slightly flex against mine with the force of my suction. My eyes slide up to hers, desperate to see if the ecstasy that once existed when my mouth was on her still exists.

When our eyes connect, I see desire, aged and different, its intensity unmatched by wisdom that could only be gained from the time we've spent apart. Not only does she like the way I'm making her feel, she's letting herself feel it without reservation. I suck again and watch her eyes darken with each swallow, and I grow harder. White-hot desire deliciously shoots down my spine, and I'm fully erect and ready for her to feel what she's doing to me every time her heels press into my ass as she rocks against me. I suck her hand hard one last time, certain I did my job and sucked the shallow splinter from her skin, before releasing it altogether. I swiftly switch arms, relieving the one that's been holding the beam, and wrap the other securely around her waist, ensuring there's no mistaking what's happening between us.

"London," her voice hitches. "We shouldn't."

I lift and thrust against her. "Use your words," I say, bringing my mouth dangerously close to the lips I want to feel against mine again. "Tell me to stop."

Her eyes hold mine, and I can't be sure of all I see in their depths. All I know is, at this moment, she isn't pushing me away. For now, hidden away from the world, she's mine again. I press into her again, and she sucks her plump bottom lip into her mouth. It's sexy as fuck, and I want to chase it. I want to suck it into my mouth, but I wait. I'm currently getting more than I ever thought I'd have again. I slide my hand down her back and grab her ass hard on the next thrust, and the sexy little whimper she tries to stifle has me going again, harder, creating waves in search of another. Her eyes close, and I keep pace, grinding against her in long, hard strokes, watching the ecstasy flit across her face and reveling in the knowledge that I'm putting it there.

Instinctively, my head drops to the crook of her neck the way I know she likes, in search of the delicate skin beneath her ear that makes her break out in goosebumps every time my lips are near. The way her body feels pressed against mine, the fire spreading through my veins, feeling her desire for me again…it's consuming.

My lips connect with her soft skin, and the trance is broken. "What about my splinter?" she pants.

"The splinter was out when I asked you to use your words." I pull back, needing to see her eyes, needing her to acknowledge what's happening between us. Her gaze wavers and then meets mine with a vulnerability that takes my breath away. Although we haven't spoken about everything that's happened and all the things that have changed, a soul-deep recognition passes between us—the same connection that has always existed, transcending the limits we put on our relationship. What has happened and what is to come are insignificant because we are right where we are supposed to be.

Our mouths slowly inch together when thunder cracks overhead, and Trigg yells, "Dallas, come on. We need to ride out."

"Shit, I forgot about the storm. We need to get out of here." Her eyes widen, and she nods. "The bees should be gone, but do you have your Epi-pen?"

"Yes, it's in my saddlebag."

"I'll duck out first, and when you feel me squeeze your hand, follow me out." She nods, and I slip beneath the surface, mourning the loss of our sanctuary—that stolen pocket of peace where the world's chaos couldn't touch us. But as I surface, hope flickers. If we can find moments like this, maybe we can find more. Maybe what we once had is still alive. Maybe it's strong enough to weather the storm.

When we reach the bank, I raise my hands and wave the others on as the first heavy drops begin to fall. We're already soaked, no one's hurt, and there's no sense in everyone getting caught in what's coming. Fisher catches my signal and gives me a quick wave before spurring his horse away with the group.

Thunder bursts overhead with enough force to vibrate through my chest and into the ground beneath us. In the distance, Laney's horse rears and whinnies, spooked by the sound. He yanks against his tether, and the rope snaps before he bolts into the storm.

You've got to be kidding me. I know exactly what she's going to say.

"London, we have to go after him."

I don't bother saying, "No, we don't." We don't have time to argue, and I need to get her out of the storm. I'm not worried about a bit of rain. I am, however, concerned about lightning and hail if the conditions worsen.

"We will," I promise, catching her hand before she can run after the horse. "After the storm passes."

"Lon—"

"No." My grip tightens. "I get you safe first. Then the horse."

Something in my voice stops her protest. Her shoulders sag slightly. "Okay."

BAYLOR'S HORSE, REINHOLD, RIDES INTO THE BARN SECONDS before we hear hail begin pelting the metal roof. We are soaked to the bone after jumping into the lake and riding back in the rain, and I'm about to lose my mind. The mix of adrenaline still coursing through my veins from jumping into the lake and then riding to beat the storm mixed with the lust is a mindfuck. Riding back with her ass firmly pressed against my cock after the scene that unfolded under the dock has immensely distorted my better judgment, and I can't be held accountable for what happens next. She's the only girl I've ever wanted. I should find my way back, regain my resolve to stay strong and say no before pursuing what I want. I should give her every sordid truth first, but the second she puts her hands on my shoulders for me to lift her down, all my good intentions are gone, and my mouth is crashing to hers as I back her into a stall and against a wall.

I don't care where things stand between her and Noah. She's supposed to be mine. Besides, if she doesn't want this, she could end all of it right now, and I'd let her go, but she's not. The way her tongue is battling against mine and taking its fill tells me she wants this too, and fuck if I wish she didn't, because I can't stop, even though stopping is what I should do. Letting this continue will only hurt worse when I have to let her go for the things I can't undo. It's that thought that has me finding a mustard seed of willpower to pull away. My lips leave hers, parting for less than a second, when a groan of disappointment escapes her sweet mouth, and I snap.

Instead of pulling away, I'm lifting her and pinning her to the wall so I can press my hard length right against her core. Our tongues and teeth clash, hungrily fighting for more, for a closeness that can't come from stolen kisses and my strategically placed hardened length, but I push forward anyway, picking up right where we left off beneath the dock. This time, when my lips trail across her jaw and down to the spot on her neck that I know drives her crazy, she doesn't get scared. Instead, she turns her head, giving me better access—an invitation to keep doing exactly what we're doing.

Her hands glide down my sides, blazing a new trail, reacquainting herself with the same map but with different markers. Those soft hands I swear I've felt ghost over my torso in my sleep the way they once did find the hem of my shirt, where they slowly test the waters, seeking permission to make this more. I don't stop her. I couldn't if I wanted to, but the second my shirt is off, and her eyes scan over my bare flesh, I find the strength to say, "Heartbreaker, are you sure this is what you want? Because if it's not, you need to tell me now. If this goes any further, I won't be able to stop."

"What gave you the impression I wanted to stop?"

The storm outside hammers against the metal roof with a savagery I've lived with every day since I left Willow Creek, but it's that cruelty that pushes me forward. My lips brush over hers. "We haven't talked."

She shakes her head. "Talking doesn't change that I want this."

That's all I need to hear to throw caution to the wind and abandon my willpower to stop. Her hands on my body, my rough skin pressed against every soft curve as her mouth devours mine, the passion behind her kisses mirroring mine, and time ceases to exist. The storm outside is washing away every doubt that this can't be the start of something new, something better than what we had before. The thunder shakes the earth, and we're a beautiful mess of skin and bones. With every crack of lightning that illuminates the darkened barn, every vibration, something shifts between us, something wild and honest, something unafraid.

Everything is fast and slow all at once. One moment, she's clothed, and the next, she's naked in my arms, and before I can overthink it, I dip my hand between us and free myself from my jeans. Her legs wrap around me, and when my tip nudges her warm, wet entrance, my stance falters. "God damn," I pant, bracing myself on the wall. I'm not even inside of her, and she has me weak at the knees. I push through the emotions that want to tether me to this moment and make it more than it is. Until she knows everything, I have to guard her heart. Making love to her will only make it all worse. For that reason, I slam in. She whimpers, and I kiss her collarbone as I catch my breath. "Did I hurt you?"

"No," she answers through labored breaths. "Don't stop."

I grip her ass and lift, finding just the right angle to use the wall to help anchor her weight and find my pace. I pull back and repeat the move, savoring the long stroke of feeling her wrapped around me as I'm balls deep inside of her.

"Fuck, why do you have to feel so good?" I growl before sliding in again, the sound of her wetness sucking me in, saying without words that I do to her exactly what she does to me, spurring me on as much as it pisses me off. When I've weighed the risks in every scenario where she runs, I let her go. I let her go because if she goes, it's what she needs to be happy, but fuck if I'm not reconsidering that stupid train of thought.

Her hips meet every one of my thrusts, her heels digging into my ass, pressing me inside, holding me where she wants me like she wants this to last the same way I do.

"The things that aren't good for us always feel the best." Her words give me pause, and I find her eyes. "Just pretend I'm another warm body, like any other you've used to replace me."

Did she really just fucking say that? "Another warm body?

You could never be that, and you know it," I grind out, unable to let her pile on another lie. We're drowning in enough of them.

I still feel her in my skin and bones. Not a day has gone by where I haven't carried her with me. Warm bodies are there to fill a void, one her absence carved inside of me. I wasn't supposed to ever see her again. She was supposed to be living a beautiful life without me. But she isn't just another warm body. She bites the corner of her mouth, and her fingers dig into my shoulders.

"Just finish what you started."

Her words hit hard, and I feel them everywhere, burning through my chest and making my pulse race. She's lying to me, to herself, to whatever we still have left. I can hear it in her voice, even when she's trying to sound like she doesn't care. I hate this. Hate the way we're acting like what we had doesn't matter anymore. Her voice sounds cold and distant, but when she speaks, I hear its tremble. She's scared, just like I am.

My hands are too rough, moving too fast. I'm being selfish, taking what I want instead of giving us what we need. I know it's wrong, but I can't seem to slow down. This isn't how we used to be together. We used to take our time, touch each other like we meant something. Now we're both fighting while we're trying to love each other. She says cruel things to push me away, and I respond by being too aggressive, too demanding. We're hurting each other in the worst way possible, and underneath it all, I can still feel how much we want this. How much we want each other.

We're barely holding on. Every word, every touch could be the thing that breaks us for good. But even as we're tearing each other apart, even as we pretend this doesn't mean anything, I know we're both terrified. If we stop pretending, if we let ourselves feel everything we used to feel, we might not be able to handle losing it all over again.

My grip tightens, fingers pressing into the curve of her ass, feeling the strength in her body, the way she fits against me like she was made for me. The thought hits me hard, and I can't shake it loose. Maybe I don't get to keep her. Maybe I've already lost any right to call her mine. But I'll be damned if she's going to forget this…if she's going to forget me.

So I pour everything I can't say into the way I touch her, into every movement, every kiss. All the words I'm too scared to speak, all the love I'm too broken to admit. If this is all I get, if this is the last time she lets me close enough to matter, then I'm going to make sure it burns into her memory the way she's burned into mine. I thrust inside, fast and deep, her moans increasing to borderline screams that have me on the edge of coming. Were it not for the storm outside, I'd have to cover her mouth. I've never particularly enjoyed it when my partners were vocal, and now it's abundantly clear that it's always been because they weren't her. I love every intoxicating crescendo.

Her pussy starts to choke my cock like a vise. "I'm going to come."

"Fuck yeah, you are. Come on my cock, heartbreaker." The words are out like a reflex because, in my head, they are. In my head, she is still mine. That nickname rolling off my lips is the last thing I needed to say, but the way her orgasm barrels down and instantly starts milking my cock, it's hard to say she hated it. My teeth sink into the base of her neck, and her nails dig into my back as I find my release.

A small piece, minuscule as it may have been…it was there all the same, thinking this could cure the years of yearning and pent-up anger. That perhaps this moment had to happen so we could find closure—so I could finally let her go. There was a chance this was what I needed to get her out of my system. The goodbye that was taken from us. But those are minor vexations compared to the gut-wrenching sensation that all but chokes out whatever soul may have remained when I feel my release leak out of her and drip down my balls.

"Shit." I slam my fist into the wall beside her before setting her down. I don't dare look at her. I can't. I'm already ruined. Seeing the flush in her cheeks from the pleasure I just gave her will be my undoing.

"Dallas… Dallas, are you in here?" Madison's voice slices through the sound of our labored breaths. My eyes flash to the window, where I see it has stopped raining.

"You don't have to worry about me saying anything. I won't tell Madison. It's not like this changes anything." Laney's voice is low, like what just happened between us is a dirty secret.

I freeze and take a second to choose my words and not lose my mind, arguing the lie in every one of her words. This has most definitely changed things. She's still deflecting. There's no way she doesn't feel anything. We are far from over. I set her down and quickly pull up my wet jeans.

"Madison is the last thing I'm worried about. Right now, I'm more concerned about the mistake dripping down your thighs."

Fuck. I shouldn't have said that. Everything is coming out wrong, twisted by anger into something cruel. Years of things we've never said to each other, secrets I've kept, and this is what finally comes out? This isn't the mistake. We could never be a mistake. But I should have been more careful. I should have protected us both.

I close my eyes quickly, focusing on my pants. "I forgot to use a condom," I say with my back to her as I search for her top and hand it to her so she can cover herself.

"Dallas!" Madison calls out again, the sound of boots pounding gravel quickly closing the distance. "Dallas, something's wrong with Titan!"

My heart drops, and I straighten, every muscle in my body tensing. Titan, my stallion, my partner for the past six years, my ear to bend through every late-night ride, for every ten-hour day spent tending to chores. He's been with me, weathering every storm since I arrived, since my world was turned on its head.

"Go," Laney's voice cuts through the silence behind me, barely above a whisper but sharp, the word carrying the weight of her exhaustion and disappointment.

My anger doesn't just rise. It erupts, flooding my veins before I can stop it. Here we are again. She's assuming the worst, painting me as the monster before I've even had a chance to explain. Before I've had a chance to be anything else.

My knuckles go white against the stall door, wood creaking under the pressure of my grip. I need something solid to anchor me, to keep me from turning around and seeing the look in her eyes, the one that says she's already written the ending to this story.

"I am what you make me." The words leave my mouth, steady and controlled, each syllable measured and deliberate. But they taste like truth and tragedy all at once, bitter on my tongue because no words have ever cut deeper or rang truer.

I want to be her knight in shining armor, her safe harbor in every storm, her always and forever. I want to be the one who makes her laugh until her sides ache, who holds her when the world gets too heavy, who loves her so fiercely that we rewrite the fate the gods decided was ours.

But if she needs a villain and casting me as the enemy is what keeps her whole, what helps her sleep at night, what makes her feel justified in walking away, then I'll wear that mask too. I'll be her darkness if it means she gets to stay in the light.

Whatever it takes. Whatever role she needs me to play. As long as she survives this. As long as she remains whole.

LANEY
CHAPTER 25

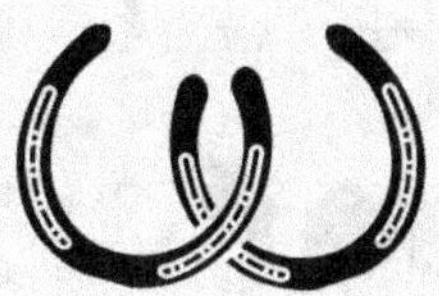

My shirt is still soaked, clinging tightly to my body as I enter the main barn. The jeans I'm wearing are heavy and cold. I desperately want to change, but I'm not at home. Seabiscuit, the horse I was evaluating on the trail ride, got spooked by the storm, so riding home isn't an option. However, the closer I get, the more what felt like punishment looks like responsibility. If I had my horse, if I were back at Fairfield, I'd be able to flee to the comfort of my room instead of facing the music and taking ownership of a choice I made.

Before we took things further, London gave me an out. He asked me if I was sure, and I said yes, and I fucking meant it. I wanted him so badly. I still do, but that doesn't mean it didn't hurt. Having him that way again, feeling him want me, his mouth covering mine as he moved inside of me, was everything. All that we had lost was suddenly alive and real again, and fuck if it didn't scare the shit out of me. It's why I pushed. It's why I said things I knew he wouldn't like—that I wouldn't like—and now here I am, still on the outside.

"Stupid," I mutter to myself as I kick a rock, entering the main barn.

"Have you noticed Titan acting any different recently?" I hear

Asha ask in the distance, the sound of her voice turning my head. Looking east, I see Trigg, Fish, and Abbey gathered in a tight cluster outside of Titan's stall. I do one more quick scan down my body to ensure my outfit doesn't scream, *I just fucked my ex-boyfriend in a stall,* and join them.

"Do we know what happened?" I ask, coming to stand on Fisher's left.

"We all reached the stable seconds before the hail started pinging off the roof. Everyone was fine. Madison was helping Abbey untack Gypsy and then went to attend to Titan when she found him lying on his side."

Peering into the stall, I see Asha crouched beside Titan with a med kit spread across the floor, her stethoscope pressed against his heaving chest as London hovers anxiously, his callused hands trembling as they stroke over Titan's coat.

"His bit was bothering him, so I switched to a new one, but otherwise, he seemed normal." London's voice is unsteady. "Just some head tossing and maybe not drinking as much, but after the bit change, he perked right up. I thought—" He swallows hard. "I thought it was nothing."

Asha's shoulders sag as she pulls back from her examination, and a telltale sigh escapes her lips, one that makes my stomach drop every time. Whatever comes next won't be good news.

"Titan is running a fever, and his submandibular lymph nodes are significantly enlarged." Her clinical tone can't mask the sympathy in her eyes. "Combined with the head tossing and difficulty swallowing you described, I think this could be strangles."

London's face crumples as raw devastation replaces hope, and his hands fall limp at his sides.

Before I can move, Madison rushes to console him, leaning over Titan and wrapping her arms around London's neck, pulling him in for a hug. The sight of her comforting him sends a vicious stab of jealousy straight through my ribs.

My hands clench into fists. She's the last person who should be comforting him. I know how strangles are contracted, and her horse is the likely culprit. Strangles spreads like wildfire, and until today, no new horses had set foot on this property except Gypsy. There's no way Titan caught this from Seabiscuit or a Fairfield horse.

"I'll need to collect nasal swabs and blood samples," Asha continues, her voice cutting through my thoughts. "I can process them at the Fairfield's clinic—"

"No need," Trigg interrupts. "We can run everything in our lab at the stud barn."

Asha nods curtly then surveys our small crowd with the calculating gaze of someone about to deliver more bad news. "This entire barn goes into immediate quarantine. Every horse that went on today's trail ride plus any animal that's had contact with Titan in the past ten days."

"We have a show next weekend," Abbey protests.

"The incubation period ranges from three to ten days." Asha's tone brooks no argument. "No horse leaves this property until we know what we're dealing with. I'll test Gypsy as well, but given the timeline..." She pauses, her meaning clear.

Madison's head snaps up, her eyes blazing. "Gypsy shows no symptoms whatsoever. How can you be sure it's not one of your horses?"

"Because none of my horses have been on this property until today's ride," Asha replies evenly. "And you transported Gypsy here using a commercial hauling service directly from California. Those trailers service multiple facilities. It's entirely possible she contracted the bacteria during transport."

The accusation hangs in the air, and Madison's face pales, her grip on London's arm tightening.

"London, I'm so sorry." Her voice breaks on the words, tears pooling in her eyes. "This is all my fault."

He immediately cups her face in his large hands, thumbs brushing away the tears that spill down her cheeks. "Hey, don't do this to yourself. I offered Gypsy a stall while you were in town.

That was my decision. We don't know anything for certain until those tests come back."

Watching him tenderly console the woman who may have just destroyed his horse and endangered his entire stable unleashes a mix of emotions I was not prepared for. Rage, heartbreak, and a possessiveness so fierce it frightens me all war for dominance. He just found out she's likely responsible for his beloved horse falling ill. Strangles is not a death sentence, but it can be.

I turn away, unable to watch and rationalize how he ran from me when I needed him most. I know these scenarios are not the same, but all of this is too much on the heels of what we just shared. He cares for her, and my stomach can't take it.

I don't even make it halfway down the barn before Fisher is at my side. "Where are you going?"

"I need to get out of here," I say, not slowing my stride.

"You're running, then? What you saw back there isn't what you think."

Those words make me stop. "What is it you think I saw?"

"I'm not sure, but it looked a lot like hurt." He furrows his brow and looks toward the barn. "This isn't the same. Madison isn't Riley. He's not playing a game."

I cross my arms, my annoyance with his speech steadily rising. "Are you saying it was a game back then?"

"No." He runs his hand through his hair, clearly struggling to find the right words, which is new for Fisher. Fisher doesn't trip over his words. One thing about Fish is that he's always been a reliable rock. Ever since we were young, he was wise beyond his years, which is why a knot starts forming in my stomach. His nerves are getting the best of him because he knows what I don't. He has information he didn't have before. "All I'm trying to say is he cares about Madison."

I roll my eyes. "I'm so glad you chased me outside to tell me that."

He reaches for my arm, stopping me from taking off. "You know what I'm trying to say. You, of all people, should know the difference between caring for someone enough that you don't want to hurt them versus loving them."

He's right. I do. I sigh. "That doesn't mean I care to witness it." I let the silence hang between us. I'm not here to argue. Am I upset? Yes, but that's of my own doing. "Look, I need to find Seabiscuit. He ran off right before the storm. I hitched a ride with London on his horse."

"Okay, but just to confirm. You're not running?"

I shrug. "Not right now," I say with a small smile. "You gonna help me find that horse?"

"Let's do it," he says as we walk, the gravel crunching heavy underfoot.

Before London left me naked and cold to wallow in what he called our shared mistake, he said, "I am what you make me." I want to make him mine, but I'm learning that won't come easily. I have to accept that being different isn't a betrayal—it's survival. Making him mine might be painful, but where there is love, there is pain, and with faith, patience, and a sprinkle of luck, I think this pain will be useful not just for me…but for us.

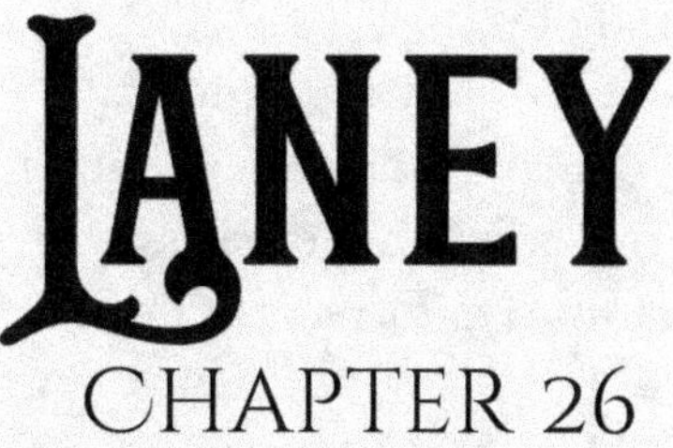

LANEY
CHAPTER 26

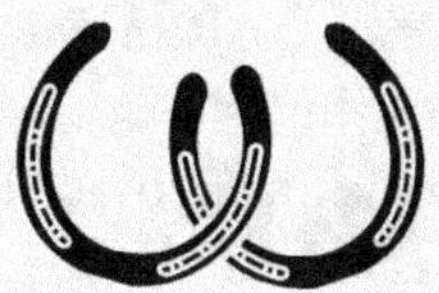

"Hey, I've been looking for you. What are you doing hiding out over here?" I ask Asha, who's standing at the top of the steps overlooking the backyard gardens, where her family is hosting their Belmont Stakes watch party featuring three Thoroughbreds from their stables in the race. That's a huge deal, and I'd think she'd be happy, but since she's up here instead of enjoying the party, I know something is up.

"I just have a lot on my mind right now," she says before taking a sip of her champagne.

I lean onto the stone wall beside her. "Want to talk about it?" I ask, not wanting to unintentionally rock the wrong boat. I assume she's talking about the future of Fairfield, but it could also be about Trigg.

She licks her lips. "My dad just bought a new property."

"That's not a surprise, though, right? You knew he was looking at land." She had to bail on Sydney and me to go tour a property with him, and while she was inconvenienced, it hadn't really come up again. I was hoping that, during that time, he'd come clean about the things I already knew.

"No, it's not that…" She draws in a sharp breath, and I recognize her familiar reluctance. We hold back from naming the things we fear. "I guess it kind of is."

Her somber gaze locks with mine, and even shrouded in worry, she remains one of the most beautiful women I've ever encountered. There's something timelessly elegant about Asha Fairfield, a grace that makes the secret I've been keeping heavier with each passing day.

"I understand why he's making these moves. If we relocate our breeding facilities to a separate location, we will significantly reduce our maintenance costs. Running a breeding operation alongside training facilities and showcase stables, keeping everything pristine and uniform, is hard on our bottom line."

My mind comparatively drifts to what I've witnessed at Hale Ranch after our trail ride. They own a lot more acreage. Hale's Cask sits isolated on the far side of the property, hidden behind rolling fields of crops and dense woodland. When we were there, I never would have imagined it was on Hale land. Then there's the main house and the showcase stables, where they house their prized Thoroughbreds, both maintained with meticulous care and ready for clients and investors to walk through. Keeping all the working parts of the business separate has its benefits for the bottom line. However, I know Asha isn't driven by money. She cares about the horses, so I know there's a *but* coming.

"Which property does he want you working at?" I cautiously press, sensing it's the root of whatever is bothering her.

"As the vet and genealogist, I'd go wherever the breeding facility is located." She closes her eyes and drops her head. "Which is currently in a nowhere town two hours past here." Laughter below draws her eyes open, and she's quiet for a beat before she says, "My mom loved this property, and when I dreamed of becoming a vet, this is where my dreams lived."

"Oh, Asha." I drop my arm over her shoulder and pull her in for a hug.

Her mom died when she was young, and finding out this piece

of information is making me physically ill. I want to tell her every-thing. It needs to be her choice. If her dad is already buying land, it tells me marrying a Hale brother was never in the cards. He'd rather lose the land than surrender his daughter, which I respect, but Asha might have a different opinion. I justified not telling her what I knew in the name of not interfering with someone else's love story. I still firmly believe that Asha and Trigg have history. Whatever it is, she has her reasons for holding it close. I don't get the sense they've ever been intimate. Had that been true, she never would have pushed me at him, but something profound happened between them.

"What if there was a way you could stay here?" I ask, my voice barely a whisper as I contemplate how to deliver my following words carefully.

"My father made up his mind, and when it comes to the busi-ness, his word is law, and there's no changing it."

"Isn't that why I'm here?" Her brow furrows in confusion. "You brought me here to show him there are other avenues for retired racehorses that can be lucrative and humane. Have you lost the faith that we're achieving that?"

"No, I haven't. He was impressed with your choice of place-ment for Casanova and the work you did identifying that Gypsy wasn't the problem with Madison and Abbey's routine."

"So, what you're saying is there's a chance," I point out.

"I guess, but moving the breeding facilities is the easiest. They must meet certain criteria, but they don't have to resemble a museum. If he wants separation, moving that part of the business makes the most sense."

"What if I told you I don't think he bought the property because he wants to move?"

Her eyes widen into saucers. "Oh my god, what do you know?"

I put my hands up. "Let me preface this with, I had my reasons for not telling you the second I found out. I was never trying to hurt you. I thought I was helping you, but that's the thing with secrets, I guess…the more you unravel them, the more you learn."

She grabs me by the shoulders. "Out with it already. I can't know if I have a reason to be mad at you if you don't spit it out."

"Your family doesn't own all of this property. The back sixty is leased, and the lease is up in a little under a year."

She releases me, her eyes darting to the ground as she thinks through the information I just dropped on her. "Okay, so we just renew the lease or buy."

"It can't be bought," I say bleakly.

Her eyes are back on mine. "And why not?"

I pull in a stuttered breath. "Hale land can't be sold."

Her eyebrows shoot up. "Are you fucking kidding me?" She starts pacing, her heels clicking against the stone like gunshots. Back and forth, like a caged predator with nowhere to run.

She whirls toward me. "And…" The word hangs between us, loaded with expectation. "I know there's more, because you wouldn't tell me this useless information if there wasn't a damn caveat."

My palms are slick with sweat as I slide them anxiously down the front of this baby-blue dress she chose for me to wear tonight. "At the end of the lease, they can reclaim the land or lease it again, but given your family's rivalry…"—I swallow hard, the words scraping my throat—"I doubt that's even remotely an option." The silence stretches taut as a wire. "Or…"—my voice cracks—"marry a Hale."

She stops on a dime, but she doesn't look at me. I can sense the inner turmoil, the war raging beneath the surface. I know her wheels are turning. I can practically see the gears grinding inside her head, but the anger I expected from keeping this bombshell of a secret doesn't come. Instead, there's just the sound of her mind working, calculating, reshaping everything she thought she knew into something new and maybe dangerous.

"Asha, please say something. Are you mad? How can I fix this? I feel like a shit friend."

She raises her hand. "You're not a shit friend. You did exactly what I asked you to do." She rolls her head from side to side. "You may have been slow on the relay, but I got the information all the same."

"What are you going to do with it?"

"Marry a Hale," she answers surely with no hesitation.

"Which one?" I attempt to make light of what I believe is a joke.

"It depends. Are you and London still not talking?" She quirks a dark brow.

"I see what you're doing there. You're trying to deflect and act like you didn't just casually agree to a marriage of convenience."

"Meh." She shrugs. "It was partially a joke, and I need time to sit with this information before I discuss it." She takes a long drink of her champagne, downing the remaining flute in one go. "Your drama, on the other hand, I'm already thoroughly invested in, so give it up. What's going on? It's been almost a week since the trail ride and escapades in the barn," she says with a smile.

"I'm not ignoring him because I want to. Like you, I just needed some time to sit with everything," I recycle her words. I told Asha and Sydney what happened the next day—well, almost everything. I left out the part about having unprotected sex in the barn, but they know about what happened under the dock.

I've thought a lot over the years about what I'd do, how I'd act if I ever got him back. But that alternate reality looked different than the one I've been given. In that world, there wasn't someone else, and I'm trying not to be selfish. The things Fisher said when I left the barn were spot on regarding me and Noah. I understood precisely what he was saying concerning Madison and London's relationship.

I care for Noah, but I don't love him. However, I've been questioning what London's life would look like if I had never shown up. Would London have built a life with Madison? When you love someone, you want them to be happy even if it's not with you.

"Have you heard from him?"

"I have. He wants to talk," I say, turning away from the party and leaning against the half-stone wall. "But I left him on read."

"As you should. It's good for men to feel pressure, especially ones with secrets. He needs to know if he wants you back, he's going to have to earn it. You weren't the one that left. He did. I know the guilt eats you alive. You feel terrible for the sacrifice he made, and because of that, it's easy to lose sight of his choice in that."

I look up toward the sky, remembering the last time I made him grovel. It forced his hand, and I became his girlfriend. The reason I haven't been worried about talking is because I know whatever he has to say won't change what's in my heart. I love him —then—now—always. Now, I only need him to realize the same thing. I'm not going anywhere, because where he is…is where I want to be.

"You might be on to something there," I confirm.

"I'm glad you agree, because he just showed up," she says coolly.

"Wait, he's on the guest list?" I ask curiously, turning around to spot him for myself. With the constant bickering and shit-slinging, I assumed London and Trigg were not making the list tonight.

"Not exactly. Madison asked if I'd take over Gypsy's care while she was in isolation. I invited her and Abbey. It would appear their plus-ones are the Hale brothers."

My pulse skyrockets when I see him. Time doesn't exactly stop, but it shifts, slowing the way it does when you're in an accident, and everything becomes crystalline and inevitable all at once. I don't understand how it's humanly possible to be so intensely drawn to someone. Every time I see him, it is like the first time. He takes my breath away, my pulse increases, my hands get clammy, and the butterflies are in a full-on flurry. Tonight is not different. If anything, it's amplified because, tonight, I'm set on ending the standoff and making him mine while I might be scared shitless. The fear of not taking this jump is worse.

"I'm going to get a refill, mingle, and possibly commit a tasteful murder," Asha jests with a sharp smile. "Care for a drink while I'm orchestrating chaos?"

"I'll be right behind you. I just need a moment to sharpen my knives," I reply, wearing my own dangerously sweet smile.

"Now you're speaking my language," she says before disappearing down the adjacent stone staircase.

I haven't even finished watching her descend the staircase when a familiar voice approaches. "There you are. I was hoping I'd run into you tonight," Madison says, joining me on my perch.

"Oh, hey, you look stunning as usual," I say, returning the hug she goes in for the second I face her.

"As a performer, I have no shortage of dresses," she laughs, her eyes already cataloging every face in the crowd before returning to mine with laser focus. Then, dipping her hand inside her bra, she pulls out a folded piece of paper. "I don't mean to keep you from the party. I just wanted to make sure I gave you this."

I take the paper and unfold it to find it's a check. Ten thousand dollars as promised. I stare at the check blankly. This money has so much potential to help me get started at the end of summer, but accepting it no longer feels right, especially when I can't help but feel like I'm taking something—or rather, someone—from her.

"Madison, I can't take this. What I did with Gypsy wasn't worth nearly this much," I say, offering it back.

She doesn't reach for it. "I had a feeling you'd say that. The truth is, I needed Gypsy healthy, he's how we make our living, but I was really paying for something else entirely."

"And what's that?" I question, not following her explanation.

"I had to know if you were the girl." She takes a slow sip of her bourbon.

"The girl?"

She raises a brow at me. "A woman knows when she's not the

girl that owns a man's heart." She smiles with the kind of sad wisdom that comes from loving someone who belongs to someone else. "We know when it's been taken by someone else." I watch as she swirls the amber liquid in her glass and wait to see if she'll say more. "For a while, I thought maybe I could steal it, that maybe he could learn to love me, but a piece of me always knew I was only fooling myself. The second Trigg introduced us at the wedding, I knew you were the ghost of a past I could never compete with."

I twist one of my rings nervously, her honesty settling like a stone in my chest. "How did you know it was me?"

"Your name," she says with gentle certainty, as though that answer is obvious, though I know it's not. London said he didn't talk about me. It's odd that she could have known who I was the first time we met. Then, as if reading my thoughts, she adds, "I'll let you piece that together in your own time, but it's why I offered you that money. I wanted your help, but I also needed your time just to be sure." Wow, that was an admission I didn't expect to hear. She literally paid to find out if I was the other woman. Her eyes trace the yard. "I'm not going to pretend I know the past the two of you share. I don't. I care about him. I want the best for him, and even though it stings a little to admit this, it was worth every penny." She nods to the party below. "It was worth it to help that tortured soul find peace. That man loves you, even if what he says tells you differently. It's a lie."

London is talking to another guest below when his eyes peer up at me. He does a double-take when he sees who's standing at my side. Even at this distance, I can see his shoulders tense.

"I don't know what to say," I begin helplessly.

"Don't say anything." She gently pushes my hand holding the check back. "A new horse would have cost me twice this, and someone else might not have figured out what you did, which could have cost me precious time with my sister. Besides…"—her gaze drifts toward the bar where an auburn-haired man raises his glass to her with unmistakable interest—"I have a feeling my story isn't over, just...redirecting." Her smile becomes genuinely warm. "I'll see you around, Laney Hart."

After all the confessions I have given and heard, I need a drink. I follow a few steps behind Madison, but instead of heading to the bar, I veer right and cut off a server carrying a tray of champagne, stealing not one but two flutes.

"For a friend," I lie with a smile before making my way to the edge of the party.

All the people I care to talk to are currently unavailable. Asha is plotting, Fisher is talking to a pretty girl across the pool, and Sydney is currently in bed with a migraine. The stress of deciding whether to continue her education is taking a toll on her. Sydney has a very carefree exterior, but inside, she's a boss bitch—fiercely independent, confident, smart as hell, and unafraid to go after exactly what she wants. I wish I could help her work it out, but this is one of those things she has to decide for herself so that she has no regrets.

"Hey," a sultry voice wraps around me like silk. "Are one of those for me?"

I take a hefty drink, downing half of the flute in one go. The champagne burns slightly but not nearly as much as the familiar warmth radiating from beside me. "No, they're for me," I say with a coy smile, finally turning to look into the eyes I've avoided for the past five days.

God, those eyes. Still a dark hurricane that can make me forget my own name, framed by lashes that shouldn't be legal on someone who already broke my heart once. He's standing closer than necessary, close enough that I can smell his cologne, and it's utterly intoxicating, just like the man.

"You didn't return my texts."

"I know. I had a lot to think about," I say before finishing off one flute.

"Do you care to elaborate on that?"

"Your aftercare is shit. I wasn't sure if I wanted to entertain another abysmal performance." He steals my extra glass of champagne. "Hey, that's mine," I grumble.

He downs it one go. "Sorry, that wasn't at all what I was expecting you to say when I walked over here."

"Not used to women telling you you're shit in bed?" I deadpan, the words sliding out before I can stop them. Apparently, small jabs are my coping mechanism of choice this evening.

His jaw tightens, and something dangerous flickers behind his eyes. He takes a slow step closer, his voice dropping to barely above a whisper. "Heartbreaker, if you have something you want to say, then say it. But don't you dare stand there and lie to both of us by pretending what we shared wasn't earth-shattering the same way it was the first time."

The air between us crackles with tension, and I hate how my pulse quickens at his proximity, at the raw honesty bleeding through his words.

Own it, Laney. Tell him everything you've wanted to say. You said you would. If you can't own your shit, you can't ask him to do the same.

"You kissed her…" I lick my lips.

His hand runs over his jaw. "I kissed her to forget you, then I kissed her to hurt you. The problem with kissing Madison is that it was never really her. It always came back to you. When you walked out of that barn, I ended things. She and I haven't been anything in a long time. That was the first kiss we shared in over a year, and I made it clear there wasn't going to be another."

His words hurt, not because they aren't the ones I want to hear, but because they confirm what's been right in front of me all along. He tried to come clean and speak his piece, but I was too scared to listen. Too afraid to hope for an us again when I'm barely surviving losing him the first time. But I'm not scared anymore.

"You didn't let me finish." My voice comes out steadier than I feel. "You kissed her, and I had to get out of there." I spin the stem of my empty flute, condensation making my already trembling fingers slip, but somehow, that gives me the courage to push forward with my own raw truth. "I had to get out of there because I wanted it to be me."

He pulls in a stuttered breath. Here we are, two people who never stopped being in love, finally peeling back the lies we told ourselves, only to discover we're still standing on the same side of forever.

"Do you want to get out of here?" He takes another step forward, nearly eliminating all the space between us.

"Just the person I've been looking for," Trigg says, grabbing London's shoulder from behind, annoyance quickly transforming hardened features that had softened for me.

"Now is not a good time," London says, not bothering to pull his eyes away from mine.

"Eh, I beg to differ. I think she likes me a little bit more than you right now."

"How do you figure?" he asks, peeved.

"Well, for starters, you told me she left you on read all week, and from what I've witnessed, you're chasing her tonight, not the other way around. Also, my face is better…" He uses his hands to frame his face. "Stronger jaw, soft face that makes the perfect seat for the ladies—not all this scruff." He goes to touch London's beard, and he swats his hand away.

"This is ridiculous," I snap, grabbing Trigg's hand and leading him away. "I'll be right back."

"Told you she likes me better," he tosses over his shoulder.

"Will you stop?" I hiss.

"Not a chance. Getting him riled up is my new favorite pastime." His grin is wolfish as he lets me pull him along. "Until you walked back into his life, nothing—and I mean nothing—got a rise out of him. The man was practically catatonic."

I drag him behind me as we weave between clusters of people who seem determined to block my path as I search for an empty table. I spot one tucked against the far corner of the garden and make a beeline for it, practically collapsing into the nearest chair. The relief that floods through my feet is immediate. "My feet are absolutely killing me. Asha picked out this dress, but Sydney…"—I gesture helplessly at the torture devices strapped to my feet —"Sydney picked out these heels, and I am decidedly not a fan. And because I already know exactly what this conversation is going to be about, you better wave down that waiter with the tray full of drinks, or I'm out."

He smirks. "So demanding."

As he flags down the waiter, my eyes naturally drift in the direction where I left London. We were finally talking, which needed to happen, and, as per usual, we were interrupted. Trigg is the last person I want to small talk with this evening; however, once I get this conversation out of the way, there shouldn't be anyone else to distract me from the one man at the top of my list.

Looking across the garden, I don't see London standing where I left him, and my heart sinks. Damn it. I told him I'd be right back. Given my track record this past week, he probably believes I'm still trying to avoid him.

"Here you go," Trigg says, sliding a tall glass of ranch water in front of me. "Hope you like salt. Looks like they went heavy on the rims."

"I love salt," I say as I bring it to my mouth. I pucker my lips as soon as lime and tequila hit my taste buds. "Oof, and they're strong too, just the way I need it." I watch as he takes a slow drink of the one he grabbed for himself, his eyes casually scanning the partygoers as they wind in and out of tables. "So, was your goal to pry me away from your brother for show, or do you actually have something you want to talk about?"

He flashes that trademark gorgeous smile. I hate when good-looking men know they're good-looking. It's like they know they can sweet talk their way out of the shittiest remarks before they make them. "You know, if you had been mine first, I never would have let you go."

I roll my eyes, not because he's being insincere; in another life,

I'd be attracted to Trigg. Hell, I was drawn to him since I first laid eyes on him, but the words now are moot. There will never be a me and him because I'll only ever belong to one man. I feel him before I see him. I don't even need to look to my right to know what caused the skin on my arms to pebble. It's him. It's always him. He may have moved from where I left him, but the man doesn't stray far from his territory.

"Sweet sentiment, but we both know that's bullshit. You're not interested in me. You're interested in winning."

"Ouch. Cold." He clutches his chest like I've wounded him. "All this time, I thought you did a number on my brother, but maybe it's the other way around. You're a fucking catch, Laney Hart, and if you don't know that, I need to drag my little brother behind the shed and teach him how to properly worship a goddess."

"You are laying it on thick tonight," I say with a smirk that naturally has me turning away so he doesn't see the way my cheeks flush from his flattery. The last thing I need is to hand him ammunition, but my eyes snag on London's intense glare from two tables over. He's pissed—that much is obvious—but there's something else simmering underneath. Jealousy? He knows damn well I'm not interested in his brother, but that's not what's twisting him up inside. No, what's eating him alive is that I'm choosing to give Trigg my attention instead of him. Any lingering doubts about their DNA connection just got torched. These two are definitely cut from the same possessive, alpha-hole cloth.

"Alright." I bite my lip, savoring the way I can still make London twitch from across the room, then pivot back to Trigg. "Since you're allergic to addressing the elephant tap-dancing in the room, I'll do it. I told Asha. Spilled everything."

"Why?" he asks evenly, which takes me by surprise. I fully expected fury or, at the very least, irritation, maybe a few threats.

"That's it? That's your whole reaction? 'Why?'" I draw out his word and I lean back, studying his face while trying to keep mine unaffected. I move to cross my legs, but before I can reposition myself, a hand grips my ankle. "What the hell..." My words feather off with an awkward high pitch when lips kiss my inner knee. My eyes immediately dart to the table London was at seconds ago, where all that remains is his hat, and I know instantly who's under the table. Shit.

LONDON

CHAPTER 27

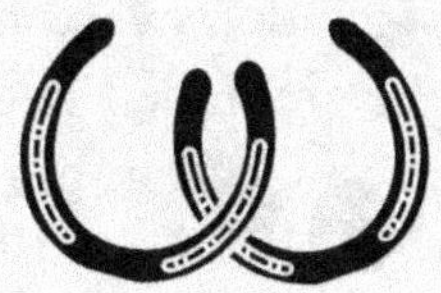

This is not where I saw this night going when I accepted Madison's invitation to be her plus-one to the Fairfields' Belmont Stakes watch party. I accepted for one reason: to see Laney. I didn't know then that "yes" would turn into crawling on my hands and knees beneath a cloth-covered table, my pulse hammering against my throat as I search for any excuse to get her attention.

I saw her the instant I walked into the party. She captured my attention without trying. It took all of a second for honey brown eyes to connect with mine and make my heart pound. I felt the electric current thrumming through her gaze from across the gardens. I wanted to excuse myself and go to her right then, but someone else has had her ear all night—everyone except me— and I'm growing tired of it.

Her legs, from this view, are impossibly long. They have haunted my every thought since they were wrapped around me under the dock and again in the barn. I grind my teeth as I think of how she's ignored me for the past five days. I know exactly why she's been ignoring me. Her reason is the same reason I'm here: Madison. Laney is determined to believe that we are a couple and that she isn't all I think about, even after I gave her those admissions.

I get it, though. I gave her words, and then she had to endure an afternoon on the back of a horse, watching me be friendly with a woman I've been intimate with. If the roles had been reversed, I would have lost my damn mind. I also know it's more than that. I'm not dense. I heard her words after we came down from one of the best orgasms I've ever had, only topped by the only other one I shared with her. I ran off. I ran to rescue the horse that had saved me, but it was the voice that called out for me that she saw me running toward, and the embrace I know she saw in the barn, that has her doubting what she feels in her bones: me. She sought comfort in Noah, and now I'm being punished for doing the same. It doesn't matter that Madison and I have shared a bed a few times over the years. I was always going to belong to Laney. I've always been all hers, all in.

This is insane. This is crossing every line we've both been carefully straddling, but I can't do it anymore. Every missed opportunity, every word that's gone unsaid…I'm done with all of them.

The moment she shifts to cross her legs, my hand finds her ankle like it belongs there. Laney goes rigid above me, whatever words were flowing from her lips cutting off in a breathless gasp that she tries to disguise as a cough. I freeze, my pulse hammering against my ribs as I wait for the inevitable—for someone to notice, for the tablecloth to be yanked away, for this moment to shatter.

But it doesn't come.

The conversation above continues, oblivious. She's covering for me, and the realization sends heat coursing through my veins. Laney asked me to stay put, and I didn't. I couldn't. I moved closer, drawn into her orbit like I always am, helpless against her pull. I saw the way she glanced over her shoulder earlier, the way goosebumps rose on her skin when she sensed I was still near. I'm certain she's spotted my hat sitting brazenly atop the table—my not-so-subtle calling card.

My thumb traces a slow circle against her ankle bone, and I feel the tremor that runs through her. Her breathing changes above me, becoming carefully controlled in that way that means she's fighting to stay composed. The knowledge that I'm affecting her, that she's as desperate for this connection as I am, makes me bolder.

I lean closer, my lips hovering just above her inner knee. My breath ghosts across her skin, and I watch, mesmerized, as goosebumps bloom in its wake. She shifts slightly, whether toward me or away, I can't tell, but it's enough permission for me to press the softest kiss there, right where her skin is warmest and most sensitive.

The kiss is barely there, a whisper of contact, but I feel her whole body respond. Her free hand drops to grip the edge of her chair, knuckles going white with the effort of staying still. Above me, her voice wavers slightly as she responds to whatever question was just asked, but she recovers quickly, too quickly for anyone else to notice.

"Are you sure you want to hear what I have to say?" my brother asks, and satisfaction curls in my chest. Here I am, literally on my hands and knees for this woman, and I get to eavesdrop on whatever was so important he had to pull her away from me.

My fingers trail higher, just barely, testing boundaries. Her breath catches—a sound so quiet only I can hear it. She knows exactly what game we're playing, knows the risk we're taking, and she's letting it happen. That knowledge makes me reckless.

He knows she's mine. We've never had the conversation, never sorted through our tangled history, but some truths don't need words. And though he let me believe he was pursuing her, I know now it was never real—just another game in the complicated dance between brothers.

But this? This is real. The way she's fighting to keep her composure while my touch sets her on fire. The way she's protecting this moment, protecting us, even as we teeter on the edge of discovery. This is everything we've been building toward. Every stolen glance and loaded silence is finally taking shape.

"I brought you to the table," Laney says, and I can hear the effort it takes to force calm into her voice as my callused hand glides up her leg. "Secrets are poison. I've lived with them for far too long, and I won't do it anymore."

I know those words are for me as much as they are for him. Their irony leaves a bitter taste in my mouth. I'm the one who asked her to coffee, who wanted to see her and finally talk through the wreckage we've been tiptoeing around for years. Then she's the one who stood me up and had the audacity to get salty about it afterward.

And tonight... Christ, that comment about my aftercare in the barn. She knew precisely what that taunt would do to me, knew it would burrow under my skin and fester, because she knows every fucking button I have. She knows the way I loved her—wholly, completely, desperately. She knows I've always taken care of her, that if she asked for five more minutes, she got them. One more kiss was never a question.

The memory of that one night six years ago burns through me. How, afterward, I collected her dress from the grass, pulled it carefully over her shoulders, smoothed her hair with trembling fingers, and ran my thumbs under her eyes to catch the mascara that had smudged. She looked so vulnerable then, so beautifully wrecked, and I treated her like she was made of glass.

Now she's too busy trying to fortify her walls, too scared to let me close enough to show her what we can be again if we're brave enough to reach for it.

I skim the backs of my fingers along the tops of her thighs, the silk of her dress hiking up as they make their slow, deliberate climb. Her muscles tense under my touch, a war between wanting to pull away and wanting to lean into the contact.

"I don't have any secrets," my brother says above us, and we both know that's bullshit, but I'm less concerned about whatever he's hiding when every nerve in my body is focused on the woman above me who's trying so hard to stay composed.

"Are you serious right now? You specifically asked me—or maybe threatened is the better word."

The word "threatened" detonates something inside of me, and I can't help but sink my teeth deep into her thigh. I'm fucking livid that she'd allow my own brother to threaten her and not come to me. It doesn't matter that we're caught in this gray space between together and apart. It doesn't matter what labels we've discarded or what boundaries we've tried to draw. There's no universe, no reality, no scenario where I would allow someone to intimidate her, not even him.

The hand that was tightly gripping the chair glides over my scalp, sending a shiver down my spine and straight to my groin. A low groan rumbles deep in my chest as her fingers twist in my hair before she tugs with force. My cock twitches hard before I relinquish her sensitive skin from my teeth. We've been apart for six years. She can take care of herself. Laney has always been fiercely independent, unafraid to dance to her own beat, never keen on conforming just to fit in. She likes being on the outside.

"Did I threaten you?" Trigg questions as Laney's hand disappears, leaving me alone under the cloak of the table cover. "Or did you not like the alternate ending?"

This week without her, this goddamn week of silence, has shown me something I can't ignore anymore. I can't do this dance again. I was already planning to lay it all out for her, all the truths I've been choking on, but I wanted them to come in the right order, at the right time.

"Does it matter?" she asks as I place a chaste kiss on her milky skin where a mark is already blooming into a bruise, the sight stirring to life something possessive—something territorial. She's mine. I've only been lying to myself, trying to make myself believe there was a universe where I'd actually let her go again if she told me no. I tried that. Living without her wasn't living at all. I'd follow her to the ends of the earth and live in her shadow.

My gaze shifts higher, following the path my forefinger dares to blaze to the apex of her thighs. Fuck. Her pussy is covered by a thin white thong. The tip of my finger slips beneath the seam, and I close my eyes for a heartbeat to rein in my own desire. I could come from just toying with her panty line, feeling the heat from the place I've visited in my head, with my hand wrapped firmly around my cock, countless times. Her hand hasn't returned to stop me. She's aware of what I'm after, and she's letting me stay. I hate that it feels like I'm taking advantage, crossing lines she might not let me cross if she knew everything. But something she said in that barn keeps echoing in my head. When I tried to stop, tried to be the gentleman and say we should talk first, she said it wouldn't change anything. That she wants this. Wants me.

Their conversation becomes background noise as I let myself get lost in her, but then I hear her say, "You knew I would tell London. You knew who I was all along, and you knew, regardless of who hurt who, my loyalty lies with him, and I would rat you out."

And I'm done. Done waiting for the perfect moment. Done letting other people interrupt what's ours, stealing time that should belong to us. Done watching her from across rooms full of people who don't know her the way I do, who don't see the fire behind her eyes or understand the way she bites her lip when she's thinking. She can ignore my texts all she wants, but she can't ignore me forever. Not when we're breathing the same air, not when I can see the way her shoulders tense every time my eyes land on her, knowing it's my gaze alighting the recognition in her veins.

There's no more teasing as her words hit a mark I didn't know I was waiting for, and I slide a thick digit into her tight hole. Damn. Her pussy clenches hard around my finger, and fuck if it isn't the hottest thing I've ever seen—her swollen pink lips greedily taking what I'm giving her. I've had her a total of two times now, but not like this. I've never had my face between her thighs. I haven't even tasted her yet, but I know there is no way I'm leaving things the way I did last time. Her thighs instantly try to close.

The intrusion came without warning, and I wish I could see her pretty face, see the ecstasy I know is there by the way her pussy is responding to my touch.

"I was counting on it," I hear Trigg say right before I run my tongue up her center. My God, she tastes better than I ever could have imagined. I groan deeply, a vibration that I know rumbles through her core when her thighs tighten around my head.

I should be focused on what my brother is saying, but so far I haven't caught anything I don't already know. I've known all along that Trigg's motives with Laney were shrouded in deception, but I've also suspected that their core revolved around someone and something else.

"Why?" I hear her ask, her tone breathy as I add another digit and pump two fingers deep.

"I guess you could say it's in my DNA. I'm the product of a secret, and I grew up in a family intent on keeping them. It feels like a survival mechanism. I have to know to be prepared."

Those words don't surprise me. I've felt similar sentiments after learning everything I didn't know existed after being dumped on my uncle's doorstep at eighteen. This show he's been putting on with her for the past few weeks was posturing, him staying two steps ahead and plotting his next move. I remove my fingers and slide both hands over her thighs until I have a handful of cheek in each hand.

The move grants her a small reprieve, and she uses it to ask, "Then I suppose you know what London is planning?"

Her voice is unsteady, and I can tell she's getting close. The thrill of getting caught, coupled with what I'm doing to her, is utterly intoxicating. My fingers dig into her flesh, and I pull her to the edge of her chair, where my tongue spears her pussy. I hear the glass on the table rattle as she braces herself. I wish I were a fly on the wall so I could see exactly what she's doing to avoid my brother's dissecting stare.

"No, but you're going to tell me," he states squarely. The demand should give me pause, but it doesn't. I can't. I have the only person I want, writhing against my lips. Whatever stunt he's pulling—score he's trying to settle—comes second to her pleasure.

"What makes you think I would do that?" Laney responds as I suck her clit into my mouth, her thighs now trembling.

"I think we both know the third person in your trifecta isn't inside nursing a migraine."

Now, that comment has me slowing my pace. There's only one person I've yet to see tonight.

"You may have noticed Sydney isn't the only person missing from tonight's festivities. Wouldn't you know Warrick Fairfield has yet to make an appearance at his own party," he says, and even I can hear the dramatic flair in his tone.

That's a big claim to make, but if I've learned anything about my brother, it's that he does his research. I'm not thrilled, but Sydney is an adult. She can do adult things with whomever she wants. I can't tell her to stay away from someone when I can't even take my own advice. I'm on my knees, devouring the woman I told myself I could never have again, my reasons evaporating with every exquisite swipe of my tongue as her legs quiver around me.

"So if I tell you what London's plans are regarding the land lease—"

My fingers push inside of her, joining my tongue, and her thighs tremble against my shoulders. I can feel her fighting to keep her voice steady, to maintain the facade that she's having a normal conversation while I'm worshiping her beneath the table.

"I won't out your best friend for sucking your other best friend's dad's cock."

"And if I don't?" I hear the sharp intake of breath she pulls through her mouth as I feel her orgasm start to take root. She's fighting it, trying to hold her composure as her pussy strangles my fingers.

"You will." Trigg shifts, his legs now facing her. "But I'm not ruthless…" Then, knocking on the table, he says, "I'll let the two of you work out the details together this time."

Fuck... I'm sure Laney is mortified right now. Her face is probably flushed with a mix of embarrassment and ecstasy, but my cock is weeping. I'm so turned on by the knowledge that my brother knows I'm under this table, taking my fill of MY woman.

Her hand returns under the tablecloth with a vengeance. I know she wants to come, but she doesn't like having an audience. Her fingers tug my hair hard, but it only makes me hold her tighter, keeping her in place. If she didn't want this, she shouldn't have taunted me earlier about my aftercare. She shouldn't have let me go this far. There's no going back.

"Oh yeah, you never answered my question earlier," Trigg adds fuel to the fire, staying put even though he knows she's on the brink of orgasm and his presence is the last thing she wants. "Do you like your seat clean-shaven, or do you prefer the added stimulation that a beard gives as it rubs against your soft, delicate skin, reddening it and leaving its mark hours after the feast is over?"

Those words shatter her completely, and I crush her against my mouth, desperate to devour every tremor, every violent quiver as she convulses around my tongue. The broken whimper that tears from her throat is mine, a raw confession I've ripped from her very core. She's unraveling beneath me, every sound a surrender she can no longer deny. With her defenses down, all that remains is pure, unfiltered truth. I still own her the same way she's always owned me.

"I'm not answering that," she finally manages to choke out, her voice strangled as I lick her through the aftershocks, not wasting a single drop and claiming every part of her surrender in this moment, despite the chaos above.

"You don't have to. Your face just did." Then, just to ensure there's no mistaking that he's well aware I'm under the table, he slaps it one more time and adds, "Have a good night, brother."

And then he's gone.

The silence that follows is deafening, broken only by her ragged breathing and the distant hum of the party. My heart pounds against my ribs as the reality of what just happened, what Trigg just acknowledged, settles between us.

Slowly, carefully, I pull her thong back into place, my fingers gentle now. I press a lingering kiss to each of her thighs, tasting salt and silk and the lingering evidence of what we've just shared. When I draw her dress down, smoothing the fabric with deliberate care, it feels like both an ending and a beginning. I emerge from beneath the tablecloth like I'm surfacing from deep water, and I know exactly what I look like: hair mussed beyond repair, lips glossy and swollen, eyes dark with satisfied hunger. The shit-eating grin spreading across my face is inevitable.

"How was that for aftercare?" I ask, my voice rough with the evidence of what I've been doing.

She opens her mouth, but no sound comes out. Instead, her gaze travels over my disheveled appearance with an intensity that makes my skin burn. I watch her take in every detail. The way my hair falls across my forehead, the way my lips catch the light, the way my breathing is still uneven. When her teeth sink into her bottom lip, my mouth is instantly jealous.

"Heartbreaker," I murmur, leaning closer so only she can hear, "the crimson on your cheeks and the flush spreading down your throat says yes louder than words ever could." I nod toward the edge of the party. "Wanna get out of here?"

She nods, the movement sharp and desperate. "Unless you want to kiss me right here in front of everyone…yes."

My hand slides possessively around her waist as I rise, pulling her flush against me in one fluid motion. The heat of her body against mine sends electricity racing through my veins, and I have to fight the urge to lift her onto this table and finish what we started.

"Don't tempt me," I murmur, my voice a low growl against her ear. "I have no problem kissing you for the world to see."

To prove my point, my lips find hers in a kiss that's deliberately slow and unhurried, a stark contrast to the energy thrumming between us. I don't care who's watching, don't care about the conversations that might pause or the looks we might draw. Let them see. Let them know she's mine.

When I pull back, her lips are swollen, and her breathing is uneven. "But I think we both know I want more than just a kiss..." My pulse hammers against my throat as my mouth trails along her jaw, tasting the salt of her skin. "I want to kiss you while you're wrapped around me. Apparently, I need to remind you how you scream for me." I taunt her with the lies she dared to spew earlier about what really transpired between us in that barn. I let my teeth graze the shell of her ear, and she shudders against me. "What's it going to be, heartbreaker?"

Taking her hand, I guide it to the evidence of my desire, rock-hard and straining against my jeans. Her breath catching in her throat is music to my ears.

"If you keep biting that lip like that," I warn, watching as her teeth worry her bottom lip again, "I won't be able to wait until we're alone."

She nods breathlessly, her voice barely above a whisper. "I want you, London. I always want you."

Her confession knocks the wind out of me, stealing the air from my lungs. Something fundamental shifts between us, the playful teasing dissolving into something deeper, more raw and honest. Her eyes search mine with an intensity that leaves me feeling exposed, and I know she sees it all: the longing I can never quite hide, the way I ache for her even when she's right here in my arms, the truth I'm too terrified to say out loud.

My forehead drops to rest against hers, and for a suspended moment, we just breathe each other in. The party fades to background noise, the world narrowing to just this, her warmth, her scent, the way she fits perfectly against me.

"Always?" I ask, my voice rough with wonder and something dangerously close to hope.

"Always," she confirms, her hands fisting in my shirt like she's afraid I might disappear.

I close my eyes briefly, letting the weight of that word settle in my chest. When I open them again, I make sure she sees me, really sees me, sees that the depth of what I feel for her lives eternally in my soul, the way she's carved herself into every corner of my heart.

My hand slides to the small of her back, pulling her impossibly closer until there's no space left between us.

"Let's get out of here," I say, my voice thick with promise. "Because I need to show you exactly what 'always' means to me."

LANEY
CHAPTER 28

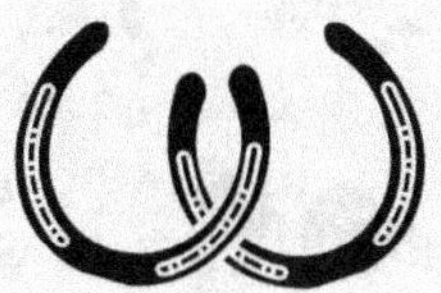

The second we left the gardens, it was like we were in high school all over again, two teenagers with raging hormones unable to keep their hands to themselves. We didn't make it to the main house, back to my room. The distance was too far, and we were too eager. I grabbed a saddle blanket as we passed through the stables and escaped up the back hill to a small clearing where I barely got it spread out before he was at my back, his hands on my hips, collecting my dress and pulling it over my head, leaving me in nothing but my soaked thong. He instantly fell to his knees and took his time kissing every inch of my body, spending extra time kneading and sucking my breasts, caressing me in ways he didn't days ago. I've been floating somewhere between Earth and the heavens, in a place I never want to leave, for time I never thought I'd have again, but it's had me on the brink of insanity. I need more. I need him.

"I want you," I moan as I reach between us and dip my hand inside his boxers, stroking his hard cock long and slow. He groans and pumps his length into my hand. "Take these off and get inside me."

"It's fucking hot when you tell me what to do." He nips my lip and follows my instructions. I only wish it wasn't dark. I can see the hard planes of his chest when the moon peeks through the clouds, but I want to see everything. My mind quickly forgets what it doesn't have when his body reclaims its position between my legs, reminding me of all that I do. The hard length he's been pressing against my swollen core for longer than I'd like is now bare and sliding through my wet lips.

"Mmm." I close my eyes, reveling in the feelings only he has ever been able to make me feel. My nipples are pebbled against the cool night air, and behind the shadows of his lust-filled gaze, I see his complete adulation.

"My God, you have no idea how many nights I've dreamed of hearing the sexy sounds you make when I'm inside of you," he says in a low, sultry tone that matches the yearning I feel.

I smile and open my eyes. "I'd like to remind you of all of them, but you're not inside of me yet."

He drops to his elbows. "I can fix that," he whispers, his nose skimming mine as he aligns himself with my entrance. With his eyes fixed on mine, I don't dare look away as he slowly pushes in, deliciously stretching me with the same tentative care he gave me the first time we ever made love. He knows he won't hurt me, but he's waiting for me to change my mind. That's why he is taking his time. He wants to reacquaint himself with a body he once knew better than his own, but he is also giving me time to reconsider.

I wrap my legs around his waist, pulling him into me and fully seating him. His lips crash to mine as he holds himself deep, our tongues battling the wars written on our hearts. I press my fingers to his face. "I want to be on top."

His eyes search mine, and I know he sees it. He sees the depth behind my ask. He gave me the control the first time, and I'm asking for it now. I'm asking him to let me show him I want this.

"Whatever you want, heartbreaker. It's yours," he mutters before swiftly rolling us over.

With my hands on his chest, I pause, taking a second to collect a memory: the man I've loved my whole life beneath me, under a sky filled with stars. I don't care what obstacles are thrown our way; I know he's the exact person who's supposed to be by my side, facing them with me. His hands glide up my thighs, his eyes softening with a slight twitch that feels like he can read my thoughts. Hoping he can, I push my hair over one shoulder and lean down, my lips taking their turn to blaze a trail. His skin pebbles with each new open-mouthed kiss as I start a slow pace and let myself get lost in him and the depths that only he has ever been.

An immeasurable amount of time is spent rediscovering each other as our unspoken love that started out slow burns hotter with each stroke, each kiss, and each caress under a moon-drenched sky.

"You're on the pill, right?" he asks, his voice strained as his lips part from my neck. Our shared breaths are labored as I lose myself riding him the same way I did the first time we ever had sex.

"No." I try to steady my breathing, but my voice comes out breathy and ragged.

"What?" He pulls his face away from my neck and steadies my hips. "You've been fucking Noah Donovan, and you're not on the pill."

It's a statement more than a question, but it doesn't alter the insinuation or the disdain. In this moment, another man's name was the last thing I expected to hear fall from his lips, but here we are. "Are you serious? You've been out of jail this entire time, and you expect me to believe you've been celibate for the past six years?"

"It's not that…" he growls, dragging his hand through his hair like he's trying to tear the thoughts from his head. "It's the recklessness. It's knowing you were perfectly fine with him being the father if an accident had happened."

Accident. The word hits me like a slap. I don't know which I despise more: a mistake or an accident. Both insinuate that I'm some naive fool, stumbling blindly through life, oblivious to consequences.

His eyes find mine again, raw and devastated. "But that's not even the worst part." His voice cracks. "It's the intimacy. I won't lie to you. There have been others. God knows I've tried everything to scrub you from my memory. That bullshit saying about the best way to get over someone is to get under someone else is a lie. Every woman I touched only made it worse, because none of them were you."

His hand trembles as it comes up to cup my jaw, his thumb brushing against my skin like I might disappear. "There may have been bodies in my bed, but never my soul. That belongs to you. Only you. You're the only one who's ever stripped me bare, the only one I've ever completely lost myself with. And knowing you gave that same piece of yourself to someone else..." He closes his eyes, jaw clenched tight. "It kills me."

I lean into his hand. "I've never given this to someone else. I'm not on birth control because it makes me sick, and technically, I haven't been with anyone in a really long time. Noah and I were never a couple. The handful of times we did hook up, I was drunk. I wanted to feel something, and he was there, but he didn't have me like this. You're the only person I'd ever let have all of me."

His eyes soften, and his hand wraps around the back of my neck before he pulls me flush against his mouth in a slow, passionate kiss, a kiss that can only come from a place of love. He still loves me. I haven't decided if that's a good thing or a bad thing yet. I know it's that love that stole him from me, and it's that same love that was determined to push me away when I showed up in Bardstown. I know what I want it to be, but I also know I can't think about tomorrow or the next day. I have to live in the now, and right now, he's here with me, choosing me, and it's everything I want.

I rock my hips, reminding him that he's still buried deep inside of me, and he groans, long and deep. The hand that never left my hip digs into my flesh. "Laney." He leans his forehead against mine. "We can't."

"Tell me…tell me why."

He closes his eyes, and I hate it. I hate that he's shutting me out when I know he still cares. He's battling his desire, but beneath his resistance burns an undeniable hunger. The chemistry between us hasn't merely lingered. It has intensified to almost painful degrees. The years apart didn't diminish what we once shared. If anything, they transformed it into something more potent, more consuming. I know he feels it. When our eyes meet, the air itself seems to crackle with electricity. Each moment we resist our connection only heightens the ones like now. He just admitted I'm the only one he loses himself with. So that's what I'll do, make him lose himself until he finds his way back to me.

"But we already did," I remind him before softly pecking his lips with another slow roll of my hips. "Your release a few days ago is still inside of me. What's one more?"

The next thing I know, I'm on my back. "I know what you're trying to do, heartbreaker."

"Oh yeah, and what's that?" I question, wrapping my legs around his back.

"Make me lose control."

"Is it working?" I seductively tease.

"You know it is." He presses in deep, and the tiniest of moans passes through my lips on a pant. "But this is it. This is the last time. This can't happen again."

Something about the words he chose doesn't sit right with me, and I can't help but feel he means all of it. He's feeling everything and pulling away—or at least I think he is.

"Which part? Sex or the unprotected part?"

"Both," he says, and my heart fractures. He said he wanted to show me what *always* meant to him. He kissed me in front of everyone at the party, claiming me publicly like he'd finally found his courage. I thought we were finally moving past the fear that's kept us circling each other since I arrived. "Or at least it should be." His voice drops, rough with something that sounds like desperation. "But I don't think I'm capable of staying away from you."

There's a pause that stretches between us, heavy with everything we're not saying. His dark eyes search mine, and I can see the war raging behind them, his want battling with whatever demons he won't name.

"Forgetting isn't an option," he whispers, and the raw honesty in his voice makes my throat tight.

I want to plead with him to tell me what's keeping him from letting go, from coming back to me, but I don't because I don't intend for this to be our last time. If he's breaking now, he'll break again, and each time, I'll collect the pieces until there's no choice for him but to come back and let me make him whole again. If he's still questioning whether we end, I have to prove that he's wrong. We don't end this time; this is just the beginning of his surrender.

"You feel so good," he pants, using his forearms to hover above me. "This body was made for me." I want to say I know. I want to repeat his words back to him until he realizes his own admissions. I'm made for him because I'm supposed to be his, and he's supposed to be mine. It's why we fit. He's taking his time with me, moving inside of me in long slow strokes, letting my body acclimate to his length in this new position. He lifts my leg over his hip. "I want to feel every inch of you," he says, pressing in deep, his tip reaching depths only he has been. His head drops to my neck, and he bites the sensitive skin at the base, no doubt marking me just like he did last time.

"Your mouth seems to know something your mind won't admit," I tease, arching into him. "Marking your territory again?" He doesn't release the skin between his teeth. He takes his time, sufficiently holding me captive until he knows his mark will remain before running his tongue over the heated flesh.

His dark eyes find mine. "You make me forget every reason I should walk away."

I blink away the sting of tears forming in my eyes and focus on the man I have now. He doesn't want to stay away any more than I want him to. If my body can break down the walls he's erected around what remains of his heart, I'll gladly use it. There's a pain in his eyes when he looks at me, but not when we're like this. Right now, there's nothing but the man I used to have, the one who looked at me with pure love and adoration.

"Don't look at me like that." His lips press into a thin line. He doesn't want to hurt me. He's still protecting me while hurting inside. His hand glides down my thigh, adjusting my leg so he can press in deeper. "Territory implies I have a claim. We both know I don't."

"I don't know..." I trail off, my words dissolving into breathless gasps as he moves inside me with deliberate precision, each thrust dragging his tip over the spot that makes my vision blur. The rhythm is maddening, and he knows exactly what he's doing to me. "My body seems to disagree with that assessment."

My words are as calculated as the relentless pace of his thrusts. I know he can hear the intoxicating rhythm we're creating, our ragged breaths filling the space between us as the sound of our arousal filters up, just barely slicing through the thunderous beat of our racing hearts. I'm drowning in sensation. The salty taste of his skin, the way his muscles tense beneath my hands as my fingers drift down his strong back, the heat radiating between our bodies where we are connected. There's no line of where he begins and I end.

I know he feels me too, the way I respond to every deliberate movement, every touch. I wrap both legs around his waist, pulling him impossibly deeper, and he responds with a growl, driving into me harder, claiming what he swears he doesn't own.

"Fuck, do you hear how wet you are for me? Taking my cock like it's yours."

"It is mine," I say before I can think better of it. He might not be ready to claim me, but I'll lay claim to what is mine, and he will be mine. I'm not letting him go.

"Yeah?" he says, his eyes locking onto mine. It is neither a question nor a confirmation.

"Maybe you should look at what's always been yours and see for yourself how I was made for you the way you were made for me." His jaw flexes, his soft stare turning hard. He knows what will happen if he looks. There will be no denying the truth.

He pushes up onto his hands before pressing back onto his haunches, pulling me by the hips so we stay connected. I watch every emotion that flicks across his face as he watches his cock disappear inside me, slickened by the wetness he created. His eye twitches, and his fingers dig into my hips. "Mine," he grinds out through clenched teeth, his eyes never straying from our connection. I watch as he pumps into me, each stroke more irregular than the last as he struggles to hold on, fighting a release he's not ready to relinquish.

It's his fear, his need to protect, and his inability to stay away from me—the person he knows he loves most—that sends me spiraling. I said he was the person meant to be at my side, battling every war, and this...this is no different. Love is an eternal battlefield. The hardest battles are fought within, between the head and the heart. I refuse to lose again.

Seconds behind me, he falls over the edge with a roar ripped from his chest, a sound that feels like complete surrender. His body covers mine in the aftermath, two hearts thundering against each other like war drums.

We lie like that for long moments, neither of us moving, silent for fear of losing what was gained. I lose track of time in the hushed sanctuary we've created. Minutes blur into eternities as I listen to the beat of his heart against my ear and the heat of his skin seeps into mine until I can't tell where he ends, and I begin. But even as my mind fights against exhaustion, desperate to memorize every detail of this night, his voice cuts through the drowsy haze.

"I want beautiful mistakes with you," he whispers against the curve of my neck, sending shivers cascading down my spine.

Unable to fight the fatigue, I fade into a deep sleep with a heart full of hope that, when I wake, those words will still be true.

LONDON

CHAPTER 29

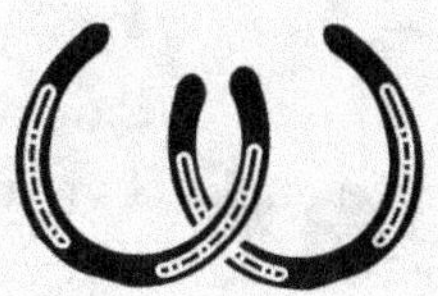

The first thing I notice when I wake isn't the obvious chill in the cool morning air or even the way my back protests against the uneven ground. It's the weight of her head on my chest. Laney's blonde hair is sprawled across it as I take careful breaths to steady the rise and fall of my chest. I've spent a small eternity dreaming of a moment just like this one, where she is mine again, one where I wake up, and she's right where I left her, in my arms.

I don't need to question how we got here. I remember every minute detail because I took my time cataloging each one, knowing tomorrows aren't guaranteed. The fear of what happened before had sunk its claws deep, and this time, I was the one throwing up walls, hurting her with words that gutted me even as I spoke them. But she refused to let them win. She fought —fought just like she did last time. Except, this time, I fought too.

Now, with her temple pressed against my chest and her arm draped loosely over my waist, something inside me cracks open. Not a breaking, rather an opening, like a door I've kept locked for far too long. Right now, in the still morning light, with her stubborn heart beating against mine and my own unyielding need to protect warring with this newfound clarity, I can see what I was blind to before.

We're not better apart. We're stronger together, and protecting her from a distance was never the answer. It was cowardice dressed up as nobility. The best way to protect her isn't to stand guard against the shadows but to stand beside her in the light, to be whatever she needs me to be. That's the man I want to be. That's the man she deserves.

A breeze rustles the leaves above us, and Laney's eyes flutter open. For a heartbeat, her eyes assess mine and her soft gaze is unguarded. It's the way she used to look at me, and I'm going to do everything in my power to ensure I get to keep it.

"Morning," she whispers, her brown eyes almost hazel as they reflect the morning sun.

"Good morning." I smile softly, pushing a strand of hair away from her forehead.

We steal a few more seconds of silence, basking in the light of a new day, one that we started together instead of apart, before the sounds of catering crews breaking down tables filter through the air.

"What time is it?" she asks, looking over her shoulder and scanning all that there is to see in the light.

"I don't know. My phone is in the pocket of my jeans and checking it would have required letting you go."

She rolls her lips to stifle the smile threatening to take over her face. Her fingers lazily trace over my chest, my skin sparking to life beneath her touch. "Last night, were you aware Trigg knew you were under the table?"

I chuckle, my fingers finding hers. "Not at first, but there were signs," I admit. I know that when I went under the table, his eyes had drifted toward the bar, where I knew Asha was entertaining guests.

Pressing the tips of her fingers against mine, she asks, "Are you worried about telling him your plan to add him to the lease?"

I pull a cleansing breath through my nose and exhale slowly.

"No, I started to tell him on our trail ride, but then you got attacked by bees. He knows I'm aware of the lease. I want to fill him in on my plan, but we haven't been able to sync up yet. Every time we're close, life happens."

"What changed? I thought you weren't sure if you could trust him."

"Hard times test your character, and watching how he's handled things since you arrived, I understand him more," I attempt to explain.

Six years. That's how long it's been since I arrived on Trigg's doorstep, a ghost from a past he didn't know existed. Beyond that first jarring moment when Baylor introduced us as brothers, we've found our rhythm, carved out a space where two strangers could become family.

The early days carried their weight of uncertainty, both of us walking on eggshells around truths, but that hesitation felt inevitable. When your entire understanding of yourself gets rewritten in a single conversation, caution becomes a survival technique. I catch myself wondering if our positions had been reversed—if he'd been the one standing on my father's doorstep with nowhere else to turn—would I have opened my door as readily? Would I have demanded explanations he wasn't ready to give, or would I have possessed his quiet patience, waiting for trust to grow organically?

These questions gnaw at me because they matter. They reveal the fault lines that run through both our lives, the damage done by a mother who chose abandonment, and the bitterness and pride that festers between our fathers. They've chosen isolation over reconciliation and resentment over family, and those choices have shaped both of us in ways we're still learning to understand. However, despite the scars of the past, we both seem to have one core value in common: our refusal to let the past repeat itself.

"Are you saying you agree with his tactics?" she questions, a little baffled by my acceptance.

We may have different temperaments and different ways of

processing pain, but fundamentally, we are both determined to be more than the sum of our wounds. We both want something our parents couldn't give us: family.

"I didn't say all that, but the more you know him, the more you understand his ways. He's good at playing the Jekyll-and-Hyde card, but he's never really the bad guy." I sigh. "I can relate to someone who'll let you assume the worst of them if it means they help you in the end. He knew you wouldn't keep his secret, and the way he saw it, that benefited both of you."

She's quiet, choosing to lay her head on my chest, pressing her ear to my heart as she processes what I've said. I know we are talking about Trigg, but I think she's heard another truth in my response—my truth.

"What about the things he said about Sydney?" she changes the subject.

I laugh and seductively drag my finger up the side of her arm. "I think that's when it became clear I was between your thighs, and he was trying to get a rise out of you." I bite my lip hard to force myself to think about the pinch of pain instead of the way she came hard all over my tongue.

Her head pops back up, and she rests her chin on my chest. "So you don't think it was true?"

"She's your best friend. You'd know better than me."

"Fair, but I know you have to have some kind of opinion. It's not like she's a complete stranger."

"I honestly don't have an opinion. Warrick and Sydney are both adults and free to do whatever they want. He isn't that old. He's only in his early forties. He and his late wife had Asha at a young age. I could see the Sydney I used to know going for an older man. She's very smart. An older man would challenge her the way men her own age can't."

Her eyes look past me, and I can see her wheels spinning. She agrees with me, but there's something else.

"I don't disagree with you, but what if Asha finds out?"

There it is. She's happy to support Sydney, but she doesn't

want to see a friendship destroyed over something that might not be forever.

"That's why I don't think Trigg's threat had any real imminence. I'm in the dark on whatever does or doesn't exist between those two, but I know he likes her, and because he likes her, I know he wouldn't frivolously hurt her."

"You're right," she says with a cleansing breath before propping herself up beside me on her elbow. It's in that one natural movement, one that should be no cause for concern, that the blanket slips, and my heart beats out of rhythm. Her eyes immediately zero in on the ink that wasn't there before. "What's this?" She sits up, grabbing her dress to cover her breasts and get a better look at the heart on my right thigh with her initials in the middle.

I close my eyes when I feel her finger trace over it. *This is it, London. You said you want to keep her, to stand in the light beside her and be whatever she needs you to be, so fucking do it.*

"It's your initials…" I start.

"We have the same initials. I'm not sure I believe you…" The spirit in her voice dims, and something else filters in. "Why here?"

I grab the shirt I was wearing last night and sit up beside her, draping it over her shoulders before saying, "It was a reminder of why I had to stay away…why I lost my heart."

"I don't understand," she whispers, and when her worried eyes connect with mine, I see the exact moment her world starts to fracture.

My chest aches as my heart thunders against my ribs. This is it, the moment I've clawed my way away from for six endless years, the reason I became a ghost in my own hometown. I'm about to bleed out a truth so raw it might kill us both, and I'm terrified she won't survive it. Terrified I won't survive watching her break.

"God, Laney, you have no idea how this is destroying me…" My voice cracks as I cup her face, memorizing every freckle, every curve, because this might be the last time she lets me touch her. "I never wanted to hurt you. Never wanted to be the one to put that look in your eyes."

Her hand comes up to cover mine. "You're killing me now by not letting me in. We're drowning in secrets, London. We can't heal if you don't trust me with your pain. We're bigger than what's broken us."

The love in her voice still, after everything we've been through, guts me. "We lost six years, Laney. Six goddamn years because I couldn't bear the thought of you living with the truth."

"Then don't let us lose any more." Her lips brush my cheek like a prayer, soft and desperate. "I love you. Nothing changes that. Give us a chance to prove it. Please."

"I lost you the night of your senior prom. I lost my heart to one fatal wound, but it wasn't my hand that killed a man…" I lick my lips, tasting salt and fear, and find the courage buried beneath six years of nightmares to add, "It was yours."

Her pupils dilate, her right eyelid twitching as if her body is trying to reject what her mind is processing. Tears well in her eyes and threaten to spill over. I pull her head against my chest before they can fall and shatter us both completely.

"No." The word comes out barely a whisper. "No, London, that's not... You took the blame. You told everyone it was you. You—"

"I lied." My voice cracks. "I lied to everyone. To the police, to you. Your stab wound hit his femoral artery. He was going to bleed out within minutes."

Her face crumples and I watch the weight of years of believing I was a killer shift into the crushing realization that she was the one who took a life. "Oh God," she breathes, looking down at her hands like she's seeing blood on them for the first time, turning them over.

"You survived." I grip her face tighter, desperate to make her understand. "Laney, you survived. He was going to hurt you. You fought back. You saved your own life."

Her eyes are wide and unfocused, and I can practically see her mind replaying that night with terrible new clarity. She presses her palms against her temples, shaking her head like she can force the truth back out.

"I'm sorry." I pull her against me, and this time, she doesn't resist, but she's rigid in my arms, her body locked in shock. "I'm so fucking sorry."

Long seconds stretch between us, her breaths coming heavy and ragged against my chest, but I never feel her tears fall. She's holding herself together with sheer will, and it's the most heartbreaking thing I've ever witnessed.

"Six years," she whispers. "Six years, I lived with the guilt of what I thought you did for me... Going to prison for my crime." She expels a heavy, stuttered sigh. "It's done," she says softly, her voice hollow but steady. "It's been done for years, and nothing I feel about it now will change that."

"I wanted to tell you so many times. Every letter I never sent, every phone call I never made... I wanted to tell you that it wasn't your fault, but I also wanted to spare you from ever having to know."

She pulls back to look at me, her eyes red-rimmed but lost, like she's drowning in her own guilt. The shock is wearing off now, replaced by the crushing weight of reality.

"You just... left," she says quietly, her voice hollow. "You let me think you were running from your own demons when you were really protecting me from mine." She takes a shaky breath. "I can't take it back. I can't change what happened that night."

"It was self-defense, baby," I quickly add when she pinches her lips together and closes her eyes.

"I know," she whispers, and there's a strength in her voice that amazes me. "I know it was." Her eyes flash open. "But if you believe that, then why did you do it?"

"Do what?" I ask as I stroke her hair.

"Why did you slit his throat to cover my crime? Why did you lie to everyone? Why did you steal my choice and make it yours?"

Her words have the air in my lungs catching as I hold my

breath. Why did I do it? Where do I even begin? I know the number one reason, but it's one I'm still not brave enough to speak aloud. It's not one I can give her without destroying what's left of my soul. I've loved her unconditionally, maybe more than I've ever loved myself. Now, then, and for eternity, I'll be her shelter, her rock, the safe place to lay her head because being her everything makes me whole.

"I didn't want you to live with the weight of taking a life," I whisper against her hair. "The eternal haunting that comes with blood on your hands. The way it changes you, piece by piece until you no longer recognize yourself in the mirror. I didn't know..." My voice cracks completely. "I didn't know my sacrifice would cut so much deeper. That staying away would hurt you more than the truth."

She's silent again, and it kills me. I can't stand not knowing what's going on in her head, feeling useless when her heart is hurting. "You asked me to trust you with the pain, heartbreaker. Your silence is killing me. Let me help you."

"It's just a lot to process. I saw things one way for so long. There's not one part of my life that night didn't change. The truth doesn't change the past, but it colors it differently..." Her head tips up, her sad, honeyed gaze finding mine. "We lost so much time."

"I'm so sorry," I manage. I want to give her so much more than sorry, and given the chance, I will, but for now, I start there.

"We should get dressed," she says, pushing out of my hold, taking the comfort of her warmth with her.

"Are you upset with me?"

"Yes and no," she says, brushing my shirt off of her shoulders to pull her dress over her head. "Even though I don't like it, I understand why you did it. I can't be mad at you for doing something I would have done."

Her response is better than I expected, though I couldn't say I planned on ever hearing one since I never planned on getting her back. But now that she's here, I hate the cold that feels like it's settling between us as she dresses. Her words say one thing, but I fear her heart isn't giving me the whole truth.

Glancing over her shoulder, she sees I haven't moved. "Aren't you going to get dressed?"

"In a minute." I lean back on my palms as she searches for her shoes. "Why does it feel like you're in a hurry to leave me?"

"I'm not," she says too quickly, her voice pitched higher than usual. The way she won't meet my eyes tells me she doesn't believe her own words. She fidgets with the cuffs of my discarded shirt. "You could... You could take me on a date?" The suggestion tumbles out, shaky and uncertain, like she's afraid of the answer.

That's when I realize why her mood has changed. We've said a lot of things, but we haven't defined what this is. This isn't some meaningless hookup with a stranger. We're exes, but not just any exes. We're the kind who used to say "I love you" like a prayer, the kind that planned on forever.

"A date," I repeat, letting the word settle between us while I study her face. A date isn't nearly enough. I want everything.

"Yes...we could go to dinner," she says meekly. I watch her shoulders tense as she misreads my silence, bracing for rejection.

"I can't do dinner."

"Oh," falls from her lips, and I see her physically deflate.

My hands find her shoulders, and I press my lips to the curve where her neck meets her shoulder, in the spot that has always made her melt.

"I can't do dinner," I murmur against her skin, "because I'd rather take you to breakfast." I feel her breath catch. "I'm not ready to let you go yet, heartbreaker. Not when we just found our way back to each other."

She turns in my arms, and I see everything I've been hoping for reflected in her eyes: relief, want, and something that looks dangerously like the love we used to share. Maybe some things are worth the risk of breaking twice. I'd break infinitely until they put me in a casket just to share moments like this with her.

LONDON

CHAPTER 30

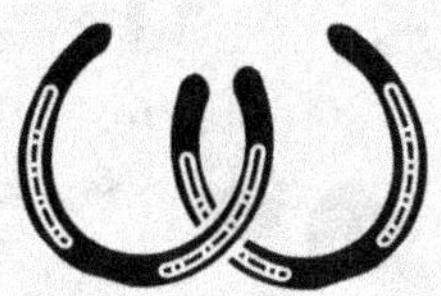

The summer has come and gone, Laney is still here, and I wouldn't want it any other way. It feels like we've finally lived the summer that was stolen from us all those years ago, but it's even better. Six years ago, we may have questioned our strength and our ability to make it through the hard times, but not now. This summer, we were able to give each other everything without reservation, because we've been tested, and we know we're stronger for it. Now it's time to make it clear: I don't want to love anybody but her.

Her hands tighten around my chest, and my entire body hums, buzzing to life, with the woman I love with everything that I am wrapped around me as we wind down a wooded road on the bike. I'm done wasting time. The things I want in my life have always begun and ended the same. They end with her or no one. I've ridden this route countless times alone, memorizing every pothole and bend, but having Laney behind me with the late-afternoon sun filtering through the canopy above transforms everything. Maybe that's because I'm about to ask for everything.

The engine thrums beneath us as I step on the gas coming out of a turn, and I feel her laugh vibrate against my back, her excitement sending a trill of electricity through my veins. I don't know why I'm nervous. I don't see a scenario playing out where she says no, but it hasn't stopped my palms from growing sweaty as I recall all the things I want to say and all the ways I want to make her mine.

The tree line breaks, and the road opens up ahead, and a rolling meadow covered in sunflowers, bordered by a lazy creek, comes into view. The first time Baylor brought me to this part of the property, I was enamored. The small cabin with overgrown vegetation is less than a thousand square feet and almost one hundred years old. It was built by my great-grandfather for my great-grandmother. It was the first house they lived in after getting married. Apparently, land with horses and a garden full of sunflowers was my great-grandmother's dream, and since my great-grandfather was determined to give her the world, he made Hale Ranch a reality.

I was young when my grandfather died, too little to remember meeting him or getting to hear his memories of growing up on this land firsthand, so it was Baylor who filled me in on the history of how my great-grandfather lost his heart years before her time because of cancer. It was because of her that this land was bought, and it was because of her that he ensured her legacy would live on for generations to come. It's why there's a no-sell clause on the deed as long as there are living descendants. This was her dream, and he ensured it would never die.

I downshift and turn onto the old dirt driveway that leads to the heart of the property. Once we are in front of the cabin, I kill the engine. There are seconds of silence as I steal a moment to etch this scene onto my heart. Being here with her is profound. I know I was always meant to live this moment with her.

"London," she says softly, pulling off her helmet. "This place is beautiful. Whose is it?"

"It's mine." I swing my leg over the bike and dismount so I can face her. "Want to see it?" I ask, extending my hand.

She smiles and nods adamantly, putting her hand in mine. "When did you buy it?"

My nerves are getting the best of me. I was supposed to say, "It's mine, but I was hoping it could be ours." I'm already fumbling this.

"I didn't. Technically, we're still on Hale land," I explain.

Her eyes widen. "Really? Exactly how many acres does your family own?"

"A little under six hundred acres."

"Holy shit. I mean, I knew the property was vast, but six hundred?" She squeezes my hand. "That's nuts."

"In today's economy, yeah, it's a lot. I can't imagine buying this much land, but this property has been in the family for a long time. My great-grandfather built this house for my great-grandmother."

"Really? That's the sweetest thing I've ever heard," she says, stepping onto the porch. "Like something straight out of the pages of a fairy tale. It's beautiful here. I think I could sit on this porch for hours." She walks over to the far end of the porch that faces west and points to a small clearing beside the creek. "Right there, I bet she spent a lot of time sitting peacefully beside that bubbling brook, reading, writing, and taking summer naps. It looks like a little slice of heaven."

"I'm glad you can envision yourself here," I say, wrapping my arms around her from behind. "Because I was hoping it could be ours," I murmur against her neck before placing a small kiss there.

"What do you mean?"

"You had only planned on staying here through August. It's now late September." I spin her in my arms so I can see her face. "I know Asha offered you a full-time position at Fairfield, but I also know that's not your dream. I know you want to run your own equine rehabilitation ranch, helping horses and people. I want to give you that dream the same way my great-grandfather gave my great-grandmother hers."

Her eyebrows rise slightly, and she opens her mouth, but no words come out. "London, I… I don't know what to say."

"Say yes," I plead before kissing her forehead.

"Can we go inside?"

That wasn't a yes, but it also wasn't a no. "Yes," I say with a hitch of excitement. "But brace yourself. This place is old, and it hasn't exactly been maintained."

The solid oak front door swings open, creaking on its hinges as Laney steps across the threshold, and I realize I'm holding my breath. I'm watching every body movement and expression that crosses her face, trying to get a read on her. I know she loves the property. Outside, she was already dreaming about the places she would sit and the things she would do, but I can sense a pause, or maybe it's my nerves.

The main room is the only room apart from the bathroom. There isn't much to this original cabin, but it still has a lot of charm. The exposed beam ceilings are twelve feet high, and the logs on the inside still hold their original honey color despite their age. In the very center of the cabin is a stone fireplace open on both sides, its mantel displaying intricate, hand-carved horse designs.

I watch as she steps deeper into the space, the wide-plank pine floors creaking underfoot as she walks toward the kitchen. "The kitchen would need to be completely overhauled as well as the bathroom, and we'd need a new roof, but the bones are solid."

She nods silently, running her fingers across the dusty dining table my grandfather built. "Asha is my friend. I can't quit, but more than that, I don't want to."

"I'm not asking you to quit. People could bring their horses to you. Remember what you said to Madison when she asked you to work with Gypsy?"

Her back straightens, and I realize I could have picked a better reference. We've had long conversations about what the past six years apart looked like. We discussed our relationships and the people that were in our lives during that time. She knows the truth about Madison and me: that despite whatever feelings existed, Madison was ultimately just someone to fill the empty spaces, a friend who happened to share my bed when loneliness got too heavy to bear alone. I know how that sounds—cold, maybe even cruel—but we were both using each other in our own ways. Madison might have wanted something deeper toward the end, but for most of our time together, I was just a convenient stop on her endless journey. She never belonged to Bardstown the way I do. Her home is the highway, the next town, the next temporary landing place.

"You turned down work because you didn't have your own space to accept a client, control the environment, and assess the horse. Here, you could have that." I walk around the fireplace and meet her on the other side. "You can still work, but you could do it here instead while also expanding and starting your own business."

I can see the wheels in her head spinning, and I can tell by the way her lips are slightly pursed that she doesn't hate the idea.

"And what would you do? What's your dream, London?"

I pick up an old candlestick and brush off the dust. When we discussed our dreams in high school, they were five-year plans. Back then, I was attending school to become a civil engineer. I liked building things, but that was before I learned about the family business. My father and Baylor may have dug their heels in and refused to put their differences aside, but somehow, they still managed to run the ranch together. Growing up, I knew my father was an accountant. What I didn't know until I moved here is that he's been balancing the books and running the financials all this time. This gives me hope that his relationship with Baylor is salvageable. Reconciliation is possible. We just have to make it happen.

"I like working with horses, but I'm not a breeder. Trigg has a knack for looking at a horse and knowing without any genealogy paperwork if a horse has winning blood. I don't have that in me, and I'm not sure it's trainable." I sigh and shrug. "I like to ride horses leisurely. I worked with Titan and trained him to be my horse hand because I needed a companion, and I felt like I could relate to him. However, at the end of the day, true contentment came from working the fields with Baylor, watching the fruit of my labor pop up in rows. I wanted to be an engineer because I liked the satisfaction that came with creating something, and if I get my way, I'm hoping that Baylor will allow me to work with him and take his small-batch bourbon to the next level."

"So when you're done working the fields all day…" She takes a few short steps to stand at my front. "You'll come home"—she laces her fingers around my neck—"to me?"

"Heartbreaker, you are my home. I want to wake up with you next to me, not in my uncle's house, but in our house. I want to build a life with you, Laney Hart. I've wanted it since we were ten years old. I don't want to live without you—"

My words die when her sweet mouth presses against mine. "I love you, London Hale." I barely have a moment to appreciate her soft lips on mine before she's pulling away, eyebrows raised. "Hey, that doesn't look old."

She releases me to grab the cowboy hat sitting on the stone hearth.

"This looks like it's at least from the past decade," she says, turning it over in her hands with the careful reverence of someone discovering buried treasure.

"That's because it is." The words scrape past the sudden tightness in my throat as memories, both painful and beautiful, pull to the forefront.

"Whose is it?" Her eyes find mine, curious and questioning.

"Mine."

"Did you forget it or something?" she asks, placing it on her head like it belongs there. Like it was always meant to be there. My chest constricts at the sight. She looks exactly like I'd imagined on all those lonely nights when missing her felt like drowning.

"No, I left it here six years ago when Baylor brought me here for the first time."

She adjusts the brim, tilting her head. "Why? It's a nice hat."

The words stick in my throat for a moment. "Because it's yours."

Her hands freeze. "I don't understand."

I drag a hand through my hair, trying to find the right words for something that's lived in my heart for years. "About a month after I got to town, Baylor dragged me to this flea market, said he needed muscle in case he bought anything heavy." The memory is more vivid now. "One of the vendors was selling hats, and the band on that one caught my eye."

She pulls the hat off, studying it with new intensity. "The tribal print," I continue, my voice barely above a whisper. "It matched the etching from my grandfather's knife perfectly."

I don't need to say more. She knew I carried that knife with me everywhere religiously...until I couldn't. "Flip it over," I say gently, knowing what she'll find but needing her to see it for herself.

She turns the hat, squinting in the cabin's golden dimness. "Look closely at the logo in the liner. What do you see?"

Her breath catches. "Our initials. LH."

"Another small detail that solidifies that we are meant to be," I say, stepping closer, drawn by the wonder in her voice. "But only one of us has them inked on their skin inside a heart, just like that logo."

Her lips part in surprise. "You already had the tattoo when you found this?"

"I wore that hat everywhere for months. It was like carrying a piece of you with me when I thought I'd lost you forever. Crazy as it sounds, it felt like fate. Like I was supposed to find it."

She traces the initials with her fingertip, and I watch her face soften with understanding. "So why is it here?"

I release a shaky breath. "Because I was trying to let you go. I thought if I left it here—left that piece of you where you belonged, maybe I could finally move on."

The confession hangs between us, raw and honest. I remember that day so clearly now: walking out that front door with empty hands and an even emptier heart, telling myself it was the right thing to do. Telling myself lies.

"But I couldn't," I whisper. "I could never let you go, Laney. Not really. That hat has been waiting here all this time, just like I've been waiting to find my way back to you."

Her eyes are soft as she places the hat back on her head, the sentiment behind it clearly striking a chord, but when she adjusts the rim and gives me her eyes, something shifts—a spark of determination mixed with desire that makes my pulse quicken. Her fingers find the thin strap of her athletic dress, and she lets it slip slowly off her shoulder. I can't breathe. Can't think. Can only watch as she reaches for the other strap.

"What are you doing?" The words come out rougher than I intended, my voice already betraying how she affects me.

"You're giving me so much. This house is special… This dream is special... This hat... You… I want to give you something in return."

Laney Hart has had a starring role in every one of my fantasies since I was old enough to start having them. But now she is every wish, every dream, every hope wrapped into one beautiful reality.

She purses her lips, a knowing smile playing at the corners of her mouth as she hooks her thumbs under both straps of the athletic dress that's been driving me crazy all summer. Those damn dresses. She looks like temptation incarnate in them, but they're also my personal torture because I know what's hidden underneath—or rather, what isn't.

"Not even a memory?" she questions, her voice dropping to that seductive whisper that undoes me every time. She starts to peel the fabric down slowly, deliberately, revealing the curves that have haunted my dreams for years. "I thought we could make a memory and christen the place we've decided to call home."

My breath catches as more of her is revealed, and I have to grip the edge of the mantel to steady myself. Years of aching for her touch, countless nights falling asleep with nothing but memories and my own hand for company, and now here she is, real, warm, mine.

This summer, we've been making up for all the lost time, and she's completely owned me from the first moment she let me back into her heart. I've had no qualms about letting her lead, following wherever she wants to take us. She tells me what she wants, and I'm more than happy to oblige.

"Laney," I whisper her name like a prayer, my voice rough with need and love and everything I've kept locked away for too long. The hat sits perfectly on her head, framing her face as she looks at me with eyes full of heat and promise.

"You're the story I'll always remember," I breathe, taking a step forward, desperate to close the distance between us. "Unforgettable in every way. You're woven into the fabric of who I am, etched into my memory, eternally mine now and always."

The crackle of energy that constantly pulses between us feels almost tangible under the weight of her dark, hungry gaze. Every cell in my body is drawn to her like a magnet, and I take another possessive step forward, unable to simply watch her stand before me, but she holds up her hand, stopping me mid-stride with a gesture that's both gentle and commanding.

"On your knees," she commands with a teasing finality that dares me to disagree, but resisting would be futile. When a goddess stands confidently before you naked, you do exactly as she says.

The wooden floor is rough against my knees as I sink down, my eyes never leaving hers. From this angle, she looks ethereal. The hat casts a shadow across her features, but I can still see the fire burning in her eyes, the same fire that's been consuming me for years.

"You're so fucking sexy, heartbreaker." I can feel the heaviness in my eyes as they trail down her body, taking in every delicious inch—inches I'm dying to put my lips on. "What now, baby?"

"Get your knees dirty," she says, pointing to the floor in front of her.

"Yes, ma'am," I say, putting one knee in front of the other and closing the distance between us.

Kneeling before her, my gaze level with my favorite place, my cock strains against my jeans. When I lift my eyes to meet hers, a wicked smile blooms across her face, one that sends lightning through my veins and makes my pulse stutter. The dangerous curve of her lips promises the kind of beautiful destruction I crave, and she knows exactly the power she holds over me.

Her fingers drag deliciously over my scalp, making every hair on my body stand at attention as their master pulls the strings. Then, with a sharp tug, she yanks my head back and lifts a leg over my shoulder, claiming her throne with the confidence of someone who knows I'm exactly where I belong.

"We're in the dining room. I thought I'd make your first meal memorable…" She catches her lip between her teeth. "Eat."

That hypnotic honey gaze holds mine as I dip my tongue and run it up her center. Her plump lips part with a gasp, her eyes never leaving mine, framed by the weight of her heavy breasts, and I lose it. She's so damn perfect. My tongue sinks into her tight hole, and I can't help but close my eyes as a deep growl rumbles from my chest. Hearing her intoxicating whimpers and knowing I'm the one who's making her feel good has me rock hard.

I grip her firm ass hard and pull her closer, practically smothering myself and loving every second. Her happiness has become my religion. I've spent months worshiping at the altar of her joy, consumed by an insatiable craving for total unity in all ways. She's always been the other half of my soul, her words already the ones in my head. All summer, we've been dissolving the last barrier between us, our bodies speaking their own fierce language, transcending something physical into all-consuming until no distinction between where I end and she begins remains. Her hand fists into my hair as she rocks against my face, desperate to hold me right where she wants me. I slip a digit inside, and her hungry pussy clenches hard.

"More," she pants.

"So greedy. You're making my cock jealous, baby," I say,

adding another digit and stealing another glance at the eyes that give me purpose.

Her milky skin is flushed as I thrust in harder. Her pussy is gripping my fingers like a vise, and I know she's close. I suck her clit into my mouth.

"I want to come, London. You better not tease me. Don't you dare stop."

Her pussy starts to clench hard, on the edge of letting go. I can feel it. Curling my fingers, my tongue works her slit, giving it to her just the way she likes it but stealing something for myself and tilting my head back to watch her come. I want to see her pretty face flushed with ecstasy when I bring her to orgasm on my tongue. But the second my eyes look up, they collide with hers, and fuck if it doesn't unlock something feral inside of me.

Watching her during her most vulnerable moment creates a profound sense of connection for me, and seeing her watch me pleasure her is a new level of unlocked. I love it. She was already on the edge, but our eyes locking sends her spiraling, and she pulls my hair hard. Fuck. I growl hungrily against her pussy as I pump her through her orgasm, lapping up all her juices until her grip loosens. I withdraw my fingers and kiss her lips before removing her thigh from my shoulder.

Her cheeks burn with a rose-colored blush I've memorized because it's the exact shade that tells me I've done my job well. Her breathing comes in deep, measured waves as she rides the aftershocks.

Her body is still humming with electricity when she points to an old shaker chair. "Sit," she commands.

I shoot a glance at the chair before turning back to her with a smirk that's all sin and satisfaction. "Yes, ma'am. You know, watching you take control like this is doing dangerous things to my self-restraint," I say, my voice a low rumble of appreciation.

Once I'm seated where she wants me, she leans in close enough that I can feel her breath on my skin, her lips barely an inch from mine. "I'm counting on it," she purrs, her words sending every nerve ending ablaze. My hands ball into fists against my thighs, fighting the primal urge to grab her hips and claim what she's dangling in front of me. But that's precisely what she wants.

Pushing me to the edge has become Laney's favorite form of foreplay. She thrives on the knowledge that she, and only she, can reduce me to something raw and desperate, something so intoxicating that I'd willingly drown in her. And fuck, do I want to drown. Every breath she steals, every second she makes me wait, only fuels the fire.

As much as she gets off on torturing me, I do the same, watching her take what she wants. I love this side of her. I love this side of us. The side that found their way back home. Her hands move down the front of my shirt, making quick work of unhooking every button before settling on my belt, where she undoes it. My cock is aching to feel her touch as she pulls it off and unbuttons my jeans before giving me another order. "Lift," she says, her hands gripping my jeans and boxers where she tugs them down and frees my cock.

Her eyes don't miss the glistening tip as it springs to attention for her. "I like how ready you are for me, cowboy," she taunts seductively before dragging her nails over my thighs. Her pink tongue wets her lips as her hand encircles the base of my cock.

"I'm always ready for you. I've had six years to fuck my hand to thoughts of you. My dick didn't forget how to worship its queen."

She looks up at me from her seated position between my spread thighs. "I'm the one on my knees for her king."

Damn. I like that sentiment. I love that she holds me in the same high regard I do her, but that doesn't shift the power.

"This chair doesn't give me the upper hand, heartbreaker. The one on their knees is the one who decides when, how, and if at all." Her eyes fall to my cock hungrily.

"You're right, and I think I'm done talking. I'm going to suck your cock now," she says, and in the next breath, her hot mouth is wrapped around my dick, her soft lips gliding down my shaft.

"Fuck," I hiss as I tip my head toward the ceiling. "You do that so good, baby." I feel her hair cascade over my thighs, and I can't help but take her hat off and gather it to get a better look. She's taking me so deep, my tip hitting the back of her throat on every bob. Her fingers dig into my thighs as she finds a punishing rhythm determined to make me lose control, and as tempting as that sounds, I want something else more. I tug her hair. "Baby, you said you wanted to give me a memory, and as much as I fucking love this one. I want another one more."

Her mouth releases my cock with a pop, and it throbs, already missing its warmth. "I want my first release in our house to be inside of you. You're my home, Laney." Her brown eyes pierce mine. "Look at it, baby. See for yourself what you do to me. I come undone in every way, every time. Get up here."

"You're good at saying all the right words when you want to, London Hale," she says, rising to her feet and straddling the chair. She plants her feet on the floor and sits, her slickness rubbing against my hard length as her mouth covers mine. Her sweet tongue hungrily dips inside, and I taste myself on it. A deep growl erupts from my chest, and she pulls away. "I love you."

"I love you so damn much," I answer breathlessly as she aligns my tip with her entrance. Then placing the hat back on her head, our eyes connect, and I say, "Ride me."

Her hands grip my shoulders as she slowly starts to lower herself. Feeling her warmth pull me in, my whole body shudders, but it's the sight of observing her as she watches me disappear inside of her that wrecks me.

"You're so fucking beautiful," I say, and her eyes snap up to mine, my praise gaining another inch as she slowly acclimates to my size. My hand cups one of her breasts before I bring it to my mouth and suck hard. Her pussy instantly clenches around my dick as she bottoms out.

I love the way she rides me, the way she feels stretched around me, but mostly, it's the way she has a way of fucking me and loving me at the same time. When she's in control, she takes what she wants, how she wants, and it's usually fast and hard. It doesn't take long for her orgasm to build; sucking me off got her ready for another. She's hungry, and I happily let her chase it, because we both know it will only be the first of many. We're alone in a house we plan to call home with nowhere else to be.

She picks up her pace, the sound of her ass slapping against my thighs every time she bottoms out picking up in an intoxicating crescendo.

Her nails dig into my shoulders as her walls start to flutter around my length, and I know she's close.

"Look at me," I demand as I pull her chin to my face, and our labored breaths mingle for a heartbeat. "I want to see your eyes when you come undone, in our house, on my cock, for the first time."

She slams down hard one final time, my words setting us both off at the same time. A loud crack echoes through the cabin, and the chair gives way beneath us, sending us tumbling to the floor in a tangle of limbs and breathless laughter.

"Well," Laney gasps between giggles, her hat somehow still perfectly perched on her head despite everything, "I'd say we definitely christened this place."

I pull her closer against my chest, both of us still breathing hard, still trembling from the intensity of what just passed between us. "Think we broke more than just the chair," I murmur into her hair, my voice rough with satisfaction and exhaustion.

"Good," she whispers, tracing lazy patterns on my chest. "Some things are meant to be broken and rebuilt."

The words hang between us like a confession, and I feel the weight of everything unsaid settling into the space where our bodies meet. Long minutes pass as we lie on the floor, a perfectly tangled mess of limbs—her leg thrown over mine, my arm curved around the small of her back. The hardwood beneath us should be uncomfortable, but somehow, it feels like the most natural place in the world.

"London?" she murmurs finally, rough with the same bone-deep weariness that's settled into my chest.

"Mmm?"

"Best memory ever."

I press a kiss to the top of her head, just below the brim of her hat, and let my eyes drift closed. "The first of many, heartbreaker."

~

"THIS ISN'T REALLY PILLOW TALK," LANEY SAYS, HER BLONDE HAIR cascading over her shoulder as she props herself up on her elbow. "But are you sure you've thought through this whole plot to get your dad back to Hale Ranch? You and I know the damage that secrets and lies can do."

I mindlessly twist her hair around my finger. "He kept this place a secret from me my whole life. You know better than anyone. I always wished I'd had cousins and grandparents growing up. Being an only child wasn't ideal. Sure, I found my mom in high school, but she was twelve years too late with a poor excuse that she believed justified the abandonment of her son. I think if I can get my dad here, if he could step on the earth he was raised on, and smell the dusty warmth that permeates the pastures in the summer and the crisp, cool air in the fall it would go a long way. He once called this place home. If a white lie gets him here and I can bring my family back together, it's worth it."

"Having Fish call and tell him there's been an accident might backfire. He could have a heart attack," she points out.

"That's a valid point," I say as I stare at the ceiling in thought.

"What if, instead, he calls and tells him you haven't come home? You and Titan rode out to check the property, and you haven't returned. It's enough to make him worry without him jumping to the absolute worst-case scenario. Plus, if you're missing on Hale land, I bet his mind would instantly drift to the places he used to go. I bet he'd start thinking of all the places he'd look first."

"You're fucking brilliant. It's one of the many reasons I love you."

"I still wish there was a way to get him here without lying."

"Me too, but I feel like something big needs to happen to end the war. My dad doesn't know Trigg's story—who his mother is and how everything went down. It's a conversation that needs to happen in person."

Her eyes look distant as she stares at the fire I started in the fireplace, and I hate it. I understand why she hates lies. I hate them too. "Hey, I can think of something else if this is going to upset you that much."

"No." She shakes her head. "It's not that. I was just thinking."

"About?" I question as I pull her closer.

"Us, this property, the future, all of it..." she draws off nervously, and I am reminded of why I brought her here at all. The words I fumbled giving her earlier—and then not at all after she seduced me to this floor. "I have something I need to tell you," she says softly.

"And I have something I need to ask you."

"You go first," she says, pulling in a shaky breath.

That has to be it. The reason for her anxiety. I told her I wanted to build a life with her here on my family's land, but I never asked her the big question. The one that ties her to me for eternity. The one where she takes my last name.

"You knew from the start, from the very first day when I begged and pleaded for my father not to take you fishing, that I'd love you. You knew I'd fall for your beautiful soul. I loved you as my best friend, as my fishing partner...until I loved you as more." I watch as her eyes well with tears. The direction of my words is clear. "I loved you when I didn't know what love was, and I loved you when I was scared to feel it. This may not be the spot where our story began, but I'd love for it to be the spot where it ends.

Laney Hart, would you make a man out of this lost boy and be my wife?"

Tears flow freely down her cheeks as silence hangs between us. Her eyes search my face as the question waits patiently to be answered. Ten seconds. Twenty. Thirty.

She closes her eyes, and my anxiety spikes. She wouldn't say no, would she?

Her eyes pop open, and her face transforms with joy. "London Hale, I've wanted to marry you since the first time I saw you. I want nothing more than to take your last name and make it mine."

I close the distance between our mouths, and a new hunger forms. Every day with her is better than the last, but hearing her confirm she wants forever is a new level. Her fingers tangle in my hair as she seeks to deepen our kiss, two people discovering a new fire. The world melts away the way it always does when I'm with her, and for long moments, I get to experience a slice of heaven on earth where all is right in the world because the only girl I've ever wanted said yes.

When our lips finally part, she lays her forehead against mine, breathless, her heart racing. I ask for one more thing. "What would you say if I asked you to go down to the courthouse and marry me right now?"

"It's the middle of the night. They're closed."

"You know what I mean. If we wake up first thing tomorrow morning, would you get on the back of my bike and let me take you downtown to get married?"

"Easy cowboy, I haven't finished judging all of your questionable life choices," she jests, swatting my chest, and it feels like a stall.

"Is that a no?"

"It's a maybe," she says, rolling her lips, and I deflate. "Not because I don't want to marry you, but because when I pictured getting married, I saw myself having a wedding with our closest friends and family. Sydney, Fisher, Asha, Trigg, and our parents…

they're all part of our story. I wouldn't want to hastily make a decision that didn't include the people I love most and hurt them." Her fingers find my chin, and she tips my face toward hers until she has my full attention. "You know I'd marry you in a heartbeat. I love you, but they love us too, and I don't want to have any regrets."

The word 'yes' had barely finished forming on her lips when my world tilted sideways. For one perfect, crystalline moment, I had everything I wanted. The future spread out before us the way we'd always planned.

I had thought the truth I finally gave her would be enough. The carefully curated version of events that let me keep her while salving my conscience. I thought it was complete, thought it was sufficient, thought it would hold the weight of forever.

But lying here, watching her eyes light up as she describes the wedding she's dreamed of, I understand with devastating clarity how wrong I was. The truth wasn't enough. It never could have been.

Because it wasn't really the truth at all.

LANEY

CHAPTER 31

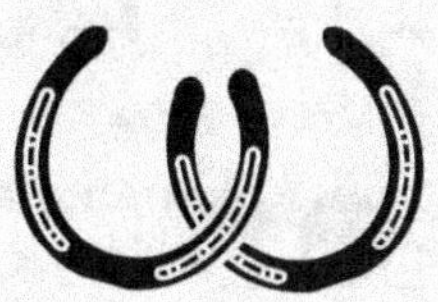

I felt it as we lay there watching the embers of the fire die out. I felt a shift.

I couldn't put my finger on it. I thought it was the high, the excitement of the night, the property, the plans, the proposal. I dismissed it for jitters and fell asleep in his arms. We woke up the same way we always do, tangled up, holding on to each other, as if one of us might disappear in the middle of the night, and this would all be a dream. But after he dropped me off at Fairfield, the shift was still there. His words were the same, but the feeling behind them, the love and excitement, the electric current, was dimmed. I went through my morning workout with a new horse in a haze, and now, as I sit in town at the local coffee shop, sipping a white chocolate mocha, I'm still there.

My eyes have been pinned on the busy street outside the window since I sat down. My head is in the clouds with unanswered questions. Is he upset I want a wedding? Did he really want to go to the courthouse this morning? There wasn't a ring. If he was truly set on getting married today, he would have had a ring, right? I just don't get it. We went from top of the world to a funk, and I feel like it's my fault. I texted him hours ago, and he hasn't responded. He always responds, so this is yet another sign something is off, and this isn't all just a figment of my imagination.

"That's it." I scoot my chair out with fierce determination. "Screw this." I'm going to ask him straight up—or I thought I was. "Shit." I grab the table to stabilize myself. I stood up way too fast.

That's when it occurs to me: I haven't eaten. Too much caffeine on an empty stomach.

When the lightheadedness subsides, I slowly turn toward the pastry case. All the usual suspects are there, but a particular apple fritter is calling my name. I don't love apples, but the thin slices and cinnamon swirls are calling my name.

"I'll take an apple fritter, please," I say, laying cash on the counter.

"Sure thing," the barista with the shiniest brown hair I've ever seen says. I watch as she reaches into the case, and my vision starts to blur.

"Fancy running into you here," I hear Fisher say, stepping up behind me.

"Hey," I answer, my voice small as I close my eyes to shut out the blurred vision setting in. I need that fritter ASAP.

"You okay?" he asks, his hand resting on my shoulder as I hold onto the counter.

"Yeah, just need to get some food in my stomach," I assure him.

"One apple fritter," the barista pushes my pastry across the counter.

I open my eyes to take it, desperate for the sugar and relief seconds away, when my heart quickens, and a ringing in my ears sets in. "Oh no," I say regretfully as I feel my knees buckle.

Strong arms catch me before I hit the ground. "Laney... Laney, can you hear me?" his voice echoes from somewhere far away, growing fainter with each repetition.

The warmth of his embrace is the last thing I feel before darkness takes me completely.

~

"Seriously, you brought me to the emergency room? Fish, I just needed to eat that damn pastry, and I would have been good. Now, I'll have to pay an ER visit bill. Do you have any idea how much this is going to cost me?" I fume as I sit in the stupid bed, staring at the ceiling, waiting for bloodwork to come back.

"Oh, so it's my fault you didn't eat today? I suppose it's also my fault you were unresponsive longer than medically acceptable. For your information, the shop called the ambulance. You were a liability." He starts opening cabinets, being nosy as one does in a tiny exam room with nothing else to do. "Don't worry about the bill. I'll pay it."

"You don't need to pay my bills, Fish. I can handle them. I'm just saying it sucks to pay a thousand dollars because I didn't eat breakfast," I groan.

"Did you tell London?"

"I called and texted…no response," he says, closing the last cabinet and turning to face me, arms crossed with boredom.

"You don't have to stay. I'm fine. You can see that."

"Stop trying to kick me out. It's not happening." His eyes roam around the room. "I'm just not a fan of emergency rooms. They creep me out."

That makes me laugh. "Are you serious? Why?"

"Are you saying you haven't been sitting there, wondering how many people died on that bed you're waiting on?"

I can feel my eyebrows shoot up to my hairline. "Umm, not until you just said that," I say, sitting up instead of lying down like I was. "Thanks for that." Trying to get my mind off the number of dead people who may have occupied this bed, I ask, "Did London seem okay when you saw him today?"

Fisher has been staying at Hale Ranch since he came to town. I'm not sure what his long-term goals are, but I know he's liked playing a hands-on role at the ranch. Before coming here, his role as a bloodstock broker was done behind a screen. I don't think he has any plans of returning to Europe or living in a city. Country life suits him.

"I didn't see him this morning, so I couldn't tell you." He crosses his legs at the ankle. "Why? Did something happen?"

I drop my eyes to the blanket. Fisher can read me like a book, and I don't want to spill the beans on our engagement yet. I know London would want to tell his best friend in person.

"No, nothing happened. He just seemed a little distant when he dropped me off, is all. It's probably just me." I shrug it off. "I mean, look at me. I'm the one who can't remember to eat breakfast," I force a laugh into my tone, one that Fish clearly isn't buying.

He opens his mouth, but before he can speak, the door swings open. "Sorry for making you wait so long, Miss Hart. The lab took longer than expected to process your results." The doctor's eyes shift to Fisher, his expression turning professional. "Before I discuss Miss Hart's test results, I'm going to need to ask you to step outside."

"It's okay; he can stay," I say quickly, and Fisher moves closer to my bedside, his presence steadying me.

The doctor nods. "As long as you're comfortable with that." He glances down at his clipboard then back up at us. "Your glucose levels came back below normal, which we expected given that you hadn't eaten before the fainting episode. Your CBC also showed low hemoglobin counts, which often correlates with low blood sugar." He pauses, choosing his words carefully. "However, since you mentioned no prior history of fainting or blood sugar issues, I ordered an additional test."

The silence stretches between us, heavy with anticipation, and my stomach knots. I know what the other test was. The doctor's eyes move from me to Fisher, something like caution flickering across his features.

"The hCG test confirmed what I suspected might be the underlying cause." Another pause. "You're pregnant, Miss Hart. Congratulations."

The words hang in the air like a held breath, and I feel Fisher's hand tighten around mine.

I lean back against the bed as the weight of the news washes over me. My periods haven't been regular all summer, light to almost non-existent, but I was having them. Then, this past week, when I should have had something, there was nothing. It's what I wanted to mention to London last night, but after the proposal, I decided to wait.

Discovering I'm pregnant is not entirely unexpected. I suspected it. I knew there was a risk when I chose to be with London unprotected, but I hoped that when and if this moment ever came, he would be the one by my side, learning it with me.

"Now that we know you're pregnant, my discharge orders have changed slightly." The doctor's tone shifts from congratulatory to one of focus. "You'll still need to eat small meals or snacks every few hours and try to balance your carbohydrates, proteins, and fats. This should also help correct the anemia, but I'm prescribing iron supplements to be safe. Take them until your first OB-GYN appointment." His pen runs down his clipboard, checking off topics as he goes. "You'll also need to start prenatal vitamins immediately."

He looks up, meeting my eyes. "Given the pregnancy, I've ordered an ultrasound. I want to confirm fetal development and rule out an ectopic pregnancy just as a standard precaution." His expression softens slightly. "Do you have any questions before I have a nurse bring in the ultrasound machine?"

"No," I manage, my voice barely above a whisper. "Not at the moment."

The reality still feels surreal, like I am watching someone else's life unfold.

I release a shaky breath, the weight of everything pressing down on my chest. This is not how I pictured my afternoon going. Fisher squeezes my hand, anchoring me to the moment.

"You want me to try calling London again?" he asks quietly.

"Yeah." I swallow hard. "But don't tell him anything. I need to be the one to tell him."

"Of course," he says, already moving toward the door.

The room feels impossibly quiet after he leaves, filled only with the steady beep of monitors and the thunder of my own heartbeat. I'm going to be a mom.

"You realize London is going to lose his actual mind with the news, right?" Fisher asks as we drive down the gravel road that leads to Hale Ranch.

Neither of us was successful in getting in touch with him from the hospital. Then, later, his phone must have died because it started going straight to voicemail, which makes me think he lost it. I know things seemed strange this morning, but not enough for him to go completely dark.

"You think?" I ask nervously.

We've talked about kids, but it's always been an in-the-future talk, one where we're settled, living under one roof, and sharing a name. We're doing things out of order, and I think he'll be happy regardless, but there's about a three percent chance he might not be as excited as I am. I've also had two hours to sit with the news. The longer I sat, the happier I got. I just know that, together, our baby is going to have the best life, full of lots of love, with two parents instead of one.

"Not even a question. If there's anything that looks different, it will be the initial shock of finding out and then piecing together that he's about to be responsible for another human life. Still, it will probably take all of ten seconds for his face to light up with sheer happiness. Laney, that man has loved you since the day you met. I know the two of you have had more than your fair share of obstacles to work through, ones that he may have created, but his heart was always in the right place."

I nod. I know he's right. He loves me like he never left me, like he never let me go, and that is because, in his heart, he didn't. I owned it all this time, just like he owned mine. There's a reason no one else ever fit. They weren't him.

"His bike is here. That's a good sign he is too," Fisher says, putting the car in park. "Let me open your door, please. I know you can do it… but please just let me get it for you."

I roll my eyes. "You can open my door, Fish, but remember, don't say anything. I'll tell him."

"I won't spoil the best-kept secret. Just don't make me keep it too long, or I can't promise I won't slip up," he says, exiting the car.

I guess I better get used to it. Fisher has been giving me the princess treatment ever since we left the hospital, and I already know London is going to do the same. It's in his nature. He's always taking care of me and predicting what I'll need before I need it.

Fish opens the front door before leaving my side. "London," he calls out from the living room. "London, get your ass out here, fucker."

I've just closed the front door when London walks out of his room in nothing but a towel, water still dripping from his dark hair. Our eyes connect, and my heart doesn't just skip—it fractures. God, I missed him.

I missed the way he looks at me like I'm his whole world, the warmth of his hand in mine, and the safety I feel with his arms wrapped around me. When he didn't answer my calls, I thought something may have happened. I take a step in his direction, eager to tell him about my day, when something on his face changes. Something that looks a hell of a lot like regret and apology, and my knees get weak.

"Where have you been? I've been trying to get ahold of you for hours," Fisher's voice cuts through the tension.

London's eyes never leave mine. He licks his lips, and I watch the rise and fall of his chest kick up a notch, and my body remembers his, every kiss, every whispered promise, every moment we shared building our future together just hours ago. "My phone died," he says, his voice hoarse.

"London, thanks for everything."

The familiar voice sends ice through my veins, freezing me in place. My stomach plummets, taking my heart with it as recognition crashes through me. The look on his face…that voice…and finally, she steps out—the girl he swore meant nothing, the girl who was supposed to be in our past. Her hair is mussed in a way that tells a story I don't want to read as she clasps a necklace around her neck with fingers that shake slightly.

Of course, it's Madison.

"Oh, hey," she says when she sees Fisher and me standing frozen at the end of the hall.

London's fists are clenched at his sides, his eyes tortured, and I know…I know without asking what happened behind that door, but I do it anyway. I can practically taste the betrayal coating my tongue like poison. But if this is how we end, if this is how he destroys everything we built together, he doesn't get to take the coward's way out. He's going to use his words and tell me to my face that we're over. There's no cop car here to drive him away this time, no murder to hide behind.

"Tell me this isn't what it looks like, London." I try to keep my tone even when, inside, I'm splintering, each jagged piece piercing deeper than the last. The way his eyes are looking at me now, with guilt and pain, only adds insult to injury. He knew what he was doing. "Say it!" I yell, and everyone flinches.

Madison's pale-blue eyes dart from me to him like she's watching a tennis match, and I see the exact moment she realizes she's witnessing our end.

London's right eye twitches, and his eyes turn glassy with unshed tears that he has no right to cry. When he speaks, his voice breaks on every syllable. "I can't tell you that."

The words hit me like bullets, each one finding its mark and tearing through what's left of my heart. This is it. This is how our love dies, with four words that reduce everything we were to nothing.

"Are you fucking serious, man?" Fisher explodes, his voice cracking with emotion. "Do you have any idea what you've just done...where we've been all day—"

"Fisher, don't," I say, panic flooding my system as I realize what he's about to reveal. I press my hand instinctively to my stomach. I don't want London to know, not like this. I don't want his pity, and I sure as hell don't want his empty apologies for the sake of our unborn child.

"But, Laney—"

"No." The word comes out sharp and clear. "He chose this. Let him have it. He's not worth it." I pause, letting the truth settle in my bones like lead. "Turns out he never was."

I watch London's Adam's apple bob as my words choke him, watch the way his face crumples like I've physically struck him. Still, he says nothing. The silence stretches between us, heavy with all the words we'll never say, all the promises he's broken, all the tomorrows he's stolen from us. I'm hurting him. I can see it in the way his shoulders shake, in the tears that finally spill over and track down his cheeks. Which means he cared. He loved me. Just not enough. Not enough to choose me over whatever this was with her. Not enough to fight for us.

I take one last look at the man I've loved since I was old enough to understand the depth and weight of the word. I let my eyes rake down his body, memorizing and saying goodbye at the same time because I need to cleanse myself of him. The next time I allow myself to look into his eyes, they will hold nothing but hate.

I hate him for hurting me, for choosing her, for throwing away everything good between us. But I loathe him with every fiber of my being for destroying our family before it ever had a chance to begin. He didn't just close the door on us; he slammed it shut on our baby, on the tiny heartbeat I heard just hours ago, on the future we'll never have.

As I turn on my heel, I hear feet pounding against the wood floorboards, then Madison screeches, and the sickening sound of fist hitting bone echoes through the house.

"You fucking idiot!" Fisher's voice is raw with fury and heart-break. "How could you?"

That's the last thing I hear as the door closes behind me with a finality that echoes in my chest. I leave Hale Ranch for the last time, carrying London's child and the shattered remains of a love that was supposed to last forever.

"Goodbye, London."

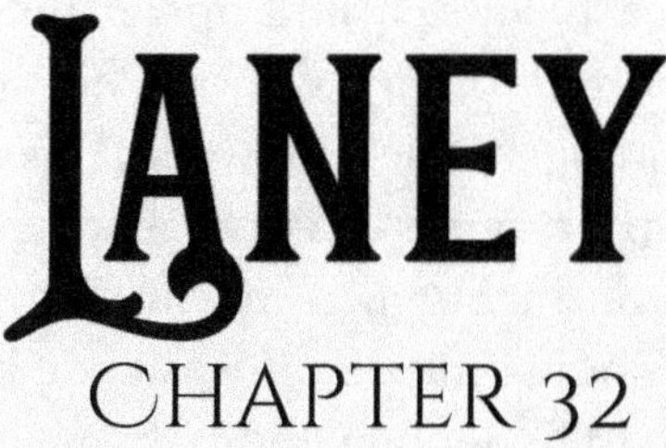

LANEY

CHAPTER 32

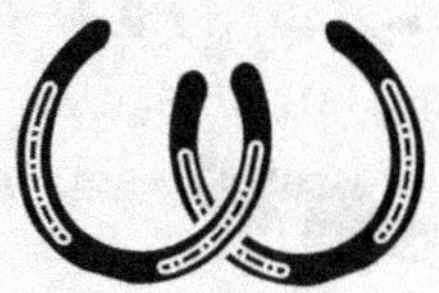

The rain soaked through my jacket ten minutes ago. I'm drenched and cold, yet here I stand, watching the water drip from my hair and pool at my feet onto the welcome mat. I want my mom—need my mom—but I'm scared to go inside, too afraid to face the suffocating memories these walls hold—the same ones I'm running from now.

My hand trembles as I reach for the doorknob, only to fall back to my side as my chest tightens with the ghost of a memory —London carrying me through this door the night I fell into the lake. Fuck. I knew this was going to hurt. I need my mom, but maybe running away to a place where no one knows my name would have been best, somewhere warm and tropical. My memories might still exist, but at least there, I wouldn't have reminders of him all around me, cutting open old wounds. How am I supposed to heal when I can't tell if the weight in my lungs is from a past that refuses to let go or the strength that comes from walking away?

The rain drums harder against the covered porch, each drop heavier than the last, out-thundering the rhythm of my heart. Through the living room window, I catch the soft glow of a lamp beside the couch. The light means she's home. She's not working a shift at the hospital, which means she's probably in the kitchen, brewing a pot of tea before curling up on the couch to read a book or catch up on one of her shows. Warmth floods through me. Memories of sitting beside her while I worked on my junk journals, catching up on our days, and sharing bowls of buttery popcorn during movie nights seep in, pushing out the pain and giving me hope, reminding me that it wasn't all bad. I just need to find the good. I have to find it now more than ever.

With a shaky breath, I raise my hand to open the door, but before my fingers can slide around the brass knob, it swings open, and there my mother stands in her faded blue robe, eyes wide in disbelief. For a heartbeat, we simply stare at each other in shock. Then recognition spreads across her face, quickly followed by relief and joy.

"Laney," she says my name like a whispered prayer, and in the next second, her arms are wrapping around my shoulders, pulling me close.

Her hold is fierce and desperate, as though she fears I might disappear if she doesn't hold me tight enough. It only takes seconds before my body collapses into her familiar warmth, finally allowing myself to be held by the woman I've missed more than I've dared to admit. Losing London broke me, but losing my mother nearly killed me.

"Come on, Laneybug. Let's get you dry clothes."

IT's BEEN HOURS SINCE MY MOTHER WALKED ME TO MY ROOM AND took her time peeling away each piece of my rain-soaked clothing as if I were made of something precious and breakable. I felt like I was five again and sick with a fever, and she was there helping me into my soft pajamas. Part of me felt shame, needing her help in a semi-catatonic state, twenty-four years old and unable to remove my own clothes. However, accepting her help felt like its own kind of strength; it wasn't surrender. It was a courage I'd forgotten existed.

She never once asked why I'd shown up unannounced, soaked to the bone, with tear-filled eyes, on her doorstep. She didn't demand explanations or apologies. She simply did what mothers do—what my mother had always done—loved me unconditionally no matter the circumstance.

Now, lying in my childhood bedroom with rain still pattering against the window, I feel like the worst kind of asshole. For six years, I carried my anger like armor, nurturing every grievance and all my hurt. I'd convinced myself that because she chose to stay in Willow Creek, she was somehow a villain in my story and one of the reasons I had to stay away. But she'd been here all along, keeping my room exactly as I'd left it, loving the ghost of me while I tried to forget memories of this place, even the ones that included her. A realization settles, one impossible to ignore. I'd been so busy protecting myself from this town, from this house, from her that I'd never stopped to consider that she might have been protecting herself from losing me too.

"Knock, knock, Laney. I just came to see if you're hungry," she says softly, entering my room.

"I'm not hungry," I say, keeping my eyes trained on the streams of drops running down my window.

I hear her footsteps as they lightly tread across the floor to my bed, where it dips when she takes a seat. "I understand if you don't want to talk. You can take as much time as you need, but I'm glad you're home." Her hand squeezes my ankle. "I've missed you so much."

I don't immediately respond. Instead, I let myself feel the warmth her presence brings to my room. I'm tired of being alone. Sure, I've had my friends by my side through thick and thin, but no one understands you more than your blood. My mother used to be my best friend, and I turned her into a stranger.

When my words don't come quick enough, I feel her stand. "Mom…"

"Yes," she answers gently.

"He asked me to marry him," I say, my voice trembling with nerves.

"Oh, honey." She reclaims her spot on the foot of my bed.

Once I completed my hours and received my certifications, I called to let her know I'd be staying in Bardstown. I caught her up on all the cases I worked on over the summer and told her how Asha asked me to work for Fairfield full-time. I had discussed all the easy stuff before finally telling her that my neighbor was once again London Hale. I could hear it in her voice. That detail caught her off guard. She could hear the happiness in my tone, and at the time, I read her trepidation as normal mom worries. She didn't want to see her daughter's heart get broken again. I dismissed it, and now I wish I hadn't.

"You said no?" she treads lightly, trying to understand and not push.

"He took me to the cabin his great-grandfather built for his wife. It was beautiful, not only the property but the sentiment behind it. The love they shared and the legacy they left for their children. It was perfect, only to be made unforgettable when he asked me to build a life with him in that very same spot and be his wife..." I pause as the sweetness of the memory tightens around my throat. How could we go from that to him sharing a bed with Madison in less than twenty-four hours? I blow out a breath, needing to finish the story and get it off my chest, release the pain so I can get through it. "I said yes... I said yes, and then the next day, when I came over after running errands, I walked in the front door and found his ex walking out of his bedroom."

I didn't even know Madison was back in town. After Gypsy was cleared to leave Hale Ranch, she and Abbey were back on the road, traveling the country and doing shows. Since London and I were officially a couple again, and she didn't have any roots in Bardstown, I didn't expect to see her again, but then there she was, just as pretty as ever, and there he was, standing in a towel. I feel the contents of my stomach rise, and I sit up, trying to push it back down.

Her arms are around me before I can blink. "Oh, Laney, I'm sure there's an explanation. London loves you. I know he does."

"No, Mom, I asked him." I pull out of her hold. "I said, 'Tell me this isn't what it looks like,' and he looked me in the eye and said, 'I can't do that.'"

"Oh—" A loud knock at the front door silences her response. "Now, who could that be? There's practically a monsoon coming down outside." She gets up. "I'll be right back."

No sooner than the front door opens do I hear him. "Where is she? I know she's here," he says, his voice laced with panic.

"London, I don't think she wants to see you right now," I hear her say seconds before my door swings open, and he's standing there soaked to the bone, with a bruised temple, dark circles under his eyes, and a thousand apologies written across his face.

I drop my eyes to my lap, unable to stomach seeing him. It hurts too much. I love him, even after he hurt me in the worst possible way. I love him. I will never stop loving him. But I have to love myself, and that means letting him go.

"Laney." He drops to his knees before me, giving me no choice but to look into his wild eyes. "I didn't cheat. I promise you. You have to believe me. It was the perfect storm, and I capitalized on it. I knew you'd think that. I knew what it would look like, but God, I swear I didn't touch her. I could never do that," he says, chest heaving.

"I asked you... I looked you in the eyes and begged you to tell me differently, and you didn't," I say, my words stronger than I feel.

"I know... I know, okay." He reaches for my hands, but I pull them out of his grip.

"Maybe you didn't cheat, but you still chose to hurt me. You hurt me with the worst possible lie ever, and I don't see how that's any better." This time, my voice cracks.

"No, no, no." He starts to lose it, tears pooling in his eyes before he drops his head in my lap, hands fisting the material of my sweatpants. "You don't understand—"

"Don't you dare." My voice is steel now. "Don't you dare give me that excuse again. That's the same bullshit that tore us apart before. I'm done, London. I can't keep doing this with you. This isn't just about us anymore. I know that's why you're here now. You were fine pushing me away again, sacrificing us for whatever fear is eating you alive, until you found out about the baby."

I told Fisher not to tell him, but I knew all bets were off when I left town. I knew he wouldn't keep my secret. Fisher was every bit as hurt and mad as I was. It's why London's lip is split, and his temple is bruised. His best friend was hurting for me.

"Two parents constantly in and out of love? That doesn't work for me. I want my baby to have stability, and if that means I have to do it alone, so be it."

The words hang in the air like a death sentence. London goes completely still—not just quiet, but statue-still, like every molecule in his body has frozen. His hands, still gripping my sweatpants, don't even tremble. He may have heard the news but not from me, and hearing the confirmation from my mouth is clearly a different beast altogether.

"You're pregnant," my mom says with a sharp intake of breath.

"Mom—" I turn toward the doorway, and she's pale as paper.

Shit. I was so caught up in London's unexpected appearance I hadn't thought through revealing my pregnancy. Of all the ways to tell your mother you are pregnant, your fiancé storming through the house, black and blue on the heels of a scandal, is not it.

She raises her hand. "London, you need to go. I need some time alone with my daughter."

Their gazes lock, but not in challenge. Instead, I see what looks like understanding. That has to be what it is, because no matter what I believe of London, I know he wouldn't chase me here to Willow Creek only to walk away before saying everything he needed to get off his chest.

His eyes swing back to me. "I'm not leaving. I love you. You and this baby are my whole damn world. I knew the risks; I always knew the risks and took them with you because this is what I want."

My lip trembles as I look into his sorrowful eyes, believing every word. But I don't say it back. I don't say anything. I can't.

He rises to his feet to exit, and when he gets to the door to pass by my mother, she says, "I'm sorry. I'm so damn sorry," as though the breath is being taken from her lungs.

I watch in confusion, not understanding what she's apologizing for. London hurt me, not the other way around. A stone settles in my stomach as I watch him give her a hug. He doesn't look back before he takes his leave, and the hot tears that had been stinging my eyes roll down my cheeks.

My mother stands frozen in the doorway, glued to her spot, until we hear the sound of the front door closing behind London. The sound reverberates through my bones, the familiar ache of his absence carving itself deep. I know this pain intimately. It's the same wound that tore open the last time I stood in this suffocating town, watching him disappear into the night. The memory strikes like a blow, but this time, I'm not the one who landed the punch. My mother is.

"Mom." My voice fractures on the single syllable. "Why did you apologize to him?"

"Laney, I think it's time I tell you my side of the story."

"I'm confused. What side? What story?"

She returns to my bed, this time taking her seat beside me. "The story about the day you killed a man."

"You know?" I lick my lips, tears streaming again. "You know it was me and not London?" She nods slowly, her eyes cast down at her hands, where she has them clasped together so tightly that her knuckles are turning white.

"Yes." The single word lands heavily between us. "I know all about the day you murdered your father in self-defense."

Everything tilts sideways, the room, reality, the bed beneath me. My vision blurs at the edges as the air turns so thick I can barely swallow. It's as if invisible hands have locked around my throat, squeezing until every breath becomes a battle, until the light starts to drain from the world around me. This can't be real. The words have to be wrong, scrambled somewhere between her mouth and my ears. Not the man I killed. Not him. Not the phantom I'd built entire fantasies around, the missing piece I'd spent my last years of high school searching for. The father I'd imagined meeting, embracing, and understanding parts of me I'd never know. They can't possibly be one and the same.

"Say that again." My voice sounds foreign, distant. "I thought you said I killed my father."

"That's exactly what I said."

"I don't—" My words crumble as I search for the right ones. "I don't understand. How is that even possible?" Panic surges upward, making it hard to breathe. "Why didn't you tell me? Why didn't you—" My chest seizes, and the room starts to spin faster. "I can't breathe." The admission comes out as barely a whisper. "I can't breathe."

"Laney, look at me." My mother is on the floor in front of me. "You're safe. This is going to pass, but I need you to breathe, slow and deep, in through your mouth…" She coaches me through the action. "Long and steady release… Another deep breath in, hold for a count of four. One…two…three…four…release."

She walks me through the breathing exercise a few more times, and the tightness in my chest starts to dissipate. Her thumbs trace gentle circles over the backs of my hands, each stroke deliberate and soothing as the storm inside of me settles.

"Why did he want to hurt me?" I ask, my voice barely a whisper.

The silence that stretches between us feels like a canyon, deep with decades of unspoken truth. I watch as she attempts to gather herself, squaring her shoulders and preparing to unload a burden she's carried alone my entire life.

"Laney, there's a reason we traveled for most of your life. I became a travel nurse so I could outrun your father. I lied when I told you I didn't know who he was."

With her admission, a second shock ripples through me, weaker but still there. I'm already too numb to feel its full impact.

"I always knew his name. But he wasn't a good man. He wasn't anyone I ever wanted you to meet. I thought—" Her voice catches. "I thought believing the lie was better than knowing the truth."

"If he was so bad, why were you ever with him?"

"Well, the one-night-stand part of my story wasn't a lie. We met at a college party, and he said all the right things. I was never that girl who could put out without a connection, but damn it, if he didn't sweet talk his way right into my bed. It was great, and he didn't take anything I wasn't offering. The next morning, he was gone, and that was that until we ran into each other a week later at a local coffee shop, and what was only supposed to be one night turned into a summer."

"So it wasn't all bad," I say, hopeful to find a slice of good.

She sighs heavily. "Things are rarely bad in the beginning," she points out before reclaiming her seat beside me. "If we saw the worst in people from the start, a lot less bad things would happen. We were good until we weren't…until I found out I was pregnant with you."

"He didn't want kids?"

"We were college students. Kids never came up in our conversations. He wasn't my soul mate, and I wasn't dreaming of a future with him that summer. I was simply happy and having fun. When I told him the news, he wasn't upset—shocked, yes, but not upset. I told him he didn't have to stay because I was pregnant but that I would be keeping you. Giving you up wasn't an option, not for one second."

I know a little bit about what that feels like. The second the doctor delivered the news that I was expecting, I was instantly in love. A love I didn't know I possessed flowed through my veins like a switch I didn't know existed had been turned on. Sure, knowing I made the baby with the man I loved made it special, but with or without love, the baby was a part of me.

"What happened? Why did the two of you split up?"

"It was little things at first," she says with a furrowed brow as she stares blankly at my dresser. "Things he never cared about started setting him off, like a cup left in the sink or a throw blanket sprawled over the couch instead of being folded. He wasn't meticulous by any means, which is what made his behavior all the more peculiar. How can you complain about a blanket on the couch but leave your toothpaste on the sink, uncapped, or your bed unmade? I never knew what little thing would set him off, because it didn't have rhyme or reason." She grabs one of my pillows and holds it in her lap, taking a few seconds to collect her thoughts. "The short fuse and insults gradually got worse...until accidents entered the picture."

"Accidents?" I repeat, my heart rate quickening with the implication.

She nods slowly. "Insults and jealous accusations turned into abusive behaviors. At first, it was something incidental, easily passed off as a mistake, like closing the door in my face when I was walking into a room. Then, incidentals started to feel like traps, like leaving things where he knew I might fall. The last straw was the night we were in the kitchen, cooking together. Music was playing, and I was chopping up carrots for a soup I was making. He came up behind me, sweet as pie, and kissed my neck before saying, 'You're doing it all wrong. Let me show you.' His hands covered mine, and he started chopping the carrots...until it was my hand."

My eyes instantly drop to the white scar that's been on top of her hand my entire life. She told me she got it cooking, but I never could have guessed its darkness. My heart aches for this woman who must have been so scared.

Her voice is ragged, and her hands begin to tremble. "That night, I didn't sleep. I couldn't. I lay there in the dark, staring at the ceiling, my mind replaying the moment over and over: the cold steel against my palm, his grip tightening over mine, the deliberate pressure as he guided the blade into my flesh." She pauses, her breathing shallow. "And then his performance afterward, the practiced innocence of a narcissist. 'My fault,' he said. 'I was holding the knife too tightly.' He couldn't guide it properly. But I knew that was a lie. We both knew."

The words come out soft and broken. "The insults had been escalating into targeted strikes. The jealousy had become a maze. Every conversation was a trap. But that night, when he crossed the line from psychological to physical violence, I understood the game he was playing. He was conducting an experiment: How far could he push me? How far would I let him?"

She takes a shaky breath before continuing. "The next day, when I knew he had left for work, I packed a bag with no plan of ever returning, but fate had a cruel sense of timing. I was halfway down the staircase when I heard his footsteps, heavy and deliberate, climbing toward me."

Her hands clench into fists. "Our eyes met through the narrow gap in the railing, and in that split second, I watched recognition dawn across his features. He knew I was leaving him."

She pauses, the painful memories she's kept locked away suffocating. I reach for her hands, intertwining our fingers and giving her strength. I'm here today not because my mother is a victim but because she is a survivor. "You don't have to finish the story, Mom. It's okay."

Her lip trembles. "No, I really do." She swallows hard and squeezes my hand. "It all happened in a blur. One second, I was on solid ground, and the next, sharp and all-consuming pain radiated from every point of my body as I lay at the bottom of the staircase. Another student came to my rescue, calling for help, and when I managed to see through a haze of agony and lift my head, I saw your father, still at the top of the stairs, and for an unguarded second, I saw him as he truly was. No mask. No performance. Just a man surveying his handiwork with satisfaction. And then it was gone as he dutifully ran down the stairs, rushing to my side to ask if I was alright. He knew I wasn't. He knew he pushed me, and I knew I had to disappear. So I did."

The silence that follows isn't empty. It's heavy with the weight of shattered illusions. I can feel the truth of her words settling into my bones like poison, rewriting my identity.

My father was a monster.

For twenty-four years, I had been crafting a redemption story from myths and scraps of nothing. In my mind, he was some phantom prince who, given the chance to know me, would have loved me. But that man never existed. He was nothing more than a mirage I'd constructed to fill the father-shaped void in my life.

The real man carved his intentions into her skin with a warning, and when she didn't bend to his will, a staircase turned into a weapon. He tried to kill her, and then he tried to kill me.

The memory surfaces with crystal clarity: his gloved hand around my mouth, the deliberate pressure, the way his grip tightened when I struggled. I had told myself it was a man unhinged by circumstance. I didn't know his story; I didn't need to. I only needed to survive that moment. But now I understand why I sensed him before I knew him, because those weren't the hands of a man losing control. They were the hands of someone who had found it. He knew all along, standing beside the stop sign as I walked into my house. He knew who I was—the daughter he failed to kill the first time. He was there, plotting his kill, and in my bones, I knew it. I knew him because I led him straight to me.

Maybe the capacity for violence is in my DNA. Perhaps the reason I was able to end his life wasn't because I'm a survivor, or because I'm strong, or even because justice demanded it. Maybe it's simply because I am his daughter, and destruction is the only inheritance he ever gave me.

The thought should horrify me. It should send me running from this room, but instead, I find myself settling deeper into this new understanding of who I am. If I killed him because his blood runs in my veins, then maybe that same blood is what allowed me to save both myself and London. Perhaps being his daughter isn't a curse—it's the reason we're both still breathing.

"Mom, I don't know where to start or what to say..." I lean my head on her shoulder and run my thumb over the back of her hand the way she soothed me with the same gesture moments ago. "I understand why you never told me, but you don't have to go through this alone anymore."

"Laneybug, I love you so much, but so does someone else. If you can find it in your heart to forgive me for keeping this inside your entire life, then I hope you can do the same for London."

"Mom, this isn't about London. This is about you, and what you endured, and the years you spent alone with no one to talk to..." I draw off, my heart breaking for my mother. She was so strong, always putting on a brave face for me while living in fear on the run.

"Oh, honey, I don't want you to feel sorry for me. I spent years in therapy to process and cope. I'm okay." Her hands cover mine. "And while I support you in whatever choice you make, that baby in your belly makes London every bit a part of our story. He loves you, Laney. I heard his plea. I saw the pain in his eyes. I know he hurt you, but he's not the man your father was. He thought he was protecting you."

Her comment makes my stomach churn. I know she's right. London does love me, but that only makes it worse. He shattered something fundamental when he let me believe such a terrible lie, something that can't be pieced back together with good intentions and apologies. Even though every fiber of my being wants to forgive him, to find our way back to each other, I'm not sure I can simply erase what was done.

There's always a way. We always have a choice. Usually, the right path is the one that requires the most courage and the most sacrifice, but it's worth taking when love is at stake. However, this cuts deeper than ordinary heartbreak or misunderstanding. This is about trust, about the foundation of everything we've built together. How am I supposed to build a life with someone who doesn't trust that I can handle the hard stuff?

What makes it infinitely worse is realizing that, for six years, the people I care about have been treating me like I'm made of glass. I've never been fragile. Not once in my life have I backed down from a challenge that terrified me. I've thrown myself head-first into the unknown, pushed past every boundary that tried to contain me, bent and adapted without breaking. I've survived things that would have destroyed others. So why do the people who claim to love me most act like I'm one strong wind away from collapse?

My annoyance ignites. "Why does everyone think I'm weak?" I throw myself on the bed. "I don't need protection."

"No one thinks you're weak, Laney. I believe when we love something so fiercely, we do everything in our power to sustain it —to protect it. When that source of light is a person, that protection can easily become a crutch, an excuse to hide our own fear. We don't protect what we love because we think it's weak. It's the opposite. We know it holds extraordinary power; it's our life source. It fills our cups, and it gives us purpose. It's that extraordinary power that stops our hands and gives us pause. You see, if we don't protect what we love and it breaks…we break too."

Her words throw water on the embers that were slowly beginning to ignite. I hadn't thought of it like that before. I've been so tired of the secrets, tired of hearing the reasons we keep them, and tired of feeling like I'm a secret away from losing everything, that I've given the idea of them more weight than the truth itself. They're not always kept in vain, and sharing them doesn't always mean betrayal. Sometimes, they're a shield, the very thing holding us together so that we have the strength to see another day.

"Get some sleep. We can talk in the morning," she says, leaning over and pressing a kiss to my temple. "I love you, Laneybug."

~

LIGHT FILTERING THROUGH MY WINDOW HAS MY EYES SLOWLY fluttering open. I don't know what time I finally closed my eyes for the last time. My head was a mess, going over everything my mother told me about my father and then replaying the days I saw him walking the streets, watching me, until finally, I ended his life. The memories of that day and the day leading up to his death have haunted me for years. Now, they haunt me in different colors. He's still the same monster, but now he has a name: Dad.

I sit up in bed and shake off the eerie feeling threatening to settle. I thought sleep would evade me last night. I thought I'd be more upset with the news my mom gave me, but I find myself unable to mourn the death of a man who tried to kill my mother —tried to kill me. I'm sad that a chapter has come to a close. I'll never find the man I spent hours, months, and years dreaming to life in my head. A father who would love me never existed at all. But that pain is a dull ache compared to the soul-deep hurt I feel in my bones from not waking up next to London for the first time in months.

I look toward his house, toward his old room that faces mine, and there's a white paper bag on the windowsill. A flurry of excitement fills my chest. I might be mad at him, and forgiveness isn't something I have to give...yet, but that little bag feels like hope. I pad over toward the window and quickly pull it inside. My eyes flash up to his window to see if he's there. He's not. Relief and disappointment hit me with equal measure. I'm not ready to see him. I still need time to sit with everything, but at the same time, I don't want him to give up. It's selfish to not have forgive-ness in my heart and want his attention anyway, to make him suffer when he's been hurting for so long. I don't like the way it makes me feel inside, but I'm trying to cope. My mother said if I can forgive her, that same understanding should extend to him. My mind is still wrapping itself around that. I do understand, and I'm hoping that's the first step toward forgiveness.

I open the bag, and on top is a note.

> *992 minutes.*
>
> *That's how long it's been since my heart stopped beating. I hate the silence. I miss its drum, but I'd rather be hollow than listen to the beat of a heart without its purpose, without you.*
>
> *I'm sorry. I'm sorry I caused you any pain, sorry I let you down, sorry I fell short of being the man you needed when you needed him most, but I'm not going anywhere. You deserve a better man, and I'm going to prove to you that I can be him. He's been here all along.*
>
> *I want to take care of my girls... Eat! I got your favorite blueberry muffin from Poppy's, along with a few others, just in case.*
>
> *I love you.*
>
> *London*

A sad smile tugs at my lips. We haven't even had a chance to talk about our baby, but he's thinking about it, and in his heart, we're having a girl.

My fingers trace the paper's edge as I whisper, "You've always been exactly the man I wanted." The admission burns my throat. I fold the note with shaking hands, setting it beside me like a fragile piece of my heart. "Love sucks." I release a frustrated sigh.

Pain and heartbreak aren't unfortunate side effects of love. They're woven into its fabric, inseparable from the joy and tenderness that make us feel most alive. Real love demands everything: your peace, your certainty, your carefully constructed walls. It asks you to hand over your whole heart, knowing it might be returned to you in pieces, and that's precisely what I did with London Hale.

I peek inside the bag and pull out the blueberry muffin. I loved these things growing up. The best muffins are the top-heavy ones.

I can't get enough of the crunch in every bite from the coarse ground sugar. I've just sunk my teeth into a hefty bite when the smell of pancakes floats across my room. I love my mom's pancakes.

"Eggs or pancakes…" my mom says as I enter the kitchen with a mouthful of blueberry muffin. "Or both. What does the baby want?"

"Both," I say around another scrumptious bite.

I couldn't have eaten if I wanted to yesterday. Everything was too fresh, but I don't need a repeat of what happened at the coffee shop happening again. London was right in his letter. I need to eat and take care of our baby.

"Mom, I have some questions," I say, softly pulling out a chair at the table.

Without missing a beat, she says, "I'd be more surprised if you didn't. I'll do my best to answer all of them."

"London knew the man I killed was my father…" I pick at my muffin. "Did he know the rest? Did he know how he hurt you?"

"No." She turns away from stirring the eggs. "I didn't tell him that story. When your father showed up in town, walking the streets, I didn't tell anyone. I did my best to ensure he never saw me. I thought if he didn't see me, he wouldn't be able to find you. I had my name legally changed before I gave birth to you. There was no way he could have known our new names, so I was careful to stay out of sight. It's why I was working so many hours. I was trying to stay away from you so he wouldn't realize who you were."

I put down my muffin and rub my temples. I brought him here. I searched for him. I made the calls to family members, trying to reach him. I never did get in touch with him myself, but since he showed up in Willow Creek, I know one of the calls got back to him.

"When you decided to go to California instead of following me to college…"

"It was to get us as far away from him as quickly as possible," she confirms.

"Why did you come back?" I ask, even though I already know the answer.

"To keep you safe and ensure you wouldn't be implicated." She flips the pancakes. "And Willow Creek grew on me. It became home."

The first part of that answer was expected after I lay awake, piecing together all that I had learned and knowing all that had happened, but the second part is a bit of news. My mom may have had a darker reason for constantly moving to new cities, but I was always by her side. She liked exploring new places and finding new favorite eateries and boutiques. It wasn't all bad, and the memory that this town has of my father's blood spilled on the street has me hypothesizing that it's not just the town…but someone.

"Are you sure it was just the town and not someone?" I ask, curious intrigue evident.

My mother has never been in a relationship my entire life. The closest thing to a date I witnessed was the dinner date she went on with London's father in high school. Now, I understand her reluctance to date, but she said she was okay. Perhaps the peace she found in knowing my father could never hurt her again allowed her to open herself up to finding love.

"There might be." She opens a cabinet to grab plates, but I hear the smile in her tone.

"Really? Who? Do I know him?" I question, surprised by her answer but thoroughly invested in her response.

"As a matter of fact—"

Ding dong, the doorbell robs her words.

"No," I whine. "Tell me first. I must know," I say dramatically as she walks past the table to answer the door.

"If it's London, send him away," I call after her.

The muffin and letter were a start, but I'm not ready to see him.

"Does Laney Hart live here?" I hear Trigg's voice carry through the house.

I drop my head to the table. "Seriously."

"Laney, you have a visitor," my mother announces as she walks back into the kitchen. "It's not London, so I let him in."

"I should have clarified and said no visitors," I grumble into the table.

"Good to see you too, sis." He pats my back before pulling out the chair next to me. "Is that pancakes I smell?"

"It doesn't matter if it is." I lift my head from the table and add, "You're not staying."

"Ouch." He makes a face.

"Laney, where are your manners?" my mother scolds before asking him, "How many do you want?"

"I'll take as many as you give me. I worked up an appetite driving straight through the night to get here."

"Yes, remind me again. Why are you here?" I rest my hand on my elbow and look at him curiously.

"Making sure my brother doesn't royally mess things up beyond repair," he explains, and I catch my mother turn around, eyes wide.

"Mom, this is Trigger Hale, London's half-brother. Trigg, this is my mom, Anastasia."

"Well, that explains the striking resemblance. Bristol never mentioned that London had a brother around the same age," she says, opening the refrigerator, pulling out a pitcher of orange juice, and setting it on the table.

"That's because he doesn't know," Trigg answers, and my mother freezes. Bristol knows Baylor has a son. The part he doesn't know is that Baylor's son is technically London's brother. "If you could keep that to yourself, I'd really appreciate it." My mother's eyebrows slightly raise, and he must see his request isn't sitting right with her, so he adds, "I plan on telling him."

She nods. "Where are you staying?"

"Umm, I haven't figured that out," he says, pouring himself a glass of orange juice. "Laney was my first stop."

"You're welcome to stay in the guest bedroom."

"Mom," I groan, perturbed that she offered him the room, not because I have anything against Trigg but because it basically invites London into our home.

"What?" She shrugs, sliding a plate of pancakes and eggs across the table to me. "He's family now. If he's London's brother, then he's also the uncle of your baby."

"Mom," I hiss. "Not everyone knows about the baby."

A satisfied, shit-eating grin takes over his face. "Oh, I heard all about the baby. Who do you think broke up the fight between Fisher and London?" My mother slides a plate to him. He picks up his silverware. "I tried to tell you—you picked the wrong brother," he jests before cutting into his stack of pancakes as I do the same.

"If my brain was the one doing the choosing, maybe I would have listened, but the brain doesn't choose who it loves. The heart does," I say before shoving a delicious bite into my mouth.

"Yeah, I think I might know a little something about that," he admits. "So, what are we doing today?" he asks as if we're back home on the ranch, and his brother hasn't completely obliterated my heart.

"I am going to go back to my room, take a hot bath, sulk, sleep, read, and repeat. Maybe not in that order, but you get the gist. We..."—I gesture between us—"aren't doing anything."

"You can't take a hot bath," my mom says, joining us at the table with her own plate.

"Why the hell not?"

Hot baths are my favorite when I'm having a bad day or need to unwind.

She points her fork at my stomach. "Because you're pregnant."

"Looks like a vacancy just opened up in your schedule," Trigg says, making himself cozy in the chair beside me.

My mother gives me a pointed glare. She doesn't want me to be rude to our new house guest, and honestly, I don't have the energy to argue.

I give him my sweetest fake smile. "Perfect. Sulking starts in ten minutes, and a chick flick marathon in twenty. Hope you're ready for *She's All That* followed by *10 Things I Hate About You*."

"Can't say I've seen either." He leans back with an infuriating grin. "I'm more of an action guy. Fast cars and high-adrenaline activities. Oh, I like that football movie..." He snaps his fingers, trying to recall the title. "*The Blind Side*."

"How very...predictable of you."

"Tough crowd." He raises an offended eyebrow. "And here I thought we were bonding."

My mom hides a smile behind her coffee cup, clearly enjoying this more than she should.

"Well, if testosterone-fueled entertainment is more your speed, you're welcome to crash with your brother next door. I'm sure he's got plenty of football documentaries."

"Nah, I think I'll stick around." He flashes my mom one of those charming grins that probably works on every woman he encounters. "Something tells me the pancakes are better over here. Plus, I've never seen someone sulk professionally before. Could be educational."

I narrow my eyes at him. "Trust me, you haven't seen anything yet."

"Looking forward to it," he says, and I can tell he's slowly winning my mother over with every word. And me too. The problem is I was never mad at Trigg. It's his brother I have a problem with.

All this is so painful. None of it makes sense: me falling for London, London falling for me. What was it all for if this is how we end? That may be my problem. I'm overthinking, trying to protect a heart that's already in pieces. But maybe that's the point. Sometimes, the only way forward is to dance in the storm. If you're not scared of getting wet, it can't hurt you. And forgiving isn't forgetting. It's letting go and choosing not to let the things that hurt you hold the power. The rain will stop eventually, but I'll still know how to dance.

LANEY

CHAPTER 33

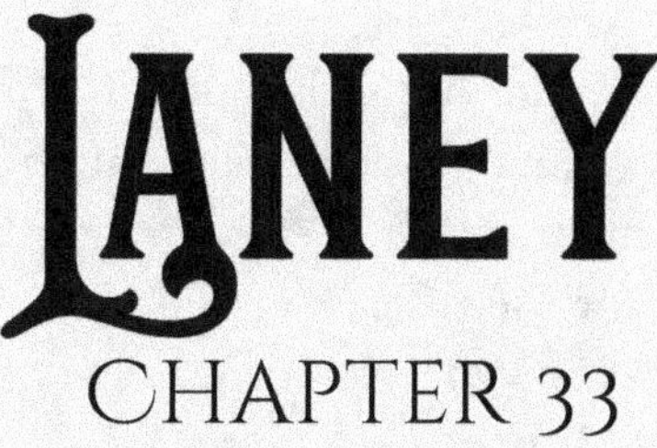

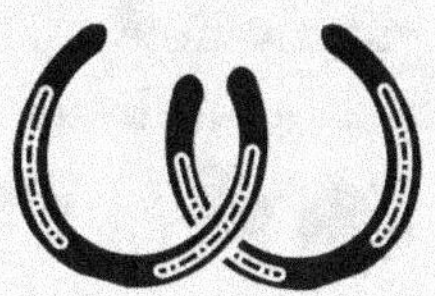

"I'm bored," Trigg says, strolling into my room unannounced and throwing himself onto my bed as I finish my morning skincare routine in the mirror.

"I don't see how this is my problem," I say, uninterested. He's been hounding me for the past three days, and while, truth be told, I'm getting bored too, I haven't been ready to face the town. Not just because I could run into London, but because of what happened the last time I was here. I haven't been home since London was hauled off in a police car for my crime.

"You refuse to leave the house," he says as though he read my thoughts.

"So…" I draw out in a bored tone as I reach for my mascara.

"So, I need someone to show me the town," he says as he picks up one of my throw pillows and tosses it in the air, only to catch it.

"Ask your brother," I retort plainly.

"He's not talking to me." He tosses the pillow up again.

His antics are needling at my nerves. Maybe growing up an only child wasn't the curse I thought it was. Right now, brothers lying on my freshly made bed, wrinkling my sheets, and carelessly tossing throw pillows around that could break something are a hard pass.

"I don't believe you," I say with a pointed glare through the mirror.

"And why not?" he questions, dropping the pillow.

"Because every craving and every little item I thought I might need, from a pregnancy pillow to a water bottle, has shown up outside my window for the past three days." I turn to him, unbelieving how he thinks I haven't connected the dots.

"I don't see how this has anything to do with me." He picks up the dropped pillow.

"You're literally living in my house. How else would London know to leave all those things outside my window if you weren't feeding him information?"

"I'm not," he argues.

"Are too," I fire back.

"What's the last thing that showed up?" He puts the pillow back where it was.

"A strawberry milkshake," I say with narrowed eyes.

"And who did you tell that you had a craving for a strawberry milkshake?"

Damn it. "Sydney," I sigh. I should have known.

"See, I think an apology is in order." He crosses his arms, vindication evident.

"I'm sor—"

"Nope, I don't want an empty apology. You can apologize by taking me out on the town."

"Fine," I agree.

His eyebrows shoot up. "Really? You're not going to put up a fight?"

"Nope." I turn in my chair to finish applying my makeup. "I'll be ready in ten minutes. Get ready to be thoroughly unimpressed."

Fuck it. I want to leave these four walls and stretch my legs. I have the truth, which is more than I had the last time I walked these streets. That's my armor now. Everything else is just noise.

"WHO ARE YOU TEXTING?" TRIGG BUMPS MY ARM AS WE SIT AT the new bar in Willow Creek.

"Why? Are you hoping it's Asha?" I tease sardonically.

"Always." He lifts his beer to me and takes a sip.

"Touché," I say, twirling the straw in my virgin daiquiri. "Are you ever going to tell me what happened between the two of you? I know it's more than some family feud between your parents."

He purses his lips and spins his bottle in thought. "It's not that I don't want to talk about it…" His eyes flash up to mine. "I just want to know if she remembers it."

That was not the response I was expecting at all. I thought I'd get the runaround again, same as always, not some ominous answer that's going to turn me into Nancy Drew until I crack the case.

"What do you think she forgot?" I pry shamelessly.

He smiles. "That is the question. The problem is, if I tell you, then she'll know."

"I don't understand. If it happened between the two of you, how could she not know? Why would confiding in me ruin anything? Think of it this way: if you tell me, then I can tell you if she's ever mentioned it, and then you'd know. But if you don't tell me, you'll never know if this secret you keep is worth harboring at all. And I think, since meeting me, you've learned secrets are poison. Nothing good comes from keeping them."

He nods in agreement. "I suppose that's one way to think about it, but as you said, if it happened between us, then I'm not really keeping a secret now, am I?"

Not much has shifted between them these past few months. They've been around each other more, but only because London and I spend time together—it's circumstantial, not intentional. There's definitely something simmering beneath the surface, but things haven't progressed like I expected after finding them asleep together on that lounge chair. Both are too stubborn to talk it out —whatever IT might be.

I roll my lips. "Fine, don't tell me. Sit there and sulk in your unknowingness." I take a sip from my daiquiri before pulling the straw out and licking the whipped cream. "It wasn't Asha."

"My brother again?"

"No." I debate not saying anything, but if I didn't want to talk about it, I wouldn't have told him it wasn't Asha holding the attention on my phone. I would have said nothing, but I want someone —no, I need someone—to talk to. "Madison left me a voicemail a few hours after everything happened, and I haven't listened to it."

I shrug. "At first, it was too fresh. Then, I just wanted to move on. Now, I don't want to look back."

"Since you haven't deleted it, the way I see it, you have two options. One, delete it. Or two, let me listen to it."

"You believe London?" I ask one more time, even though I already know what he'll say.

"I do. My brother might be the biggest moron on the planet forever thinking what he did was better for anyone, but while he might be ignorant when it comes to his decision-making abilities, he's not a cheater. I think you know that too. His heart is too good for that to ever be true."

I slide my phone to him before I can think better of it. "You decide. Put yourself in my shoes. You know the entire story. What would you do?"

I watch as his finger hovers over the message. When it meets the glass of my screen, it takes all of two seconds to learn his choice when her voice rings out on the speaker.

"Laney, hey, it's Madison. Look, I don't mean to overstep. This phone call feels awkward, because all of what I'm about to say is speculation on my end, but I would want to know if I were you. Plus, I want to clear my name... I am not that girl.

The other day, when you walked into the house as I was walking out of London's room, you got the wrong impression of what had happened. I walked into the house a minute before you arrived. I had a layover and stopped by to pick up my grandmother's necklace. I mistakenly left it in the barn when Gypsy was being quarantined. I'm never in one place long enough to receive mail, so I popped in. It caught London off guard as well. I wanted to say something right then and there, but honestly, it all happened so fast, and I was just trying to keep up. I knew after you walked out of the house and Fisher and London got into a fight that it was clear I had unknowingly become a game piece. But if I ever play the role of the other woman, you better believe it's because I didn't know I wasn't the only woman. I'm not a cheater, and I respect you. Anyway, I just thought you should know... And woman to woman, if you take him back...make it sting first."

The message ends, and we sit there in silence, staring at my phone. My heart wanted to believe London. It did. But watching her put on that necklace is one of the images I can't get out of my head. It feels the most damning. A woman putting on something personal, something she had removed during intimacy—even if it wasn't that day, then another. Even thinking about it now, knowing her account of that day, it still hurts. I don't want to think about London with someone else.

"Thank you," I say quietly before he presses delete.

"If I were in your position, that message would eat me up longer than it had any right to. Not to mention, there's a show every spring that comes through Bardstown, and it features her act. Life is too short to hold a grudge, and if you work things out with my brother, which I'm counting on, you don't need that hovering over your head, casting doubt."

"You know, I really wish you'd tell me what happened between you and Asha," I say, meeting his eyes with a small smile. "You're not as prickly as you let on. Asha might be missing out on one of the best things that's ever happened to her."

He smiles softly, hearing my words and accepting the compliment. That lasts for all of five seconds before his cocky, self-absorbed persona returns. "Of course she is. Glad you're finally catching up. But don't worry about me and her. I'm handling it." He takes a long pull off his beer.

I think about asking him what "handling it" means, but I

don't. Part of me doesn't want to know. I'm still processing that bit of information he shared at the Belmont Stakes watch party about Sydney and Warrick. He hasn't mentioned it since, and Sydney has never said anything, but I've noticed Warrick has been staying at his Louisville property. It could be coincidental with the estate situation still unresolved, but a house isn't the only thing in Louisville. Sydney is there too. She decided to go back to get her master's degree.

While getting lost in their drama is a distraction from my own, I want the peace that comes from being oblivious. I understand now, more than ever, the tremendous burden that comes with knowing.

"Well, if it isn't Laney Hart back in the flesh." The voice I'd prayed I wouldn't hear slices through my thoughts. I don't need to turn around. I know that voice, and now I know the secrets it carries. My eyes close as every muscle in my body goes rigid.

My mother's confession about my father didn't just bring things to light. It exposed a web of complicity that reached deeper than I could have ever imagined. London bore the weight of my father's identity because he took the fall for me, but he wasn't the only one carrying that burden. As mayor, Noah's father knew every sordid detail. And Noah… Gah, there's no universe where his father kept him in the dark.

Four months of London and me reliving every buried truth, laying our souls bare until nothing remained hidden. That's how I learned Noah wasn't just a bystander in London's initial rejection of me. He was the architect. He wasn't just threatening to expose the truth. He was threatening to take me down. "But would you trade places with her?" Those words echo in my mind. Noah wasn't just threatening to reveal that my hand delivered the killing blow—he was threatening to put me on trial for my father's death.

But Noah miscalculated. He thought that fear would keep London in line, and the truth would remain hidden, but his lies ran just as deep. The entire senior class heard him claim he witnessed London's hand wielding the knife. However, it would only take me a few keystrokes to take him from liar to accessory. He helped hunt down my father. He helped lure him to Willow Creek. If he aims a gun at my head, there's a double-barrel shotgun pointed straight back at his.

I always wondered what kept him coming back time and time again. The soul-deep connection to be anything more than just friends with benefits was never there. For years, I questioned if he truly felt it, and now I know it was never about love. His father never pushed harder for him to stay away from me, because keeping me ignorant satisfied his goal of ensuring the Donovan name remained untarnished.

"Can we talk?" Noah asks, placing his hand on my back.

"I don't think she wants to talk to you," Trigg answers for me.

"I have to say I'm surprised to see you occupying the stool beside Laney," Noah subtly pushes back.

"You shouldn't be. I'm a Hale. I thought you would have learned by now…we don't lose," Trigg says with a challenging undertone. He may have been fine with entertaining Noah's company before, when he was trying to make his brother jealous in hopes of us getting back together, leaving him as the only Hale heir available for an alliance, but Noah is no longer of use to him. Still, Trigg will always have his brother's back, even when they don't see eye to eye.

Noah rolls his eyes. "Whatever…seriously, can I have a minute?" he tries again.

"I'm not sure we have anything to talk about," I sigh.

"If you're home after six years, I think we both know that's not true. You learned a truth, and I want to give you mine." His baby-blue eyes hold mine, and I can see his request is genuine.

"Fine, one minute," I confirm before turning to Trigg. "Do you mind giving us a minute alone?"

His eyes dart from me to the man standing on the other side. "Sure, I'll be over by the pinball machine if you need me."

Noah is quiet as he sits in Trigg's vacated seat, confirming my speculations are accurate. I can practically feel the weight of the truth I know radiating off him in waves. It's in that silence that I realize I owe him an apology too. He wouldn't have had to bear the burden of these lies if I hadn't asked him to help me.

"I'm sorry—" I start, but he cuts me off.

"Don't… you have nothing to be sorry for. Just let me get this out." He takes a deep, cleansing breath before continuing. "When I left you in Bardstown, I was angry, but not for the reasons I'm sure you've assumed after learning the truth. I was angry because I felt like I failed you. You may have asked me to help you look for your dad in high school under the guise of a biology project, but I could have said no. I could have suggested we choose a different project, but I didn't. Instead, I offered my assistance willingly. I was hoping to steal more of your time by helping you look for your dad because I liked you. I never could have predicted how that one, yes, would irrevocably change our paths. The night everything went down outside the ice cream shop, I lied… yes, part of me saw it as a way to win a game I had no shot at winning otherwise, but over time, that changed. It was no longer about winning. It was about being a reason to make you smile…" he pauses and taps his thumb on the bar.

"Laney, I felt terrible for my role in helping you bring that monster into your life. For the past six years, I wanted to be the man to make it right, to correct a wrong. I wanted to make you happy. I would have done anything to make those picture-perfect moments last; the way you smiled for a camera broke me because I couldn't make it last. I didn't understand that I would never be able to give you that until I found the strength to leave. Coming back home, I figured out that the only way to keep that smile on your face was to give you back the other piece of your heart. The piece that I tried to own but never could because it was never yours to give. It already belonged to him."

Wow, that was not the confession that I saw coming. I expected anger and resentment, perhaps even a hint of entitlement. Hell, I was holding my breath for a threat. I didn't expect the guilt. What kind of friend does that make me?

"It wasn't all bad, Noah. I just wasn't in love with you. You did make me happy. Your friendship was a pillar of strength through some of my darkest times, and I will forever be grateful that you stood by me for taking on that role and helping me, even though it was hurting you."

The silence that follows feels different, heavier, but cleaner somehow, like we've finally laid our ghosts to rest.

"How are you doing with everything now that you know the truth?" he asks on a long exhale, cutting through the lingering tension.

"The truth is a bitch. I'm not gonna lie. It hurt. It cut deep. It's definitely gonna leave a scar, but I feel like nothing is holding me back anymore. I feel like the choices I make from here on out are mine. They're fully informed, and knowing I've left no stone unturned is empowering. There are no more secrets to haunt me. No more unknowns about that part of me."

I slurp down the last few drops of my daiquiri. "What about you? How has running your father's businesses been going?"

"Honestly, it sucks. I don't want to do it. I don't want to be his gopher or ride his coattails. I just want to do what I want to do," he says firmly, like he's saying it out loud for the first time.

"And what does Noah Donovan want to do?" I ask, licking the remnants of whipped cream off my straw.

"Fuck if I know. I'm still trying to figure it out." He hops off the stool beside me and rounds the bar. "However, for tonight, I am the bartender. Can I get you another?"

"Wait, this bar is a Donovan establishment? How come your name isn't on the front like it is on every other store in town?" I ask with a teasing tone that makes us both laugh out loud at the absurdity, and it feels good. It feels like the old us, the us before the night that changed everything.

"Yeah, I think he drew the line at putting his name on a place that sold liquor while holding a seat in public office," he says with a playful, wry smile that hints at the distaste.

"That's probably a solid call." I laugh as he slides me another strawberry daiquiri. This time, it's not a virgin. Before I have time to slide it back and think of something to say, someone else is doing it for me.

London snatches the glass from my hand and takes a long drink. His face morphs as he tastes it. "This has alcohol in it." His dark eyes find mine in horror.

He tosses the drink into the sink behind the bar, the glass shattering on impact, drawing the attention of everyone seated nearby.

"What the fuck is your problem, Hale?" Noah bellows from behind the bar, his face flushed with fury.

London turns around, his body tense. "My problem is you. It's always been with you." His voice is low and threatening. "You're always trying to take what's not yours, but you're not gonna take her this time. She's mine. It's my fucking baby she's carrying, not yours." The words come out harsh and angry, his neck muscles tight as he clenches his fists.

"London, oh my God, you're making a scene," I hiss, feeling embarrassed.

"No, you're doing that by entertaining a date with Donovan. It hasn't even been a week since I asked you to be my wife... In case you forgot, you said yes." His voice wavers slightly on the last words.

My eyes widen as anger renders me speechless. "I'm here with your brother." I gesture to Trigg, who appears beside us, placing his hand on London's shoulder.

London's expression shifts as he realizes his mistake. His lips press together, and his left eye twitches as the error in judgment hits him. We haven't talked since I came home, and it's killing him. It's killing me too, but I needed time. I'm trying to work through everything I feel. Everything that's happened. He took six years. I can take a few days.

"I'm not doing this with you here," I say firmly, getting off my stool and grabbing my purse. "Let me know what I owe for the drink and broken glass," I tell Noah before heading toward the exit.

"Laney, don't walk away from me," London calls after me, his voice more pleading now, but I'm already halfway across the bar.

How dare he? How dare he fucking assume the worst of me when I've done nothing but attempt to navigate this impossible situation he put us in. I gave him my heart, not once but twice. Coming home, I thought there was a chance I might get it back, but now I don't even know if I want it at all because I'm starting to question its true colors. He embarrassed me back there, made me mad as hell, but as I exit onto the sidewalk, all I can think about is the traitorous part of me that felt a sick thrill when he called me his. When he claimed our baby with such fierce possession. God help me.

"You're just going to run? You're not going to stay and work this out?"

I whip around, fury crackling through every nerve. The audacity of him calling me a runner. He wrote the damn book. I'm just stealing a page.

"No, that's your specialty," I bite out, my lip trembling as emotions shred me. "You perfected it six years ago when you vanished without a word, and you mastered it again when you strolled out of your room half-naked, letting me drown in assumptions while you knew the truth. This isn't running. This is you not giving me a reason to stay."

The words hang between us, each one cutting deeper than the last. I finally let my eyes connect with his. I'm not trying to hurt him. I don't want to hurt him, but I don't know what to do with all this pain. He fucking hurt me. "So don't you dare stand there and call it running when you taught me how to walk away."

I turn on my heel before he can see my tears. I thought I was strong, but I'm not. I'm not strong enough to survive him.

London

CHAPTER 34

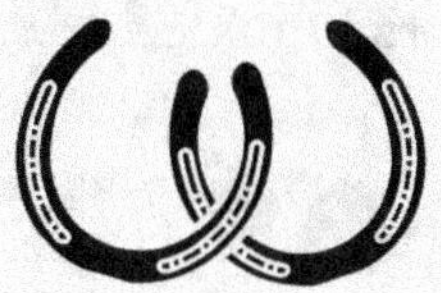

"London, do you mind getting the door?" my father calls out from the kitchen. "I'm elbow-deep in chicken wings."

"Yeah, Dad, I'll get it," I call out from my bedroom, where I've been staring at Laney's window for the past two hours, waiting to see if she'll open the curtains.

I can't believe I ever told her to close them. I pinch the bridge of my nose in annoyance at how I've so carelessly let my fear steer my path. I asked her to close her drapes when we were teens so I wouldn't have to watch her exist without me, when all along she was waiting for me to give her a sign—give her a reason. She never listened to me; they stayed open. And deep down, I loved it because I still got to see her. Now they're closed, and I hate it.

"London," my dad calls my name again when the doorbell rings for a second time.

"I'm coming," I say, padding down the hall, upset I have to leave her window and miss her finding the last gift I left on her windowsill. Her curtains might be closed, but it hasn't stopped her from collecting her snacks and everything she asks for. Even if she didn't ask it of me, I make sure it shows up.

I know I messed up. I intentionally messed up, and that is the worst kind of mess-up. There's a special kind of betrayal in deliberate harm, in looking at someone you love and deciding to wound them because you've convinced yourself it's somehow necessary. It doesn't matter that I told myself it was the lesser evil. It doesn't matter that I was trying to protect her. In that moment, I became the mastermind of her pain, and that truth cuts deeper than any consequence I'll face.

The door is closing for what feels like the last time, and I'm terrified, not just of losing her, but of who I became in that moment of choosing cruelty over courage. She has every right to walk away. She has every right to decide I'm not worth the risk of trusting again. I've earned whatever judgment she sees fit, whatever distance she needs to heal from what I've done.

But even in this darkness, even as I accept the weight of my choices, I refuse to surrender. My love for her isn't conditional on her forgiveness. It exists in her absence, in the quiet moments where all that's left are the memories of who we were together. She is my home. She's where I learned what it means to be fully seen and entirely accepted. I love her in the light of our best days and in the shadows of our worst. I love her enough to let her go if that's what she needs, but I also love her enough to fight for us when she can't find the strength.

This is a storm, but they don't always come to break us. Sometimes, they are there to test us so they can reveal us. And maybe, if we can survive what we're learning about ourselves in the wreckage, we'll emerge not just intact but transformed. Stronger, not because we avoided the break, but because we chose to heal together despite it.

The doorbell rings one more time right before I reach for it. "Lon—"

"I got it," I yell only to slam it shut when I see who is on the other side: Trigg. "Solicitor," I call out.

He rings the doorbell again. "London." My dad appears in the doorway separating the living room from the kitchen with his hands covered in seasoning and chicken guts. "Just buy a damn pizza. The new select youth baseball team is relentless."

I stand frozen in my spot. It's not a baseball player on the other side of the door. It's his brother's son, who also happens to be my brother. His eyebrows rise as though he's waiting for me to open the door. Fuck my life. "Sure, I'll buy a pizza," I say, grabbing the doorknob and squeezing out before he can see who's on the other side.

"What do you want? My dad is inside," I hiss as soon as the door clicks closed behind me.

"You've been ignoring me all week," Trigg states, his voice maddeningly calm, like standing on my front porch, announcing our family secret to the neighborhood, is the least of his worries.

"I'm aware." The words come out sharp. "You gave me no choice. You're staying with Laney." I step farther onto the porch, the old boards groaning under my feet like they're protesting this conversation as much as I am.

"So?" he questions, and the genuine confusion in his voice makes me want to shake him.

"So, you don't think my dad would notice a resemblance if he saw you?" My voice cracks slightly on the last word. "We look like fucking brothers, Trigg. Because we are. And yeah, I'm a little pissed that you're there and not me." The admission tastes bitter, but it's been eating at me all week. Watching from the sidelines while he gets to be close to her, while he gets to be the one she turns to, hasn't been easy to stomach.

His expression shifts, and for a split second, hurt flickers across his face before he masks it. "You actually think I would try to take your girl?"

"No," I say after a beat. "I know you don't have a death wish." I cross my arms tighter across my chest, a futile attempt to hold myself together. "But it doesn't mean I like it. It doesn't mean I like watching you be everything I can't be for her right now."

"Well, actually, that's why I'm here. I wanted to know if you wanted to grab a beer and talk before we have dinner tonight." He shifts his weight against the railing. There's something almost apologetic in his posture, like he knows he's about to drop a bomb and is bracing for the explosion.

"What do you mean have dinner tonight?" I furrow my brow incredulously. "We are not having dinner."

"Yes, we are. Your father invited us over for burgers and wings." The casualness in his voice makes me want to punch something.

"That's not going to happen," I say, each word deliberate and final.

"It's happening, and you're going to let it happen because Laney is coming. She's making apple pie." There's a practiced ease in how he delivers this, like he's been rehearsing the exact words that would make it impossible for me to say no.

"Laney is coming," I repeat slowly. My heart does something stupid and gets hopeful, betraying every rational thought in my head. Maybe she'll end this silence. Maybe seeing me here, in my space, will remind her of what we had. "She agreed to come to dinner at my house tonight?"

"Yes, dinner was her idea. Your father insisted on hosting."

"And you didn't object?" I exhale annoyance through gritted teeth, the sound harsh in the evening air. "Now I have to play the role of asshole again with the girl I love because dinner cannot happen. You can't be here. We have the same damn jawline." My hand instinctively goes to my own jaw, tracing the angular line that marks us both as family. "My dad will notice, and—"

"I know," he cuts me off, and for the first time since he's arrived, his shoulders sag with the weight of what we're dealing with. "I'll take full responsibility if this all blows up, but to be honest, I wasn't a fan of the original plan either."

He runs a heavy hand through his hair. "The elaborate plan we concocted to get your dad back to Hale Ranch would have worked. I'm sure he would have booked the first flight back to Bardstown when he received word you didn't come home after riding out to do chores." His voice carries a heaviness that wasn't there before, like he's been wrestling with this decision for days.

"But I don't think getting him there with another lie is the best move, even if its intent is in the right place."

He's not wrong. The divide that exists between our fathers was built on lies, betrayals, and stubborn pride. It has lasted decades, and adding another deception—even one born from desperation and love—would have only been salt in a wound that's never properly healed. Trigg and I are laying the groundwork for a new future, one where blood bonds mean something, and family is strength. That shouldn't start on the back of a lie, no matter how small.

"Yeah, I get it," I say, my voice quieter now. "A lie wrapped in good intentions is still a lie." We've both seen the wreckage that well-meaning deceptions can leave behind. I'm currently a walking fucking billboard.

I push off the door with a long exhale—the kind that carries years of frustration and the weight of decisions I never wanted to make. "Let me grab my keys. I needed to head into town anyway. Asha told me she suggested that Laney start using body butter sooner rather than later, something about preventing stretch marks." I shake my head at how much lighter I feel, focusing on something I can actually control. "I want to swing by the drugstore and pick some up to leave on her windowsill."

"Body butter?" he questions quizzically, his nose scrunching up like I just suggested buying her a stick of actual butter from the dairy aisle.

"Yeah, it's expensive lotion," I say, rolling my eyes after supplying the obvious answer.

"Then why don't they just call it lotion? Butter is something you put on toast, not your body," he says with a visible cringe.

"Because *expensive-ass lotion that will cost you more than your grocery bill* didn't fit on the label," I say dryly, unable to keep the corner of my mouth from twitching upward despite everything.

"Maybe this time you should write in your note that you'd be happy to apply it," he jokes, waggling his eyebrows in a way that would've made me laugh under different circumstances.

My hand freezes on the doorknob, and the lightness in my chest evaporates. "She tells you about the notes?"

He can tell I didn't know that and that the notes are personal. I'm not upset that she's sharing them. If she's sharing them with him, that means she's thinking about me, but God, I wish it were me she was talking to, not him. I wish I were the one hearing her thoughts about the words I pour onto paper at three in the morning when sleep won't come.

"I know you leave the packages on her windowsill." His voice is quieter, recognizing the wound his flippant comment just made. It's not his fault that the only woman I've ever loved is pushing me away but still opens her window to take what I leave there. "Sometimes she tells me about the notes..." He shrugs. "But not always. When she doesn't tell me about them, I assume she doesn't want to talk about what they say."

The admission gives me confirmation that my words are reaching her, that they matter enough to keep private sometimes. That maybe, in those moments she chooses not to share, she's holding something of mine close to her chest.

"Help me get my girl back," I say, my voice fracturing on the last word.

"Why do you think I'm here?" His response comes without hesitation, but there's something raw underneath the certainty. He steps closer, close enough that I can see the circles that have formed under his eyes. He's losing sleep too. "She became the sister I didn't know I was missing these past few months." His voice drops, weighted with something more profound than mere affection—he loves her.

I can't blame him. She's hard not to love. The way she hums while making coffee, how she picks up after us just to check our trash for items to put in her junk journal, and the Sunday dinners she started making at the ranch. Having her at the ranch made the place feel more like a home than it had in years.

"I love her like family," he continues, his jaw tight. "She's carrying your baby, which makes her family." He turns toward the street, and I know it's to hide the intensity of emotions threatening to crack his composure. "She is family."

The silence stretches between us, heavy with everything we're not saying. This is new territory for us. The scent of apple pie floats through the air with the breeze, and when he finally looks back at me, his eyes are glossy with unshed tears.

"So yeah," he says, his voice rougher now, "I'm here. And I'm not leaving until we bring her home."

Sure, Trigg and I talk, but never like this. This level of depth is new for us. We're revealing ourselves, brick by careful brick, showing what we want to see rising from the ashes of our fathers' mistakes. All week, I've been focused on my regrets, the mistakes I made that drove her away not once but twice. I've struggled with the word and its weight, especially as I confront the stark truth: I wounded someone whose love runs deeper than my own veins, someone I would die to protect yet somehow still managed to destroy. The cruelest irony is that I can't say I'd wish it away.

How do you mourn choices that felt like salvation in the moment? How do you regret the very decisions that kept you breathing when drowning felt inevitable? How do I regret the choices that led me to my brother? Were it not for my missteps, the man standing next to me might still be a stranger, and I may never have gotten this chance to heal a decades-old family divide that has festered like an untreated wound.

"I'm glad you're here," I say, even though when he showed up on my doorstep, I wasn't.

Do I have regrets? Yes. But what's worse than my regrets is knowing I'd probably make them again, knowing that love some-times means choosing the wrong thing for the right reasons. But finding Trigg and blazing a new trail for our family's legacy has opened my eyes to another thought. To be human is to be flawed. Breaking a cycle isn't about perfection but rather being brave enough to face the wreckage and sift through the ashes of your mistakes. It means having the humility to say I was wrong and the strength to try again, even when failure feels like certainty.

He snorts, his amusement a welcomed contrast to the heaviness of our conversation. "Yeah, well, your welcome was about as warm as a January funeral. Good thing I'm stubborn as hell." The corner of his mouth quirks up. "Must run in the family."

Despite everything, the weight crushing my chest, the fear clawing at my throat, I feel my mouth twitch. It's the first smile I've managed in days.

"I'll get my keys."

Standing here with him, feeling the weight of shared understanding, I realize that redemption isn't about erasing the past. It's about refusing to let it write the ending. It's about having the audacity to believe that broken things can be made whole again, that love is stronger than the mistakes that nearly killed it.

I smile, and this time, it reaches my eyes. Time to prove how strong our love really is. She said I didn't give her a reason to stay. Time to show her I am the reason.

As soon as I returned from having a beer with Trigg and picking up Laney's body butter, my dad sent me to the backyard to set up the table. The nights have just started to cool down as summer comes to an end, and he had me bring out the gas fire pit that runs down the center of the table for ambiance. Aside from setting up the table, putting out the plates and napkins, and filling the drink cooler with beverages, there wasn't too much that needed to be done. My father has always taken pride in keeping a well-manicured lawn, with every hedge trimmed just so, and Edison bulbs strung across the patio to create a cozy atmosphere. The only thing that's changed since I left is that he does all the heavy lifting himself, whereas I used to be the one helping to keep the yard immaculate.

"London, can you run inside and grab the condiment tray from the refrigerator," my dad asks as he walks out the back door with a tray of buns.

"Yeah, anything else?" I ask, running back inside so I can rush back out. I've been on pins and needles ever since I got home, my anxiety practically eating me from the inside out. I'm so damn nervous about this conversation, but I know it needs to happen. I take all of ten seconds to collect the condiments before returning to the backyard, anxious to see Laney.

I'm just setting the carrier down on the table when the hairs on the back of my neck perk up, my body feeling her before I see her, and my heart instantly starts racing. I release a long, steady breath, attempting to calm my nerves, before straightening to greet them.

My hand grips the back of the chair I'm standing closest to when I see her. It's only been a few days since I've seen her, but it feels like a lifetime. Fuck I've missed her. She's wearing a new sundress—or at least I think it's new. It could just be the hue the setting sun casts, or maybe it's the glow of pregnancy changing her skin and the way the breeze catches its hem, but it's different. She's different. Her hair still falls in soft waves past her shoulders, the same thick mess of blonde that I've spent countless hours with my fingers tangled in, but it's the way she tucks a strand behind her ear that has my chest constricting with the memory of the last time I made that same gesture on the floor of what is supposed to be our new home.

This isn't the Laney who used to sneak out at midnight and curl up next to me on a blanket in the backyard. This isn't the girl who collected my clothes to keep me close. This is the Laney who's been finding reasons to shut me out. But God, she is still devastating, still the same woman who makes me forget my own name with a sideways glance.

Walking beside her with a six-pack of beer is Trigg, and flanking her on her right with a bowl of salad, her mom, who'd been saying something in her ear as they walked down the back porch steps, keeping her from looking my way until now, until she's feet away, the distance between us half of what it was. Her brown eyes connect with mine, and even at this distance, I can see the way the pie dish trembles slightly in her hands, so slight I might have missed it had I blinked. That has to mean she's nervous too. That means something, right? I can't be sure. What I am sure of is that this tension between us somehow feels sharper in the clear air with nowhere to hide.

She's ten feet away now, close enough that I can see the way she is biting her lower lip, the same tell she's had since we were kids, the one that meant she was working up the courage to say something that scared her.

"Hey," I say when she reaches the table, walking straight for me with the pie dish clutched in her hands.

"Hey," she says with equal measure of unease.

A heartbeat of silence stretches between us as we drink each other in for the first time in days, the space crackling with electricity, all our unsaid words, everything we've broken.

"Let me take that," I say, grabbing the pie dish from her hands and placing it carefully on the table between the mason jar candles and the plate settings. When I turn back, the breeze shifts, carrying the scent of shea butter to my nose. "You used the butter?" I say, grasping for something—anything—to break the tension between us.

"I did. Thank you for getting it for me..." She twists her hands nervously at her front, fingers knotting together. "And for all the other stuff."

Behind us, the sound of my father's laughter drifts over from the grill where he's talking to Anastasia.

"I want to take care of you," I say, taking a step closer, desperate to bridge the distance she's put between us. I want to hold her in my arms, kiss away all the pain I caused, smooth her hair back from her face the way I used to. If she'd just let me hold her, half the battle would be won.

"I know you do," she says before averting her gaze to Trigg, who stands rigid, thoroughly engrossed with whatever is on his phone across the table. "Where are you sitting?"

"I suppose here," I say, lifting my hand from the chair it's resting on.

"Okay, then I'll sit here." She pulls out the chair beside mine, its legs scraping against the brick patio.

"You're going to sit next to me?" The surprise in my voice is filled with cautious hope.

With the distance she's put between us lately, this closeness is both welcomed and disorienting. I don't know where her head is. Is she ready to let go and move forward, or is this something else entirely?

She looks over her shoulder, at my father plating the wings beside the grill, before finally giving me her eyes. "I figure I should be sitting next to you when we tell your father I'm pregnant."

"Oh," I say, unable to hide my disappointment.

She doesn't want to sit next to me because it's me. It's business. Strategic positioning for the conversation that will change everything. When I went to lunch earlier, Trigg filled me in on her plan for tonight. Our baby will be a reason to add an heir to the land title. If Dad talks to his brother about adding his grandchild, then Baylor can also add Trigger.

"And I want to sit next to you," she says, stepping into me to slide between our chairs and stealing the breath from my lungs. Her proximity is intoxicating.

God, she has no idea what that admission just did to me. My goal tonight was always clear: get my girl back. Watching her walk across the lawn, I thought maybe I'd disillusioned myself with the ease of the task. I'd make it happen regardless, because I know this is all my fault, and winning her back won't be easy. It's not the first time she's put me in the doghouse for getting shit wrong, but I'm grateful she's tossing me a bone, because I'm done with safe distances and cautious steps. Hearing her say she wants to be close, feeling the gravitational pull between us that she's finally stopped fighting, changes everything.

I'm not chasing her anymore. We're moving toward something together.

"Laney—" I start, only to be cut off as my father and Anastasia join us at the table.

"Is everyone ready to eat?" my dad says as he sets the tray full of wings beside the burgers in the center of the table.

"Yeah," I say, flustered. I didn't get the chance to say more to Laney, but the night is young. Pulling out my chair, my eyes fall on Trigg, who's sliding a chair out across the table. "Dad…" I pull in an unsteady breath as I take another leap. "This is Trigger Ha—"

"I know who he is." He waves his hand as he takes his seat. "You think I wouldn't recognize my own nephew?" he says as Trigg and I share a wide-eyed, bemused expression.

"Wait, you know who I am?" Trigg asks cautiously.

"Yes." My dad puts his napkin in his lap, as if this conversation isn't anything of significance, unaware that Trigg and I have been discussing ways to introduce him to my father and bring up making an addendum to the property title for months.

"How long have you known about me?" Trigg sits forward in his chair, elbows on the table, wholly invested in this conversation.

"I suppose as long as your father," my dad answers, peering down the table. "Anastasia, do you mind pulling an ale out of that bucket in front of you?"

"Sure." Laney's mother twists the bottle from the ice and passes it down. Laney's fingers brush over mine, her soft skin divine against my callused hands. I linger a second longer than necessary before passing the beer to my father.

He's just twisted the top off when Trigg asks, "Do you know why I'm here?"

My father leans back in his chair, taking a long pull off his ice-cold beer, before answering. "Since you're asking, I'm guessing it's not to get to know your uncle."

"No," comes out easily before he's tripping over his words. His eyebrows rise. "I mean, yes…" He pinches the bridge of his nose.

"Well, which is it?" my father prompts.

"It's both. I didn't expect this kind of reception. I was

expecting to meet resistance, not acceptance," Trigg answers honestly.

I get it. Being dumped on Baylor's doorstep left me completely out of my depth. He was a stranger who shared my blood but nothing else. I had every reason to expect the cold shoulder, not a warm welcome. After all, if I'd never heard of him, there was probably a damn good reason why.

"And the resistance... I suppose you believe I wouldn't willingly acknowledge another heir on the lease?" He rests his beer on the table.

This time, I cut in. "Can you blame him? Not once in my eighteen years did you mention anything about having a brother. If you've known about Trigg all this time, why isn't he already on the lease? You had over twenty years to make that happen."

"My brother never asked," he says, his tone even.

My eyebrows rise. That tracks. They don't talk, but damn. I would have never expected that my father would have it in him to hold a grudge and sacrifice a relationship with his blood. It's not the man I know.

"Okay, back up. How do you know all this?" I start with that question before I ask the harder one. I lean into Laney and say, "Can you pass me a beer?"

It's a natural move, having her at my side again, and it doesn't go unnoticed how easily we fall back in step. Just being next to each other fills the space. It fills it because neither of us wants it. I know this is killing her as much as it is me. I know she feels me in every cell. Her love for me runs through her veins the same way it does me. She passes me the pale ale, knowing it's my favorite, before pulling another out of the bucket and silently offering one to Trigg, who happily takes it.

"As you are now aware, Baylor and I run the family business together. He tends to the horses, and I handle the books and our online presence. However, since my brother refuses to communicate directly, preferring to nurse old grievances, I'm forced to get most of my information secondhand through Rupert Downs."

"So, you're saying my father is the only one refusing to let bygones be bygones?" Trigg's voice cuts through the evening air, irritation sharpening each word. "Your son has been living at Hale Ranch for the past six years, and you only made one call, and in the twenty years I've lived there, you haven't visited once. You're an heir. It's your land too. You grew up on that dirt. You came from it, but you refuse to return to it." He leans forward, firelight dancing across his face. "You can't tell me that's all because of my dad."

My father drains half his beer in one long pull, flames from the table's fire feature reflecting in his distant eyes. When he finally speaks, his voice carries the weight of decades. "You're not wrong—phones, planes, and automobiles work both ways." His gaze finds mine, raw and unguarded. "I never wanted to be a stranger to him. But he gave me no choice, and maybe...maybe I'm just built wrong. When I love someone, I convince myself I'm poison in their lives, that they're better off without me contaminating their happiness." His laugh is bitter, hollow. "But perhaps I should have fought instead. If you truly love something, it's worth bleeding for. And I love my brother."

His gaze drops back to the table, and I know those words were true for him, but they were also for me. He's not just talking about Baylor. He knows exactly what I sacrificed for the woman beside me. How I walked away believing she deserved better than the truth I couldn't keep if I stayed.

"What happened between you and Baylor?" Laney's fingers find mine, and electricity shoots up my arm. "Why did you stop talking?" Her touch is gentle but deliberate. She can sense the old wound my father's words have torn open, and she's anchoring me, reassuring me that no matter where we are, she's here for me, ready to pull me back from the edge if I need her.

"That is the question..." He nods toward the bucket of beers, and Anastasia passes another one down the table. "Growing up, we were as thick as thieves." His voice carries over the chorus of crickets. "Growing up on that ranch is a little boy's haven. We had endless adventures—creeks that ran cold even in August, lakes where we'd skip stones until our arms ached, and animals that knew us by name. We had it made." His eyes grow distant and unfocused, as if he's watching those memories play out in the dancing flames of the fire.

"In high school, everything changed my senior year. I met London's mother, and she stole all my time—every spare moment, every breath." He rolls the cold bottle between his palms, the label peeling under his thumb. "But that's expected when you're in love, isn't it? It's natural to want to be with your person when you find them, to orbit around them like they're the only source of light in your world."

Anastasia passes a bowl of salad around the table, and Laney scoops some onto both our plates.

"In the beginning, I could tell Baylor wasn't a fan of our relationship. The way his jaw would set when I'd cancel our plans, how he'd go quiet when she'd show up at the creek where we were fishing. I went out of my way to include him, tried to make it work, but he didn't like being the third wheel, and she..." He pauses, choosing his words carefully. "She didn't like having him tag along, which was hard. My best friend and my girl not getting along put me in a rough spot, and I myself was still learning how to navigate the new territory as well."

The sound of Laney's fork clinking against her plate cuts through the silence, and I see her hand still. I reach for her knee under the table and squeeze it gently. If she's hungry, I want her to eat. She needs to feed our baby. I don't know what it's like to be pregnant, but I imagine if you're hungry and there's food in front of you, you want to eat it; your appetite now doubles.

"A month after London was born, she said she couldn't live at the ranch anymore, and she wouldn't give me a reason. She just stood there in the kitchen where I'd eaten breakfast every morning of my life, holding our baby, and said she had to leave. When I offered to build us our own house on the land, somewhere we could start fresh but still be close to family, she said no. Said she couldn't stay in Bardstown, and that was that."

The silence stretches between us, only the sound of Laney and Anastasia enjoying the dinner they helped prepare exists as Trigg and I stay intently focused on every detail of my father's story.

"So, we left. Leaving was the hardest thing I ever did. I left behind my entire support system, but I did it for my new family."

Trigg and I share a knowing look across the table, our eyes meeting over the flames of the fire pit. The weight of what we know—what he might not—presses down on us like the humid air before a storm. We know why our mother couldn't stay, but the question that matters now is whether he does too.

"Do you know the real reason Mom left?" I already know the answer, but I'm searching for his truth now, wondering if it's the same story he's always told me or if tonight the story might finally change.

"She didn't love me anymore," he says with a furrowed brow, surely reflecting on the day she left. "The story I told you was true. She left, without a word, on a regular day, for a mundane errand, and never came back. A person that loves you could never do that." His eyes find mine. "I could never walk away from you. It's why I chased a woman who wasn't worth chasing." He gestures toward the house. "She knew the house that she left us in. I never left it, and she never looked back."

Well, that's not exactly true. She called when I turned fifteen and asked my father to put me on a plane. And he did. Just like that, without asking what I wanted, without preparing me for what I'd find when I got there. I'm still mad about that.

"Why did you guys move to Willow Creek, of all places?"

He chuckles, the question clearly lightening his spirits. "Honestly, it's a fate straight out of a country song. It's where the car broke down. We were nineteen when we left the ranch. Back then, I wasn't balancing the books. If I had stayed, I had a job, but there wasn't much I could do to help the business from states away back then."

I lean forward. "Why didn't you move back after Mom left" — I pause, holding up my fingers to count off the years she actually stayed—"two years after I was born? You could have gone home then."

"I searched for your mother. I thought maybe I'd gotten it wrong, maybe there was an accident that kept her from coming home, but then I received a summons for divorce, and the paperwork was filed in a Florida county court." He puts some wings on his plate. "By the time that paperwork was filed, another two years had passed, and Grandpa passed, which meant I was no longer just an heir to the ranch. Baylor and I were in charge. You're too young to remember, but you went on a week-long camping trip with the Downs family the week I went to settle the estate and bury your grandfather. Baylor and I didn't handle losing our dad well. We got in a fight, and he said a lot of things…" he draws off, and I can't help but wonder if any of those things were about my mother. He shakes away the memory.

"What kinds of things?" Trigg pressures.

My father looks between us and takes a drink of his beer. "It doesn't matter. He said them out of anger. We lost our dad. I know he didn't mean them. I don't hold them against him." His shoulders sag, and I don't know if I believe him, but I can tell he wants to believe the words.

Laney's hand tightens around mine. She knows those summers spent with my mom were brutal. I always knew my mom had left, but knowing and understanding are different beasts. At eight years old, I was already manufacturing reasons why she chose to walk away, reasons that had nothing to do with me being too much trouble, too loud, too needy. When Laney walked into my life, I watched her walk through the world, collecting pieces of Seattle like they were sacred relics. Every one of her junk journals had multiple pages dedicated to the city because she knew that was where her mom and dad met. Laney had never actually lived in Washington state, yet she had pages upon pages of clippings, bar coasters from places she'd never been, napkins from restaurants she'd never eaten at, magazine cutouts of a baseball team she hadn't watched, Pike Place Market, the Puget Sound. You name it. If it was Seattle-related, she found a way to weave it into her journals somehow. I know it's because all those items were rooted in dreams of her father—this mythical man who might still be out there, might still want her.

Watching her create stories with junk and craft alternate endings around a family that didn't exist had me doing the same on afternoons when we shared the same blanket on a patch of grass in the backyard. It's an innate human need, this desperate want to know who you are, where you came from, to be part of a nuclear family where the DNA that created you actually wants to stick around.

When Laney found out where I'd been spending my summers, I told her how much I hated them. But talking about hurt and living inside it are two very different kinds of torture. I kept those summers I spent with my mom a secret because I wanted to hold onto the dreams Laney and I had spent hours creating about the parents who were out there waiting to love us. Those were good dreams. Reality fucking sucked.

My reality for those three summers sucked the life out of me one day at a time. And when I found out the truth about the man who tried to hurt Laney, when I realized her father wasn't some romantic figure waiting in Seattle but a predator who'd already tried to destroy her once, I couldn't break her heart the way mine had been shredded. I couldn't watch her beautiful dreams crumble into the same ash mine had become. But now, sitting here listening to my father's story, I see that living in fear of breaking hearts in the name of protection isn't really protecting anything at all. It's just another kind of abandonment, another way of saying someone can't handle the truth of who we really are.

"Dad, Trigg isn't my cousin." The words hang thick in the air. "Baylor didn't say those hurtful things to be cruel. He said them because he loved Mom first. Trigg is my brother."

For a moment that stretches like an eternity, he sits frozen. I watch his eyes, see the exact moment Baylor's words begin their relentless replay, every barbed comment, every bitter accusation suddenly reshaping itself in his mind, taking on new meaning and weight. The woman he married and planned to build a life with had kept the cruelest secret of all. She hadn't just slept with his brother; she had his child.

"How old are you?" The question comes out strangled, directed at Trigg.

"I'm one year older than London."

His face drains of color as he grasps at straws. "You weren't there." His voice breaks on the words. "When I went to bury my father, you weren't there."

The funeral. The one time in twenty years the brothers might have reconciled, when grief should have brought them together. Instead, pride and misunderstandings kept them apart.

"She put me up for adoption." Trigg's voice carries the weight of abandonment, steady but laced with an apology that isn't his to give. "Baylor didn't know I existed until I was five years old."

I can see him struggling, his world tilting on its axis as twenty years of assumptions crumble to dust. But beneath the shock and betrayal, I catch something else flickering in his eyes—regret.

He sets his napkin down with the careful precision of a man trying not to shatter completely. When he rises, he says, "If you'll excuse me"—his voice is barely recognizable—"I think I've lost my appetite this evening."

"THANKS FOR HELPING ME CLEAN UP," I SAY AS LANEY PUTS THE last container of food in the refrigerator after boxing up the leftovers from the dinner that was barely touched.

"Of course." She closes the fridge door with a soft click. "I mean, helping clean up has its advantages. I got to eat more food while putting it in containers." The smile she offers is genuine but cautious, like she's testing the waters between us.

I can't help it—it comes as natural as breathing. I step into her space and slide my arms around her waist, drawn to her like gravity. It's the closest we've been in days, and God, I've missed this. She doesn't push me away, but I can feel her hesitation, the way she's holding part of herself back.

"I'm glad you came tonight," I murmur, my eyes drinking in her face like I'm memorizing it all over again, cataloging every detail I've been starving for.

"Me too," she whispers, her palms settling on my chest. But there's something careful in her touch, like she's reminding herself not to fall too easily back into this.

"Laney." Her name comes out rougher than I intended. "I hate this distance between us. You're all I think about, and waking up without you next to me is torture. I don't want to keep doing it."

Her expression softens, and I watch her resolve waver. She wants this as much as I do. I can see it in the way her eyes linger on my face, the slight lean of her body toward mine despite herself. "I know," she admits quietly. "I don't like it either. I miss you."

Those three words make my chest tighten with a mix of relief and longing. I want to kiss her, to close this unbearable gap between us, but I can sense she needs more than just my touch right now.

Leaning my forehead against hers, I breathe in her familiar scent. "Then talk to me. Don't shut me out. Let me be there for you." Those are the same words she gave to me the morning we woke tangled up in each other after the Fairfield's watch party. Her strength and certainty fueled me.

Her eyes flutter closed as she leans into the contact, and for a moment, we just exist in this space together. When she opens her eyes, they're soft but guarded. "It's not that simple, though." She presses gently against my chest, not to push me away but to create just enough space to think clearly. "I want to trust this. Trust us again. But I'm scared."

Her hands fist softly in my shirt, torn between pulling me closer and protecting herself. "I love you," she whispers, the words both a gift and a confession. "I love you so much it scares me sometimes." She takes a shaky breath. "You have this power over me, London. When you hurt, I hurt. When you're gone, I'm lost. And I can't...I can't be that vulnerable and broken when I need to be strong. I need to be strong for our baby."

The revelation hangs in the air between us, tender and enormous.

"You love me the same way I love you," I say softly, my thumb tracing her cheek. "That's not something to be afraid of."

"But you left before," she says, and there's no accusation in it, just hurt that hasn't fully healed. "When things got complicated, you chose to go."

"I was eighteen and terrified," I admit, my voice thick with regret. "I thought I was doing the right thing, protecting you and your pretty heart. But Laney, leaving you was the biggest mistake of my life. I've regretted it every single day since."

I can see her wavering, love and caution warring in her beautiful eyes. She wants to believe me, wants to fall back into us, but she's protecting her heart.

"And at the ranch," she continues softly, "you pushed me away again. You hurt me because you thought it was easier than fighting through the hard parts together."

Her words aren't angry. They're just achingly honest, and somehow, that makes them cut deeper. "I know," I say, my hands tightening on her waist. "I know I hurt you, and I hate myself for it. But I'm here now, trying to fix what I broke. I want to fight for us, with you, not against you."

She bites her lower lip, a gesture I know means she's trying not to cry. "How do I know you won't run again when things get hard? How do I trust that you'll stay when being here gets difficult?"

"Because I came after you," I say desperately. "Before I even knew about the baby, the second you turned away from me at the ranch, I knew I'd made a terrible mistake. I couldn't let you go—

not again. I ran after you. I would have begged you to forgive me right then and there if Fish hadn't stopped me—"

"Wait." Her brow furrows as she attempts to process my words. "You came after me? I heard the fighting in the hallway and assumed Fish went after you. I didn't realize you were the one who was running."

"Does it matter?" I ask as I study her face.

Her eyes hold mine, and in their piercing gaze, I can see healing. She didn't know until this moment that I fought for her—for us. I hurt her, but I was ready to fall to my knees and beg for her forgiveness. Ready to take it all back.

"It matters," she says, her voice breaking at the end.

"Laney, I know I messed up, but what I've found at the core of it all is fear. I spent years living in fear. Fear I was unlovable because my mother walked out on me and my dad. Fear my dad regretted me, believing I was the reason my mom left. Fear of never being good enough because, at every turn, I felt like I was five steps too short. Fear of falling for a girl at eleven years old..." My voice grows thick with emotion as I continue. "Freshman year, I got it wrong when I caught you TPing my house. Sophomore year, I got it wrong when I kissed you and disappeared. Senior year, I got it wrong again when I stole your crime. But at the root, all my actions were motivated by fear. I was scared of hurting what I cared about most."

I pause, my hands trembling slightly against her waist. "You. I was scared of hurting you."

But standing here now, holding her, feeling the steady rhythm of her breathing against my chest, something shifts inside me. The fear that's lived in my bones for so long...it's still there, but it's not driving me anymore. I'm not that scared eighteen-year-old boy who ran because he thought love meant inevitable loss. I'm not the man who pushed her away at the ranch because facing the mess felt impossible.

I'm tired of being afraid, tired of letting fear make my decisions for me. Because the truth is, losing her—really losing her—is the only thing that truly terrifies me. And I almost did that by trying so hard to protect us both from getting hurt.

"But I'm not scared anymore, Laney," I whisper, my voice stronger now, more certain. "Not of this. Not of us. The only thing that scares me now is living without you."

Her eyes start to glaze over with unshed tears, and I watch as her carefully constructed walls finally begin to crumble. The sight of her trying so hard not to cry, of all that love and pain shimmering in her eyes, breaks something open inside me.

I can't stand the distance anymore.

In one swift movement, I pull her fully into my arms, crushing her against my chest like I can somehow absorb all her hurt and fear into myself. She melts into me instantly, her arms winding around my neck as a soft sob escapes her lips. I bury my face in her hair, breathing her in, holding her like she might disappear if I let go.

"I love you," I murmur into her ear, the words desperate and reverent. "I love you so much."

When she pulls back to look at me, her cheeks are wet with tears, but there's something different in her eyes now…hope…or maybe surrender. Before I can second-guess myself, before either of us can overthink this moment, I cup her face in my hands and kiss her.

It's deep and desperate, full of all the longing and love we've been holding back. She kisses me back with equal fervor, her fingers tangling in my hair, and for the first time in days, everything feels right again. Like we're finally home. "Stay with me tonight." I break our kiss, and her eyes fill with apology. "I don't mean it like that. I mean, just stay with me."

"I want to…" Her fingers run through the hair at the base of my neck. "But I need to take it slow, and that means sleeping in my own bed tonight."

I growl out my frustration before kissing the tip of her nose. "What about tomorrow?"

"I don't know. I suppose I'll take it under consideration," she says teasingly, and my heart soars. That's the sound of my girl coming back to me. Her soft lips press against mine, and I melt. God, I've missed us. Her hands brush down my chest before she pulls away and slowly walks backward toward the door. "An egg-and-cheese sandwich on a bagel with avocado sounds excellent. If someone were to leave that on my windowsill, it might help sway the judge."

I press my teeth into my lower lip hard and watch her flushed cheeks walk away from me with a playful glint in her eye. "It'll be there," I say as she reaches for the doorknob. "Oh, and heart-breaker..." Her eyes flick up to mine when I use her nickname. "Open your curtains tonight so I can sleep."

LANEY

CHAPTER 35

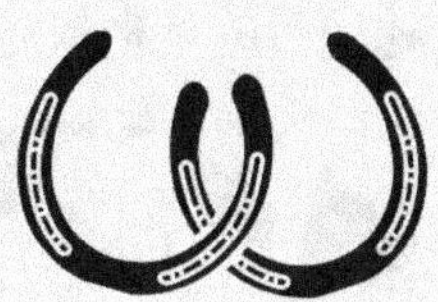

"Hey, I know this is completely last minute," I say, pushing open the door to London's bedroom unannounced, "but I was wondering if you wanted to go to—"

My words die in my throat when I look up and see him standing across the room, frozen by his dresser, water droplets still clinging to his shoulders, and a towel wrapped dangerously low around his waist.

His eyes widen momentarily, my presence catching him by surprise as much as his state of undress has me rooted to my spot beside the door. The air between us shifts, charged with the same electricity that's been crackling under the surface for days.

"I didn't know you were coming over," he says, his voice rougher than usual as he rolls his lips before running a hand through his damp, messy hair. The movement makes his bicep flex, and I have to remind myself to breathe.

"Umm...your dad let me in," I manage, unable to keep the nerves and want out of my voice.

London Hale has the body of a god, and I fucking miss it. I miss him. The past few days since the dinner have been great. We're falling back in step, but we haven't been together intimately. I said I wanted to take things slow. I needed to take them slow. I

449

owed that to myself to process everything that had happened, to listen to not only what was in my head but my heart. I've done that, and he still hopelessly owns them both.

For a moment, neither of us moves as the air turns electric, and my heart starts to race, and the way his dark eyes are drinking me in tells me he knows the exact thoughts that are running through my head. The hunger there mirrors my own. I want to lick every drop of water off his toned stomach and trace the V that disappears beneath his towel with my tongue.

His gaze drops to my lips, then lower, lingering on the slight curve of my belly before traveling back up to meet my eyes. The look he gives me is pure fire.

"You said you were going somewhere." He clears his throat, but his voice is strained, like he's fighting the same pull I am.

"Ah, yes. I was wondering if you want to go to the doctor with me. My mother set it up at the hospital, said I need to start figuring out my birth plan, deciding if any tests or screenings are necessary, and discussing my job..." I pinch my nose to stifle the stress of the list she ticked off as we discuss the baby. But right now, all I can think about is how badly I want to close the distance between us. "Riding horses during pregnancy is apparently a problem."

"It's not even a question." He takes two steps toward me, happiness written all over his face, ready to crush me with one of his hugs, until he realizes he's still practically naked. The movement makes the towel shift lower, and my breath catches. "I want to be at every appointment." His hand tightens around the towel, knuckles white with restraint. "Just give me two seconds to get dressed."

I nod, but I don't move. I can't move. The way he's looking at me like I'm something precious and dangerous all at once has my pulse thrumming.

"You can wait in the living room," he says casually, but there's nothing casual about the heat in his eyes as he turns to his dresser to rummage through his drawer.

I purse my lips and consider doing just that, but my feet carry me to his bed instead. I don't want to wait in the living room. He's the man responsible for putting this baby in my belly, and right now, that thought has heat coiling low in my stomach, making me ache for his touch. The living room is distance. I'm tired of distance. Besides, looking isn't touching, even if every fiber of my being is screaming to do exactly that.

"The bed will do," I say, flopping onto his mattress, and I'm immediately surrounded by his scent. His head snaps to me, and the look that crosses his face when he sees me stretched across his sheets is pure hunger wrapped in warning. I arch one eyebrow with a smile. "Watching isn't touching."

A slow, wicked smile spreads across his face. "Heartbreaker, you can watch anytime. I like it when your eyes are on me," he says, voice dropping to that low register that makes my toes curl. Then he drops the towel.

And I see everything.

My breath hitches as I squeeze my legs together, fighting the wave of desire that crashes over me. When my eyes fall upon the marks on his shoulder from the last time we were together, faint but still visible, a possessive heat flares in my chest. Mine. He's mine, and I marked him to prove it.

He doesn't move to get dressed right away. Instead, he stands there, letting me look, letting the tension build until the air feels thick enough to drown in. His eyes never leave mine, reading every reaction, every catch of breath. He knows exactly what line he's toeing, and I'm letting him.

"See something you like?" he asks, voice rough with want.

I bite my lower lip, letting my gaze travel slowly down his body before meeting his eyes again. "Maybe," I say, trying to sound casual, even though my voice comes out breathier than intended.

He chuckles, low and dangerous. "Maybe?" He takes a step closer to the bed, and I have to tilt my head back to maintain eye contact. "Your pulse is racing. I can see it from here."

"That could be from anything," I counter, though we both

know it's a lie. "Pregnancy hormones. The shock of walking in on you naked. General anxiety about the doctor's appointment."

"Uh-huh." Another step closer. Now he's at the foot of the bed, hands braced on the mattress as he leans forward slightly. The position gives me an even better view of his chest, of the way water still clings to the hollow of his throat. "And the way you're looking at me right now? That's just...medical curiosity?"

Heat flames across my cheeks. "I'm allowed to appreciate aesthetics."

"Aesthetics," he repeats, amused. "Is that what we're calling it?"

I sit up straighter, chin lifting in challenge. "What would you call it?"

His eyes darken further. "Hunger." The word hangs between us like a confession. "The same hunger that's been eating me alive for days, watching you, wanting you, respecting your need for space, even when all I want to do is—"

"What?" the question slips out before I can stop it, barely a whisper.

He moves around the bed slowly, predatorily, until he's standing beside me, close enough that I can feel the heat radiating from his skin. "Touch you," he says simply. "Everywhere. Until you remember exactly how good we are together."

My breath catches. "London..."

"But you said slow," he continues, voice dropping to that rumble that makes my insides melt. "So I'm being good. Even though right now, with you on my bed, looking at me like that, being good is the last thing I want to be. I want you in the worst way."

I swallow hard, my hands fisting in his comforter. "Maybe I'm tired of slow."

The admission hangs in the air between us, heavy with possibility. His jaw tightens, as his control wavers.

"Don't say things like that unless you mean them, heartbreaker," he warns. "Because I've been holding back, and my restraint isn't infinite."

I lean back on my elbows, the movement deliberate, knowing exactly what it does to the neckline of my shirt. "Who says I don't mean it?"

He makes a sound low in his throat, somewhere between a growl and a groan. "You're killing me."

"Good," I say, surprised by my own boldness. "Now, are you going to get dressed, or are we going to be late for this appointment because you're too busy showing off?"

His grin is pure sin. "Oh, I'm definitely showing off. The question is...are you complaining?"

"I didn't say that," I murmur then flash him a wicked smile. "But we really should go. Wouldn't want to keep the doctor waiting."

I stand up from the bed and brush past him toward the door, making sure to let my fingers trail across his chest as I pass. "Besides," I add, glancing back over my shoulder with deliberate innocence, "I'll have plenty of time to look later."

The sharp intake of breath behind me tells me I've won this round.

~

London: Is that MY t-shirt?

I DON'T EVEN NEED TO LOOK DOWN TO KNOW THAT IT IS.

Laney: Maybe... It looks better on me, though.

London: You literally stole it from my room this morning.

I smile as I set my phone down to take out my earrings. This morning, while he was giving me a show before our appointment, I snuck the shirt that was crumpled up on his bed into my bag.

Laney: I don't like the word stole. I prefer "borrowed indefinitely."

London: I want it back.

My eyes narrow on my screen. He's never once asked for his clothes back.

Laney: I thought you like it when I wear your things.

London: You look incredible in anything you wear, but my favorite is when you're wearing nothing at all.

London: Come on, heartbreaker. Take it off. It's only fair. I showed you mine, now you show me yours. 😈

Laney: Don't you have something better to do than watch me through your window?

It's a tease. I know I'm stoking the fire, but I like how easily I can get him riled up. Plus, he's right. After his show this morning, it's only fair I get him hot and bothered.

London: Nope. Watching you put lotion on every night are my plans.

Laney: Such a creeper.

London: This coming from the girl who has left her curtains open on purpose since high school.

I can't help but smile. He asked me to close them once, and I never did. This past week was the only exception. However, even then, closing them revolved around him. I couldn't leave them open and let him see that I was sleeping in his old shirts because I missed him.

Laney: I need to put lotion on after my shower. It's not a show for you.

Fighting sucks, but the making-up part is fun. Like now, when I know he's probably over there biting his fist to temper his reaction to the images I know are flashing vividly across his mind.

London: Could've fooled me with the way you were looking right at my window last night.

Laney: That's because you were being so obvious about staring.

London: Like I said, it's hard to focus when you're putting on a performance.

Laney: It's not a performance. 😊 Maybe I just like attention. 😊

London: Then come over here, and you can have all of it.

Laney: Tempting...but I still need to moisturize.

This time, I toss my phone onto my bed across the room. With the jar of body butter in hand, I settle onto the edge of my bed and prop my leg up on the cushioned ottoman near the foot. Starting at my ankle, I apply the butter in slow, deliberate strokes, my fingers tracing every curve as I move up my calf and finally to my thigh, where I linger, kneading the muscle with a firm pressure that makes me sigh.

This might have started as a show for the boy next door, but it's quickly becoming something more. The day's tension is ebbing, and I can't deny how good it feels to touch myself this way. It's a fact that massages release endorphins. They're natural mood boosters, but the rush I get knowing he's watching me from across the way...that's something else entirely.

I lift his shirt over my stomach, but I don't remove it

completely. It smells like him. I warm the butter between my hands before splaying my fingers over my stomach and hips. The combination of my own touch, his scent, and his burning gaze sends heat pooling low in my belly. My hand begins to drift lower without conscious thought.

What began as innocent teasing, matching his earlier display, has me hungry for more. My fingers trail over my heated skin, and suddenly, I'm aching with need. It's been days since he was last inside me, days since I felt the perfect connection that exists when our bodies are intertwined. My hand slides over my underwear, one finger tracing my center through the thin fabric before I pull the material aside. The first touch of skin on skin makes me gasp, and I let my middle finger glide through my wetness. Spreading my legs wider, I brace one arm behind me and let my head fall back with a slow, breathy moan.

The tension I've been carrying melts away as my thumb finds that sensitive bundle of nerves, stroking in slow, deliberate circles that make my toes curl. I know exactly what I need and can feel my body climbing toward that perfect release, but just as my fingers prepare to dive deeper, a sharp knock slices through the air.

I don't need to look to know who I'll find there, and a satisfied smile curves my lips. I was wondering if he'd stay put like a good boy, if he'd touch himself while watching my private show, or if temptation would finally break his restraint and drive him to my window. When our eyes connect, his eyebrows are raised slightly, as if he wasn't entirely sure I'd actually dignify his presence with a glance. But there's also something vulnerable in his expression. He nods toward the latch, and I reach across my bed to flip it open, my pulse quickening.

He lifts the window, and I ask, "What are you doing?"

"Looked like you were trying to get my attention. I'm just making sure you know you have all of it," he says with a lopsided grin. "Can I come in?" I nod and watch as he climbs through, his broad shoulders barely fitting through the frame. "I think that window got smaller," he teases, glancing back at the opening with a rueful smile that makes my heart clench with bittersweet familiarity.

"Or you got bigger." I let my eyes trace the way his old t-shirt now stretches tight across his back, emphasizing muscles that weren't there before. "We're not eighteen anymore." The reminder hangs between us, heavy with everything that's changed, everything we've lost. "Is there something you wanted? Because I was in the middle of—"

"Yeah, I saw what you were in the middle of." His voice drops, rougher now, and he gestures toward his joggers, where the evidence of his reaction to my "little show" is impossible to ignore as it strains against the fabric. "That's why I stopped you."

I furrow my brow, confusion cutting through the haze of desire unfurling inside of me. "I don't understand—"

The words die in my throat as he drops to his knees before me, and his playful confidence is replaced with vulnerability.

"I don't want you to replace me." His hands settle on my thighs, warm and steady despite the tremor I can feel beneath his skin. "If you have needs..." His voice cracks slightly on the word, and he swallows hard before continuing. "I want to take care of them."

I've dreamed of his touch for days, craved it with an intensity that bordered on madness. But this isn't the sensual reunion I imagined in my fantasies. This is something rawer, more desperate. His hands on my skin aren't a seduction. They're an anchor. This is a plea wrapped in desperation. He's on his knees, begging me not to erase him from my body the way I tried to erase him from my heart.

But what he doesn't understand, what breaks something inside me as I look down at him, is that I never could. I may have pushed him away, needing the space to heal from wounds that felt too deep to survive, but I haven't explored this. I haven't wanted to— not without him. This is the first time in days I've felt this way, and

I know it's because his eyes were watching my every move, spurring me on.

The sleepless nights we've spent apart have hollowed him out and stolen every last shred of his willpower as he's waited for whatever we're supposed to become. This space between us has been killing him slowly, one lonely night at a time. He can't wait anymore, and neither can I.

His thumbs pause their gentle movement, and he takes a shaky breath before meeting my gaze. "I've been dying to put my hands on you again," he admits, his voice filled with raw honesty and desire. "Please don't make me stop."

"I've been dying for you to touch me," I whisper back, my voice just as honest. "I don't want you to stop. I never wanted you to stop."

His hands burn a slow path up my thighs as his eyes stay locked on mine. When his touch disappears under my shirt, my body comes alive. He hasn't touched me intimately since finding out about the baby. The slow push as his hands travel higher exposes the gentle curve of my stomach. His breath catches, and my chest tightens as his eyes drop to the slight swell he hasn't seen up close—the evidence of what's growing inside me. Our baby.

When his gaze lifts to meet mine, something fundamental shifts in his expression. The desperation is still there, but it's tempered now by something more profound. One hand spreads flat against my stomach, fingers splaying wide. His touch is achingly gentle.

"God," he whispers, voice thick with emotion. "You're really… We're really…"

Sure, he was by my side for our first official doctor appointment today, but he was beside the bed watching the doctor examine me in a sterile environment, taking in everything she had to say about what comes next. There was weight in that moment, the clinical reality of charts and due dates and medical terminology that made everything feel official and overwhelming. However, this moment has an intimacy that one never could.

Here, it's just me and him, no doctors, just his hands on my skin, feeling the subtle changes in my body with his own touch rather than through someone else's explanation.

He doesn't finish the sentence, but he doesn't need to. The truth is there in the way he looks at me, in the tremor of his hand against my skin, in the careful way he touches me. This is when it becomes real for him. His other hand moves to his pocket, where he pulls out a small black velvet box, the sight of it momentarily stopping my heart.

"I've been carrying this around for weeks," he admits, his voice barely above a whisper. "I had it in my pocket at the cabin. I planned on putting it on your finger when I asked you to go to the courthouse, but then..." His words trail off, and I know where his thoughts went.

Talking about the wedding that day triggered him. London has always listened. He knows me better than I know myself. He remembers dreams I've forgotten, and when he heard me talk about a wedding with friends and family, he assumed I wanted to find my father, and he knew that wasn't possible.

"Hey..." My hand caresses the side of his face. "It didn't matter that you didn't give me the ring. You asked, and I said yes."

He takes a shaky breath. "You know what I realized?" His voice hitches. "We've been through everything—hell, heartbreak, and loss that should have destroyed us. We've hurt each other and walked away, convinced it was over."

He opens the box and lifts out the ring, and my lungs forget how to function. "But fate..." He shakes his head, almost laughing through the tears threatening to spill. "Fate kept dragging us back together. Every time we thought we were done, it was there, pulling us back together, waiting until we were brave enough to try again. We dared to prove that our story wasn't finished, that it was still being written. That our future, our love, is so much louder than our fear ever was."

He picks up my hand and places a delicate kiss on my ring finger. "Laney Hart, marry me. Not because our love is perfect, not because we have all the answers, but because we've already survived the worst of it. Marry me because I'd rather fight through life with you than live peacefully without you. Marry me because our love story isn't over. It's just beginning."

"I meant it the first time," I whisper, my voice breaking with emotion. "The ring doesn't change anything. I was already yours the moment you asked. I've been ready to marry you since I was ten years old, London Hale. With or without a ring, my answer has always been the same."

He slips the ring onto my finger like it was always meant to be there, but before I can even look at it properly, he's rising from his knees, and I'm launching myself into his arms. The collision of our bodies is desperate and hungry as the days of separation, fear, and uncertainty explode into this single moment of absolute certainty.

His lips bruise mine with fierce possession. Years of loving him are poured into this one kiss. I can taste the salt of my tears as his tongue sweeps against my lower lip, seeking entrance that I grant without hesitation.

The kiss deepens and becomes something primal and consuming. His fingers thread through my hair as he tilts my head to take the kiss deeper still. I melt against him, my body remembering every curve and angle of his, every way we fit together perfectly. His other arm wraps around my waist, pulling me flush against him until there's no space left between us.

The intensity of our embrace sends us tumbling backward onto the bed in a tangle of limbs. He catches himself on his forearms above me, his body caging me in, and for a moment, we just stare at each other, drinking in this moment.

"I love you," he whispers, his voice raw with years of wanting, of fighting fate and losing. "I've loved you since before I understood what love meant, carried you in my chest like a prayer I didn't know how to say. You're the constant in every version of my story, Laney, the beginning, the middle, and every ending I'll ever want," he whispers against my lips.

"I love you too," I whisper back, my voice breaking on words that carry the weight of every sleepless night I've spent loving him, every moment I thought I'd lost him forever. "You're written into my soul, London. You always have been. You always will be."

His mouth covers mine, hungrier than before, like he's trying to devour every word I just spoke and make them part of himself. His hands tangle in my hair, holding me to him as our tongues dance, both desperate for more.

"I need to feel you," he murmurs against my lips, his voice rough with want. "All of you." His hand glides up my side, pulling my shirt with it.

"We can't," I moan with disappointment, but his hand doesn't relent.

With my breast fully exposed, he cups it before pinching my nipple. "And why not?" he questions before sealing his lips over the peak. Fuck. My entire body arches into him. "My mom and Trigg are down the hall sleeping," I say, holding his head to my breast while rocking my hips against his, my body contradicting my words.

"If you're asking me to stop because of those intoxicating moans you make when I'm inside of you...you're going to lose. That's not a reason." His hand drifts to my leg, where he lifts it over his hip so he can press his hard length where I need it most. "My brother refuses to leave until he knows you're coming home with me." He presses against my clit, the sensation making me gasp. I'm so sensitive. "You screaming my name when you come undone around my cock accomplishes that."

His hands reach for my panties, but he doesn't pull them down. Instead, he fists the fabric in his hand before pulling hard and ripping it from my body, the sharp sting against my skin only making me burn hotter for him.

"What about my mom?" I pant as he drags his tongue up my stomach.

"This sexy body is growing my baby. I think she's well aware that you enjoy bouncing up and down on me."

The vulgarity in his words paint a vivid image I want to replicate. I need him. I'll suffer through whatever mortification I see on my mother's face tomorrow, because it pales in comparison to the desire I'm fighting now. I need him more than I need air. I push him back, and his wild eyes search mine, unbelieving that I could possibly reject him. My teeth sink into my bottom lip as I stifle a smile and reach for the hem of my shirt, slowly pulling it over my head.

"I don't care who hears. I'm looking at the only person who matters."

He falls on top of me, careful not to put weight on my body as his hands frame my face and his expression shifts. "What's wrong?" I ask as the eagerness that was there seconds ago slightly ebbs.

"Nothing, just taking a second to admire my whole world." His mouth drops to mine, and he kisses me long and slow, like he's savoring the feel of his lips on mine and the love between us. I feel his hand snake down my stomach before he pulls his joggers down and brings the tip of his cock to my entrance.

"You've been my every thought since the first time I looked through this window and saw you." His voice breaks on the words, years of buried longing spilling out. "I'm sorry I didn't tell you that from day one."

"We were kids, London. We didn't know anything about life and love." But even as I say it, my heart hammers against my ribs, because part of me had known too.

"I always knew." His confession comes out raw, desperate. His nose skims mine, and I can feel him trembling. "You've always scared the hell out of me, heartbreaker. The way you could destroy me with just a look, the way you made me want things I didn't think I deserved."

My breath catches. "Falling is always scary..." I search his eyes, seeing all the pain we've caused each other, all the time we've lost. I wrap my legs around his waist. "But it's also the easiest thing I've ever done."

I press my heels into his ass, and he slides in, fully seating himself, and we both groan, the connection not only satisfying our carnal cravings but reuniting our souls. His lips brush against mine, but he doesn't kiss me as he slowly starts to move inside of me. These past years carved valleys between us and left scars we're still learning to trace, but we survived. We found our way back to each other.

With every deliberate thrust, I feel him reaching deeper, not just into my body but into the very core of who I am. His heartbeat thunders against my chest, the rhythm mirroring mine. This is more than desire, more than need. This is recognition, physical proof of a love that refused to die despite everything that tried to kill it. This isn't our first time, but it might as well be. Having him this way, after baring every wound, after exhuming all the ghosts that dared to haunt and keep us apart. This feels like the forever we were always meant to claim.

Each movement is purposeful as he finds that spot inside me that makes me see stars. The friction builds, and I wrap my legs tighter around him, anchoring him to me as my body begins to unravel.

My toes curl, and my back arches as pleasure coils tighter in my core. "Don't stop," I gasp, the words torn from my throat. The sounds spilling from my lips grow louder, more urgent, as he drives me toward the edge.

"I couldn't if I wanted to," he breathes, his voice rough with desire, eyes heavy-lidded as he hovers above me. "You feel too good. We feel good."

Before I can take another breath, his mouth claims mine with brutal need as his hips surge forward, driving deep with a force that makes us both cry out. His knees spread wider, bracing himself as he drives harder, each stroke reaching places that make me forget my own name. The rhythm becomes relentless and determined, as if he's trying to brand himself into my very soul. My walls begin to flutter around him, the telltale tightening that signals my approaching undoing, and his mouth tears away from mine as his breathing turns ragged.

"That's it, baby," he growls against my throat, his voice thick with possession. "Take everything I have."

The words shatter what's left of my restraint. My nails drag down his back as my climax crashes over me in waves that have me crying out his name. He follows me over that edge a heartbeat later, his body going rigid as he buries himself deep and collapses against me, his weight a welcomed anchor as we both struggle to remember how to breathe. I run my fingers through his damp hair, feeling the rapid thrum of his heartbeat against my chest, a rhythm that matches my own.

Countless heartbeats stretch between us in perfect contentment until exhaustion finally claims me, and for once, I welcome its pull. Fear no longer steals these moments, because I know we have forever to build new ones. Finally, there's nothing left but the reality of our dreams we dared to chase.

LONDON
CHAPTER 36

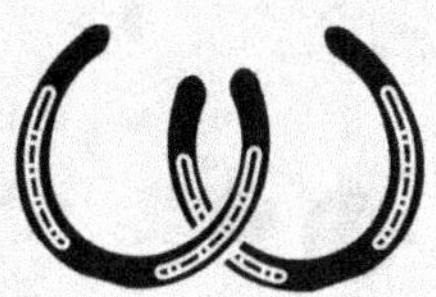

"Laney... Laney, where are you?" my voice echoes through the cabin as I throw the door open. She texted me she wasn't feeling good and was taking the rest of the day off. The text would be laughable under any other circumstance, but not while she's pregnant. Laney doesn't complain. She doesn't exaggerate. She once worked a full day in the training ring with a fever of 102 and insisted she was "just tired." The fact that she even acknowledged feeling unwell prompted me to abandon my meeting with my father and Baylor mid-sentence.

"Laney!" The desperation bleeds into my voice as I round the stone fireplace, scanning the empty living room, the lack of response putting me on edge.

"I'm in here," her voice drifts from the bathroom, strained but enough to slightly settle my anxiety.

"Laney." My hands grip the doorframe so hard my knuckles go white as I find her in the clawfoot tub, her hair plastered to her neck with sweat.

"What?" The single word comes out between pants, her eyes squeezed shut. "I said I didn't feel good. I just needed a bath. Baths always make me feel better."

"You're not supposed to take baths this late in pregnancy," I remind her, already moving toward the tub.

She waves a dismissive hand. "My belly isn't submerged. It's fine. I just needed the warm water. My stomach hurts."

"What do you mean your stomach hurts?" I drop to my knees beside the tub, water soaking through my work pants. "Laney, you're nine months pregnant. If your stomach hurts, that's not nothing."

Her face crumples, a flush of embarrassment coloring her cheeks as she looks away. "It's not *that* kind of hurt." Her voice drops to barely a whisper. "My stomach is upset. I've been running to the toilet every few minutes."

"Baby…" My hand finds the curve of her spine, feeling the tension coiled in every muscle. "Don't be embarrassed. You're growing our baby. You're fucking beautiful. There's nothing you could say that would change that. But I think we need to go to the hospital."

Her eyes snap to mine, wide with panic. "We don't need—" she cuts off abruptly, her body going rigid as she grips the sides of the tub. For ten endless seconds, she can't speak, can't breathe, can only endure whatever's happening to her. When it passes, she's paler than before. "—to go to the hospital. I'm not due for another three weeks. It's just an upset stomach and some back pain."

"Back pain?" The words come out sharper than I intended.

"Yeah," she grinds out through clenched teeth, irritation and pain warring in her voice. "Why do you think I've been practically living in the bathroom?"

That's when I see it, the way she's bracing herself against the tub, the shallow, controlled breathing, the white-knuckled grip on the porcelain edge. This isn't an upset stomach. This isn't back pain.

"Okay." My hands slide under her arms, gentle but firm. "We're going. Right now."

"But I'm not—"

"We're going to let the doctors tell us it's nothing." I meet her eyes, letting her see the fear I've been trying to hide. "But we're going. Please, Laney. For me. For our baby."

She stares at me for a long moment, and I can see the exact second she stops fighting the truth her body has been telling her. Her shoulders sag in defeat.

"Okay," she whispers.

"Okay," I repeat, my voice steadier now that we're moving forward, my panic shifting into focused determination. *We're having a baby.*

~

"You're doing so good, baby," I murmur against her temple. "Just breathe through it. In through your nose, out through your mouth. Just like we practiced."

She nods weakly, sweat-soaked hair sticking to her forehead. The epidural wore off an hour ago, and they can't give her another one—not this close to delivery. Every contraction now is raw.

Fourteen hours. Fourteen hours of watching Laney's face contort with pain, of counting breaths between contractions, of being her anchor. My hand is probably permanently shaped to hers now, crushed and reformed by her grip through each surge, and I couldn't care less. I want the scar. She's so strong, but I wish I could take the pain from her. If reshaping my hand helps her through it, it's hers.

"I can't," she gasps, her nails digging crescents into my palm. "I can't do this anymore. I'm so tired."

"Yes, you can." I brush the damp strands from her face. "You're the strongest person I know. Remember that wild Mustang we found this summer? Everyone said she was too far gone, too broken to trust again. But you spent three months earning her trust, one gentle touch at a time. You know how to fight through the impossible. This is just like that. Except, at the end, we get to meet our baby."

Dr. Martinez checks the monitor again, and her brow furrows. Something shifts in her expression, a tightening around her eyes that makes my stomach drop.

"Laney, I need you to give me everything you've got with this next contraction," she says, but her voice has an edge to it that wasn't there before. "Baby's heart rate is dropping. We need to get this little one out now."

Her words slam into Laney like a freight train, and her eyes snap wide, wild and terrified, darting between Dr. Martinez and the monitors.

"What do you mean dropping?" Her voice cracks. "Is my baby okay? What's wrong with my baby?" She tries to sit up despite the contraction building, her hands instinctively moving to her belly. "Please, tell me my baby's okay!"

I grab her by the shoulders and gently press her back. "Hey, look at me. Look at me, heartbreaker." But I can see the panic taking hold—exactly what she doesn't need right now. "Our baby is going to be perfectly healthy because her mom is going to give it everything she's got on this next contraction." I give her my hand. "Give it hell so we can meet our little girl."

She closes her eyes, and her head rocks from side to side as tears slide down her cheeks. "You don't know it's a girl," she reminds me.

We decided to wait until the baby arrived to find out the gender. All that mattered to us was bringing a healthy baby into the world, and with everything else on our plate—between renovating the cabin, building a barn for Laney's business, and planning a wedding—she didn't want to stress over names, themes, and clothing.

I squeeze her hand. "Give me one more big push and prove me wrong."

She nods, and I watch as she starts to breathe through the next waves of another contraction, her hand tightening around mine as she grits her teeth and prepares to give it everything. I watch the monitor over her shoulder. The baby's heartbeat, which had been a steady gallop, now stutters and dips with each contraction.

"Push, Laney!" I'm practically shouting now, my free hand supporting her back as she bears down with everything she has left. "You've got this. Come on, baby, push!"

But something's wrong. I can see it in Dr. Martinez's face, in the way the nurses are moving with sudden urgency, checking machines, adjusting equipment. Laney's face is gray, her lips tinged blue, and when I look at the monitor showing her vitals, my blood turns to ice.

"Blood pressure's dropping fast," one of the nurses says, her voice calm but clipped. "Heart rate's irregular."

"Get me two units of O-neg, stat," Dr. Martinez orders then turns to me with an expression I've never wanted to see. "Sir, I need you to step outside."

The words rip through me as the room tilts, and suddenly, I can't breathe, can't think, can't process anything except the terror clawing its way up my throat. This can't be happening. This isn't real.

"What?" The word comes out strangled, broken. "No. No, absolutely not. I'm not leaving her."

"Sir—"

"I said NO!" The scream tears from somewhere deep in my chest, raw and desperate. My hands are shaking, my entire body vibrating with panic. "She's my wife! That's my baby! You can't make me leave!"

But even as I'm shouting, I can see Laney getting paler. The room is full-on spinning now, or maybe I'm spinning, and there's a blaring in my ears like I'm standing right next to a fire alarm.

Dr. Martinez grabs my arm, her grip surprisingly strong. "She's hemorrhaging badly. Her blood pressure is crashing, and if we don't get this baby out in the next few minutes, we could lose them both. Do you understand me? Both of them."

The words punch through me like bullets. *Lose them both.* The phrase echoes in my skull, bouncing around until it's the only thing I can hear. My knees nearly buckle, and I have to grip the bed rail to stay upright.

"No," I whisper. "No, this isn't happening. She was fine. She was fine an hour ago. People don't just—" I can't finish the sentence, can't say the word *die*, because that would make it real.

"Sir, please." A nurse appears at my other side, and I realize distantly that I'm being surrounded. "The surgical team needs space. Every second we spend arguing is a second we're not saving your family."

Dr. Martinez moves closer, her voice dropping to a whisper meant only for me. "She's hemorrhaging. We need to get this baby out immediately, and I need my team to have room to work. If you want to help her, you need to let us do our job."

Hemorrhaging. The word detonates in my soul, tearing through every hope I've carried for the past nine months. *Lose them both. Lose your family.* My God, why is this happening? This isn't supposed to happen this way. We were supposed to go home together, all three of us. No. I refuse to accept any scenario where we don't walk out together as a family the way it was always meant to be.

"Laney?" I squeeze her hand, but her grip is weaker now, her eyes unfocused. "Baby, look at me."

Her eyelids flutter open, and for a moment, she's there—really there. "Don't leave me," she whispers, and it's barely audible over the chaos erupting around us.

"Sir, please." A nurse has her hand on my arm, gentle but insistent. "The surgical team needs to come in."

I lean down, pressing my forehead against hers, memorizing the feel of her skin and the scent of her hair beneath the hospital's antiseptic. "I'm not leaving you. I'm going to be right outside that door, and when you wake up, I'll be the first thing you see. You and our baby. You hear me?" I grind out, fighting back tears, emulating strength when, inside, I'm shattering.

She nods weakly, and I press a kiss to her lips—soft, desperate, tasting of salt and fear and fourteen hours of shared breath.

"I love you," I whisper against her mouth. "Fight for us, Laney. Fight for our baby."

"Sir!" Dr. Martinez's voice cuts through everything. "Now!"

I force myself to let go of her hand, to step back as the surgical team floods in. The last thing I see before the door closes is Laney's face, pale and beautiful and fighting, as they wheel in equipment I don't want to recognize.

And then I'm in the hallway, my back against the cold wall, sliding down until I'm sitting on the floor with my head in my hands, listening to the controlled chaos on the other side of that door and praying to every god I've ever heard of that I won't lose them both.

"I'll do anything," I whisper to the empty hallway. "God, please, don't take the girl." The tears fall freely now as I bargain with a god I've never met. "I know I've asked for a lot over the years. I've prayed for nights with her I don't deserve, so you can make this my last request." My hands are shaking so hard I can barely form the words. "Take me instead. Take my breath, take my heart, take every year I have left, and give them to her. Give them to our baby."

I run my hands through my hair, surrendering to the sobs I was fighting to hold back. "She's good," I choke out, pressing my palms against my eyes. "She's pure and kind, and she makes the world better just by existing in it. Please, God. I'll spend the rest of my life on my knees if you just let me hear her laugh one more time. Let me see our baby take their first breath." Another sob breaks from my chest, ugly and desperate. "Please don't take my girls. Please don't make me bury my heart."

My words dissolve into sobs, and my entire body shakes as I rock back and forth, completely broken, completely lost, completely at the mercy of forces I can't control or understand. And then, like someone pressed pause on the world, the chaos behind the door falls silent. It could be an answered prayer, or it could be the end.

The quiet stretches, heavy and terrible, pressing down on me like a weight I can't bear. I know that silence. I've heard it before in movies, in stories, in nightmares I never thought would become real. It's the silence that comes after. The silence that means it's over.

One way or another, it's over.

~

THE FIRST THING I SEE WHEN I WAKE UP IS SUNLIGHT. REAL sunlight, not the fluorescent glare that's been burning into my retinas for what feels like forever. It streams through the window of what I slowly realize is a different room, quieter, softer, with pale-yellow walls instead of sterile white. I'm still in the same clothes from yesterday, wrinkled and stiff with dried sweat and tears, but none of that matters because there, in the bed not three feet away, is Laney. Alive and breathing.

Her color is back, not the terrifying gray that has haunted my thoughts every time I close my eyes, but her real color—warm and pink and beautifully alive. And cradled against her chest, wrapped in a soft pink blanket, is our daughter. I must make some sound, because Laney's eyes flutter open and find mine immediately. When she smiles, it's like watching the sun rise after the longest night of my life.

"Hey," she whispers, her voice hoarse but real…so fucking real.

"Hey, yourself." I can barely get the words out past the lump in my throat. I'm afraid to move, afraid to breathe too hard, afraid this might all be some cruel dream my exhausted mind has conjured up.

"Come here," she says, shifting carefully to make room on the narrow hospital bed. "Come meet our daughter."

Our daughter. The words hit me like a miracle, and suddenly, I'm moving without thinking. The bed dips as I settle beside them, and for the first time in what feels like years, I can breathe again. She's perfect. Tiny and wrinkled and absolutely flawless, with blonde hair that's definitely Laney's and little fists that are already reaching for the world around her. When I touch her cheek with one finger, her skin is soft and warm. It's that same warmth that solidifies this is real and not a dream.

"She's been waiting for you," Laney murmurs, adjusting the blanket so I can see her better. "The nurses said she wouldn't stop fussing until they brought her in here where she could hear your voice."

That makes me smile. Last night, I wasn't able to see Laney right away after they wheeled her down to an ICU unit for further observation. I spent those hours praying and telling our baby girl all about her mom, how amazing she is, and how hard she fought to meet her. I filled the space until she came back to us, and my little girl listened.

"I get to keep you," I whisper, the confession spilling out before I can stop it. It's not a statement. It's a prayer of gratitude for a gift I thought had been taken away. "I get to keep you both."

Laney's hand finds mine, her fingers intertwining with mine in a way that feels like coming home. "I wasn't going to leave you," she says softly, squeezing my hand. "Not when we just got our little miracle." She looks down at our baby. "Plus, I promised I'd take your last name. I couldn't leave you stranded at the altar," she says, attempting to lighten the mood, and I smile softly, grateful I get the chance to listen to her voice.

In my mind, we're already married. She's wearing my ring, we're building our home, and she just gave birth to our daughter. She's always been my forever, but we haven't made it official on paper. Once I slipped the ring on her finger, her mother and the girls began bombarding her with questions about dresses, venues, and themes. I thought it was overwhelming. It is overwhelming, but seeing the smiles that planning it has put on everyone's faces, I see how right Laney was to turn down my courthouse wedding. We would have missed out on something special if we hadn't included our friends and family.

"I thought I lost you." The confession tumbles out before I can stop it. "Both of you. I thought..." I can't finish, can't voice those fears now that they're safely in the past.

"But you didn't." Her thumb traces over my knuckles, soothing and sure. "We're right here. We're not going anywhere."

Our daughter makes a tiny sound, not quite a cry, more like she's testing out her voice, and both of us look down at her in wonder.

"Have you thought of a name?" I ask. We've had names picked out for months, but we never settled on one. We knew we'd wait until the baby arrived to see what fit.

"Grace," Laney says without hesitation. "Grace Elizabeth, after your grandmother. Because if last night wasn't proof that we live by grace, I don't know what is."

Grace. It fits perfectly as if she was always meant to be Grace, like the name was waiting for her, just as much as we were. She's living proof that hearts, even when shattered, possess extraordinary capacity. They can break and grow back stronger, not in spite of their cracks, but because of them.

"Grace Elizabeth," I repeat, and when I say it, she opens her dark-brown eyes. "Hi there, sweetheart. I'm your daddy."

The smile that spreads across my face feels foreign after the hell of the last twelve hours, but it's real, and it's mine, and it's for them. My girls. Both of them safe, both of them here, both of them mine.

"I love you," I whisper to Laney, pressing a kiss to her temple. "I love you both so much."

"We love you too," she whispers back.

Sitting beside her now, I allow my eyes to close, and I find it: peace. Not the fragile, fleeting kind that slips away at the first shadow, but something deep and unshakeable...complete, overwhelming, grateful peace. I finally understand that love isn't about avoiding loss. It's about choosing each other despite the risk. The scared boy who once ran from the possibility of loss has learned that some things are worth fighting for, worth staying for, worth rebuilding from broken pieces. We've taken the shattered fragments of our first love and forged something stronger, something that can hold the weight of forgiveness and the promise of tomorrow. Our baby girl will know a love that knows its own fragility and chooses itself anyway, a love that understands that the deepest healing comes not from avoiding the wound, but from tending to it together. And as I hold her now, I know with absolute certainty that this—this messy, complicated, beautiful love—is the greatest risk I'll ever take and the only choice I'll never regret. We were brave enough to try again, and now I have my family. My heart is whole.

THE END

EXTENDED EPILOGUE

C an't say goodbye to London and Laney? Good news - you don't have to! 💜 Their love story continues in the extended epilogue...

Get a front row seat to their wedding NOW.

ALSO BY L.A. FERRO

Summer Nights

DIG: A Second Chance Romance

Trope list: Sports Romance, College Romance, Dark Secrets, Emotional Scars, Second Chance, Redemption.

Fade Into You

Trope list: Arranged Marriage, Sports Romance, Small Town, Single Dad, Mistaken Identity, Unrequited Love.

SALT

Trope list: Age Gap, Best Friend's Daughter, Protector, Angsty, Secret Romance, Forbidden, Sports Romance.

~

Copper Falls

Rewriting Grey: Romantic Thriller

Trope List: Reclusive Author, Siblings Ex, Forced Proximity, Secret Identity, Small Town.

Scoring Grey: A Hockey Romance

Trope list: Golden Retriever MC, Boy Obsessed, He Falls First, Secret Past, Reunited Lovers.

~

Shades of Dark

The Delicate Vows Duet - A Billionaire Romance

Trope list: Billionaire Romance, Off-limits, Age-gap, Secret Virgin, Different Worlds, He Falls First.

Wicked Beautiful Lies: A Taboo Romance

Trope list: Taboo/forbidden, Mistaken Identity, Enemies to Lovers, Dark Secrets.

Sweet Venom: A Why Choose Romance

Trope List: Taboo, Enemies to Lovers, Friends to Lovers, Dark Secrets, Different Worlds, Unrequited Love.

ACKNOWLEDGMENTS

To my Beta Team: Thorunn, Mindy, Lakshmi, and Brittany—I know I've said this before, but repetition doesn't diminish its truth: you four are absolutely incredible. The polish and brilliance in my writing comes directly from the insights you share with me.

Mindy, your enthusiasm for the story keeps me going. You share my passion for both tension and intrigue, and your encouraging words push me forward more than you know.

Lakshmi, my night owl companion, I adore how you're always available when everyone else has gone to bed. You're someone I can talk through ideas with and bounce thoughts off of as I develop character storylines.

Thorunn, your feedback is incredibly detailed—you spot issues that would fly completely under most people's radar. Sure, some might seem small on their own, but those seemingly minor problems have a way of snowballing into complete chaos if left unchecked.

And Brittany, my detail detective—definitely not forgotten! Thanks for keeping me inline and making sure I don't repeat myself.

I'm truly thankful. Please don't ever abandon me. I value each of you immensely!

To my ARC Team: You all are absolutely amazing to me. I'm deeply thankful for this crew with each and every launch. Your feedback fuels my spirit and empowers me to champion my book with pride. My gratitude for each of you runs so deep.

Shoutout to these amazing readers!

Aliyah Smith, Allison T, Amanda Fenech, Amanda G, Amanda Sewell, Amber Long, Angela McManus, Angie Large, Book Witchling, Ashlyn Romero, Becky Jaegle, Bekah Saulmon, Bettyandabook, Blair W, Maz, Jennifer Borner, Breana Molina, Bree Jones, Brenda Smith, Raeann Wolfley, Brittany S Fraser, Brittany Vitu, Brooke Jiral, Caitlin Loggins, Carla Dionne, Casey Pettey, Catherine Boudreaux, Chelsye Lopez, Cheryl L, Cheyenne Yowell, Chloe Rosenbaum, Christina S, Christine Harris, Cierra H, Court Anne, Dania Diaz, Danielle Beckham, Danielle Coon-Davis, Dawn Litwiller, Dawn Wilson, Deborah Dow, Elizabeth Satala, Emily Cherry, Erin, Faith Jones, Fiona Wilson, Hailey Amos, Hannah Wells, Heather Douglas, Hilary Litzinger, Jackie A, Jacklyn Banyas, Jane Litherland, Janelle Sequin, Jasmin Aguilar, Jenn Maryk, Jenn Trocine, Jenna Crumpton, Jessica Stroup, thespicybooknerd, Jordan Fiest, Kaelea, Kailey D, Kaitlyn Dorman, Kat, Karla Rendon, Kass B, Kassandra Lopez, Kat schumacher, Kat Parkins, Kayla, Kayla Price, Kaylen Trejo, Kelani, Kimberly Blackburn, Kimberly Weber, Kristi D Haynes, Kristin Graves, Leah Edwards, Lisa Swartz, Lu (an Ecuadorian fan) Mandi S, Meagan, Merrit Townsend, Michelle C, Michelle (@bellesbooktique) Michelle Berger, Emily Cuen, Nancy A. Pasquale, Nayalee Scarborough, Nicole Scarborough, Nicole Wheelbarger, Nikki Johnson, Nina Harris, Olivia Rose, Olivia Pace, Rachael Davis, Sabrina Latulipe, Sarah Lloyd, Sarah Provenzano, Shannon Tori, Shawn-Joy Martin, Sherrece Tanner, Shianne, Novels_recommended, Tabatha Slagle, Taylor Nobles, Kim Greene- @the_romance_regent, Tianna Delgado, @bookjourneys.at.tiffanys, Tina Howell, Victoria Shelton, Wendy K.

Thank you all from the bottom of my heart.

About the Author

L.A. Ferro has had a love for storytelling her entire life. For as long as she can remember, she put herself to sleep, plotting stories in her head. That thirst for a good tale led her to books, where she became an avid reader.

The unapologetically dramatic characters, steamy scenes, and happily ever afters found inside the pages of romance novels irrevocably transformed her. The world of romance ran away with her heart, and she knew her passion for love would be her craft.

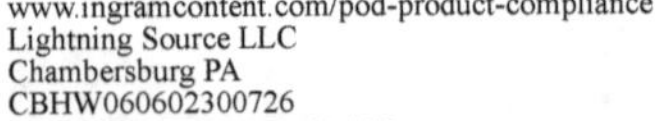